CW00502143

ENGAGED IN
TROUBLE

BY
JENNY B. JONES

Copyright ©2017 Jenny B. Jones
Print Edition
Sweet Pea Productions
Cover design by Seedlings Design Studio

All rights reserved. Without limited the rights under copyright reserved above, no part of this publication may be reproduced, stored in or introduced into a retrieval system, or transmitted in any form or by any means without the prior written permission of the copyright owner.

This is a work of fiction. Names, characters, places, brands, media, and incidents are either the product of the author's imagination or are used fictitiously. The author acknowledges the trademarked status and trademark owners of various products referenced in this work of fiction, which have been used without permission. The publication/use of these trademarks is not authorized, associated with, or sponsored by the trademark owners.

DEDICATION

This story is for anyone who hears a voice whispering, "It's time for something new." For the person who thinks about taking a chance, pursuing something a little scary, a little different.

Do it.

Take the risk.

Life's too short to wonder . . . *what if?*

Change happens outside our comfort zone. So try that new thing.

And if you fall, then fall gloriously.

FREE EBOOK OFFER

Sign up for my newsletter and be the first to know about my new releases,

book discounts, giveaways, and as a bonus, receive a **FREE** ebook!

Sign Up For the Jenny B. Jones Newsletter!

www.jennybjones.com/news

CHAPTER ONE

T HEY SAY HOME is where the heart is.
I say home is where my cheating ex-fiancé is, so I really
hadn't ever planned on making a move anywhere near the same
time zone as Evan Holbrook.

But then that certified letter came and changed everything.

Sugar Creek, Arkansas, hadn't been home to me since I'd left
town just two weeks shy of high school graduation on a plane to
Los Angeles, fueled by the promises of a talent agent and my
own youthful arrogance. That had been ten years and many
failures ago. And at some point, the failure gets so big, you can't
fit it all in a suitcase and bring it home. So you stay away,
promising to return when the favorable winds shift your
direction once again.

Sure, I'd been back to Sugar Creek a few times. Like when I
let my fiancé talk me into holding our wedding here for some
small-town charm and good press.

How was I to know he intended to practically light that press
on fire, using my good name as kindling?

My green eyes now lingered on every familiar sight as I drove
through this town I'd avoided. The elementary school where I
broke my arm in the third grade, attempting a master-level
double Dutch move. The two-story Victorian home with a

1

manicured exterior as uptight as the owner, Mrs. Mary Lee Smith, whose claims to fame included being a descendant of Robert E. Lee and surviving five years of me in her cotillion classes. (She told my momma a Lee never had it so bad.) The vacant field near the VFW where they held the summer fair, and where I stood on a flatbed trailer at the age of ten and sang Beyoncé songs to a corndog-eating crowd and knew I'd found my life's work. Then the Sugar Creek Chapel, a beautiful glass structure that had landed in every bridal magazine as an ideal, quaint wedding location. It had certainly been ideal to me once upon a time.

But then Evan decided to throw some drama into our wedding, leaving me at the altar and bringing shame down on my head, heavy as that ugly veil his momma talked me into wearing. Half the town had been invited to those nuptials. Evan and I had pretty much been the Will and Kate of Sugar Creek. But my prince stopped our ceremony mid-vow, let go of my hand, told me it was over before God and gape-mouthed man, and walked away. The only wedding gift I kept was a chrome toaster—with aspirations of tossing it into Evan's bathwater.

Fed up with the Southern-drawled whispers and speculative looks, I'd hightailed it back to my beloved LA.

Two years later I found myself back in Sugar Creek. Desperation was the only thing that could slip its hold around my neck like a lasso and drag me back. And desperate I was.

Snap out of it and focus on where you're going, I told myself, shoving aside memories and broken dreams, bitter as unripe berries. I sounded like the therapist I could no longer afford.

My car, named Shirley, was an old Camry that was a daily

insult to the Mercedes convertible I'd had to surrender. Shirley was loud and sassy and liked to shimmy at inappropriate moments, but I guess she got me where I wanted to go. Or in this case, where I didn't want to go.

The old car shook with a rusty palsy while I did a loop around the square. The heart beating beneath my cotton T-shirt warned me that Sugar Creek was where people dropped by for a visit and never left, buying themselves the corner lot and the picket-fence dream they hadn't even known they'd wanted. Like many downtowns across this fine country, Sugar Creek had recently begun the process of a restoration, rejuvenating the ghostlike, boarded-up ruins of the past into a bustling community that looked like something straight out of a Norman Rockwell painting. The square and its surrounding streets were dotted with small shops, a few bed-and-breakfasts, a bank that still passed out lollipops to your kids.

"Come on, Shirley. You can do it. Just a few streets more." Perhaps it was my weary imagination, but the car seemed to rally.

A familiar house came into view, a marshmallow-white Queen Anne with a wraparound porch, and a smile lifted my lips.

I might not want to live in Sugar Creek forever, and I might be resentful of why I was there, but nothing compared to finally returning to the sweet, gentle embrace of your beloved grandmother.

Wondering at the cars lining the street, I parked in the driveway of 105 Davis Street, hopped out of Shirley, and ran to the door. Oh, grandmothers. They bake cookies. They play pretend. They tell bedtime stories and sing lullabies and slip you a five-dollar bill when nobody is looking.

And then there's my grandma.

"State your business," came a voice from the shrubs. "Or I activate the home security yard gnomes. They'll shoot pepper spray from their hats and Taser darts straight outta their knickers."

"Stand down, Agent Hot Stuff." I grinned. "It's your beloved granddaughter. I've returned to kiss your wrinkled brow and make your life complete in your golden years before we ship you off to Shady Acres."

Sylvie Sutton, the woman who refused to let me call her *grandma* to her face, stepped from the shadows. "I've paid good money to make sure there are no wrinkles in this brow." She held out her toned arms. "Come here and give us a kiss, Paisley."

I ran into her embrace like our own reenactment of *The Notebook: Grandparents' Edition.* "I've missed you," I said.

"You, too, shug." Sylvie stepped back and took a measured study. "Are you eating? Sleeping? You look a little peaked."

"I look a little broke." And brokenhearted.

"You've come to the right place." Sylvie slipped her arm around my waist and drew me onto the porch. "Come on inside. You're just in time for book club."

Oh, no. The last thing I wanted was to see people and have to make small talk. "I've driven a really long way. I just wanted to see you, then grab the keys to the rent house and crash."

"Uh-huh." Sylvie held open the screen door. "About that rental . . ."

"Look who's finally here!" My cousin Emma appeared in the

foyer, her eyes bright, her hair perfect, and her hands making little claps of delight. She tackled me in an impressive bear hug. "Run," she whispered in her ear. "Run while you can. Aunt Maxine's visiting."

"I heard that." Sylvie escorted us past the formal living room and into what she liked to call her parlor. And if parlor meant a place where coasters weren't required and folks gathered around the giant-screen TV, then parlor it was. "Nobody's leaving. Paisley just got here."

"Hello, sweet pea." My grandmother's sister, Maxine Simmons, scooped me into a hug, her hands patting all over me as if she were airport security. "Tanned and trim. Could you be any more of a Hollywood cliché?" My crazy great-aunt clucked her tongue. "Someone get this girl a burger. She's OD'd on salads and tofu."

"Quit hogging her, Maxine." Frannie Nelson stood, her lips pulled into a smile that could power the streetlights. "Girl, you bring some of those hugs to me."

"Hi, Aunt Frannie."

"You been gone too long." Frannie could speak five languages, but Southern was her dialect of choice. "It's about time you got right with Jesus and came on home."

Frannie and I didn't share DNA, a last name, or even the same skin color. But she was as family as any blood relative of Sylvie's. The two shared a unique bond, one that could be trying in the worst of times, entertaining in the best. The two had recently retired from the CIA, having devoted their entire adult lives to intrigue and espionage. To say retirement was going well was like saying World War II was a little historical hiccup. Both women had been mysteriously recruited into the bureau at the age of seventeen under a top-secret program when women were more likely to take care of a home than take a bullet for their country. Sylvie had married her high school sweetheart two weeks before graduation, given him five children by the age of twenty-five, then left most of the child-rearing to her husband. She knew more about bomb detonations than diapers and more about Middle Eastern spies than spaghetti dinners.

And, as Emma had warned me, Sylvie was spending her newfound free time on helping her grandchildren down the aisle. So far Emma had taken the bait, as she was now engaged to the handsome Sugar Creek mayor. But Sylvie would not get me. No, sirree. You could bet your nukes on that one.

"Welcome to Sexy Book Club," Emma said. "Frannie and Sylvie already have a husband picked out for you."

"I told Paisley all about him," Sylvie said. "Have you given my plan any more thought?"

"No," I said. "I'm still not up for an arranged marriage to an Israeli diplomat."

Sylvie shared a look with Frannie and Maxine. "Some people just have no sense of romance and peacekeeping."

The room held a handful of other women of various ages, each clutching tablets or paperbacks in their laps, and all greeting me with familiar warmth or unbridled curiosity.

"You look like you could use some punch and cookies." Sylvie handed me a plate as I settled onto the couch.

"Thank you." I blew my limp red hair out of my face. My long locks had started out beautifully straight this morning and were now a hot, humid disaster of curls and frizz. "I really can't stay, though."

"What's brought you back home, toots?" Aunt Maxine asked.

"I'm just here for a little while," I said. "Home is in Los Angeles."

"She's inherited her great-aunt's wedding planning business," Sylvie said.

My weird great-aunt Zelda, who'd had no children, had left me and my two siblings all she had. My brother had received money. My younger sister a bunch of stock held in a trust. Me? The woman had strongly disliked me and willed me her dying business. Such was my luck.

I caught my grandmother's eye. "I'm dead on my feet. Can I just get the keys for the rental and—"

"Let's talk about Cordero." Sylvie held up her iPad like a chalice, her voice booming in the room. "Did everyone read the whole book this time?"

Every head nodded.

"You might as well settle in," Emma said from her spot beside me. "Sylvie won't let anything get in the way of book club night. Not even her exhausted granddaughter. I speak from experience."

"What book are you discussing?" I asked.

Sylvie smiled. "*The Cowboy Lassos a Peasant.*"

I blinked.

"This is Sexy Book Club," Sylvie said. "When we retired last year, Frannie and I decided we'd try out some hobbies. So far this is the only one that's stuck."

"We started with some classics," Frannie said. "But we got

bored."

Sylvie nodded. "Lots of big words."

"So we started reading some of those hot romance novels." Frannie lifted her dark brows high. "Woooo-weee."

"Romance novels?" I frowned.

"Or as we like to call them"—Sylvie patted her iPad—"the *unsung* classics."

"Twenty-first century literature at its finest," said Aunt Maxine.

I melted into the couch cushions and stuck a cookie in my mouth.

"Now, let's begin." Sylvie swiped at her tablet. "Does anyone have anything to say about the theme?"

Blank stares from every lady in the room.

"Any poignant symbolism?"

Total silence.

"Okay," Sylvie said. "Any comments about our hero, Cordero?"

All hands shot toward the ceiling.

"Ooh, me!"

"I want to go first!"

"He was dreamy!"

"I'd like to visit *his* prairie!"

"He can rope my doggies anytime!"

As the chatter swelled about this fictional paragon of sexy, I leaned toward my grandma. "I've been driving for two days, and as much as I'd love to stay and hear more about the main character's pecs and kissing techniques, I'm about to fall over from exhaustion. Could I please have the keys to the rent house?"

Sylvie poked an entire cookie in her mouth, eyes wide.

"What are you not telling me?" I asked.

My grandmother chewed thoughtfully, shouted out an amen to something dirty Frannie said, then finally looked at me, her face a little too innocent. "Nothing. Nothing at all. I was just hoping you'd stay a night or two with me. But I know you're tired. You've got a big day tomorrow."

That was an understatement. Tomorrow would change my life. Turn everything around.

"The garage code is the chest and waist measurements of Vladimir Putin's body double."

My head hurt. "Can I just get a key instead?"

"So change in plans. You'll be staying at the house on Bowen Street. It's a bit smaller and has some issues. When Emma gets married and moves out, you can have her rental. It's a bit more deluxe."

Emma chimed in. "We could bunk up. You can help me with wedding preparations."

I'd rather have a unity candle shoved up my nose. "That's sweet, but I don't mind being cramped."

"The wedding's not for another six weeks," Sylvie said. "I told Emma to shack up with her sweetie and swing from the chandelier of sin, but they're not having it."

"How much is rent?" I lifted my cup to her lips.

"Minimal."

"Okay." I stood and stretched my aching back. "I'm waiting for the catch. There's always a catch with you, Sylvie."

"Uh-huh," Frannie said. "That's exactly what I told her

when we got captured in Cairo in '82."

Sylvie ignored this. "No catch. Goodnight, shug." She kissed my cheek, then her lips curved into a curious smile. "Get some rest. You, my dear, are going to need it."

CHAPTER TWO

I PULLED UP to a darkened house and briefly rested my head on the steering wheel in the quiet of the night.

Two months.

I had to stay in this town two months.

There had to be a way around that. To get what I wanted and return to LA before my beloved city had forgotten me. But the terms of the will, something I'd read at least twenty times, stated that I had to keep my great-aunt's business afloat for eight weeks, then I was welcome to sell. The business itself wouldn't be worth a dime, but the old building in the growing downtown area would bring in some much-needed cash.

Yanking a suitcase from the backseat, I slammed the car door shut and heaved the best of my belongings toward a gray two-story with black shutters and enough Victorian personality to charm but not intimidate. Sylvie owned a handful of rent houses in Sugar Creek, and this one boasted two side-by-side front doors. I tried the key she'd finally given me in both doors, but to no avail. Seriously? I just wanted a bed, to slip beneath cool sheets and let my worry-ridden head fall into a fluffy pillow.

Leaving my bags, I walked around the back of the house, using my phone for a flashlight. Crickets chattered and mosquitoes rudely buzzed their welcome in my ear. I tripped on a step to the back deck but climbed on up, only to be faced, yet again, with two doors. The key refused to fit into one lock, but the weathered door on the left opened with no effort at all. I could practically feel the cool, crisp sheets already.

My flashlight illuminated a small kitchen with granite countertops, white cabinets, and a dining set tucked into a nook. The hardwood floor beneath my feet creaked as I stepped into the room and—

A large shadow flickered a millisecond before five hundred pounds of solid bulk slammed into my body and threw me to the ground.

Lightning exploded in my head as it hit the floor, and my scream pierced the air. I kicked and struggled, desperate to get this intruder off me, while panic overrode any rational thought. I'd taken a self-defense class years ago, but I couldn't recall a single move. Still screaming, I thrashed wildly and tried to claw this person's face, but he took my hands captive.

"Get off me!" I yelled. "My husband's in the car! He has a gun!"

The intruder stilled. With one large hand still wrapped around both my wrists, he reached for my dropped phone and shined the light right in my face. My thunderous heartbeat couldn't drown out the loud sigh from the person hovering over me.

"Husband, huh?" a deep voice said. "Maybe we should wait for him."

Oh, geez.

I was pretty sure I knew that voice.

My attacker released my hands and rolled to his feet, the

light revealing one familiar face.

"Beau Hudson." My volume escalated with each word. "What in the name of all that's holy are you doing in *my* house?"

"You're in *my* house, Paisley Sutton." He flicked on the overhead light, illuminating a tableau I would forever call *The Time I Faced Death and Didn't Wet Myself.*

"This is my grandmother's home, and I have the keys to it." I pulled myself up to a seated position, my skull throbbing.

This interloper was the brother of my childhood best friend. His hair was the color of toffee, and those eyes, blue as sea glass. Back in the day, just to look upon him made a girl want to write poetry and compromise every moral she had. None of that had changed. He'd been the hero of the Sugar Creek football team years ago, before picking up his high school diploma and heading off to the Army. He was tall and trim, his body contoured with muscles he clearly still maintained since his military days. I only spoke to his sister about once a year, but she always gave me an update on Beau. I knew he'd come back to Sugar Creek within the last few years, lucky to be alive—yet, as his sister put it, "not quite the same."

Beau had been the older, mature fourteen to my twelve. After sharing a plate of macaroni and fried chicken, we'd kissed at a church social. Then he ran back to school to tell everyone it had been a slobbery disaster.

He took a knee beside me, and I scooted away.

"Let me see your head." His voice was as gruff as the stubble on his face. I'd just been attacked by a lumberjack. "Quit squirming." He reached out a hand and skimmed it over my cheek and temple, his eyes intense on my face. "I could've hurt you."

My skin tingled beneath his touch. "You *did* hurt me."

His hand began an inspective crawl into my hairline. "I mean I could've killed you."

I rubbed my aching shoulder. "I was two seconds away from ruining your life with a well-placed knee to your manly bits, so I don't think so." My pulse had yet to return to normal. I tried to shrug out of Beau's grip, but he wasn't having it. "I'm okay."

Those blue eyes still on mine, Beau's fingers slowly slid through my hair to the back of my head. "Does this hurt?"

"I . . . I think I'll live."

His gaze darkened. "You want to tell me what you're doing in my house?"

"I told you, it's my grandmother's house, and I'm living here for a couple months." Good heavens, his fingers were magic. "So I think I'm the one who should be asking the questions."

"For the love of—" Beau's expression darkened—"*You're* the new neighbor Sylvie was so cagey about."

I frowned, certain I had the right address. "Neighbor?"

"The house is two units. The back door you came in? It's mine. I assume you're living in the other half."

I slapped away his hands and attempted to stand.

"Easy." One strong arm curled around my waist. "We should probably get you to the ER. Have someone look at your head."

I was related to Sylvie. We were used to people suggesting we needed our heads examined. "I'm fine. I just want to get to my side so I can sleep. Apparently Sylvie gave me the wrong keys." Probably on purpose.

"I can get you in there."

"Is this going to involve brute force as well?"

Brow furrowed, Beau gave my form another assessing look before he walked away, a slight limp marring his gait. He returned shortly holding a silver key. "Let's get your luggage."

A few minutes later I stood behind him as he opened the door to my side of the house, carrying three bags as if they were no heavier than my purse.

He took a few steps inside. "Welcome home."

I stood in the doorway, my feet unable to carry me any further.

Welcome home.

This town had been home. Before I got plucked from a high school choir competition to round out a girls' band. Before I traveled the world and lived large. Before life said, "Never mind!" and kicked me off the train of success.

"I hope you're not waiting for me to carry you over the threshold," Beau said, interrupting my maudlin thoughts.

I mustered up a smile. "You'd do anything to cop a feel."

"Paisley?"

"Yes?"

"It's going to be okay."

"Is it?" I couldn't see how.

"Sugar Creek's not such a bad place. You loved it once."

"It's no longer my home."

"We could re-create a certain church picnic—if that would make you feel any more welcome."

"So you can go and tell your friends I'm a bad kisser?"

"Are you saying you want to refresh my memory?"

I laughed, took a deep breath, then stepped inside the living room. I tiredly took in the charming setup. Old wooden floors, gorgeous white moldings, original light fixtures, and a vintage fireplace that had more character than my last few dates combined. It was a lot nicer than the Los Angeles apartment I'd been living in. Minus a tackle from an old flame, probably a lot safer too.

"So, you're moving back." Beau didn't sound any more excited than I was. He had taken a severe disliking to me in our high school years, claiming my wild ways were a bad influence on his sister. And they were.

"It's temporary. I have to keep Sugar Creek Weddings and More afloat for a while, then I'm selling it and heading back to LA."

"And how is the music world treating you?"

Everyone knew the music world had long since spit me out. "Great," I said. "While I'm here, I hope to work on my next Grammy speech in peace and quiet."

He nodded slowly, not even bothering to hide his smile. "So this shop you inherited. Have you seen it lately?"

"No. Is it worse than I think it's gonna be?"

He grinned, a dimple forming in one stubbled cheek. "I'm sure you'll handle it just fine." Beau carried my big suitcase past a dining table with four chairs the color of driftwood. A vase of wildflowers sat in the middle like a little hello. "Master bedroom's back here." He led me down a short hall to a spacious room straight out of a HGTV show.

A giant king-sized bed occupied the center of the bedroom with matching whitewashed lamps on either side. A fluffy comforter covered the bed, a gray throw draping the end. A slipcovered chair sat in the corner with a burlap pillow emblazoned with my last name. Just waiting for me.

"Don't get any ideas." Beau gave the bed a meaningful glance and set down my bag. "I know you want to throw yourself at me tonight, but I'm just not in the mood."

"You haven't changed a bit, have you?"

I watched his smile fade so slightly, and his eyes darkened. "We've all changed, Paisley." He absently rubbed his right leg, as if a memory had pained it. "This town has a way of reminding you pretty often."

CHAPTER THREE

W ITH COFFEE IN one hand, I pulled Shirley into a tight spot on Main Street. Cars circled around the square, jockeying for parking spaces like buzzards searching for prey. What was everyone doing downtown this morning? Was there some event Sylvie forgot to tell me about?

Without bothering to lock the car, I grabbed my purse and coffee and walked the flower-lined sidewalk to Sugar Creek Weddings and More.

Located in a storybook house the color of cotton candy, the little business had held its ground near the square for fifty years. Owned by my great-aunt Zelda, the place was known for putting on some of the worst weddings in the history of the state. If you wanted glam and glitz, you traveled a few towns down the road. If you were okay with sweating through your gown at Sugar Creek First Baptist and drinking watery punch in the basement, Zelda was your gal. She wasn't known for quality, but she was known for her ability to throw a cheap wedding together in days. If a couple had reasons for a hasty, classless production that wasn't even accompanied by some good cake, Great-Aunt Z could fix you right up.

I noticed the sign first.

Enchanted Events.

When had Aunt Zelda changed the name? I guess it was better than Sugar Creek Weddings and More, since everyone in town knew the *more* was the complimentary eau de mothball smell.

The door chimed the same familiar tune as I stepped inside the lobby.

But that brass bell above me was the only thing I recognized.

"Excuse me." A woman sailed past me, carrying three wedding magazines thick as encyclopedias and speaking into her headset. "Yes, we have the governor's vow renewals scheduled for the twenty-fourth, and then *Elegant Weddings* magazine has their photo shoot here on the twenty-fifth. Can you hold? Enchanted Events . . ."

I did a slow turn, wondering if the bump on my head from last night had addled my brain or sent me to some alternate reality. This didn't look anything like Aunt Zelda's shop. Where was the faded orange hotel carpet? The samples of polyester wedding dresses on zombielike mannequins? The lobby chairs that looked like the spoils of a bad dumpster dive? The Merle Haggard tunes on the crackling stereo? The shop had been totally renovated. It looked like . . . a real business. Walls of white shiplap, aged wooden chandeliers, seating areas with plush chairs, dark walnut floors. Workstations flanked the corners with sleek white laptops, where waiting brides-to-be sat and flipped through gleaming photos on iPads.

"I don't understand," I whispered to no one in particular.

A dapper man who could've been Idris Elba's twin stopped beside me. "Is something the matter?"

I blinked my eyes and sniffed the air. "I don't smell mothballs."

"Enchanted Events is now known for more than smelling like granny's attic."

"What's happening here?" I couldn't even find the right questions to ask. "I'm—"

"Paisley Sutton," he supplied.

"Uh-huh. And I'm supposed to be taking ownership of—"

"Sugar Creek Weddings and More. We're now called Enchanted Events."

"And I'm really—"

"Confused and overwhelmed."

"Exactly," I said. "And also—"

"Rudely late."

Not what I was going to say. "I'm here to meet the current manager of"—I waved my hand around—"this. But maybe I'm not in the right place?"

"You're where you're supposed to be. Alice, get us some tea," he yelled over his shoulder. "And you might want to spike one of them."

"This is not my Aunt Zelda's wedding business. Her shop was a musty, dated, relic of a thing that she hung onto for a tax write-off."

"Then she hired me." He stuck out his hand to shake. "Henry Cole."

"I was in Sugar Creek two years ago. I would've noticed someone totally transforming her business."

"I started not too long after your wedding debacle. But we don't have time to revisit your travesties or hear of my miracle-working powers right now. You have at least five brides sitting out there."

I dumbly followed him down a hall, taking in all the hustle and bustle, the charm and class.

"And those are just the ones who could score an appointment. Word of mouth is a powerful thing."

This wasn't word of mouth. This was voodoo. This was sorcery. "Why didn't my family tell me about this?"

He turned a corner. "Sylvie swore us all to secrecy. Said you'd never come back if you knew the shop had gone big-time bridal, given your own nuclear bomb of a wedding."

"My grandmother is right—I want nothing to do weddings. I'm the last person you want making bridal decisions. So I'm just going to go on home and—"

"Not so fast." He stopped in front of a door bearing his name. "You're our boss."

"But I don't want to be." My voice sounded small, whiny.

He slipped into his office and headed toward his desk. "And I don't want to be a devilishly handsome black man who's freakishly good at wedding details and rocking the business world, while simultaneously canceling out any hopes of the female population thinking I'm straight."

"Uh-huh. Sounds like we're both hitting hard times." I fumbled in my purse for my car keys. "So it appears you've got things under control here, and I'd just mess things up. I'm gonna be one of those bosses who lets her employees do what they do best. Nobody likes a micromanager."

"You don't have a choice," Henry said. "I'm quite familiar with the terms of the will. You have to show up to work at least eight hours to get a paycheck while you're here—plus, Lisa's on maternity leave, so we're shorthanded and could use you."

"Is a newborn a good excuse to miss work? You should really be questioning Lisa's loyalty." I felt as if I'd requested a ride on a carousel, yet somehow wound up in the front cart of a roller coaster. This was so not going according to plan. On one hand, when I sold the business, it would clearly bring more money than I expected. But on the other hand, I was going to have to work in this frilly sponge cake of a store. "I have a lot to think about. Permission to take the rest of the day off?"

"Permission denied."

"I'm the boss here!"

"With a house full of employees who need you."

"They have you."

"They . . ." Henry sat in the leather seat behind his desk. "They don't really like me. They've been waiting for you like it's Zelda's second coming. Your great-aunt was the heart of this place, and I'm the brains."

I was supposed to fill in for Zelda's heart? Didn't she know wedding plans made me break out in hives?

"Here's the deal," Henry said. "You need me as much as I need you."

I lowered myself into the seat in front of Henry's desk. I thought of the money required to get back to LA, to invest in my career comeback while not having to worry about rent and shutoff notices. "I'm listening."

"You shadow me, and I show you the ropes. We'll have you cross-train in every department. And you can be the bridge between the employees and myself. Maybe counsel me in areas of . . . sensitivity, humility."

"And what makes you think I know something about that?"

"I'm guessing from your last job as a cruise ship singer you know a thing or two about humility."

"I had unlimited access to the dessert bar on that boat."

"Also our dress code here is a black or gray top, black pants or skirt." With open distaste, he took in my pink stilettos, the turquoise skinny pants, my glittery off-the shoulder Rolling Stones T-shirt with authentic band autographs, and the multiple gold necklaces around my neck.

"I don't wear head-to-toe black, but y'all go ahead."

"It's protocol."

"We'll discuss it later." Like never. I had a closet full of designer and custom-made pieces from my rocker days, and it made this poor girl happy to incorporate my concert clothes into my poor girl daily wear.

"Your first assignment is to help a bride-to-be select her bridesmaids' dresses," Henry said.

I blinked in confusion.

"We're now one-stop wedding planning here. We handle tuxedos, dress selections, music, flowers, venues, catering arrangements, wedding cakes. We work with all the best vendors. Should I go on?"

"Please don't." I felt as queasy as the first few days on that blasted cruise ship. "I know nothing about wedding planning."

"That's not true. Sylvie said you organized your big nuptials all by yourself."

"Let me rephrase that: I have *no interest* in planning weddings."

"If you don't work the business, you don't get to own the

business."

"What difference does it make to you?"

"I know you want to sell when your time is up. And when you do, I want to be first in line. I have big plans for this place, so I'm going to make sure you don't run it into the ground. Here's my proposition for you—I make sure Enchanted Events stays afloat, and you let me buy the business from you for a fair market price."

Not even noon, and I was already wanting to clock out.

"Without me," he said, "this place sinks within a month."

"Okay, fine. Deal. The place is yours when I leave." The sting of someone expecting me to fail was a refrain that never got easier to hear. It would always be a pointed arrow to the heart, even if I *didn't* want this stupid business.

"You won't regret that." He smiled unevenly, as if out of practice. "We've done a few parties and gatherings. It's time to go beyond weddings and offer large-scale event planning. I'll spare you all those proposals, but for now—we do weddings. And you're going to learn every nuance of what we do. I coach you on the business, and you rein me in when I'm a bit—"

"Of a jerk?"

"When I'm a bit insensitive. Ready to get started?"

"Do I have any other choice?"

"No." Henry was not in the mood to be my crying shoulder. "This morning you'll start by walking yourself down the street to Sugar Creek Formals. It opened about a year ago and is already quite renowned in the South for its bridal wear. Our client, Sasha Chandler, is selecting bridesmaid dresses today, and I want you there to advise." He handed me an iPad. "Here's a file with her wedding details. Read it before you go and be fully knowl-edgeable on the event."

Great. I already had homework.

"Oh, and beware," Henry said. "This bride has claws."

"Bad manicure?"

"What I mean is she's a holy tyrant."

"I have absolutely no idea how to run a wedding business." I surged to my feet, suddenly craving another cup of coffee. "But I *was* in the hottest girl band of this decade, and I've met divas that would make you cry." I gave a confident smile. "Compared to pop stars, this bride will be an angel."

CHAPTER FOUR

THE BRIDE WAS a demon.

Sasha Chandler sat in a Tiffany blue chair in Sugar Creek Formals like a queen on her throne and watched her bridesmaids step from the dressing rooms. "I said blush taffeta, ladies. Raven, you've erroneously selected a pink one."

"The blush makes me look washed-out."

Sasha looked up from her cell phone. "Is this about you?"

No. Clearly it was all about the bride. The vapid, tiny-waisted, shrill-talking bride.

"Hi." I pulled myself from the shadows and walked fully into the room. "I'm Paisley Sutton from Enchanted Events." I'd practiced that at least ten times. "I'll be helping you today."

Sasha's flawlessly lined eyes traveled from my pink spike heels to the humidity-flattened hair I was ready to throw in a topknot. "I wanted Henry to handle this," she snipped.

"I did too." Believe me, sister. "But you'll have to settle for me." My lips pulled into a thin smile. "The new owner."

At that, Demon Bride's scowl lessened, and some of that judgmental scorn dimmed. "I see. And do you know what you're doing?"

I was a washed-up pop star who couldn't even get a gig to sing on the county fair circuit. If I knew what I was doing, I'd have an accounting degree instead of two dusty Grammys packed away in a storage unit and a twenty-two-year-old agent who wouldn't call me back. "I think I can manage."

I consulted the file on the tablet Henry had shoved into my hands. Sasha was twenty-four, a local, and getting married in six months. There was also a note that she was WBE, but I had no idea what that meant. "So today we're picking out dresses and shoes for your bridesmaids, correct?"

"Yes."

"Sounds easy enough," I said more to myself.

"It should be." Sasha tossed her wavy blonde hair and regarded her bridesmaids as peasants. "This is my sister Zoey. She's my maid of honor."

"*Step*sister," Zoey corrected.

"And Raven and Phoebe are my bridesmaids and best friends from college."

I glanced at her attendants and noticed no one looked too enthused to be there.

"Do you have your dress picked out?" I asked Sasha.

"Of course I do."

"I designed it," said Zoey. "I'm still working on it."

"Do you have a picture so I can get an idea of the style you're going for?" I asked.

"It's not relevant right now." Sasha whipped her attention back to her ladies-in-waiting. "Today is about the bridesmaids' dresses, and so far no one is cooperating. Phoebe, quit tugging on that bodice. Stand up straight."

Phoebe, a short girl with inky black hair, dropped her hands to her sides, her flushed cheeks as pink as her glossy lipstick. "I don't look good in strapless." She turned and surveyed herself in the mirror, her face as mournful as a funeral hymn. "The girls need straps." She did a slight shimmy. "Asking them to hold up an entire dress and stay put is asking too much."

Sasha's tone was pure saccharine. "That's what duct tape is for."

Raven shuffled out, holding the back of her dress together. "Mine won't zip." She looked to Sasha. "I need the next size up."

"No." Sasha's lip curled. "That's the size we're ordering. You have six months—lose some weight."

Raven's eyes teared up as she exchanged a look with Phoebe.

Five minutes later Zoey eased out of her dressing room looking like a vision in her gown. She was tall, something I envied since I was barely five foot five with my best heels. Zoey's willowy figure and model's cheekbones would make her a stunner in any dress. Surely Bridezilla wouldn't have a problem with her.

"Zoey," Sasha said from her command post, "take your glasses off. This isn't a hipster wedding."

"But I can't see without them."

"Can't you get some contacts?"

"I'm allergic to them."

"It's one day."

"My eyes will be swollen for a week afterward."

Sasha shrugged. "Consider it your wedding present to me. Along with a setting of my china."

Zoey straightened her red-framed glasses. "You're being unreasonable."

"Oh, am I really?" Sasha stalked to her posse of bridesmaids.

"Does anyone else have something to say?"

From there the scene deteriorated into a cacophony of yelling, insults, and tears.

"You're so demanding!"

"This is my wedding!"

"I am not wearing feathers!"

"Don't you even care that I'll get conjunctivitis?"

"I'm not going on some cabbage soup diet!"

"My boobs deserve better than this!"

I knew I should intercede, but conflict resolution was so not my strong suit. Conflict *avoidance*? I pretty much had a PhD in that.

I had dealt with countless diva tantrums from our lead singer Jaz, and I'd come back the loser in every instance I'd spoken up. The Electric Femmes had been a girl band of three, but from the beginning Jaz was the sun the other singer and I were expected to orbit around.

Okay, I could do this.

But before I could take action, Henry walked into the shop like an avenging angel, wearing a knowing, smug grin. "How's every little thing?"

"I have a feeling you know perfectly well how it's going," I whispered. "You sent me in here on purpose."

He shrugged his shoulders and lifted one dark brow. "These are your clients."

"So you just throw me to the wolves on my first day?"

"If you can handle Sasha Chandler, you can handle anything."

"What does WBE stand for?"

"Worst bride ever." He ignored my silent outrage. "What do you want to do about her?"

"Let's throw her out." I took a step forward, but Henry's hand on my arm stopped me.

"Not so fast. These are paying customers. And besides, if we threw out every difficult bride, we'd be bankrupt by the end of the month. Enchanted Events has never lost a bride."

Bankruptcy was definitely not what I wanted. The volume of the fighting swelled around us, and I rubbed my temples. *Think, think, think.* What were some of the demands on Jaz's rider for her concerts? Truffles imported from Sweden, water from a spring in France, green juice freshly squeezed with zero froth, and—

"Champagne," I said. "We need to serve them champagne."

"It's ten a.m."

"Mimosas, then."

He frowned. "We don't have any champagne."

"That needs to change." *I could use a bottle it myself right now.* "Ladies!" I yelled above the din. "Girls!" I put my fingers to my teeth and whistled, finally gaining their attention. "I'm seeing a lot of beautiful dresses." Truly, the store's selection was incredible. It was like something out of an upscale Manhattan boutique.

Plucking a tissue from a box on the floor, I handed it to a teary Phoebe before continuing. "Sasha has some excellent ideas and lovely taste." As I watched the bride preen like a pageant contestant, I knew I was on the right track. Sasha was like Jaz— and the way to get through to a diva was not with logic and reason, but by appealing to her ego. "I think the color she's chosen is very on trend and flattering to everyone. You've done a great job, Sasha." Even if she was a total witch.

"Thank you." Sasha's voice was a prideful singsong.

"But perhaps we can try on some others just to be certain we have *the* ones."

"What I picked out for each one is exactly what I want."

"And you have excellent taste." I unclenched my teeth and slipped my arm around Henry, giving him a squeeze for good measure. "But Henry here has been dying to tell you about some brand-new dresses the store's had in mind *just* for your wedding, Sasha." It was important to make the diva feel as if she was the most important person in the room. "He said they haven't let anyone else even try them on."

"What are you talking about?" Henry hissed.

"Oh." The hand bearing Sasha's megawatt diamond fluttered to her chest. "Well, I guess we could take a peek."

The bridesmaids all nodded their agreement.

"Wonderful," I said. "Henry, show them the new dresses while I go get everyone a coffee from next door."

Henry's voice dipped venomously low as the ladies walked away. "If you don't come back, Paisley, I will call your grandmother and have her hunt you down and bring you back. I know she has all sorts of contraband weapons and can make it painful."

"The girls need caffeine. I'm just being hospitable." I gave his shoulder a friendly pat. "I'll bring you something back, boss."

"You're the boss," he called out after me.

"And don't you forget it!"

IT WAS ALREADY a scorcher in Sugar Creek, and the sun seared right through my T-shirt as I stepped onto the sidewalk and hoofed it three doors down to Perky's Coffee Shop. I passed two antique stores and one new restaurant before opening the doors of the shop and inhaling the magical aroma. Surely heaven would smell like a double-shot latte.

"What'll it be?" the man at the counter asked. "Hey, aren't you Sylvie Sutton's granddaughter?"

"I am."

"The one who inherited the wedding business?"

"Yes." I eyed the arsty chalkboard menu behind him. "I'd like to order two—"

"Word on the street is you're probably gonna run it into the ground."

The town was talking about me? "Definitely not my intention."

"What do you know about running a business?"

"Not much." Though apparently I could handle crazy brides. "So I'd like to order a macchiato and—"

"Enchanted Events provides jobs for quite a few folks. I'd hate to see them out of work."

My desire for coffee was dwindling by the second. "Can I just place my order, sir?"

"Are you gonna sell it and leave? Let it die like that band you were in?"

The words delivered an unexpected bolt of pain.

I had to get out of here before the tears came.

"The lady would like to order some coffee, Frankie," came a deep twang behind me.

I turned and found my nose planted right in the chest of Beau Hudson.

"Hello, neighbor," he said.

I looked up to see him smiling down, his gaze narrowing at my watery eyes. "Beau."

One of his strong hands squeezed my upper arm. "Skipping out on work already?"

"I'm . . ." I cleared my throat and shook off the barista's barb. "I'm doing a little coffee intervention. Ordering for a wedding party." My gosh, Beau smelled wonderful. He wore a mint green T-shirt with a retro advertisement for Beaver Lake, a navy baseball cap, and a total disregard for a clean shave. "We're dealing with a barracuda of a bride right now."

"Something tells me you can take her." His smile was slow, full of the same kind of arrogance and mischief that I remembered from when he was the town's high school football legend. "Frankie, Paisley's in a hurry to get back to all that wedding crap. Why don't you take her order real quick like and put it on my tab?"

"You got it, Beau," the man said, as if Beau still possessed the ability to take the team to state.

"Thank you." I pulled my eyes from Beau's and rattled off my lengthy order. I had no idea what anyone would actually want, but espresso shots seemed a necessity.

"How was your first night back in Sugar Creek?" Beau asked as we waited, still standing closer than a casual conversation required.

"Best sleep of my life," I lied. "Sweet dreams and all of that."

"You were probably dreaming about me." He shrugged. "It

happens. I think there's a support group that meets on Wednesday nights."

"For people who dream of you nightly? Probably lots of pretty men and regular drug users."

"Nothing wrong with a diverse fan base." That wicked gleam in his eye was enough to disrupt any girl's heart rhythms. "Don't let Frankie get to you. He insults everyone. It's how he shows love."

"I'd rather have it in the form of extra whipped cream."

"Order up for the pop princess!" Frankie yelled a few minutes later.

When my order appeared on the counter, I questioned the logic of a drink run. Seven coffees. Two hands. "I don't suppose you have a delivery service, sweet Frankie?"

"I'll help you." Beau picked up four of the steaming cups and jerked his chin toward the door. "Lead the way to Ladyville."

As he held the door open, I balanced the coffee ever so precariously and stepped onto the sidewalk.

And plowed right into someone.

Mochas, lattes, and Americanos went airborne. Hot liquid splattered on me, on my skin, and on—

"Hey, watch out!" cried a man.

After I looked up, I ignored my burning skin, my dripping shirt, my stained shoes, the litter of now-empty cups around me.

"*Evan Holbrook.*" The name slipped from my lips like a hot curse.

The man swiped his hands over his blue button-down shirt, his frown severe. Until his eyes locked on mine.

"Paisley?"

"You." A fury filled my vision, made my blood go hot as a tin roof at straight-up noon. "What are you doing in this town?"

Beau's arm brushed mine as he stood closer. "You know this guy?"

"He's my former fiancé." My gaze remained locked on Evan like one of Sylvie's Beretta pistols. "Surely you know the story. Everyone does. Evan's version, that is. Because he left me standing at the altar to go running to the tabloids."

"Can't say I've heard this tale." Beau gave an easy shrug. "Fighting wars and all that."

Evan held up his hands as if in surrender. "That was two years ago. It's time to let this go. Move on with your life."

"Evan here broke our engagement *during* the ceremony, then sold the story to three different tabloids. Except the story he told wasn't the true version of a man leaving an embarrassed and humiliated woman in the Sugar Creek Chapel. It was some fabricated delusion about a man victimized by a mentally unstable pop star who needed medication to handle her tanking career and who verbally abused him. Is that about right, Evan? Did I miss anything?"

Evan pulled off his sunglasses, his eyes blinking rapidly. "Things got out of hand. Those tabloids are vultures."

"Oh, really? Do explain. Did someone tell *your* entire hometown that you're certifiable?" I took a menacing step forward, my pointer finger jabbing Evan's chest with each sentence. "Did *your* own mother call you daily for three months to ask if you needed to borrow money for a treatment facility? Did *you* lose a German recording contract you had *just signed*?

Did you?"

He shook his head. "No."

"No, you didn't."

"I'm sorry you're still hurting," Evan said quietly.

"Hurting?" I took another step, my nose nearly touching his. "Oh, I'm so far past that. Don't even kid yourself."

Beau nudged me with an elbow. "Coffee's getting cold, Paisley. Why don't we get you back to the shop?"

"I heard you inherited Enchanted Events," Evan said.

"Yeah, turns out I'm back in town for a while. And if you feel the need to call the press with that, trust me: They no longer care."

"Okay, good talk," Beau said. "But we need to get Paisley back to work before she pulls out her nunchuks. We don't want her arrested on her first day." He held his carton of coffees in one arm and wrapped his other around my shoulders.

But I wasn't done.

"You really have no idea what you cost me, do you, Evan?" I watched this weak man in front of me and wondered how I could've ever loved him. "Here's some advice for you." I stuck a finger in his pretty face. "Sleep lightly. I've spent a lot of time thinking of how I'd repay you, how I'd get you back for all the damage you caused. Pretty soon I won't be the only one who regrets you ever opened your mouth to all those tabloids." I had waited forever for this moment, and this small victory soared through my veins. "You won't know the day or the hour, but do know this—I'm coming for you. I'll make the Bridezilla I'm dealing with today seem like a saint in comparison."

"Sasha!"

I stilled. How did Evan know? "Is her behavior that renowned?"

"Um, Paisley?"

I turned at Beau's tap on my shoulder.

And found a small army of very interested townsfolk standing behind us.

Including a wide-eyed Sasha Chandler.

Evan heaved a sigh as Sasha rushed into his arms. "Paisley, I'd like you to meet my fiancée."

CHAPTER FIVE

"THE WITCHING HOUR begins at noon today." Henry handed me a coffee as soon as I entered his office the next morning.

I inhaled the comforting scent and took my first sip. "Do I even want to know what you're talking about?"

"Sasha Chandler. She has a twelve o'clock appointment for her cake tasting. The Measuring Cup Bakery brings samples daily, so our brides can taste-test here."

"Two days in a row with the WBE. Are you sure you're not trying to run me off?"

"The town is abuzz after your throwdown with Evan Holbrook yesterday."

"Discussion. We merely had a discussion." A very loud one. In which I did all the talking.

"The newspaper's already called for a statement, so back off on the public meltdowns during working hours, okay? This place was like granny's scary basement before I arrived, and I don't want to see a reverse transformation. Am I clear? This is a business, not *The Jerry Springer Show.*"

"Yes, sir. And I found out today is Alice's birthday, so do something nice for her."

Henry scrunched his nose. "Like what?"

"I'll email you some ideas, Mr. Crabby."

"I'm not jumping out of a cake."

"And for that she's probably grateful." I plucked a glass bottle of champagne from my bag and set it on his desk. "Here's my idea. We offer a coffee service until noon, then champagne 'til closing. What do you think?" My red fingernail tapped the label. "It's even locally sourced."

Henry nodded slowly. "The idea has potential. We can do a trial period. But let's get back to Sasha Chandler."

"Maybe some Sugar Creek label champagne will help her disposition." Or a lobotomy. Whatever. "Good luck to the poor soul who deals with her today."

He sat down at his computer and tapped at his keyboard. "That would be you."

I sputtered on a swallow of coffee. "I don't think so."

"I do," he said. "She's our only cake tasting today, and I want you to see how it works. Cupcakes representing the cake choices are delivered by ten each day. You'll need to review your notes about this topic, of course."

"I don't want to brag, but I know cake." Mostly the eating of it. "Let someone else take this."

Henry raised one dark eyebrow. "Why?"

"Because she's my ex-fiancé's fiancée. Something you no doubt knew."

"Maybe." He brushed a piece of lint from his charcoal pants. "Even if I wanted to help you, I can't. I have a twelve o'clock with a senator's daughter, Layla's out sick, and everyone else has appointments. It's all you."

I rested my forehead on the desk. "I should fire you."

"Uh-huh." He chuckled. "I dare you to try it. By the way, I'll have you a desk here by the end of the day. We'll share the office."

"Can we put a couch in here for twice-daily naps? Maybe a lava lamp or two?" At my suggestion of a jumbo TV and popcorn machine, he walked out.

The next few hours passed with my shadowing Henry. He gave me a crash course on our payment plans and the latest trends in wedding themes, then updated me on local venues. I watched him defuse a powder keg of a momma not getting her way, deal with two suppliers who were late on shipments, then give one of our employees a talking-to for being repeatedly late. Though his tone could be a little harsh, the man had business skill coming out his every pore. Meanwhile, I was saturated with information and completely overwhelmed. This was a lot harder than learning a melody and shaking my tush behind Jaz on stage. Not that tush-shaking didn't have its challenges.

"Okay, you're up," Henry said as twelve o'clock neared. "The Dragon Bride's in the parlor room."

"Henry—"

"You tend to Sasha today, and I'll make sure it's the last time. You're taking one for the team, and your staff knows it."

"Fine. But I'd feel better going in with a garlic necklace or holy water."

The parlor was a cozy room with antique dining chairs around a few white tables. Pale sage walls hosted framed vintage bridal prints, and white chandeliers hung from the ceiling. Violin music softly played, and the air smelled of sugar and dreams.

When I walked in, Sasha Chandler sat in one of those chairs.

I approached her like a woman given the task of routing a bear from its cave. "Good afternoon, Sasha."

She looked up, and I expected hate to flare from her pretty brown eyes and venom to spew from her lips.

But she simply said, "Hello."

I set a bottle of champagne on her table and began to ease out the cork. "So . . . I'm sorry for the scene with Evan yesterday. I can't stand your fiancé, but I want you to know that it won't affect the service you'll receive at Enchanted Events." I poured her a flute full of bubbly and recited the words Henry had written out for me to memorize. "You'll still get the same top-notch care from the staff here, and—" I couldn't do it. I couldn't continue with the drivel. "Look, I'm just gonna go grab the cupcakes, okay?"

She mutely nodded before picking up her champagne. Her hand shook slightly as she lifted it to her lips and drank. The entire thing.

I hesitantly refilled her glass. "Um, Miss Chandler, is everything okay?"

She swiped at her eyes and sniffed. "Just go get the cake."

I returned a short while later with a plate of cupcakes and gave her the spiel I'd been coached to say. "The Measuring Cup Bakery has prepared a selection of five cake samples for you today. We have the white cake with a layer of strawberry—"

"First of all, stay away from Evan." Sasha's voice snapped with fierce warning. "Never speak to him again. And second, leave this bottle." She tapped the champagne. "I think I can handle tasting cake without your hovering."

"Oh." What a peach this one was. She and Evan deserved each other.

"You would never have made Evan happy, you know." She poured her own glass this time. "You never had what he wanted."

I froze at the door and slowly turned. "I guess that's something I'm eternally grateful for."

"Really?" Her face pulled in mock-pity. "Seems like losing Evan was the beginning of the end for you. You never really recovered, did you?"

Who did Sasha Chandler think she was? "I'm just here to help you pick a cake flavor. If you'd like to verbally assault someone, maybe you could try another business."

"Stay away from Evan. Do you understand me?"

"Gladly."

"And furthermore, I want to work with someone else today—not you."

"I'm sorry," I said, "but my employees are busy with other clients." I hoped she caught the little detail that this was *my* business.

"Unacceptable."

Sasha reminded me of my bandmate Jaz—how she enunciated each word with confident disdain. "I know this is not the most comfortable situation," I said, "but I think we can be adult about it, right? I bring you cupcakes, you eat them and make a decision, and I stay out of your way. Sound good?"

"No. It does not." She stood up, a good four inches taller than I was in heels. "I am not paying all this money to Enchanted Events to be subjected to my fiancé's throwaway girlfriend."

I tried to deflect the barbed wire prick of her words, but it hit the mark anyway. "Evan was my fiancé, not just my boyfriend. And if you want to marry a spineless man who lacks any shred of integrity, have at it. As for me, I'm grateful I dodged the bullet of becoming his wife, so don't think I'll be serving you jealousy with those cake samples. Now, are you ready to begin?"

Her shiny lips parted in outrage, Sasha bore her brown eyes into mine, as if trying to melt me with her ire. "Go. Get. Henry." She pointed toward the door. "*Now.*"

"If you think that I'm going to—" I clamped my mouth shut on the rest of my words. What I wanted to do was kick Sasha out, but that probably wasn't best for a business I desperately needed to succeed. I set my jaw. "I'll relay your wishes to Henry." My legs couldn't carry me fast enough to the door.

"I told you, leave the champagne."

I slammed the bottle down on the table and all but ran out of the room before the Dragon Bride could fling another insult. My feet barely stopped moving when I collided into Alice in the hall.

A wide-eyed Alice clutched my shoulders and eyed me like a bomb seconds away from detonation. "Everything okay in there?"

"No, it's not." I jerked my head toward the parlor. "Sasha Chandler is *awful.*"

"I couldn't help but overhear some of your conversation. You know the customer is always right, don't you?"

"Well, she's all wrong for me. Either someone else can deal with her, or I want her out."

"The Chandler account is huge—maybe the biggest event

we've ever had. We can't afford to lose it."

As peaceful instrumental music played overhead, I took three cleansing breaths. *Serenity now. Serenity now.* "Can you take over?"

"It's simple cake samples, Miss Sutton."

"I'm aware of that, but—"

"I have two back-to-back appointments already. You can talk to Henry or the other girls, but we're all swamped." She patted my arm. "You can do this."

I could, but should I have to?

I next sought out Mary, who was midappointment and did not appreciate my even suggesting she step in for me. My last hope was Henry, who handed a tissue to a crying mother-of-the-bride before glaring at my interruption.

"What is it?" His smile faded as he pulled me aside.

"Sasha Chandler is evil."

"We know this. It's why we have prayer meeting before all her appointments. Now go back in there."

"I'd rather not."

"Paisley, dealing with difficult brides is part of the job."

I knew I sounded pitiful and childish. "She's incredibly rude and mean—trying to rile me up about Evan."

"I see it wasn't very hard."

"You honestly expect me to take abuse from a client?"

"When her last name is *Chandler*? Yes." He held up a hand in greeting to a couple walking in the door, then fixed his impatient gaze back on me. "Go outside and cool off. Walk around the building a few times. Take a few moments to collect yourself, then go back in there and get it over with."

"I'm never working with her again, Henry."

"Duly noted."

"And I wasn't invited to any prayer meeting."

"Then you'd better have one on your own." He pushed me toward the back exit and left to greet his next clients.

The hall echoed with my heels hitting the floor in angry stomps. That woman! That arrogant, shrew of a woman. Who was she to talk to me like that? The way she treated people was deplorable. How had she survived high school without being stuffed in a locker?

Two laps around the block simply wasn't enough, but I didn't want to sweat through my jacket—so I gave up speed-walking and sat in a lawn chair behind the building. I contemplated clouds until I no longer had steam coming out my ears like a runaway locomotive.

After a quick breathing exercise a former manager had taught me, I walked back to the front and through the main entrance of Enchanted Events. Taking the long way back to the parlor, I made a detour through the shop and greeted a few brides. I had a lovely conversation with a teary-eyed grandmother who had the honor of being her granddaughter's matron of honor, then assisted another customer as they picked out napkins for an engagement party.

Finally, I returned to the parlor.

Where I found the bride facedown in her icing.

"Sasha?"

Rushing to her, I stopped short, nearly tripping over a champagne bottle. Something was horribly wrong. Blood covered her temple, her hair. "Sasha!" My brain struggled to comprehend the scene. "Stay with me. Come on." I fumbled beneath her hair 'til I felt her neck, searching for a pulse.

Nothing.

"Someone help us!" I yelled. "Call 911! Henry!" What should I do? CPR? Did I dare move her?

I whispered a prayer for help. For divine intervention. For the girl to open her eyes, draw a deep breath, and say something cutting and cruel.

"Paisley, what in the—" Henry rushed into the room, his whole body jerking to a halt as he took in the chaotic scene. "What's happened?"

I lifted my hands from Sasha's neck, my fingers covered in her crimson blood and met his frightened gaze. "Henry"—black spots danced before my eyes as the room tilted—"I think we just lost a bride."

CHAPTER SIX

I STOOD WITH the Enchanted Events staff in a bewildered huddle as the coroner drove away hours later. My stomach lodged somewhere in the vicinity of my feet, I could barely swallow the thick panic. Though now clean, my hands tingled as if Sasha's blood still covered my fingers. Shaking my head, I tried to dislodge the images in my mind of her battered face.

A tall, lanky officer used his spindly arms to pull yellow tape across the door of the parlor.

"Miss Sutton?" Police Chief O'Hara, still the same portly walrus he'd been during my childhood, slipped his phone in his pocket and ambled toward me. "We're going to have to talk to everyone here."

"Okay." My head bobbed with excessive nodding. "Anything you need."

"Who was the last person to see Sasha Chandler before this unfortunate event?"

All eyes went to me. "I was." Why had I taken that extended break outside? Maybe if I'd just done my job like a grown-up, none of this would've happened.

A navy-suited officer appeared at O'Hara's elbow and whispered painfully long sentences near his ear. Chief O'Hara nodded once, ran a hand over his wooly mustache, then pivoted back to me. "I'd like to offer you a ride in my patrol car to the police station."

My eyes went round as wedding bands. "Why?"

"I think we might have a lot to talk about."

"I didn't do anything," I said weakly.

"Then let's discuss it."

I followed Chief O'Hara outside, the cheery glow of the sun an insult to our somber scene. "I could just take my car and meet you there," I suggested.

"And let me miss my chance to ride with a pop star?" He opened the back door to his Dodge, looking none too impressed. "Hop in."

"Can't I at least sit in the front?"

"Against policy."

"Am I being charged with something?"

He waited 'til I was tucked into the backseat. "Not yet."

The ride couldn't have been more than a couple of miles, but it took an eternity. Officer O'Hara did little talking, instead taking calls on his phone and sending me pointed glances in his rearview, as if fearing I'd lower my window and make a wild leap.

The metal building that housed the police department sat at the edge of town, an eyesore compared to the Victorian charm of downtown and someplace I never thought I'd need to visit.

Chief O'Hara pulled into a parking spot marked with his name, shut off the car with what I thought was a little too much gusto, then opened my door. "Out you go."

This was like going to the principal's office—something I had lots of experience with—yet so much worse.

I followed him inside the building, and the outer office buzzed like a beehive.

"Come with me." O'Hara led me down a dark hall, then pulled open a door to a small room. "Let's step in here."

"Is this the interrogation room?" I sat down in a metal chair at a small table, pushing away a mop and bucket for some space.

"Yeah, except we're pretty tight on space, so it's also where we keep our cleaning supplies and toilet paper."

I inhaled Pine-Sol and bleach, the clean scents not the least bit of comfort.

Chief leaned back in his chair across from me and folded his arms over his ample stomach. "Tell me what happened from the time you greeted Sasha Chandler to the moment you found her nonresponsive."

Alarm shimmered across my skin. "I swear she was alive when I left her alone."

"Just answer the question."

"Sasha was escorted into the parlor—the room where we do things like cake testing."

"By you?"

"No." I licked my lips and worried it was a guilty-looking move. "By Alice, I think. I'm not sure." Someone needed to turn the thermostat down. It was burning up in here. "I greeted Sasha, then—"

"And did she seem well? Upset? Bothered?"

"She seemed . . . distracted initially. Then she lit into me about Evan, her fiancé."

"Because he's *your* ex-fiancé, correct?"

"Yes."

He jotted notes down in a laptop. "Continue."

"Sasha got very rude."

"So she said things that made you mad."

"Yes." Oh, geez. "I mean, no!" This was going about as well as my last solo album. "I mean, what she said bothered me." I filled him in on Sasha's exact words. "I tried to brush it off and told her we needed to simply move along with her cake testing. That's when she asked me to go get Henry."

"And you did?"

"I tried, but he was too busy to help her. Everyone was. Henry told me to go cool off outside."

"Go cool off in ninety-three degree temps? You must've been really furious."

O'Hara was spinning webs, hoping I'd screw up and step into one of them. "I was upset, but I walked some laps outside the building and just sat down for a bit."

"Did anyone see you outside?"

"Not that I know of."

"You served her the champagne, am I correct?"

"Yes."

"You left her with two bottles?"

"No, just one."

He stared at me for an uncomfortable stretch of time. "Does Enchanted Events always serve champagne?"

"We do now." I explained our new service.

"So today was the first day for the beverages—and it was your idea."

"Yes." And clearly a stupid one. "Do you think someone bashed her on the head with a champagne bottle?"

"Miss Sutton, how did you feel about Sasha Chandler?"

"I only met her yesterday."

"Answer the question."

"I wasn't a fan, but nobody in the office seems to be. She was quite unkind to everyone who encountered her."

"Who else had access to the champagne bottles?"

"Everyone on staff."

O'Hara jotted some notes on a legal pad. "Under what circumstances did you meet Sasha Chandler?"

"I assisted her and her bridesmaids with their dress selection." I explained in detail everything I could remember from the day before.

"And you walked out of Sugar Creek Formals for coffee because you were upset with Sasha?"

"No." I watched him scribble something else on his paper. "Not at all. I just thought all the ladies could use—"

A knocked preceded the door opening and a woman with extra-frizzy hair stepping inside. "You said to let you know when Detective Ballantine is here, sir."

"Right. Thanks, Marge." O'Hara gathered his notebook and stood. "You stay here, Miss Sutton. I'll be back in a few minutes."

Those few minutes turned into thirty, then forty-five, the seconds ticking on a wall clock like death knells. If this delay was a stalling tactic to wear me down, it was working. I needed to pee, I was in serious need of caffeine, and I wanted my grandma. Left alone with no one to talk to but brooms and mop buckets, fear slipped into the seat beside me and presented frightening scenarios for my consideration. Did they think I had hurt Sasha?

What if they wanted to arrest me? What if they locked me in a cell and threw away the key?

When the door finally opened again, I straightened in my seat, my nerves buzzing. In walked Chief O'Hara with another man behind him.

"Miss Sutton, this is Benton County Detective Scott Ballantine."

Detective Ballantine shook my hand like he meant it, then sat down, his beady brown eyes watching me behind rimless glasses.

"Is there anything you'd like to tell me, Miss Sutton?" Ballantine asked.

I looked to Chief O'Hara. "I don't know what else I could possibly say."

"Well, let me tell you something," Ballantine said. "Sasha Chandler was murdered in your shop today."

Murdered. The unreasonable part of my brain had hoped the obvious hadn't been true. "I'm truly horrified to hear that."

"Had you made any threats toward Miss Chandler?" Ballantine asked.

"No, of course not."

Detective Ballantine pushed a button on his phone, and my voice filled the small space. *"Sleep lightly. I've spent a lot of years thinking of how I'd repay you, how I'd get you back for all the damage you caused."*

"I didn't threaten Sasha," I said. "In anger, I said that to my former fiancé—"

"Did you or did you not use the words, 'Pretty soon I won't be the only one who regrets you ever opened your mouth to all those tabloids'?" Ballantine removed his glasses. "Sounds like a threat to me. Sounded like a threat to the ten good people of Sugar Creek who came to this police department to report it. Five of them already have it on YouTube."

Everyone was a paparazzo these days. "I did threaten Evan. But I meant I'd let the air out of his tires or write a 'lonely man seeks circus clown' type of personal ad on his behalf. I sure didn't mean I'd kill his fiancée."

"Who served her the champagne?" Ballantine asked.

"I did. It's my job."

"You must've spoken to her while she was in your shop," Ballantine said. "What did you say?"

I carefully recreated my conversation with Sasha. "So you see, she's the one who was antagonistic." I regretted my words immediately, as the energy in the room shifted. The two men suddenly looked like leopards who had just sniffed an unsuspecting gazelle. "I certainly didn't harm Sasha after our heated discussion."

"What did you do?" Ballantine asked.

"I went looking for someone else to take care of her. No one could—or would. Then . . . then I went outside."

Ballantine frowned. "Why? It's blistering hot out today."

"I just needed a break." I edited each word before releasing it in to this room of toilet paper and doubts. "I thought Sasha needed to cool down as well."

"How long were you outside?" Ballantine picked up his pen and twirled it between three fingers.

"I'm not sure. Fifteen to twenty minutes, I guess. Probably too long to be considered good customer service."

"You must've been pretty upset."

I didn't appreciate the detective's tone. "I was outside the entire time. When I left the room Sasha was alive and barking orders. When I returned, she was—well, slumped over the cupcakes." Surely Chief O'Hara didn't think I'd committed murder. "Chief, you've known me since I was a kid. You know I wouldn't murder someone."

"No one said we're accusing you of murder." His gaze flitted to the table then back to me. "But folks do change, though, don't they? I do hear LA can be a mean town. How's that music career these days, Paisley?"

O'Hara was raking hot coals right over my heart, my pride. "The music career is fine." Everyone knew it wasn't. But how did I explain all the blood, sweat, and prayers I'd poured into its revival? The one that was always within my reach, but never finding its place in my hands? Nobody cared about how hard I'd chased it, how hard I'd worked. All they saw was that my career was gone, as if I'd opened a window and carelessly thrown it into the wind.

But I cared. And now my failure was being held against me in a whole new way.

"Evan Holbrook drug your name through the mud pretty good, didn't he?" Detective Ballantine posed it as a question, but he already knew the answer. "Humiliated you in front of your family, the whole town. The press ran with his idea that you were living pretty high on the rock star life and had lost control."

"That wasn't true." My words sounded fragile, lifeless. "I'm here to run Enchanted Events for two months. Its success is vital to mine, so the last thing I want is someone dying in our place of business. And I certainly gain nothing from murdering anyone."

"Even for revenge? Even if it's Evan's intended?" Ballantine asked.

I looked him square in the eyes. "Even if."

Ballantine considered this a moment before rising to his feet, his black shoes making a *whoosh-whoosh* as he and Chief O'Hara crossed to the door. "Miss Sutton?" Ballantine said.

"Yes, sir?"

"Don't even think about leaving town."

CHAPTER SEVEN

"SO SASHA CHANDLER is dead." Sylvie plopped into the chair in front of me at her kitchen table as the sky dimmed outside. "What a day, huh?"

More like what a nightmare.

I took a long drink of iced tea, then pressed the cold glass to my cheek. "I don't understand." It was as though I was right back in the parlor. My heart had liquefied as the coroner wheeled her out and panic filled my every cell. "She'd been talking to me only fifteen minutes earlier." Okay, twenty. I'd left her to her own devices for longer than necessary. "One moment Sasha was snipping at me, and the next she was nose-first in some buttercream frosting."

"Not a bad way to go," Sylvie said. "Though I'm more of a ganache person myself." She arranged some shortbread cookies on a plate, quirking a brow when I refused one. "Word from the underground is Sasha died from a blow to the head—most likely a nearby champagne bottle. You probably want to lawyer up."

"I did nothing wrong. And how can there be a murder *here*—in Sugar Creek? The town was one of *Newsweek*'s top-ten safest communities last year."

Sylvie poured her special sugar syrup into her tea and stirred. "You know what that article was? Just one big invitation to criminals. *Come on down to Sugar Creek. We make it easy for you.*"

"You're the only one in town who even locks her back door." And had a military-level alarm system, owned spy cams, was an early drone adopter, and probably had a secret bunker beneath the basement. "Murder does not happen here." My head fell into my hands. "Why did it have to happen in a business I've just inherited and to *my* client?"

"Have you called your folks?

"Are you crazy?"

"So you want them to hear about this on the news?"

My parents, Matt and Ellen Sutton, were world class motivational speakers. They traveled the globe giving pep talks on how to lasso the world in sold-out arenas, and their followers were in the zillions. For birthdays my parents usually gave me some of their books, hoping some of their can-do principles would sink in. The last book, *Sutton's Signposts for Success*, had entire passages highlighted for viewing pleasure. I'd have to check my collection to see if any of their tomes addressed finding a dead body.

"If you become a prime suspect, I can make you disappear. You know"—my grandmother patted her wrinkle-less face—"get you some work done. This guy I know in Canada's a real artist. He can make you look just like George Clooney."

"I don't want to look like George Clooney."

"Your scars would be totally invisible. Get you a new identity, new passport. We could even arrange a husband and a few kids for you. Make it look authentic."

"Can I get a new grandma?" I didn't even want to think about where a fake family would come from.

We had shut down Enchanted Events for the day and re-scheduled all our appointments. Henry assumed we'd be back open tomorrow, but really, who knew? Nobody at the office had a lot of experience with crime scenes and brides dropping dead. I doubted the Sugar Creek Police Department did either.

"What if the police truly think I did it?"

Sylvie bit into a cookie, then patted my hand. "You're not going to prison."

"You don't know that!" The hysteria in my voice sounded foreign, as if coming from someone else. "I just don't understand how this could happen."

"The woman was a tyrant. She had a lot of enemies, I hear. The police will talk to all of them."

"Can we trust them to do that?"

"A suspicious nature." Sylvie nodded in approval "I like that. And the answer is no, we don't trust them to handle the investigation themselves. That's why we're going to conduct one of our own."

"If it involves plastic surgery on my part, I'm not interested." It still burned to think that I could even be considered a suspect. I was third-generation Sugar Creek. "How could anyone think I'd kill Sasha? I've been back in town three days. I haven't had time to unpack my underwear, let alone plan a murder."

"They would assume you did it in a fit of passion. You did say she was egging you on."

"There's a big difference between getting mad enough to take a walk and mad enough to pop someone on the head with a glass bottle. Oh, gosh, and poor Evan. I can't stand the guy, but I certainly wouldn't wish this on him."

"Don't feel sorry for him. The significant other is often the culprit. For all we know, he's a cold-blooded killer."

I contemplated Sylvie's words and watched the next-door neighbor mow her grass in the remaining daylight. "Surely Evan couldn't kill someone. But then again, I never suspected he'd dump me at the altar and run to the tabloids with fabricated stories, either."

"Steer clear of him," Sylvie said. "I always knew he was trouble. Any man who spray tans that much can't be of sound mind."

I reached for my grandmother's hand and held it, taking comfort in the coolness of her skin, the ever-present gloss of her nails, and the strength that radiated from her bones. "What if the police get so focused on proving me guilty they fail to pursue other suspects?"

She squeezed my hand. "That's where Frannie and I come in. We won't let them take you down, shug."

"I didn't kill her, Sylvie."

"I know. And if we need to, we'll prove it to the whole world." She pulled me to her and kissed my cheek. "Or surgically alter your face and send you to my friends in Nairobi."

CHAPTER EIGHT

WE MIGHT AS well have renamed the shop Murderers R Us.

The Monday after after Sasha's murder, Enchanted Events finally reopened its doors and resumed business. Cancellations from concerned brides came in like a rain of torpedoes, with nowhere to run to avoid it. With each phone call and email I worried I had single-handedly shut down the business just by coming to town. Outside our doors, reporters hid in cars and shrubbery, hoping to get first crack at an interview. Curious townsfolk peeked in our windows on their way to the diner to get their coffee and bacon. The gossip would be extra spicy today.

"We need to serve the remaining brides-to-be with the same amount of attention and quality," Henry said as he paced the office, where we gathered for our pre-opening meeting. "But there's no time to dawdle. Don't rush the clients, but do work fast because we've lost nearly a week. Help them make decisions. Steer them in the ceremonial way they should go. Also what do you say when asked about the investigation?"

"We have no comment," they chimed like a doomed church choir.

Henry let his eyes rest on each of the four employees. "Does anyone have anything to say?"

"I do." I stepped forward. "I'd like to say that I didn't kill anyone." I hoped my face was as innocent as a heavenly angel's. "That's all."

Henry rolled his eyes. "Way to set the tone."

"We don't think you did it," Alice said. "Well, Layla and Mary do, but two out of four ain't bad."

And didn't that just warm a heart? "Thank you." I gave a tight smile, even to Layla who stood in the corner, her arms crossed over her ample bosom, eyeing me as if I was picking my next victim. "Thank you all."

As soon as Henry flipped the Closed sign to Open, we were off on a race. I shadowed Alice, taking notes as she helped a client build her wedding website, a newly added service. Later I trailed Layla as she counseled a bride on suggestions for live music. I then pulled up my chair beside Henry at his computer as he reviewed the pros and cons of the local wedding venues, including our outdoor options. This was the part where I felt my skin tingle and my brain engage. I was intrigued by the logistics of the actual event and loved the idea of orchestrating the time, place, and details, watching them come together to create one magical ceremony.

"It's kind of like our concerts," I said to Henry an hour later, as I picked at a ham sandwich.

He speared a cherry tomato in his salad. "How so?"

"We had to do a lot of our own stuff the first few years in the band. Jaz was never going to be bothered with any of that, so it was left up to me and Trina, our other bandmate. I helped pick out costumes, decorated to make our venues more intimate, created flyers for bulletin boards, and made sure everyone got where they were supposed to be on time."

"You were the unofficial manager," Henry said.

"Yep. Until Jaz's older sister took over." And that's when things went south. "She still had me doing lots of grunt work to free up the queen's busy schedule." I pushed the dark memories aside and focused on a beautiful photo of a nearby glass chapel. "So, anyway, I may not have much experience planning weddings—especially a successful one—but putting on a show, I totally understand."

"I think you're doing pretty good, Paisley." Henry patted my shoulder. "Just don't let anyone else die."

"Right. You do believe I'm innocent, right?"

Henry hesitated a little too long for my liking. "Aside from your music career and the tabloids, I don't know you. But I do know I sent you outside to cool off, and that's what you did. Could you have come back in and hurt Sasha without our seeing it? Yes. But did you? I doubt it."

It was quite an impersonal theory. "Okay. It's a start. But I want you to understand I'm not the erratic crazy woman the gossip sites have made me out to be the last few years. I'd never hurt Sasha. I've never physically harmed anyone. Well, minus one moment at the altar when I kicked Evan Holbrook in the squishy parts."

Henry almost smiled. "Our focus needs to be on Enchanted Events. We can't lose any more business, Paisley."

We turned at the loud commotion coming from the hall. Heavy footsteps punctuated with yelling sent Henry and me surging to our feet.

"Mr. Holbrook! Sir! Please stop!"

Evan appeared in the doorway, hair disheveled, cheeks flushed, and eyes radiating a seething anger he directed right at me.

"How could you?" He stepped inside the office, a hand-wringing Alice behind him.

"You can go, Alice," Henry said calmly. "We'll take care of it."

"Were you really so desperate?" Evan's chest rose and fell rapidly as if he'd sprinted there from Missouri. "Are you so bitter at your own life that you could take someone else's? And ruin mine?"

"Evan, I—"

"I loved her, Paisley." His voice broke and tears filled his eyes. "I loved her."

I walked to him, looking him right in his bleary eyes. "I did not kill your fiancée."

"You stood there on Main Street and threatened me. Did you have one of your rocker henchmen do it?"

"No," I said. "My posse's been on an extended vacation for quite some time. Evan, I know you're hurt and reeling. I'm sure you want answers."

"When we get the autopsy back, it's going to confirm you killed her. The lab's working extra fast on my behalf. You were the one who brought her champagne. You just couldn't stand for me to be happy, could you?"

"How did you know I served her champagne?"

"It's a very small town, Paisley. I suggest you remember that. You've been gone a very long time, but I've never left. I'm one of them in a way you'll never be."

His words stomped laps in my head with spiky little cleats. He was right. Aside from my family, these were no longer my people.

I was desperate for every living soul to believe I didn't commit this crime. "You know me, Evan. I'm still the girl who cries at the sight of roadkill. The one who has to plug her ears when folks talk about their successful day in the deer woods. The one who's never seen *Titanic* because they've yet to change the ending to include show tunes and floaties for everyone. You know I'm not capable of killing another person."

"I know you were mad. And Sasha could be . . . difficult."

Difficult was like saying terrorists were a little moody. "I was not happy to see you, I'll admit. What you did to me was despicable." I paused long enough for those words to sink in. "And Sasha was a bit of a challenge. But I swear to you, I'd never dream of harming her." Okay, maybe I'd dreamed about it. But follow through? No way.

"I want to believe you," he said. "I'm just not sure I can. You threatened me. You stood outside and threatened me in front of witnesses."

"Okay, that's enough." Henry stood at my shoulder like an imposing bodyguard. "Enchanted Events is terribly sorry for your loss, and we're all doing everything we can to cooperate with the authorities. But this isn't the place to have this conversation. Mr. Holbrook. You have our sincerest condolences, sir. Paisley and I have a meeting we must get to, so if I can walk you to the door—"

"This isn't over," Evan said. "The truth will come out, and

Paisley, if you had anything to do with this, I'll use all my political powers to make sure you're locked up for a very, very long time."

I watched Henry escort Evan out the door, as my former fiancé's words hovered in the air like angry wasps.

I knew I didn't kill Sasha.

But what if no one could prove my innocence?

What if I *did* go to prison?

It was time to put Sylvie and Frannie to work and get to the bottom of this.

CHAPTER NINE

W ITH THE SUN still cooking in the six o'clock sky, I drove the hilly road home, my brain numb. Somehow I had gotten through the workday. I'd held it all together because Henry had commanded me to, telling me that the boss had to be a leader, had to wear her game face, and had to convey that it was business as usual. Plus he'd plied me with chocolate by the hour.

But in my head, it was not business as usual. It was a total party of chaos. A drunken college rave of fear and what-ifs smothering every positive thought that happened to pop up. I stopped at a drive-thru on my way, bought two bags of fries, then stuffed them in my mouth as I drove, tears blurring my vision. I'd deprived myself of junk food for so many years in LA, but surely I could take a break from eating all that unholy healthy stuff.

Relief poured through me as I stepped onto my front porch. I had my bra unhooked and my heels kicked off before I'd even shut myself inside. I leaned against the door, a fierce ache pressing against my temple. I sniffed indelicately just as there came a pounding at the door.

Noooo. Couldn't the world just go away?

Pressing my squinty eye to the peephole, I spied a familiar

scowling face. Scowling, but obnoxiously beautiful.

"You okay?" Beau asked when I opened the door.

What did he care? This was the guy who'd spent most of our adolescence making it clear I wasn't good enough to hang out with his sister. "I'm great."

"You want to talk?"

"No." I sniffled. "Thank you."

He considered this. "Maybe I do."

"Send me a text. It's what all the cool kids do."

"Invite me in, Sutton. I need to change the air filter in your house."

I frowned in question.

"Part of my rent is doing upkeep on the house. Let me in."

"Can't you do it later? I just want to cut myself out of these Spanx, take a warm bath, get into bed, and never come out."

"Uh-huh," he said dryly. "I hear the blatant invitation there, but I'm going to hold firm to my morals tonight. How about we talk about what's going on instead?"

My sigh fluttered my bangs. "Go away, Beau."

"I got a little visit from a Benton County detective today. Wanted to know about the woman living beside me."

I shoved open the door. "You could've at least brought me something to eat."

He slipped by me, an air filter tucked beneath his arm. He stepped so close his chest brushed my shoulder. Pausing right in front of me, Beau lifted his hand toward my face and brushed a tear from my cheek. His voice went low and soft. "One of the last times I saw you cry, you were ten and I'd accidentally decapitated your Barbie doll in the lawn mower."

"Accidentally?" I swiped at my damp cheeks, all too aware of his nearness, the light scent of his cologne teasing my senses. "Your sister and I always wondered how our favorite dolls got into the yard."

"The dog must've carried them out there."

"You didn't have a dog."

His cheek dimpled with a lopsided grin. "Details." Beau lowered his long legs onto the leather couch and rested his arms on his knees as if we were about to huddle. "Talk to me, Sutton."

I slid into a chair and clutched an afghan to my chest. "Basically the whole town thinks I killed Sasha Chandler."

"Did you?"

"No."

"Okay then."

"Just like that? You believe me? You could be in a room with a dangerous murderer right now."

"I've known you since you were five. You didn't kill anyone. Besides, if you try anything funny, I'm pretty sure I can take you."

I found myself returning his smile. His faith in me meant a lot. I needed all the support I could get.

"I'm sorry I nearly got your sister arrested in tenth grade." I'd snuck her backstage at a boy band concert, and when they'd invited us on their tour bus and broken out the booze, things had gotten wild. As acting head of the family, Beau had banned her from associating with me.

"She turned out okay anyway," he said. "Though she's married to a dope of a guy."

I left that one alone. "What did the detective ask you?"

"Wanted to know our history, what I knew about you and your ex-fiancé, if I'd ever seen you sticking needles into Sasha Chandler–shaped voodoo dolls. That sort of thing."

"And what did you tell them?"

"That we'd grown up together, and I had every confidence you wouldn't harm anyone."

"Thank you."

His eyes softened, and I was suddenly regretting ditching my bra.

"So." I cleared my throat and pulled the blanket to my chest like a shield. "We know I didn't kill Sasha, but the police probably think I'm the most likely candidate. How am I supposed to sleep at night knowing there's a killer on the loose *and* the Sugar Creek PD is helping with the case? They have zero experience with a crime of this level."

"They've turned it over to Benton County. Sugar Creek police are just helping. If it makes you feel better, Chief O'Hara is pretty good at giving speeding tickets and tracking down kids who egg houses on Halloween."

"That doesn't make me feel better. The last time someone was murdered in this town, Andrew Jackson was president, electricity hadn't been thought of, and moonshine was the drink of choice."

"I think you should trust the authorities to do their job."

"Beau, I publicly threatened Evan, I'm the one who initiated champagne service at Enchanted Events *and* delivered it to Sasha, and I was the last person to see her alive. Do you know what those things add up to? Me, as a jailbird. I can't stand still and let this happen. I have too much of my grandmother in me to let others take sole charge of my innocence."

"You could make things worse," Beau said.

"What would you do if you were me?"

"Offer me a beer?"

"You'd get out there and get to the bottom of it. That's what you'd do."

"Paisley—"

"It wouldn't hurt to talk to a few people. A girl as difficult as Sasha must've had an enemy or two." I startled at yet another knock at the door. "Now what?"

Flinging open the door, I found my grandmother and her partner in crime standing beneath the glow of the porch light.

"Hello!" Sylvie and Frannie stood there like a geriatric Lucy and Ethel. "We're here to console you, dear," Sylvie said, shoving her way inside. "Frannie brought pie."

I was never getting that hot bath. But I also wasn't going to turn away Frannie's coconut cream.

Sylvie rushed to Beau, her arms open wide. "Hello there, sweet thing."

"Sylvie, good to see you." As Beau hugged my grandmother, she gave me a sly wink.

He then bestowed a hug, a kiss, and a hair compliment on Frannie. Hearts and lovebirds frolicked around the ladies' heads.

Frannie sat down on the couch, her kitty cat socks peeping out from her brown Birkenstocks. While my grandmother was still fashionable and fighting age with every weapon in her arsenal, Frannie had taken to dressing as though she selected her outfits at a thrift store while blindfolded.

"Did we interrupt anything?" Frannie glanced at my sagging bra strap.

"Yeah." Sylvie plopped down beside her. "Like something hot and tawdry?"

"Nothing going on here," I said.

"What a waste." Frannie gave us the side-eye.

Beau threw his arm around me and gave my shoulder a squeeze. "Paisley was just telling me how she's going to leave Sasha's murder investigation to the professionals."

"And that's why we're here." Sylvie reached into her purse and withdrew her iPad. "It doesn't get more professional than us."

Frannie nodded. "We're here to talk strategy."

"I don't even want to know." Beau gave my shoulder another squeeze before releasing me. "I'm just gonna check a few things upstairs."

"Stay out of my underwear drawer," I called.

"Woo, isn't he a little cupcake with sprinkles?" Frannie fanned herself.

"You two are supposed to be finding a hobby," I said, watching Beau walk away.

"Meh." Frannie flopped a dismissive hand. "We've tried. Yesterday it was yoga, which apparently makes Frannie gassy."

Frannie nodded. "The things you learn about yourself."

"And last week it was throwing pottery," I said.

"Apparently you don't literally throw it," Frannie said. "We thought it was a new form of target practice."

"Yeah," Sylvie said. "FYI—Glocks are *not* welcome at that meeting."

Frannie harrumphed. "Artsy snobs."

"So once again we have nothing to do," my grandmother said. "We can devote all of our attention to clearing your good name. Well, your mostly good name. It's a tiny bit tarnished thanks to your years of wearing booty shorts. And that rat fink ex-fiancé Evan. But we know the real you, and the real you does not murder people."

"At least not in that tacky, cliché way." Frannie's lip curled as though she was smelling an amateur. "Girl. Tell me you'd have more ingenuity than that."

I couldn't even find the words to respond.

"So Sasha's memorial has been set for Wednesday." Sylvie typed on her tablet. "The three of us ladies will attend and work the crowd, if you know what I mean. See what we can learn and observe."

"They'll never let me in the door," I said.

"It's like she's not even related to you," Frannie said to Sylvie. "Where's your imagination? Between the two of us, we have enough wigs, costumes, and stage makeup to serve a drag queen convention. You'll go incognito."

That sounded like a terrible idea. "A simple hat will be enough."

"We could bug their phones."

"We're not doing that."

"We could install hidden cameras."

"Also not going to happen."

Sylvie was just getting warmed up. "Satellites? Drones? Tap into their smart TVs?"

"That all sounds completely frightening," I said.

Sylvie stood with a wide grin. "This case is exactly what I need. I feel invigorated already."

"Could be those burritos we just had at the Taco Hut." Frannie rubbed her stomach. "I know they're invigorating something in me."

"Toodle-oo, shug." Sylvie pressed a kiss to my cheek. "It's going to be okay."

Frannie gave me a parting pat on the bum. "We'll make sure of it."

I was still standing at the door a few minutes later when Beau reappeared.

"Are Boris and Natasha gone?"

I almost had the energy to smile. "They mean well."

"Your grandmother's right, you know."

"About hacking people's emails?"

"No." Beau stepped onto the porch as the crickets serenaded. "That everything's going to be okay."

"I hope so."

"Get some sleep, Paisley. Tomorrow will be a better day."

It would. A brand-new day to take my life back. Clear my name.

And find a murderer.

CHAPTER TEN

"NOT ONE BAG or body search to get in the door." Frannie shook her head in disgust as she crossed her legs beside me in the church pew at the Sugar Creek Community Church. "There's a murderer running loose, and nobody thinks to pat us all down?"

"I was looking forward to it." Sylvie used her compact mirror to check out her lipstick as well as the row behind her.

From our uncomfortable seats in a side wing, I watched the crowd filter in for Sasha Chandler's memorial. My gray pencil skirt pinched in all the wrong places, and there was an inkblot of a coffee stain beneath my fitted jacket. A black hat with a demure bit of veil perched sideways on my head, with the goal of covering part of my face and giving me a British fascinator appeal. But the hat made my head itch, the lace tickled my nose, and as I'd borrowed the thing from Sylvie, I was pretty sure there was an extra compartment underneath it for a small pistol. I assumed I wasn't packing heat, but my hat could've easily been locked and loaded.

As a string quartet began to play a hymn, the family walked in together, with Evan right there with them. A heaviness settled around my heart at the sight of Sasha's mother crying into her tissue, leaning into her husband. Brat or not, Sasha left behind a family who loved her. At least, I think they did. I peered through the netting hanging from my hat and studied them all. Her mother wore her highlighted blonde hair in a tight French twist, and judging from her taut face, she was quite familiar with the words *nip* and *tuck*. Mr. Chandler wore a dark suit and a cranberry red tie. He still had a head full of brown hair, though it was peppered with gray.

"What does Sasha's dad do?" I asked Sylvie.

"That's actually her stepfather." Sylvie fanned her face with a program. "Owns some big construction business. Obviously has done very well at it, but lately there's been rumblings of money troubles. Zoey is his daughter. She occasionally goes to my church."

To Mr. Chandler's left sat Zoey. She wore a sleeveless black sheath dress that showed off her enviable toned arms, and I couldn't help but notice she wasn't crying. I wasn't much of a cryer myself, unless it involved animals, Hallmark commercials, or being accused of murder. So maybe her lack of tears meant nothing.

I filed these observations away as Pastor Mulroney took to the pulpit and began the service. As he spoke about Sasha's accomplishments and better qualities, I let my eyes roam the church. With a quick glance at Frannie and Sylvie, I noticed they were doing the same. We pretty much looked like a row of socially inept weirdos.

Sylvie nudged me with her elbow. "I do not get a good vibe about that one." She subtly pointed across the way to a pew near the front. "The girl in the pink dress."

"It's Phoebe Chen, one of her bridesmaids," I whispered.

"She's nicer than all of us put together." But Sylvie was right. Phoebe's face was as white as the Chantilly lace gown hanging in the Sugar Creek Formals display window. Her eyes were wide, and her brow furrowed as she worried her bottom lip with her teeth.

"That's not grief," Sylvie said. "That's guilt. I can smell it from here."

I lowered my volume. "Phoebe did not kill anyone." But she did look quite uncomfortable. "I'll talk to her first."

Pastor Mulroney spoke for an additional fifteen minutes on the virtues of Sasha before moving on to a brief sermon on getting one's key to the Pearly Gates. The string quartet played a final song, a family member spoke a moving prayer, then we were dismissed to the melody of "Amazing Grace."

"Let's divide and conquer," Sylvie said as we emptied into the courtyard.

"I'll take Phoebe," I said.

"I'll talk to that man in the navy suit." Frannie pointed two aisles over.

"What's he got to do with this?" I asked.

"Nothing." Frannie adjusted her skirt and gave her boobs a little boost. "But if he's lucky, he could be my next Friday night date."

Weaving through the crowd, I kept one eye on Phoebe and one on Evan. I definitely didn't want to run into him and get chased away. Plus he was at the bottom of my suspect list, right next to a vagrant bum or a rabid raccoon who could make evil use of his opposable thumbs.

Phoebe joined her fellow bridesmaid Raven Arnett, and the

two exchanged a brief hug. By the time I got to them, I could hear their frantic whispers, and I immediately went on alert. Sylvie probably had some listening device in her purse that would've come in handy.

I slowly moved toward them, praying they wouldn't call me out. "Hi, ladies. Lovely service, wasn't it?"

Phoebe startled. "Paisley?"

Raven propped a hand on her hip. "Should you be here?"

"I wanted to pay my respects." Someone needed to alert our justice system this whole innocent-until-proven-guilty thing was kind of a joke. "Such a tragic end to a life. I didn't know Sasha well, but I'm sure she was a wonderful person. I'm very sorry for your loss."

My comment was met with silence more awkward than an eighth grade slow dance.

"I mean, it sounds like she was just a beacon of humility and grace," I continued, watching their reactions. "All that charity work. Her heart for her family and friends. The way she—"

"She was a mean-spirited viper, and most of that crap Pastor Mulroney said wasn't even accurate," hissed Raven.

"Raven!" Phoebe whacked her arm.

"It's true. I wouldn't wish anyone dead, but it's ridiculous for all of us to pretend Sasha was this kind, giving saint. She wasn't. She made us all miserable, she couldn't be trusted, and she'd do anything and hurt anyone to get what she wanted."

Now we were getting somewhere. "You sound like you're speaking from experience, Raven . . ."

"She's hurt all of us," she said. "You could poll this whole churchyard and you'd be hard-pressed to find anyone Sasha didn't betray."

"How long have you both known her?" I asked.

"Since kindergarten," Phoebe said. "Sasha shoved me into a mud puddle on the first day of school because I was wearing the same dress as her. Then she forced me to push her on the swings at recess. We were pretty much best friends since day one."

"Because you had no choice," Raven said.

"We had a lot of good times."

"Usually at our expense." Raven turned stormy brown eyes my way. "I met Sasha my sophomore year in college. We rushed together and were sorority sisters. She stole two of my boyfriends and frequently 'borrowed' my homework."

"Then why be in her wedding?" I asked.

The girls exchanged a fleeting look.

"It was the right thing to do," Phoebe said.

That sounded weirdly ominous.

"If you want to know who really suffered, that's Zoey," Raven said. "That poor girl's been on the receiving end of Sasha's torment more than anyone."

I followed the line of Raven's gaze to where Zoey stood next to her parents and shook the hands of well-wishers. She didn't look like a killer, but what did I know? The finer points of murder were still pretty new to me.

"Do you have any idea who would've wanted to hurt Sasha?" I asked.

Raven studied her fingernails and shook her head. "I should go. I need to get back to work."

"But if you had to guess . . ." My question went ignored by Raven as she darted away, weaving in and out of the crowd until she reached the parking lot.

"Funerals make her nervous," Phoebe said. "I really need to go too."

"What about you, Phoebe? Who do you think might've killed Sasha?"

"Grab a Sugar Creek phone book. There's your suspect list."

"If you and Raven disliked Sasha so much, why continue to be her friend?"

Phoebe turned grave eyes to me. "Because we didn't have a choice."

CHAPTER ELEVEN

THE NEXT MORNING I walked to my car in a sleepy trance, clutching my coffee cup as though it were liquid survival.

"How was the memorial?"

I turned at Beau's husky voice. Men were off-limits to me right now. I was only passing through Sugar Creek, and I needed to keep my mind on more important things. Like not rotting in a prison cell. "It was interesting." I took a sip of coffee as he walked toward me. "Why didn't you go?"

He lifted a broad shoulder, pulling his aqua T-shirt taut against his chest. "Didn't know her well, and not my scene."

"What is your scene, Beau Hudson?"

"Maybe I'll show you sometime."

I laughed. "I've fallen for that one before."

His full lips parted in a grin. "I was referring to the outdoors. Someplace with trees and birds and nature. Space to breathe. I bought my grandpa's land back a few years ago, and I'm running an outdoor retreat. Added cabins for folks to stay in. They can hike, ride four-wheelers, swim in the waterfall, fish the sweet spot where Sugar Creek meets Lee River."

His grandfather's land was beautiful and probably had over five hundred acres. "Sounds perfect for you. What's this business venture called?"

"Fox Falls."

"Was it hard finding a new career after you came back?"

And just like that, the light in Beau's eyes snuffed out like a candle. "I like what I do."

In that moment a memory surfaced from the night before. "Were you sitting on the porch in the middle of the night?"

Beau rested a hand on the hood of my car. "Just keeping an eye on the neighborhood."

"At one in the morning?"

He stepped closer, his face hovering over mine. "You keeping tabs on me, Sutton?"

"When a creepy shadow falls across my bedroom floor, I can't help but notice." Just as I was noticing the way my heart picked up its tempo. "Plus, I was awake myself."

"Couldn't sleep?"

"The fact that you're diverting the topic does not go unnoticed." I took a step back so I wouldn't smell the citrusy scent of his shampoo. "But no, I couldn't sleep. Instead I made a list of possible suspects in Sasha's murder, as well as motives. Actually, I don't have a lot in the motives category. But I'm working on it. So were you haunting the grounds at night like one of the Civil War ghosts at the battlefield?"

"Nothing wrong with taking a midnight stroll."

"Says every good serial killer."

He rubbed a hand over his stubbled cheek and laughed. "Who's on your suspect list?"

"Why can't you sleep, Beau?"

"Anyone ever tell you that you dress crazy?" His gaze did a lazy inspection of my cherry red stilettos, black leather pants, and a glittery gray tank.

"You're changing the topic." Thank God I wore my good bra today.

"I have a business to run," he said. "It keeps me wired."

"I don't think that's all there is to it."

"You're not my therapist, Sutton." He took the coffee from my hands, pressed the cup to his lips, and drank.

"Do you have one—a therapist?"

He looked at me for a long moment before speaking. "Sasha's stepdad owns Chandler Construction. They filed for bankruptcy this week."

"Oh."

"Probably not related to Sasha's death at all, but as long as you're collecting information, I thought you might want to add that to your list."

"Thank you. Good to know." I would definitely be checking into that. "Now back to—"

"Have a good day, Paisley." Beau handed me my coffee and walked toward the house. "Try not to get arrested."

"TWO MORE BRIDES cancelled their appointments."

Henry met me at the door of Enchanted Events with another cup of coffee. At his dire announcement, I took his offering. I was going to need a double dose of caffeine.

"Did they reschedule?"

"No. Totally cancelled. They both said they didn't feel safe here."

"Me and my dumb champagne idea." I followed Henry back to our office. "Who's on our agenda today? Anyone left?"

"Your cousin Emma's in at ten. You and I will take care of her, of course. Little tip—don't kill her."

"Not serving her so much as a drink of tap water."

"Cecily Blackwell has a twelve o'clock, as does Grace Philpot. Those are both introductory meetings. Then we have three reception appointments, and a consult on a bridal luncheon."

"Maybe the best thing for Enchanted Events is that I don't work here anymore."

"Then you lose the business. The terms state you run it."

"I can do administrative tasks from home. I'm a whiz at the computer." My Candy Crush score was something of a marvel.

"Paisley, now is not the time to cower. If you didn't kill Sasha, then don't hide your face as if you did. Hold your head up high and show the good folks of Sugar Creek you have nothing to be ashamed of."

"They look at me like I'm a criminal."

"Maybe that's less about Sasha's death and more about those diarrhea jingles you did last year."

"Those medicine jingles paid for three months of rent." Never mind that singing "You'll feel like a champy when your bowels aren't crampy" completely brought me to a new level of humility.

"That Detective Ballantine is on the warpath," Henry said. "He stopped by here while you were at the funeral yesterday."

"What more could he possibly have to question you about?"

"Had questions for all of us. Mostly about you this time."

"What about me?"

"Wanted to know about your temperament, for one thing."

"I hope you told him I'm chock-full of peace and tranquility."

"Also asked if any of us could verify your location at the time of the murder."

"And you said no."

"I'm sorry."

"Did he ask about anyone else—Mary, Alice, Layla—or even you?"

"No."

"Why am I the only employee of Enchanted Events he's focusing on?"

"Because we were all with clients who've confirmed our whereabouts."

"And to think I thought stepping away from Sasha was a helpful thing to do. I should've stayed in the parlor and chewed her out like I'd wanted to. I should've kicked her out at her first insult."

"Ballantine is just doing his job by gathering information," Henry said. "It's procedure. Don't fret over it yet."

That was easy for him to say. His neck wasn't on the line.

HENRY SPENT THE next hour reviewing information on the day's brides, from their personality quirks to their family histories. As usual, I was amazed at the details he gathered on each of his brides. It gave him the ability to see their vision, shape their ideas into a wedding they loved, and make everyone involved happy.

He was good at what he did, and he knew it. But he was also a good teacher, giving me regular tips and tutorials that made each day more and more doable. Minus the cloud of murder hanging over my perfectly innocent head.

Some time later Layla poked her head into our office. She shot me a glance as if I was on par with Freddy Krueger and Jason Voorhees, then spoke to Henry. "Your ten o'clock is here."

Emma walked in seconds later, arms extended. "Paisley! You poor thing." She crushed me to her with a fierce hug. "How are you holding up?"

Right now I was struggling to breathe. "Hanging in there."

She stepped back with a comforting smile. "Noah and I want you to know we're here for you. We have absolute faith in your innocence. If there's anything we can do at all, just say the word."

"Thank you."

"Do you have a lawyer lined up? I know a few."

"Um—"

"Not that you need one. But you should have one. A total beast of an attorney, I say. One who can lunge for the jugular and—"

"How about we focus on happier matters?" Henry interjected. "Let's talk about your wedding. It's only *the* event of the year." He made every bride feel like theirs was the wedding of the year.

"I'm up to speed on your ideas," I said. "The venue you've chosen is beautiful."

"Thanks." Her lips twisted in temporary distaste. "The Sugar Creek Chapel isn't big, so we had to cut out so many people on the invitation list. With us both working for the city, it's caused some hurt feelings."

"I'm excited to have made the short list," I said. "Take a seat and let's go over a few questions I have."

"Okay." Emma's smile returned as she sat down in the white chair at my desk. "I can't believe we're only three-and-a-half weeks away." My cousin Emma had moved back to Sugar Creek last year during a career crisis of her own. She hadn't planned on a long stay either, but she'd met the handsome mayor, fell in love despite her best efforts, and left a lucrative job in broadcasting to stay here. I was grateful Enchanted Events could at least count on Emma not to back out.

Henry's phone played a loud minuet, and he reached into his pocket. "Just going to step outside and take this."

"So how are you really doing?" Emma asked as I pulled up her file on my laptop.

"I'd be lying if I said I wasn't concerned," I said. "But I have Sylvie and Frannie on the job, and you know they'll have the murderer bound and gagged before the police department can even question their next suspect."

"We're not just a family, Paisley. We're a team. We're going to make sure your name is cleared and you don't spend one second in jail."

I braved a smile. "I have no shoes that match an orange jumpsuit."

"I doubt that." Emma leaned in and put her hand on mine. "But let's talk about the good stuff. What's it like living next to Beau?"

My face unexpectedly flamed. "Oh. Um, fine."

"That's no answer. Come on, he's a blast from your past—someone you've always had a thing for."

"No, I haven't! One childhood kiss doesn't mean I committed my heart to him. We've spent years hating one another."

"You were kids. And he's still very handsome," Emma said. "He's got that whole war hero ruggedness."

"I hadn't noticed."

"Mmm-hmm. Right. Every woman in town from infant to *centenarian* has noticed."

Well, as long as Emma was here. "I did wonder if you had any inside information on what happened to him in the service. I read the paper, scoured the internet. It sounds like he was very close-lipped about what brought him home. Other than an ambush at a military checkpoint, I really don't know much."

"I've just heard bits and pieces. He was Army Special Forces, you know. A captain. According to his men, he saved their lives. Something about a Libyan checkpoint being infiltrated. The enemy started shooting as they neared the checkpoint, and Beau somehow saved the day. That's the simple version, but he came back home not too long after that—with a faint limp and that brooding, quiet demeanor that makes a girl sigh a bit."

"Just in the short time I've been here, I've seen him walking the backyard in the dead of night."

"He took a bullet or two in the leg, I think. No doubt he still has a lot of pain, poor guy."

The kind that mangled body and soul.

But it was none of my business. By August, I would be rolling out of town, so I definitely didn't need to get too invested in a friendship with Beau. But still, I couldn't help but be concerned for him.

"Oh, look at this wedding planning book." Emma picked up an artfully decorated three-ring binder from a pile on my desk. "Someone really put some time into this." She ran her hand over the illustrated cover as I entered some additional data into Emma's file.

"Henry likes to keep them for a few days to get to know the brides and their ideas. I don't even know whose that is."

"I think it's bigger than mine, and Noah says my planning binder's heavy enough to hold a tin roof down on a trailer house."

I glanced up from my laptop. "Oh. I haven't even begun to tackle the clutter on this desk. Henry can't bear to look at it." His desk was ever spotless, while mine resembled more of a mini-landfill.

"Mind if I take a peek?" Without waiting for an answer, Emma opened the book and turned some pages. "Oh, it's Sasha Chandler's. Her family hasn't asked for it yet?"

"I guess they've had bigger things on their minds."

"She had exquisite taste." Emma continued to flip through the giant tome. "I love her fabric samples. She's even illustrated her bouquet choices in charcoals. I've never seen anything quite like this. And look at these photos—her venue, her dress selections—the photography is almost better than the subject. Did you create a binder when you were engaged?"

"No. My agent hired a wedding planner who took over the details. I actually had very little say." It should've been an omen of the disaster that would follow. "I wanted a private destination wedding in the Caribbean, but Evan insisted on a big public event. He said it was good PR for his career." But it sure ended up being bad PR for mine.

"This is quite the keepsake." Emma handed the book back to me with a pointed look. "Maybe you should drive it over to her family today."

"Yeah, I'll have Layla or Alice do that later."

"No, I think *you* should."

Emma's words sank into my overwhelmed brain. "I should do it, shouldn't I?"

"Yes." She nodded her head thoughtfully. "Give the book back, offer your condolences, ask a few leading questions." She studied her manicure. "Inspect a medicine cabinet. Rifle through a dresser drawer or two . . ."

Well, my goodness. I had no idea my sweet cousin had this in her. "You are *so* Sylvie's granddaughter."

"As are you, Paisley." My cousin lifted her chin and smiled at me like a partner in crime. "It's time to start acting like it."

CHAPTER TWELVE

"PERHAPS I SHOULD have worn gloves." Sylvie checked her lipstick in the passenger-side mirror of my car.

"For what?" It was hotter than my straightening iron today, and I had the air cranked to a setting I called Antarctic Wind Tunnel.

"So I won't leave fingerprints when I'm snooping."

"You're not going to snoop." I made a left onto McCullough Street. "You're just going to help me carry the conversation."

"I don't think you understand the perks of having me for a wingman. Did I mention Zoey occasionally comes to my Sunday school class?"

Braking the car, I stopped right in the middle of the street. "No, you did not tell me that."

She pressed her lips to blot on a tissue. "I guess it slipped my mind."

"You still remember classified nuclear codes from the sixties. It did not slip your mind."

"An agent never gives away all her information at once."

I didn't know whether to kiss my grandmother or toss her out the car.

I'd swung by and grabbed Sylvie on my way to visit Zoey Chandler, having chickened out on dropping in on either of

Sasha's parents. It just didn't seem appropriate to barrage them with questions yet. Especially if they thought I killed their daughter.

I checked my directions and pulled into a small driveway. "Is this right?"

"This is it," Sylvie said. "Didn't you get the aerial photos of her house I texted you?"

"It's so . . . small." We parked the car in front of a brick duplex with a tidy yard and black shutters in need of a coat of paint. "Not where I expected the daughter of a wealthy construction company owner to live."

Sylvie reached for her purse. "My sources at church and at A&M say Zoey's pretty different from her family. Lives very modestly. She's finishing out her second senior year, and supports herself from what I've heard. She and Sasha have nothing in common."

"Well, here goes." I checked my own reflection in the mirror and patted down some flyaway hair. "Let our first interrogation begin."

"Let's review our safe phrase in case we need to exit this mission."

"I'm not shouting 'Lady Liberty isn't wearing undies.'"

We walked up a meandering sidewalk to the front step. I pressed my finger to the doorbell and inspected a pot of red geraniums blooming from a nearby planter. I could hear voices inside, as well as feet moving, but it was a full minute and two more ring-a-lings before the door finally opened.

"Yeah?" A college-aged guy eyed Sylvie and me with all the enthusiasm given to traveling vacuum salesmen.

"Hello. I'm Paisley Sutton. Um, I'm from Enchanted Events. This is my assistant, Sylvie." I looked past him into the house. "Is Zoey home?"

"For what?" He glanced behind him before answering. "She's not receiving guests."

"And you are . . . ?"

"Max. Her boyfriend."

Max looked like a guy who chugged a lot of protein shakes when he wasn't lifting weights. "I know this is probably a bad time, but if we could just chat with Zoey, we promise to make it quick."

He frowned. "Didn't I see your picture in the paper?"

I needed a business card to pass out that said *I solemnly swear I did not kill anyone.* "I have something to return to the Chandler family. I was hoping I could talk to your girlfriend."

"She's busy."

Sylvie stepped up to the plate. "And I'm with the Sugar Creek Community Church. On behalf of the congregation, I'd like to extend my sympathies. I have a little gift from our Sunday school class." She dug into her purse and produced a beautifully wrapped loaf of some baked good. "It's banana bread. Homemade with love."

"That's very nice of you, but we don't eat carbs."

Sylvie's gentle smile hardened.

"Another reason we stopped by," I said, "is to deliver Sasha's wedding planner and—"

"You have the book?" Zoey suddenly appeared beside her boyfriend. "I didn't know where it was." She grabbed the binder from my arms and hugged it to her chest, closing her eyes for a moment as if being reunited with a friend she thought she'd never see again. "The book is actually mine."

"Yours?" Surely she was mistaken. "It's a very thorough plan for a wedding. Very detailed." And I'd inspected every page for any bit of information I could glean about Sasha.

"Yeah, they're my details."

"The artwork and photography are amazing," Sylvie said.

"Hello, Mrs. Sutton," Zoey said. "Nice of you to visit. We're kind of busy right now though, so—"

"Could I use your bathroom?" Sylvie chuckled. "Old age and weak bladders, right?"

"Not now." I nudged my grandma with a sharp elbow. "Zoey, I . . . I wanted to tell you I'm very sorry about the terrible loss of your sister."

"*Step*sister," Zoey corrected again.

"Oh." Right. "Well, Enchanted Events is committed to getting to the bottom of what happened in our shop. I know her death must've come as a shock to you and your whole family."

Zoey's face was bland as oatmeal. "Yes. I understand the police have spoken to you at length."

"They've spoken to everyone who was there at the time of the incident," Sylvie said. "I assure you, as one Sunday school sister to another, my granddaughter did not hurt Sasha." She patted my back like a dear, old granny with nothing up her sleeve. "Paisley's a rock star, you know. Between her music career and inheriting Enchanted Events, she couldn't possibly have time to kill anyone."

Zoey didn't look impressed as she considered me. "I don't think I've heard of you."

"It's been awhile since I've been on the radio."

"My grandmother and I are . . . trying to help the police a bit." I hoped that sounded believable. "If you don't mind my asking, had Sasha been in an argument with anyone lately?" Someone besides me.

"Had she talked to any communists, religious extremists, cult leaders, or ex-boyfriends?" My grandmother was as smooth as sandpaper.

"I don't know," Zoey said.

Sylvie placed the banana bread offering in Zoey's hands. "Can you think of anyone she'd ticked anyone off lately?"

"Had you even met Sasha?" Max laughed mirthlessly. "She ticked people off on a daily basis."

"That's enough," Zoey warned.

"No, I'm through being quiet about this. Sasha was a monster to Zoey. Had been since they were little girls. So do we know people who might've disliked Sasha? Pretty much everyone below the Mason-Dixon Line."

"This is not a discussion for my front porch." Zoey sighed as she held the door open. "Come on inside."

We followed them through a small, sunny foyer and into a cozy living room. Walking to the fireplace, I studied the painting over the mantel. "Wow, this is beautiful." It was a watercolor rendering of an Arkansas cotton field in a storm. I thought of the fabulous art from my own collection, which I'd had to sell off in the last few years. "Is this a local artist?"

"Yes." Zoey sat on the gray tufted couch next to her boyfriend. "It's by Carson Fielding. He's an art professor at Arkansas A&M. His paintings sell like wildfire in galleries around here.

They can't even keep them in stock. I think he might even have one on display at Crystal Bridges Museum."

"Impressive." I settled into a black leather chair, letting the zebra-striped pillow press into my aching back.

"So you're helping the police?" Zoey pulled her legs beneath her.

Sylvie placed a stilling hand on my arm. "Yes," she said. "The town simply isn't equipped to deal with a case of this size. I am retired from the CIA, you know."

"Yes," Zoey said. "I recall the time you filled in at Bible study and brought in real weapons to teach on spiritual warfare. Quite memorable."

"The bazooka might've been a bit extreme. And illegal." Sylvie avoided looking my way. "Now, hon, if you're up for it, we'd like to ask you a few questions. It would really help with the . . . investigation."

Zoey glanced at her boyfriend. "I guess it's okay."

"What was Sasha's behavior like in the last week or so?" I asked.

"Normal, I'd say." Zoey reached for a throw pillow. "What you saw at Sugar Creek Formals is pretty much how she always was."

"I couldn't help but notice your sister was a bit demanding that day at the shop," I said. "I'd hoped her unkindness toward you was just bridal nerves."

"It wasn't." Zoey's laugh was brittle as a November maple leaf. "Sasha's mom and my dad got married when I was six." Zoey's eyes wandered as if she were seeing those days gone by. "I remember being so excited, thinking I had won the sister lottery.

Finally some happiness after losing my mother. She was two years older than I, beautiful, and she came with a lot of toys. I was this quiet, shy thing and didn't have a lot of friends. When Sasha became my sister, I knew I'd have a friend for life. It wasn't long before that fairy tale shattered."

I knew all about shattering fairy tales. It was the only kind I'd read lately.

"Sasha was mean and manipulative," Zoey said. "She'd steal money from her mother or break something in the house, then find a way to blame it on me. She stole my boyfriends, my clothes, even my wedding plans." She nodded toward the book. "I'd been planning my wedding since preschool—the music, the dress, the decor. When she suddenly got engaged, I was honored she chose me to be her maid of honor. But as the wedding plans unfolded, I realized they were *my* wedding plans. Right down to the last detail." She held up the book. "These are my sketches, my photos, and my ideas. Last week I found her wearing my mother's pearl earrings. She said it was her 'something borrowed.'"

"More like her something stolen," Max said.

"The detective has talked to me too. I don't know if he thinks I'm a suspect because Sasha and I didn't get along, but I didn't kill her," Zoey said. "I didn't withstand sixteen years of being her doormat just to suddenly do her in before her wedding. Did I hate the way she's always treated me? Yes. Have I fantasized about getting back at her a million times? Absolutely. Would I ever truly hurt her? Definitely not." Zoey reached for her boyfriend's hand. "My new fantasy was that she would marry Evan, he'd make his way to the US Senate, they'd move to DC, and I'd only have to see her at Christmas."

"So about that bathroom, dear," Sylvie interrupted. "Mind if I use yours? I had a huge slushie on the way here."

"You can wait 'til we get home," I said through clenched teeth.

Zoey pointed over her shoulder. "Down the hall and to the left."

Sylvie removed my hand clamped to her knee and flounced away.

I just hoped she didn't blow up anything in there. "So . . . your dad and stepmom must be very torn up."

"Martha is. My dad's a pretty stoic guy."

"It's probably like losing a daughter to him, I would imagine."

Zoey said nothing.

"I mean, nothing like the pain of losing you would be." I kept talking, hoping Zoey would jump in at any time. "But I'm sure he has years of happy memories with you and Sasha. He was her father figure, right?"

"He did what he had to do."

What did that mean? "So they weren't close?"

Max threw an arm around Zoey. "Nobody's close to Sasha. Just her adoring mother."

"Were you and Sasha treated differently?"

"Yeah, but I got used to it."

By the angry flush on Zoey's cheeks, I rather doubted that statement. "How is Mrs. Chandler holding up?"

"I haven't talked to her since the funeral." Zoey's lips quivered, and tears pooled in her blue eyes. "My stepmother says the maid of honor should've been at the cake tasting with Sasha. That maybe if I had been there, I could've saved her. Apparently Sasha was left alone for a long time."

Now *I* was turning pink. "It was very busy at Enchanted Events that day." Moving on . . . "What about the other bridesmaids?"

With tears still falling, Zoey swiped at her cheeks. "What about them?"

"Did they have hard feelings toward Sasha as well?"

"Paisley, my stepsister was unkind to pretty much everyone she met, and that included the ones she considered her closest friends. I don't know Raven and Phoebe well, but they'd be worth talking to, I suppose."

"Any bitter ex-boyfriends in her closet?" I asked, just as Sylvie reappeared.

Zoey opened her mouth to answer, but her phone began to ring. "It's my dad," she said, reading the display. "I should take this. Thank you for rescuing my wedding planning book. Good luck to you."

Max showed us to the door, holding it open with an arm as large as a tree trunk. "Thanks for stopping by."

"Again, I want to extend my condolences on behalf of Enchanted Events," I said. "Zoey and her family are in our thoughts and prayers and—"

The door shut, cutting off the rest of my heartfelt sentiments, my kind encouragement, and most importantly, my question about where Max was the morning of the murder.

"Well?" I followed Sylvie to the car and got in. "Did you find anything in the bathroom?"

"She has excellent taste in moisturizer." My grandmother buckled her seatbelt. "Though her window is a security hazard, and her prescription bottles are just crying for identity theft. Oh, and Max lives there. His stuff was everywhere."

"I meant anything useful?"

"No. Unfortunately not. I searched her medicine cabinet, sink plumbing, and the air ducts in the ceiling. Did you glean anything else?"

"Not really."

"Use your Sutton intuition. Do you think Zoey has motive to kill Sasha?" Sylvie asked.

"Yes," I said. "But she doesn't strike me as the type."

"We certainly can't count her out yet."

"No." The car jerked into reverse, and I slipped on my sunglasses. "I'd never underestimate the consequences of an annoying family member."

CHAPTER THIRTEEN

"DISGRACED BACKUP SINGER Suspect in Murder."

I sat at my desk Friday morning waiting for a vendor as Henry read the front page headline of the *Sugar Creek Gazette*. "I wasn't a backup singer," I mumbled. "I was an equal member of a girl band that rocked its way to pop stardom."

"When your lead singer is on par with Beyoncé, you're bound to play second fiddle," Henry said. "Or third." He held up the paper. "Nice of them to include an action shot to accompany the article."

The photo, the only thing in color on the page, showed me standing on the sidewalk, finger pointed at Evan, my face twisted in anger. The caption included my threat that had been "witnessed by a handful of concerned Sugar Creek citizens." I missed the anonymity of my life in Los Angeles. Unless you were an A-list celebrity committing a major crime, nobody cared. In small towns, you couldn't scratch your nose without someone spinning it into gossip.

"Henry?" Alice stepped into the office. "Bailey from Bailey's Blooms is here to see you."

"Did you offer her some coffee?"

"Yes." Alice shot me a worried glance. "But she said she doesn't want to eat or drink anything we serve."

"Escort her back here." Henry folded up the newspaper and stuck it in the top drawer of his desk. "Oh, and Alice?"

"Yes?"

"You have a stain on your shirt." He pulled up a file on his iPad. "Please take care of it."

Her eyes dropped to her chest, and her shoulders slumped. "Yes, sir."

"She's a single mom, you know," I said as Alice departed.

"So?"

"*So* every morning she's getting two kids ready for school all by herself."

"And that leaves her no time to look in the mirror?"

"That means, Mr. Insensitive, that mornings are chaos, and with three kids under seven, Alice is doing good to make it out the door with her sanity, much less a clean shirt. Accidents happen."

He looked up from his work. "Is this one of those things I'm supposed to be tolerant about?"

Whew, boy. "I've really got my work cut out for me."

"*You* do?" Henry stood and straightened his paisley tie. "My trainee's accused of Murder One."

Before I could respond, a woman hesitantly walked inside. "Good morning, Mr. Cole."

"Bailey, hello." Henry's cheeks lifted as he smiled and crossed the room to take her hands in his. The petite blonde blushed prettily. The man could certainly turn on the charm when he wanted to. "And you know our new owner, Paisley Sutton?"

"Yes." Her eyes darted my way before she lowered her voice.

"I had hoped to speak to just you, Mr. Cole. About a business matter."

Henry swooped a hand toward me. "Paisley's now my boss, so all business matters include her, of course."

The three of us stood in the midst of a long, smothering pause, as if a foul fourth person had joined us and we didn't know how to send him away.

Bailey clasped and unclasped her hands. "I . . . I wanted to tell you that next Saturday will be our last wedding to work with Enchanted Events."

Henry's brow furrowed, and alarm pierced his words. "We're booked with you through December."

"I know. And I'm sorry this doesn't leave you much time to find another florist."

"What's going on here, Bailey?" Henry asked. "We've brought you a lot of business in the last year and a half."

"And I'm grateful," the woman said. "But I think right now is not a good time to align our name with Enchanted Events."

"Because of me." I walked toward the florist and watched her take two steps back as if I were brandishing a cleaver. "Because people think I might have killed Sasha Chandler?"

"I'm just getting my little flower shop off the ground, and I don't need bad publicity."

Well, neither did I, but it was all I could seem to attract.

"Tell you what." Calm and cool Henry had returned, and he gave Bailey his most reassuring smile. "You take a few days to think about it. Don't make a hasty decision right now. You know we have a mutually profitable partnership, and it's just going to continue to expand. Take the weekend to really consider it before pulling the plug."

Bailey swallowed and gave a sad shake of her head. "I'm sorry, but I'm done." Her eyes flitted to me. "Good luck to you, Miss Sutton. Maybe when this all gets straightened out, we can work together again." She walked out, her sundress swishing around her fast-moving legs.

Like a deflating balloon, I slowly descended into my desk chair. "We lost two more weddings yesterday afternoon and now this. I'm ruining Enchanted Events, Henry."

He paused, as if editing his thoughts. "She said she'd reconsider when this all got straightened out."

Despair was as bitter as the cold coffee in the mug next to my hand. "She means when I'm in prison and you're the new owner."

A few hours later, I had yet to sidestep the cloud of gloom hanging over my head. I sat next to Henry in a plush chair and took furious notes while he helped a bride-to-be with her venue decisions. The bride's mother had barely let her daughter get a word in.

Henry consulted his client's list of preferred locations. "Grace Cathedral is a great pick."

"It's beautiful, isn't it?" Alyssa Compton, the young bride, gushed. "My fiancé and I both love that one."

"It's much too small and much too country," her mother said. "I'll not have my daughter getting married on a farm." Her laugh struck an annoying octave. "Next you'll be wanting attendees to sit on hay bales."

"I think it's quaint and comfortable," Alyssa said, head down and eyes toward her shoes.

"Comfortable is *not* the word people will use for my daughter's wedding."

Alyssa sniffed and dug in her bag for a tissue. "But it's what *I* want."

"All of her venue picks are completely unacceptable." Mrs. Compton handed Henry a list of her own. "I'd like you to check the availability of these instead."

Tears welled in Alyssa's green eyes.

"Mrs. Compton, how about you and I go to my office so I can show you some photos of our weddings." Henry helped Mrs. Compton to her feet. "I think you'll be pleasantly surprised how our team can transform any location."

The two walked away, with Mrs. Compton complaining loudly about her poor daughter's wedding choices. I pretended not to hear and smiled at our bride. "If anyone can convince your mother, it's Henry," I said. "He's designed some stunning weddings."

Alyssa sagged into her chair. "Can I be honest with you?"

Foreboding tapped me on the shoulder. "Um, yes, of course."

"Tyler and I just want to run to Vegas."

"Oh." My brain scanned for the right thing to say. "You don't want to do that. Think of the memories you'll make with a beautiful local wedding. I'm telling you, Enchanted Events is going to bring you a fairy tale."

She scrunched her nose. "I don't want a fairy tale."

I looked around for someone to step in and help me, but everyone was busy. "What is it you want?"

"Elvis."

"Pardon?"

"I want Elvis to marry us in the tackiest chapel we can find on the Strip."

"I don't think your mother would care for that."

Alyssa lowered her voice to a conspiratorial whisper. "She has terrible taste."

"But she wants the best for you, I'm sure."

"No, what she wants is a fancy wedding because my dad is a big deal attorney in Fayetteville, and she wants to show off for all her snobby society friends. But this isn't her wedding, is it?" Alyssa waited for a response to what I assumed was a rhetorical question.

"It is your wedding, but—"

"Exactly." Alyssa sipped from her Enchanted Events water bottle, a service we were now providing in lieu of champagne. "I knew you'd understand. Seeing how your wedding got horrifically ruined and all." She leaned my way. "I read about you in the tabloids for months. Juicy stuff."

I unclenched my teeth. "What I understand is that your mother cares for you, and she wants you to have a top-notch experience, which is what we provide."

Alyssa sat straighter, as if a new energy pulsed through her veins. "An experience is exactly what I want for my wedding. A memory. A fun, zany memory."

"We can do zany." My voice rose on a desperate note. "In fact, we're currently running a special on zany. Ten percent off." Oh, my gosh. This session was going down the toilet.

Alyssa clasped my hand as if we were partners in bridal hijinks. "You only get to do your wedding once, right?"

"Well, maybe not if you're from Hollywood or—"

"This should be *my* wedding and not my mother's."

"And it can be. Henry is a pro at balancing your family's expectations with your own list of wants."

"What I want is Vegas."

I swallowed hard. "No. No you don't." I could not lose this wedding. Why did everything I touch crumble into ruin? "Lots of feathers and cleavage. Mobsters, rigged slot machines, and watery booze."

"Exactly!" She clapped her hands in glee, her engagement ring flashing like a warning beacon. "It sounds wonderful, doesn't it?"

"No! No, it does not!"

Alyssa jumped up and pulled me into a spastic hug. "Oh, thank you! Thank you, Paisley. I knew you'd understand."

"Alyssa, no. I don't—"

The bride-to-be lifted her hands to heaven. "The big wedding is off!" Her declaration rang out like a call for human rights. Like she had been to the mountaintop . . . and pushed me right off of it. "Cancel everything!"

My lips wobbled into a plastic smile, hoping to reassure our room full of onlookers they weren't witnessing a total implosion. "Let's just take a deep breath." I patted Alyssa on the back. "Would you like more water?" A Valium? A mute button? A tranquilizer gun?

"No, no time." She squashed me in another quick hug, then picked up her purse. "I have plans to make! Oh, Paisley. Thank you for making me see the light."

"What light?"

We both turned to find Henry and Mrs. Compton behind us, the two sporting matching frowns.

"Ah . . ." My brain remained frozen in neutral. "Alyssa seems to be a little confused about her wedding details. Probably just the nerves talking."

Alyssa giggled. "Or my independence! Mother—"

Oh, no. Here it came.

"I'm canceling the wedding."

If looks could kill, both mom and Henry would have me speared to the wall.

"No, you're not." Mrs. Compton's eyes went as wide as the Botox would let them. "I left you two alone for ten minutes." Mrs. Compton turned that fire-breathing face on me. "What did you say to my daughter?"

"It was all her decision," I said. "Truly, I had nothing to do with this. I—"

"Paisley has inspired me to go my own way. Make this wedding what *I* want it to be. Goodbye, church! Goodbye, caterer! Goodbye, puffy dress I don't even like!"

I watched in horror as Alyssa Compton skipped out of the shop, singing "Viva Las Vegas" and high-fiving everyone she passed.

"You." Mrs. Compton pivoted like a firing cannon and pointed her finger at me. "You've ruined *everything!*"

I said a prayer to just disappear. "I'm so sorry."

"You will be." Mrs. Compton lifted her chin, her voice resolute. "By the time I tell everyone I know about this, you won't have a customer left. You haven't begun to be sorry!"

She left in a blaze of tears and more threats.

As the door slammed, a heavy hush hung over the room like a fog.

Henry rubbed a hand over his face, as if trying to erase his dire thoughts.

"Henry, I—"

"Go home, Paisley." He sighed heavily, his voice hollowed with defeat.

"I didn't tell her to elope."

"Take the rest of the day off." His gaze barely met mine. "We'll handle things here."

"But we have to get ready for Saturday's wedding."

"We'll see you Monday."

"But—"

"We've got it," Henry said. "Just get some rest."

The employees stood like mannequins, their heads angled my direction, unmoving in a frozen scene. Humiliation burned through me and unshed tears stung my eyes.

I grabbed my purse and escaped out the back door.

CHAPTER FOURTEEN

I TOOK THE long way home, driving through bumpy back roads dotted with the former homes of childhood friends who had moved on to mature, productive lives. Lives that didn't involve ruining businesses by mere association or becoming a murder suspect. The sun shone golden and proud, oblivious to any broken people beneath it. Though it was only noon, I stopped and got a chocolate shake at Dixie Dairy, not returning to my house 'til I had emptied the cup of every last frozen calorie.

When I pulled into my driveway, I spied Beau standing on a ladder beneath our porch, working on my outside light. Dressed in his usual jeans and T-shirt, he still inspired a moment of pause for appreciation. His every move flexed a muscle I couldn't name, but enjoyed, nonetheless. His brown hair had always lightened in the summer, just as his skin had tanned, and time hadn't changed that. But it had changed other things about him. Softened him in some ways and certainly hardened him in others.

Beau stopped what he was doing as I approached, leaned an elbow on his ladder, and regarded me. "You get sent home from school?"

"Something like that."

He nodded toward the light above him. "Just fixing this before I head back out to Fox Falls. If Sylvie knew you were without a porch light, she'd chew me out something good."

"I can change my own lightbulbs, Beau."

"You could, but that's what Sylvie pays me the big bucks for." Something behind me caught his attention. "You expecting company?"

I turned to see Detective Ballantine's car easing in right beside mine. I knew it was too much to hope that he was personally delivering me great tidings of my proven innocence.

"Detective Ballantine." Beau climbed down from his ladder. "To what do we owe the pleasure?"

"Hey, Beau. Heard Miss Sutton was home, and I wanted a word with her."

Beau stepped closer to me, his light cologne both familiar and a comfort.

"Miss Sutton, we have the autopsy back." The detective stood in front of me, his body rigid, as if he was prepared for me to bolt. I wondered if the man was going to arrest me, and if I'd regret my outfit choice for the mug shot. If my parents would even take the time from their speaking tour to visit me in prison.

"That was a fast turnaround," I said. Sylvie had told me it could take weeks, but Evan had also said his money and influence could speed things along.

He watched me with unmasked scrutiny. "Sasha Chandler died of blunt force trauma to the head."

Just as we had suspected. "That's truly awful."

He stepped closer. "How much alcohol did you give Sasha to drink?"

"What do you mean?"

"I mean, how many glasses of champagne did you give her?"

"A few." I would've done anything to shut the woman up.

"Her blood-alcohol level was pretty high." Ballantine watched me like a hawk ready to swoop down on its prey. "Sasha must've drunk a lot prior to her death." He paused, letting his words build suspense. "It's probably easier to hit a drunk person over the head with a bottle than a sober one. Especially if you want to catch her unaware."

The porch spun like a rickety Tilt-a-Whirl. "I did not hit Sasha with a bottle, and I certainly didn't intentionally get her intoxicated."

"It certainly looks that way," Ballantine said.

"I would never hurt her. I didn't even know her. Maybe somebody slipped something in her cupcakes. Did you test every one of them? That icing looked a little off to me."

"We tested the remaining cupcakes."

"You can't trust bakers! Some of them are on a constant sugar high." I threw out rambling words as if I was no longer tethered to reason. "The insulin spikes probably alter their brains. Raging ketones. Impaired judgment. And don't even get me started on the Jekyll effects of high-fructose corn syrup."

"The baked goods have no bearing on this case, Miss Sutton." Ballantine rocked on the back of his heels. "Did you or did you not allow the victim to drink more than one glass of champagne?"

"Paisley." A forgotten Beau flanked my side. "Don't say anything more."

"After she drained her second glass, Sasha Chandler demanded I leave the bottle." My voice wobbled pitifully. "I have no idea how much of it she drank. What I'd like to know is if you're pursuing other suspects, Detective Ballantine. There are people out there with motives to kill Sasha."

"Yours is especially interesting." He held up a copy of the newspaper, his fat pointer finger right on my face. "Broken hearts and humiliation do funny things to people."

"I'd never even met Sasha before that week. When I threatened Evan, I didn't even know she was his fiancée."

"Right."

"I came back to Sugar Creek because I inherited Zelda's business. If it tanks and I can't sell the building, I gain nothing. Nothing. Why would I interfere with that and murder someone? Plus, I have an alibi. I was at Enchanted Events—running my tail off."

"Your employees verified you were alone for a long stretch of time. You had plenty of time to let Sasha get liquored up, then hit her."

"I think that's enough for today." Beau's voice lost all hospitality. "She has nothing more to say without her attorney."

But the detective wasn't done. "Miss Sutton, your prints are on the champagne bottle, as well as the glass."

"I served her. Of course they would be. And the person who actually hit Sasha wouldn't be stupid enough to leave prints." Geez, I'd watched enough *CSI* reruns to know that.

"It had to hurt—Evan standing you up at the altar." Ballantine angled his head and regarded me with faux concern. "Embarrassing, I'd imagine."

In my mind, I yelled at the old shame to stay back, rebuked it for the demon it was. But that dark tormentor overrode my thoughts and flooded my heart until my skin prickled and I tasted its bitter defeat on my tongue. "Evan walking away from our wedding was the best thing he ever did for me." It was a line I'd settled on and repeated at least once a week. "If anything, I owe him gratitude."

"He maligned your character. Dragged your name through the mud."

"I'm in the entertainment business." I struggled for a light, airy tone. "We're used to people believing the *Enquirer* version of our lives."

"He said you were unstable." The detective's eyes bored into mine. "A washed-up musician unable to cope."

Tears clogged my throat and made words impossible. Lies. Most of that was lies, but some days I had trouble remembering which was the truth.

Beau slipped an arm around my shoulders and pulled me in as if I were his to protect. "I said that's enough, Detective. You can talk to her lawyer if you want any more information."

But Ballantine didn't seem in a rush to leave. "Did you visit the residence of Zoey Chandler?"

My brain instantly cramped. "No. Maybe. I mean, yes. Yes, I did."

"For what purpose?"

"To offer my condolences and return something Sasha had left at Enchanted Events."

"I'd advise you to stay away from the Chandler family. And let me warn you now: You and your grandmother had best keep your noses out of this investigation. Am I clear?"

I met his intimidating glare. "Are you arresting me today?"

His lips pinched, as if he tasted regret. "No."

My knees nearly buckled with relief.

"But my handcuffs and I might be back tomorrow." Ballantine tipped an imaginary hat. "Beau, let me know when the catfish are biting."

ALL OF LIFE'S questions could be answered at the library. At least that's what my eleventh grade English teacher Mrs. Comiskey had told me years ago. She'd also believed in unicorns and an imminent alien invasion, so sometimes it was hard to filter the wheat from the chaff when she'd doled out advice. But since I had precious little data left on my cell phone, time to kill, and a furious, nervous energy, I settled in front of a computer at the Sugar Creek Library to see what information I could unearth on Sasha and the people in her life. Ballantine's threat to carry me off in handcuffs cycled through my mind until I was nearly sick with it.

As a little investigative warm-up, I first conducted a quick search of my own name to see if news of my assumed guilt had reached the outside world. It was always humbling to type in your own name. Immediately new photos and headlines popped up, none of them flattering. "Former Pop Star a Murderer?" "Will Paisley Sutton Be Singing the Jailhouse Blues?" "Where is She Now? Possibly in Prison!"

Good heavens.

I barely refrained from responding to a few of the incendiary comments, and instead pulled out my list of murder suspects and typed in the first name: Zoey Chandler.

My search pulled up a photo from college (annoyingly

good), an article about her work with the Junior League (very altruistic), and a series of family Christmas cards her father had posted annually on his company website.

I clicked on a news article from last December. "Daughter of Prominent Businessman in One Car Crash."

Apparently Zoey had been booked on a DUI after wrecking her car, but I found no other strikes against her, no more red flags, or skeletons leaping from her online closet.

But what if Zoey have a drinking problem? Maybe she'd been in a drunken rage last week and attacked her sister?

I typed in Phoebe Chen's name next.

"I'm sorry to interrupt."

I minimized my screen with lightning speed as a woman carrying a stack of large-print hardbacks appeared beside me.

Her library name tag read Anna Grace. "Weren't you in Electric Femmes?" she asked, smiling.

"Yes, I was." I glanced around, hoping this admission didn't send anyone scurrying away in fear for their life. "I'm Paisley—"

"Paisley Sutton," she gushed. "I know. I'm Anna Grace. Back in high school I saw the Electric Femmes at least five times. Y'all were so awesome." I wondered if she knew her voice had risen above a library whisper. "The costume changes, the choreography, the songs that spoke right to my heart." She laid her hand over the general direction of that heart. "I cried for a month when Jaz broke up the band to go solo."

"That makes two of us." Then Jaz went on to be bigger than we ever could have, as if our little band had held her back.

"Any plans for a reunion tour?"

"I don't think so." Jaz was a little too busy being an entertainment deity and a billionaire recording artist.

"I was so excited when I heard you were in Sugar Creek. What an honor to live in the town an Electric Femme grew up in." Anna Grace pushed up a plaid headband that held brunette hair. Her pink tips were in desperate need of a touch-up. "I work here three days a week if you need any help." She gestured to my computer screen. "I'm an excellent researcher. I'm in my last year of grad school for my info science degree."

"That's great. Thank you."

She covered her mouth as if to shelter the words that followed. "If it's any consolation, I don't think you did it. You know—the murder."

"Thank you."

"Are you sure there isn't anything I can help you with?"

"Positive," I said. "I'm just Googling some things. Trying to reacquaint myself with the town. Get to know some folks so I can be a better business owner." And find a killer. You know, normal search stuff. "Did you know Sasha?"

"I saw her occasionally." Her face rippled into a scowl. "Occasionally she'd represent the Chandler family at some of our library charity events. We had a fund-raiser a few weeks ago, and she brought one of her bridesmaids. Sasha was so mean to that poor girl. In fact, the friend left early—in tears. If that's how Sasha treated a best friend, then there's no telling how she treated an enemy."

Unless the best friend was the enemy. "Do you know the bridesmaid who was with her?"

"Sure," Anna Grace said. "Phoebe Chen."

CHAPTER FIFTEEN

AGAINST MY BETTER judgment, I picked Sylvie up that evening on my way to chat with Phoebe.

I found my grandmother and her best friend in the dining room. Or what should've been my grandmother's dining room. Gone were the family photos that had previously decorated the walls. In their place hung giant whiteboards with lists of possible murder suspects, their photos, and info about each. Laptops sat in mini stations with blinking, flashing screens. A television was perched on a Chippendale table, the screen a collage of blurry images.

I squinted harder at the TV and saw one of those images was the exterior of Enchanted Events. Another appeared to be a live-stream of someone's house. Holy spy cams! "Do you have cameras posted all over town?"

"Quit yelling!" Sylvie hushed me with waving hands. "You never know who's listening."

"My gosh, what is all this?" I did a slow turn. "Where are all the family pictures?"

"Meh, who needs 'em?" Sylvie put down her dry erase marker. "I see your faces all the time on the Facebook. Consider this investigation central."

"Yeah." Frannie clicked away at her laptop. "And so far you

haven't brought us much intel. Are you Sylvie's granddaughter or not?"

"I am." With the minor difference that I had the sanity gene. "Is any of this legal?"

The two women looked at each other. Then burst into raucous laughter.

Sylvie dabbed the moisture away from her eyes. "Okay, enough with the irrelevant stuff. Who have you talked to since Zoey?"

"No one."

Frannie, wearing a new bobbed haircut, shook her head. "Lord have mercy on this lost soul."

"Hey, I have a job. I put in ten hours a day at the shop, then come home and—"

"Make out with your neighbor?"

"No, Frannie," I snipped. "I stay up past midnight reading about floral arrangements, displays, music choices, lighting, budgets, decorating, bridal trends, and everything else I don't know about running a wedding planning business. And what is this?" I pointed to the headings on one section of a whiteboard. "Bridesmaids, groom, father, sister . . . *jilted ex-lovers*? Who's the jilted ex-lover?"

"I dunno." Sylvie chewed on the end of her marker. "But if there's anything Sexy Book Club has taught me, it's that stable hands can be dukes in disguise and everyone has an angry old flame lurking in the shadows."

"I know that's right." Frannie held up a right hand to testify. "Though most of our old flames have been snuffed out by international espionage or enlarged prostates."

I had to sit down. "Why isn't Sasha's mother on your list?"

"She was at a spa vacation all week," Frannie said. "Translation: plastic surgery. Lady was totally out of commission."

"How do you know that?" I asked.

Sylvie smiled. "I sometimes vacation at that same . . . spa. I have sources there."

Frannie nodded. "They give her discounts, gossip, and plumpy injectables."

"I try to get Frannie to go, but she won't have it."

"The men love this face." Frannie patted her cheek. "Mess with this God-given gift? Girl, I don't think so."

"It's time to get to work," Sylvie said. "Let's move along."

"Y'all go on." Frannie plugged in some earphones to a computer that looked a little too military to be from the local tech store. "I'm going to troll around on the internet, peek into some accounts, search some files."

"It's best you don't ask, Paisley." Sylvie pushed me toward the door. "And I'm driving. Your lack of window tint is just asking for detection from a Soviet satellite."

RIDING WITH SYLVIE behind the wheel was like driving with a blind Indy 500 racer. On our way to Fayetteville, her sports car zipped and zagged, reaching speed limits that made police officers pull you over and light your license on fire. At multiple points on the half-hour trip, I thought I'd never have to worry about prison because I wasn't going to survive the car ride.

"Here we are." Sylvie pulled up to a small brick home, as her

British-voiced GPS confirmed we had, indeed, arrived at our destination.

"You let me do the talking." I jumped ahead of Sylvie on the sidewalk, speed-walking to beat her to the door.

"You have no skill at this yet." My grandmother tapped her foot in irritation as we stood on the front step. "No instinct to suss out false information. You're not even packing heat!"

I gasped and turned. "And you *are?*"

The door opened before my grandmother could respond, but I threw up a prayer to the patron saint of No Bullets just to be safe.

"Paisley, hello." Phoebe extended her hand and waved us inside. "Come on in. I was just making some tea." I noticed Phoebe's smile wavered as much as her voice.

"I hope it's okay I brought my grandmother with me." I shot Sylvie a glare, still angry that she was basically a walking WMD. "It was Bingo night at the nursing home, and she has trouble following along."

Sylvie just grinned.

As we settled into the living room, Phoebe returned in short order bearing a tray of dainty cups and hot tea. It was June. And nearly one hundred degrees. I wanted ice in that stuff.

Phoebe set the tray down on a dark oak coffee table. "You said you wanted to speak to me about . . . Sasha's death?"

"Yes," I said, watching the steam rise as she poured. "I have a few questions."

She set the teapot on the table with a clunk, descended beside me on the sofa, then buried her hands in her face and sobbed.

Sylvie's eyebrow lifted as she mouthed *I'm recording this.*

Of course she was. Probably with some gizmo the size of a Tic Tac dangling from her bra.

"Phoebe, what's wrong?" I awkwardly patted her back. "I know it's hard to lose a close friend." *Pat, pat, pat.* "I'm sure the absence of Sasha's friendship is terribly painful."

She sniffed and blotted her nose with a tissue she pulled from her pocket. "Uh-huh."

"I find it always helps to talk about the good times," Sylvie suggested.

"Yes, let's do that. Good idea." Phoebe flicked a piece of fuzz from her jeans. She studied the geometric rug on the floor before moving her attention to the fan swirling overhead. Drumming her fingers on her knees, she sighed. "I can't think of any good times."

"Not one?" Sylvie asked.

"Well, there was that one time I choked on a cookie at Starbucks, and she slapped me on the back until I coughed it up."

"She saved your life?" I smiled for encouragement. "That's very heroic."

"Actually she just hit me really hard a few times before asking this cute fireman to intervene."

"So she was thinking of your safety and getting you a handsome guy," I offered.

"After making sure I was breathing, she left with that handsome guy."

Sylvie handed Phoebe another tissue. "I'm struggling to see why you'd be best friends with her."

"I think *best* friends is probably not an accurate description,"

Phoebe said.

"You were only one of three bridesmaids." I waited for a response, but got none. "Phoebe, I'm sure no matter how Sasha treated you, you can at least take comfort in knowing you were a great friend to her."

A pitiful wail burst from Phoebe's lips, and she clutched her stomach. Ugly Cry overtook her once again. "I killed her. Paisley, I killed Sasha!"

My whole body froze. Five minutes and fifteen seconds into this conversation, and I already had a confession? My word, I was *amazing* at this sleuthing business! I did a mental victory dance involving great skill and impressive hip pops. "Tell me all about it."

"I can't. It's too awful."

"It will make you feel better." I gave her hand a bolstering squeeze. "I can't imagine carrying that burden around another moment longer."

She blew her nose and looked at my blank-faced grandmother, then at me. "You're so right. This has been eating me alive."

"Go on," I said.

Phoebe took a deep, shuddering breath, her eyes sparkling with tortured tears. "I . . . I'd been giving Sasha my anxiety meds for weeks. She was driving us all nuts, and I'd tried to talk to her about getting a prescription to help her stress level. But she refused. So I just . . . slipped her some of mine. I'd crush them up and put them in her food when we'd go out, slip them in her drink. And it helped. It really did."

Sylvie and I exchanged confused looks.

"So you drugged her and then knocked her over the head?"

Sylvie asked.

"Of course not!" A frown marred Phoebe's ivory skin. "I didn't even see Sasha the day of her death. The last time I'd given her a little happy pill was three days earlier when I met her for coffee. But what if it was still in her system? One of the side effects is grogginess. Maybe she was so out of it from the meds that she fell, hit her head, and died. And I'm responsible!"

My confessional victory dance wasn't going to warrant anything more than a few finger snaps and awkward head bobs. "How much did you slip her?"

"One pill. I was running low."

"And what was this prescription?" Sylvie asked.

"Prescription?"

"Yes." Sylvie was losing patience. "What did you give her?"

"ZoCalm."

"That's it? That's all?" My volume rose in an off-key quiver. "That couldn't harm anyone."

"Maybe it caused an allergic reaction! A freak response. One time I took a sinus pill and burped for three days straight."

I pinched the bridge of my nose and huffed my deep disappointment. "Sasha died of a blow to the head."

Phoebe covered her gaping mouth with a hand. "I . . . I didn't do that." Her volume rose like a squeaky cartoon character. "I didn't do that!"

"I know." Disappointment spiraled with the velocity of a crashing jet.

Sylvie uncrossed her legs and leaned toward Phoebe. "Do you know of anyone who wanted to hurt Sasha?"

Phoebe glanced about and lowered her voice, as if she were

in danger of being overheard. "It would be easier to tell you who *wouldn't* want to hurt her. She had a list of enemies longer than a North Korean dictator's. She was an angel to me compared to how she treated others."

"I can't understand why any of you put up with her," I said.

"Why hang around someone like that?" Sylvie asked. "Did she have something on you?"

Phoebe picked up a terribly ugly couch pillow and ran her finger over the wavy green pattern. "Sasha . . . Sasha was the nosiest person ever."

Phoebe *clearly* didn't know my grandmother.

"She made it her life's work to acquire dirt on everyone in her life," she continued. "Not only did she thoroughly enjoy it, but she used it to her advantage. She kept your secret in return for favors."

"Like being in her wedding?" I asked.

"That was the least of it."

Sylvie's voice went grandmother soft. "And what was she holding over your head, dear?"

Phoebe again made a lengthy study of the carpet beneath her feet.

I looked to Sylvie for help, but she chose that moment to get up and do a slow walk around the room, checking out photographs and knickknacks on the shelves. I could only hope she wasn't planting a bug.

"We can't bring her real killer to justice if you don't speak up," I said.

Phoebe nibbled her bottom lip. "You promise you won't repeat what I'm about to tell you?"

I had to level with the girl. "I could be charged with a murder I didn't commit. I won't abuse your information, but I also can't assure you I won't share it with the authorities if I need to."

She quietly took a sip of tea, then returned her cup to her saucer. "My parents own Herbal Remedies Clinic. They're two very successful naturopathic doctors. Surely you've seen our ads on TV? My brothers and I have been in them since we were babies." At my head-shake of no, Phoebe sang, "You don't need drugs to get rid of those bugs! Can you trust Herbal Remedies to heal you? *Naturally!*"

"Catchy."

"If it got out that they couldn't heal their own daughter's anxiety, they'd be humiliated. And lose the confidence of their clientele. People come from all over the country to see them."

"So Sasha knew you had a prescription for ZoCalm?" Big deal.

"I would do anything to not bring shame on my family. My parents have worked so hard for their practice. They don't even know I take medicine."

This had gotten me nowhere. I just wanted to slither away and go eat my feelings. "You didn't kill Sasha, Phoebe. And now your big secret is buried with her."

"Is it wrong to say I feel relieved?"

"No." Sylvie returned to her seat. "Quite normal. What about Zoey and Raven?"

"What about them?" Phoebe sat up straighter, as if her burden had been lifted. "I hope the other bridesmaids can find some peace as well."

"For what?" Sylvie asked.

"Everyone has secrets," Phoebe said. "Sasha held them over us all like a ransom we couldn't pay."

And just how far, I wondered, would those people have gone to keep Sasha quiet?

CHAPTER SIXTEEN

"Darn it, Sylvie. I do not have time for dinner and book talk." I let my grandmother give me a gentle shove inside the doors of the Bayonet, a restaurant housed in a Union blue clapboard building that had served as a hospital during the Civil War. The original floors and light fixtures remained, as reportedly did the ghosts who were known to roam the halls late at night.

Sylvie waved toward Emma and Frannie, who sat at a large table enjoying a platter of fries. "If you can't make time for steak and smut novels, then your priorities are seriously out of whack."

"Your brain is whack." Fatigue pinched and punched every muscle in my body.

Sylvie grabbed me and pressed a loud kiss to my cheek. "But you love me anyway." She slid into her seat across from Frannie and Emma and slapped the empty chair next to her. "Every other week we meet here. The three of us eat the first hour, then book talk with the whole crew the second. You'll love it."

"I'm sure."

"Oh, got a call from your mother. They're in DC all week before moving on to Seattle. Sold-out shows every night. Said you weren't returning their calls."

"I've been really busy." Of course the shows were sold out.

When were they not? Everyone clamored for my dad's message of living your dream, setting goals, and becoming super-achievers. If I were smart, I'd buy tickets and go myself.

"They're really worried about you, shug."

"But I've got you to keep an eye on me."

She leaned back in her seat. "Pretty sure that's the part they're concerned about."

"We have intel." Emma turned to Frannie. "Is that what I call it?"

"Sure, hon." Frannie handed me a menu. "Our waiter's Cal Patton's son."

Sylvie squeezed a lemon into her water. "The one who quit high school to do acrobatics off the backs of cows?"

"That's the one. It's not very profitable, so he needs a side gig."

"I'm sure the cows are relieved," Sylvie said.

I turned to my cousin. "Did you say you guys had information or just a livestock report?"

"Tell her, Frannie," Emma said.

"Jordie Patton says he was waiting tables in here the night before Sasha died." Frannie leaned in to weave her story. "According to him, the whole Chandler family came in to dine. He says he took a break to call home about Betsy, his prized Holstein who had the sniffles, and who did he see in the lobby arguing?" She paused so long for effect that I wondered if I was expected to raise my hand with a guess. "Mr. Chandler and Sasha. Jordie said they were arguing something fierce."

Emma picked up the report. "He doesn't remember what the fight was about."

"He's been kicked in the head a lot," Frannie said mournfully. "But Sasha left the restaurant crying." She looked at Sylvie. "Left a perfectly good six-ounce filet and a piece of pie."

"Good evening, ladies."

I lost all appetite as Detective Ballantine approached our table. Wasn't one appearance a day from the man enough?

"Hello, Mr. Ballantine." Sylvie's glossed lips curved into a smile, and she all but batted her eyelashes. "What's got you out and about tonight?"

"Taking a dinner break. The Bayonet has the best homemade fries in the county."

"Should you be taking dinner breaks?" I asked. "There's a killer on the loose in this town, and you have a crime to solve."

"Do I?" He leaned a hand on the back of Sylvie's chair. "I'm not sure this one is that difficult."

"Apparently it is," I said. "And I'd feel better if you were out on the mean streets, talking to every person who's stepped foot in Sugar Creek in the last two weeks. We should be searching houses, administering lie detector tests, and waterboarding every suspicious person until we get this thing resolved."

His left brow lifted. "We?"

"You," I corrected. "Your team. Your people. People who are not me."

"You've been warned to stay out of this investigation."

"I solemnly swear I haven't waterboarded a single person." Yet.

"Did you or did you not visit Phoebe Chen?"

"I was just checking on her. On behalf of Enchanted Events. And how did you know that? Are you following me?"

"Are you following Paisley?" Sylvie swatted his hand off her chair. "She has a right to talk to anyone she chooses. It *is* a free country," she said. "Thanks to our military. *And* thanks to women in secret branches of the CIA that often go unrecognized."

"You tell him." Frannie glared.

Sylvie nodded once. "So if Paisley wants to talk to this Phoebe person, she certainly can. The question, Detective Ballantine, is have you spoken with Phoebe yet? I'm sure you already have, right?"

His gaze hardened. "She was on my list."

"Who else in on that *list*?" Sylvie asked.

The detective's smile was as friendly as an alligator's. "How about you fill me in on how your little chat with Phoebe went?"

"It was a good opportunity to console a new friend." I picked up my water glass and took a drink before saying anything more.

"You were telling us who else is on this list of yours," Sylvie prodded.

"I assure you we're doing our job, ma'am." He leveled those intimidating eyes on me. "And stay out of our way while we're trying to do it."

"He wants this case tied up quickly, with a neat bow," I said as Ballantine sauntered away. "He's chomping at the bit to read me my rights, throw me in a cell, and call it good."

"That's not going to happen," Emma said.

I gave the waiter my order, then handed him the menu. "We did find out something interesting from Phoebe."

"Do tell." Emma leaned in.

"She said Sasha had dirt on all the bridesmaids, and that's

why they stuck around and put up with all her crap."

"Must be some serious stuff she held over their heads if they continued to pose as her friends," Frannie said.

"But how serious could it be? I mean, this is sweet Phoebe," Emma said.

After getting their oath of silence, I quickly explained Phoebe's anxiety medication shame.

"That's such a minor thing to care about." Frannie grabbed a fry. "So what did the other girls do—cheat on a test or take someone's parking spot?"

"I wouldn't underestimate Sasha," Emma said. "According to our intern down at city hall, the girls in the sorority house feared her. Her professors kept their distance. During her freshman year she outed a teacher who was moonlighting on weekends in a cross-dressing cabaret."

I snagged one of her fries and swooped it through the ketchup. "Would this professor be angry enough to kill?"

"I dunno," Emma said. "According to the intern, he left school and is now very happy in Tunica, Mississippi, doing a Marilyn Monroe tribute at the Lucky Jackpot Casino."

"That's no help."

"It sounds like Sasha had an uncanny knack for uncovering the most sordid dirt on people," Frannie said. "The hold she had on her friends should definitely be something we investigate."

"So who are we talking to next?" Sylvie asked.

"I feel like this is a question you already know the answer to," I said. "A test."

"And what's your answer, shug?"

"I'd like to talk to Mr. Chandler."

"A fine pick." My grandmother smiled. "Frannie and I will do a little spying on Evan. See what we can dig up."

"I'm not sure how to make contact with Mr. Chandler," I said.

"That's where I come in." Emma stirred her drink. "Chandler Construction is one of our top sponsors for the Mitchell Crawford Gala next Friday, so he's sure to be at the event. How about I get you a ticket?"

"As your plus one?"

"Sorry, my plus one is a hot mayor. But do find yourself a date so you look, you know . . . less stalkery."

"Words every single woman loves to hear."

"I have a nephew in Little Rock who might be available on short notice," Frannie said. "He has one lazy eye, four pending paternity suits, and just a touch of that narcolepsy stuff."

"Thank you." Was it too late to cancel my burger and go straight for pie? "I'll keep that in mind."

NOT HAVING READ their book club pick, *The Billionaire Boss Who Loved a Curvy Librarian*, I left the ladies after dinner and walked to Sylvie's to get my car. I turned down all offers from the girls for a ride, grateful the mile walk would give me a chance to catch an Ozark sunset and get some much-needed air. But halfway into that trek, that calming air dropped ten degrees, the trees blew with the rising winds, and the sky darkened like a Wes Craven movie as the heavens opened and let the pelting rains fall.

Of course it would rain on me right now. What better way to end a horrible day? What I wouldn't give for some sweet LA weather. And an umbrella.

My feet slipped in my stilettos as I trudged on, my hand over my eyes as a shield from the torrential downpour. I'd left my jacket in the car, and my thin Aerosmith T-shirt didn't stand a chance against the rain. With my other hand, I held down the back of my skirt, afraid I was about to add indecent exposure to my potential list of crimes. With only a few more blocks to go, I ran the rest of the way, only twisting my ankle twice and nearly stepping on a dead armadillo once. My limbs shivered with cold, and I wasn't sure all the water drops on my face were from the rain.

When I finally reached Sylvie's driveway, I threw open my car door and dove inside. My arms wrapped around me, I rested my head on the steering wheel—grateful for the shelter, for the warmth. Somewhere there was an hourglass of sand, unstoppable and running out of time before the police crowned me most likely to have murdered Sasha Chandler. I wished I'd never come back to Sugar Creek, wished I'd never met Evan Holbrook. He dumped me, ditched me at the altar, and totally humiliated me. Hadn't I been punished enough? And yet I was still paying for once loving him. Sometimes adulthood was just a series of events to remind you life wasn't fair. Like breaking a heel on Watie Street while sidestepping roadkill in a pop-up storm.

I jammed the keys into the ignition and fired up Shirley the Camry. Defrost on full blast, windshield wipers working like gladiators, I backed out of the driveway.

Until the warning light dinged.

And the car lurched to the left.

Crap! I had a flat tire. That had to be it.

Leaving the shelter of Shirley, I ran a full circle around the car, the rain slapping at my skin. The driver's side tires looked fine, but when I got to the passenger side, I knew doom had dropkicked me once again. Both tires were as flat as that armadillo on Watie.

Dashing back inside, my fingers fumbled with the phone.

I called Sylvie. Straight to voice mail.

I called Emma. No answer.

I called Frannie. No answer.

I repeated the process three, four more times. They were all probably discussing the chapter in which the billionaire boss kisses the librarian and talks dirty Dewey decimal. My phone call in distress couldn't compete with that.

I had no one else to call. Nobody in this world. In this town I never wanted to be back in.

Except.

There was one person.

I picked up my cell phone again and sighed with resignation.

Because he was my very last hope.

CHAPTER SEVENTEEN

B EAU HUDSON ANSWERED on the third ring.
"Yeah?"

My teeth chattered as I pressed the phone to my slick cheek. "Hi, it's Paisley. I wondered if you were busy and—"

"Are you okay? Paisley, are you okay? I can barely hear you."

The rain pounded the roof of my car. "I'm stranded at Sylvie's with two flat tires. Do you think you could—"

"I'll be right there."

I closed my eyes, dissolved into the seat, and let myself appreciate the moment of being taken care of. With my luck, it wouldn't last long, and I wanted to savor the rare gift. I'd been on my own since I left Sugar Creek, barely old enough to drive. These last few years had been the worst, living month to month with a sporadic income, chasing empty promises and paralyzing disappointments. There was no one in Los Angeles looking out for me. Few I could count on. I didn't miss that part of my life back in California.

Ten minutes later a familiar truck pulled up, and Beau limped out, the rain still falling as though it was angry at the world. He held a dark umbrella with one hand and a flashlight with the other. I watched him stoop down and make a thorough inspection of the tires before opening my car door. He'd yet to shave, and his stubble was fast approaching beard status, which was an unexpected addition to his manly appeal.

"What happened to you?" He stood there and let his eyes slowly roam over me, as if we both weren't getting completely soaked again.

"I had a little run-in with Mother Nature." I grabbed my purse.

"I'd say she won." With a hand lightly holding my upper arm, Beau helped me to my feet. "Nothing you can do about your tires tonight. I'll take you on home."

As Beau gallantly held the umbrella over my head, I hobbled beside him to the waiting truck and opened the passenger side.

Where a pretty blonde sat in the front seat.

Beau stared blankly for a moment, as if she were a surprise to him too. "Oh, yeah. Paisley, why don't you hop in the back," he suggested, then pulled open the door. "Easy there."

His arm came around me when my broken shoe slipped, and my eyes met his for a brief moment, rain dripping off both of us. I climbed inside and Beau jumped into the driver's seat, only to reach into the back and grab a denim shirt. "Here. It's mostly clean. Throw this on."

Slipping my arms into the sleeves, I resisted holding the material to my nose and inhaling the scent of it. "Hi, I'm Paisley." I leaned toward the mystery date. "Beau's neighbor. I'm really sorry if I interrupted your evening."

"It's okay," the woman said, but her smile didn't quite reach her brown doe eyes, which were highlighted by the most perfect winged black eyeliner. I was pretty sure any eyeliner I had left was smudged all over my cheeks like tribal war paint.

I remained in Poised for Conversation Posture for a full minute before settling back in my seat when no further chitchat came. Beau's friend didn't seem interested in small talk.

"Paisley, this is Haley Madewell," Beau finally said, breaking the silence.

She certainly was made well. While I resembled a woman tossed overboard, Haley wore a slender sundress that revealed toned arms and a golden tan. Her hair had not been assaulted by the sudden storm, and it lay in gentle, thick waves down her back. She was no bigger than a size two, and she looked like the type who routinely forgot to eat lunch—and told people about it. I disliked her immediately.

"Nice to meet you." I pulled Beau's shirt tighter around me.

Beau turned at the stop sign. "Haley's dad owns Madewell Grocery, a chain of stores all over the state."

Ah, so a trust fund baby. Nothing impressive about riding on your parents' coattails.

"And she's finishing up her PhD in biochemistry at U of A Med School in Little Rock."

Oh.

"How nice," I said as a droplet slid from my hair and plopped on my nose.

"You might remember Paisley from a band. The Electric Femmes?"

At that the woman turned. "Oh, my gosh! You know Jaz?"

I shoved a swath of hair out of my eyes. "Uh-huh."

"It must've been an incredible experience to work with such a legend." Haley didn't even bother to temper her awe. "What a gifted singer she is."

"Paisley's gifted as well," Beau said quietly. "She's got a voice that could rival Adele's."

My head lifted, and my heart caught. Beau's gaze landed on mine from his rearview mirror.

A cell phone trilled from the front seat, and the moment was over. But there for a few seconds, I was someone besides Paisley the Screw Up.

A few minutes later Beau pulled into our driveway, and I bid him and his girlfriend goodbye. "Thank you for the ride. Sorry to interrupt your date."

I exited the truck as gracefully as a one-heeled drowned kitten could, only to find Beau at my side holding his umbrella.

"You don't have to walk me to the door."

"Don't be ridiculous." His hand pressed at my back.

"Ridiculous is your lack of shaving." Though I didn't mean it.

He took my house keys and opened the front door. "Ridiculous is your shoe choices."

"Like I knew I'd be doing a little track and field tonight."

He flicked on the living room lights. "Go change into something dry."

I stood in a puddle on the hardwood floor. "You don't like this look?"

His eyes slid over my wet form. "The look is . . . fine." He cleared his throat and glanced elsewhere. "What I don't like is the way you're shivering."

Beau's voice was as rough as magnolia tree bark. But I still smiled. "Beneath all that gruff, you're a good man, Beauregard."

"Go change, Paisley."

"I will. Bye now."

"I'm not leaving just yet. I'm going to check out the house first."

"Why?"

"Make sure you don't have any leaks." At my frown he added, "It's an old house. It happens."

"Your date is waiting."

"She's fine. She's used to interruptions."

With the skeletal remains of my heels in hand, I sloshed back to my bedroom, peeled off my clothes, and slipped on a T-shirt and shorts that fit my only requirement of being dry.

Padding out to the living room in my bare feet, I found Beau coming from the kitchen.

"Any leaks?" I asked.

"Didn't find any." He frowned. "Paisley, there's no fixing those tires."

"Come on, they'll be fine. Is Gus still down at Delta's Garage? He can fix anything."

"Not this time."

"But I can't afford new tires right now. I just need a little patch to hold me over until—"

"Your tires were slashed."

"Slashed?" Lightning cracked outside and rattled the windows. "As in with a knife?"

"Something like that."

"Someone intentionally cut my tires? This is Sugar Creek, for crying out loud. That doesn't happen here."

"Maybe Sylvie's security cameras will pick up the perpetrator. Probably just kids." But Beau didn't sound so convinced.

"Or someone wanting to send me a message."

"To stop wearing high heels and sparkles?"

"To stop nosing around. That's a classic mystery movie plot. Girl gets accused of a murder she didn't commit. When she starts talking to people connected to the case, the killer gets mad. So he tries to scare her into keeping quiet."

"Or it's just kids."

"I talked to Phoebe Chen today. Maybe someone saw me at her place."

"I think you're reading way too much into this." He checked the locks on my living room windows. "What did Phoebe say?"

I quickly filled him in as he walked down the hall, his boots thunking on the hardwood. "Where are you going?"

"To your bedroom."

I followed right behind him. "If this is a cleaning inspection for Sylvie, I will fail."

He turned around, and I nearly collided into his chest. "Leaks, remember? Go back to the living room."

"No," I said. "My bathroom's a mess."

"Am I going to find unmentionables hanging from weird places?"

My gosh, his eyes could still distract me from any rational thought. "Maybe." His smile lit those baby blues, and any lingering chill from the rain steamed away. "You're not checking for leaks, are you, Beau?"

He turned on his heel and walked into my bedroom.

"You're checking to make sure no one's in the house because you know it wasn't just a coincidence that my tires were slashed." I stood in the middle of my sunshine yellow bedroom as Beau inspected the windows. He moved on to the bathroom before coming back out and peering beneath the bed.

"Is this a framed picture of me under here?" He stood and dusted off his pants.

"Only if it has darts stuck to it."

His lips quirked. "I'll take your car to the tire shop tomorrow."

"Thank you." I walked to the man, his scent a faint caress on my skin. Reaching up on tiptoe, I pressed a quick kiss to his cheek. "Thank you for everything."

Beau's smile slipped away, his face impassive. "If you need anything else, call—"

"Sylvie?"

"You can call me. You know that."

"I do need one more thing."

He already looked suspicious.

My hair dripped on the tops of my bare feet. "Are you going to the gala for Mitchell Crawford?"

"No. Why would I?"

"Because you're a big landowner. He's a big rancher. You used to work on his ranch in high school, right? I thought you two might be friends."

"We are friends, but I don't do galas."

"Don't have the right dress to wear?"

"You got a smart mouth on you, Sutton."

"I have an extra ticket if you'd like to go."

"I'm busy."

"Doing what?"

"Organizing my tackle box."

"I get it. You're dating someone, and it would be weird." Beau didn't deny it, and I sensed he was ready to get out of my crazy, drippy presence. "Sometime you'll have to tell me about your lady friend out there."

He shrugged a dismissive shoulder. "It's complicated."

"What other kind of relationship is there?"

"Goodnight." His eyes lingered on mine for three patters of my heart before he moved to the door. "Oh, and Paisley?"

"Yes?"

"Lock your doors."

CHAPTER EIGHTEEN

THE INCESSANT KNOCKING on my door Saturday morning woke me up hours before I was ready to rise.

I checked the peephole, then eased open the door.

"What are you doing on my front porch at this unholy hour?" I yawned and rubbed my bleary eyes.

Sylvie slipped past me carrying two coffees and a brown bag from Bugle Boy Bagels. "It's ten o'clock. Either you're still on rock-and-roll time, or somebody spent the night with a bottle in one hand and a lampshade in the other." She blew a kiss my way. "Either way, I don't judge. As long as you give me details. And party pics."

I shut the door with a loud thud. "There was no party. I didn't sleep last night." I held up a hand before Sylvie could get in a wisecrack. "And not for glamorous reasons."

"Were you lying alone in your empty bed all night yearning for a tall, dark, handsome, military-serving, outdoor-retreat-owning neighbor?"

I reached for one of the coffees and took a hot sip. "No. No, that is not what kept me up. And seriously, you have got to start reading something besides smutty romance."

"I read sci-fi for a bit, but people got tired of me asking about their quasars and wormholes."

More coffee. This conversation definitely required more coffee.

"Well, that hot neighbor of yours was over at my house bright and early to get your car. Said he was taking it to Delta's Garage and would have it back to you by this afternoon." Sylvie wiggled her eyebrows. "One second he's taking care of your automotive needs, the next he'll be taking care of your—"

"No, there is nothing between Beau and me. And there's not going to be. In fact, he's got a girlfriend."

She snarled her pink lips. "That Haley girl? All brains and boobs and no personality. They've been off and on for over a year. You can take her."

"I have no intentions of competing."

"Want me to make her disappear? Call some of my Italian friends?"

"That's a no. What's in the bag?"

Sylvie set the food on the granite counter in the kitchen. "Bugle Boy Bagels' famous Bull Run Croissants. Egg, pepper-jack cheese, thick-cut bacon from the Miller farm, and their own special sauce on a homemade croissant." She unwrapped one and handed it to me. "I haven't had a croissant this good since I went undercover as a poetry-writing Parisian cocaine smuggler in '84."

I smiled at the familiar tale. Some kids grew up with fairy tales for bedtime stories. My grandma had lulled me to sleep with gruesomely vivid details of her CIA escapades.

"So why the puffy eyes this morning?" Sylvie inched her way onto a yellow barstool.

"Just anxious, I guess. I didn't have two flat tires last night. I had two slashed tires."

Sylvie slowly lowered her coffee cup. "Intrigue."

"And you're not going to get involved."

"I have a friend in Mexico who's created a security system that can shoot dynamite straight at an intruder's tochus."

Lord only knew how they'd product-tested that one. "Not interested."

"He has another model that propels fire ants—"

"Remind me why you stopped by this morning?"

"Fine." She let herself fume for another moment before speaking. "I thought you might need a ride."

"To where?"

"The salon."

"I don't have a salon appointment."

"You do now."

I touched the tips of my messy ponytail. "Why?"

"I have it on good authority that Raven Arnett will be there for her cut and color." She consulted her silver watch. "And frankly, those grown-out highlights of yours need to go, so I pulled a favor and got you in with my boy Armando." She blew on her steaming coffee. "I promised him a signed photo of Jay Z. I do hope you can get that for him."

A half hour later, it was already hot enough to melt butter and wake up the mosquitos when I got in the car with Sylvie. She drove us to her salon, which occupied the entire second floor above Easley's Hardware Store.

"When did Sugar Creek graduate from beauty shops to salons?" I followed Sylvie up the wooden stairwell.

"Since Armando moved to town last year. He's a true artist. No poodle perms allowed in his shop."

I carried my doubts with me as we stepped inside, but they soon vanished into the cedar beams above us. The salon was designed in a loft style with cottage wooden accents contrasting against a color palette of hot pink and metallics. R&B competed with the sounds of scissors snipping and gossip percolating.

"Good morning, Mrs. Sutton." A young woman behind a marble counter smiled at my grandmother.

"Good morning, Gretchen," Sylvie said. "You're looking beautiful as ever." She leaned toward the girl. "And thanks for the hot tip."

Gretchen, dressed in black pants and lacy top, had model-gorgeous blonde hair and looked as though she frequently dined on ice cubes and lettuce leaves. She adjusted her tortoise-rimmed glasses and turned her gaze to me. "Welcome to Ratify. Can I get you an organic, responsibly sourced coffee, or perhaps a fruit-infused water? Today's selection is mango-peach."

What had become of my humble little hometown? I remembered getting my hair cut as a child a half-mile away at Maida Pearl's Shears and Beers. Part beauty salon, part liquor store, the place eventually added a third component of tattoos before Maida retired at the age of eighty-five.

"Nothing for me," I said, still trying to take in the scenery. This salon could easily hold its own in Los Angeles.

"Would you like to start with your manicure or pedicure?"

Sylvie stretched her neck to peer toward the back of the salon. "She'll start with a pedi." My grandmother rested her hand on my back. "Go enjoy yourself. Relax." Her lips hovered near my ear. "And by relax, I mean interrogate."

"Right this way, please." With a dainty hand, Gretchen motioned me to follow. "Sylvie took the liberty of picking your color." She handed it to me as we walked, and I read the color label: Magenta-men Prefer Redheads.

"Here we are." Gretchen stopped by a pedicure chair that looked nearly space-age. "Lilac, here, will take great care of you."

"Welcome! Your first time at Ratify?" Lilac was a good half-foot shorter than Gretchen, but at least twice her weight. "Sit. Sit. We give you best seat in house. I listen to your band all the time when I young. 'Caged in a Love Zoo' was Lilac's makeout song, you know?"

"That's so . . . nice to hear."

She nodded like her head was caught in a spasm. "You still sing?"

I picked up the chair remote and mashed one of the fifty buttons. "Not as much as I used to."

"Too bad. That too bad. But Jaz real big star now, no?"

"Yes. She's a very big star."

And my own star had flickered 'til it eventually flamed out.

I searched for Raven and was finally rewarded minutes later when I saw her being escorted my way. Another Ratify staff member, who could've been Lilac's twin brother, led her right to the empty chair beside mine. Her hair freshly cut and blown-out to shiny perfection, Raven eased into the cushy seat and placed her nail polish bottle on the table between us. Her nail tech turned on the bubble jets to Raven's footbath and chattered with Lilac in a language I didn't understand.

"Love that shade you picked." I nodded toward Raven's bottle of polish.

She startled as if I'd pulled her from a deep thought. "Oh."

Recognition tightened her features. "Hello."

"Deciding on a color stresses me out. I stand in front of that wall of choices and deliberate like it's life-or-death."

Her smile was indulgent and forced. "Me too."

Lilac massaged my left foot, and I briefly closed my eyes and breathed in the bliss. "So, Raven . . . how are you doing?"

Raven watched Lilac's twin at her feet. "I'm fine."

"I know it must be hard."

She took a sip of her fruity water. "I'm getting by."

"Tell me, if you were a betting person, who would you put money on as the prime suspect?" So far, finesse was not my strong point in this crime-solving gig.

Raven let her head fall into the cushion behind it. "At the moment, you're my first guess."

Understandable. "Let's talk about your runner-up."

"I'm not sure." Raven spoke slow and deliberate, as if her lips were too lazy to fully participate. "Lots of people hated Sasha, but I can't imagine any of them being cold-blooded killers."

Well, of course they could. It was how Lifetime movies got made. "Maybe Sasha finally pushed someone too far."

She shrugged. "Maybe."

"Where were you at the time of the murder?"

Raven set down her drink with a thunk. "I've already told Detective Ballantine."

"Just for kicks, tell me."

"I was at work."

"And where is that?"

"An attorney's office in Fayetteville. On that day I was doing research for one of the lawyers."

"Where?"

"The Sugar Creek Library."

"Why not use Fayetteville's or the university's?"

Her bland facial expression matched her monotone. "Because our library had what I needed."

"Can anyone verify you were there?"

"I went alone."

"Interesting."

She straightened in her seat. "What does that mean?"

I didn't know. It just seemed like the Jessica Fletcher thing to say.

"You have pretty feet," Lilac's twin said to Raven. "You want sugar scrub, honey? Make skin real soft."

"Yeah, sure." Raven returned her attention to me.

"Did anyone see you while you were doing this . . . research?"

"I'm not certain." She didn't act like she cared.

"Phoebe said Sasha had dirt on everyone she knew, and *especially* the bridesmaids. What was she holding over your head, Raven?"

"Nothing." She frowned as her nail tech coughed behind his mask.

"How close would you say you were to Sasha?" I asked.

"Close enough to be her bridesmaid." Her exasperation was as loud as the neon polish she'd chosen.

"Had you known her long?"

"I already told you we met during our sorority rush. Look, can I just sit here and enjoy my pedicure? I've worked a million hours this week, my friend just passed away, and I'm starting to get a migraine."

"Yes, sure. Of course." I could feel the sweat beading beneath my armpits. This sort of thing stressed me out. How did Sylvie do it all these years? And yet, I still hadn't learned any new information. "Can I ask you one last thing?"

Raven's exasperated huff could've lifted the beams from the ceiling. "Yes?"

"My life is on the line here. I'm being accused of murdering a person I did not even know. So if I'm being obnoxiously nosy, it's because I don't want to go to prison for a crime someone else committed. If you were me, who would you focus on? Who would be *your* prime suspect?"

Lilac and her brother stopped chattering, and their hands stilled.

Raven inspected a pinky nail, her French manicure glossy and white. "I don't know. I guess if I had to choose, I'd say Professor Carson Fielding."

"Who?"

"He's an art professor at the college."

"Why would I talk to him?"

She pulled her feet from the hands of the wide-eyed tech and shoved them into some flip-flops. "That's enough. I have to go before this headache gets any uglier."

"But what's this professor got to do with—"

It was too late.

With three toenails painted, Raven hobbled off, threw some cash at the front desk, and blasted out the door.

Lilac's brother propped a hand on one hip. "She no like my pedicure?"

"I don't know what that was," I said. "But I'm definitely going to find out."

CHAPTER NINETEEN

W HEN SYLVIE DROPPED me off many hours later, Shirley the Camry—washed clean and shining in the dimming sun—sat proudly in my driveway with two new tires. That Beau Hudson sure was swell. Who would've thought?

Telling myself I was only giving the wheels a test, I got in and drove to the edge of town until I came upon a crooked dirt road that took me over a one-lane bridge, past three dairy farms, two chicken houses, and a log cabin that used to belong to a white-haired widow who liked her tobacco. Jostling over a rusted cattle guard, I drove under a sign that read Fox Falls and followed the worn gravel path. Green fields and trees as far as the eye could see. It reminded me of the Irish countryside a bit, one of my favorite touring stops. I meandered for another mile before I saw a group on four-wheelers zooming toward the sunset. Another quarter of a mile, and I met some guys pulling a boat, no doubt headed out for some night fishing.

Finally a two-story brick and stone structure that said Fox Falls Lodge came into view, and I pulled into a small adjacent parking lot.

The inside of the lodge looked like a grown-up tree house. Natural wood everywhere and huge windows that took up entire walls so the outside could come in. Antler chandeliers hung suspended from a planked ceiling, and paintings of wildlife adorned pine walls.

My polka-dotted espadrilles slip-slipped on the hardwood floor as I made my way to the front desk. Beau stood behind the natural stone counter, talking to three guys decked out in what appeared to be brand-new hiking gear. They were almost too stylish, as if looking like hikers was more important than actually *being* hikers.

"So if you come to the point where Sugar Creek meets Lee River, you know you've come about a half-mile too far." His voice sounded weary, as if he'd already explained this a few times. "Happens a lot."

"Do we get cell reception out there?" A redheaded guy asked. "I need to FaceTime with Tokyo at seven."

Beau pressed his lips together in a smile. "Not likely."

"This wasn't in the brochure."

"You're in the middle of the woods," Beau said. "Mother Nature's gonna interfere with cell towers."

"Any wild animals out there?" another man asked.

"Probably."

Redhead looked up from his phone. "Also not in the brochure."

"It's a good night for camping," Beau said. "The fish are biting, it's a full moon, and the humidity's dropped a bit. Stick to your maps, keep your food supply off the ground, take lots of water breaks, and you should be fine."

The threesome grumbled as they walked away, each of them tapping furiously on cell phones as if they were breaking up with technology forever.

I stepped forward. "I'd like the four-wheeler tour. But you can't mess up my hair, I don't want any bugs to touch me, I expect complimentary drinks, and it had better be air-conditioned."

Beau scrubbed a hand over his face and laughed. "We're all sold out of the Princess Package today. What else can I get you?" He leaned his tanned arms on the counter, fatigue shadowing his eyes. "Can I rent you a cabin for all your hunting needs?"

"I only hunt in malls."

His smile deepened. "Need a fishing guide?"

"Not the least bit tempting."

"Maybe some archery in the back forty?"

"Is that where you dispose of people you don't like?"

Beau watched me for a moment, then walked around the counter until he stood before me, leaving little space between us. I thought about that space. I didn't seem to mind him standing in it, and that did not bode well.

His voice was as easy as the breeze outside. "So tell me how can I help you."

"You already have." My fingers itched to brush that shock of hair from his forehead, and he'd yet to shave. "I wanted to thank you for getting my car fixed." I reached into my purse and extracted a folded check. "I called Delta's to find out how much it was."

"Keep it."

"Definitely not."

"Consider it my welcome-to-the-neighborhood present."

"You know I can't let you buy my tires."

"The deal is done."

I stood there juggling pride, gratefulness, and a healthy dose of attraction I needed to ignore. "Thank you." He knew I was broke. Everyone in town knew I was broke. "I'll just have to find some ways to repay the kindness."

"Remember me fondly when your next solo album hits the big time."

My smile slipped, and I focused on the giant elk head hanging on the wall. "Nice place you have here. Very . . . *National Geographic.*"

"You okay?"

His words all but caressed my wounded spirit. "Right as rain."

"You didn't have to come all the way out here. You could've just sent a text." His Southern accent made everything out of his mouth both a comfort and an allure.

I shrugged. "It seemed impersonal, given the gift."

"You could've waited 'til I got home."

Now I just felt silly. He was probably waiting for his girlfriend to drop by at any moment. "I wanted to see the place, as well as thank you." I drew a circle pattern with the toe of my shoe. "And now I have. So I'll just be off—"

His hand lightly captured my arm. "Paisley?"

"Yes?"

"Do you want a tour?"

"Nah. I just got my hair done today. I don't want it to melt in the humidity."

"While you're taking your seven o'clock call with Tokyo?"

Or spending the rest of the evening in my pajamas eating ice cream directly from the carton.

"If you have the time," he said, "I'd love to show the place off. It's had quite the makeover since we were kids."

Hadn't we all? "I guess I have a little time."

An hour later, I sat on the back of Beau's four-wheeler, my salon-straightened hair melted into curls, at least two bugs stuck to my skin, and my hands loosely anchored to his hips. Violet pink and lilac purple covered the sky as if God had airbrushed his favorite colors across the it. The moon hid in the distance, not quite ready to report for the night shift.

Beau gently braked the four-wheeler, causing my body to lean into his. He glanced back at me, then pointed ahead. "That spot right by the low water bridge? Troops camped there during the Civil War. It's said they had to move on or risk an attack, but they were loathe to leave it due to the prime fishing. It's still one of the best fishing holes in the state of Arkansas."

"And it's all yours." I marveled at the scene around me, a landscape so different from the hustle, bustle, and smog of Los Angeles. "This is all yours."

He climbed off the ATV, then held out a hand for me to do the same. "Easy. The rocks can trip a girl in fancy shoes."

His fingers closed over mine as I slipped off the seat. When he let go, disappointment fluttered light as butterfly wings.

Walking toward the creek, I inhaled the fresh air, letting my chest expand and fill with what could be my first cleansing breath in years. Birds chirped amid the border of trees surrounding us, frogs called out throaty demands, and crickets tried to outshout them all.

"I've missed this." The words tumbled out of my lips unbidden, a surprise to my own ears. But I knew it was true.

Beau's arm brushed mine as he came to stand beside me. "You thinking about staying?"

"No." I couldn't. My life, all that I wanted was back in California. "But this town isn't the torture I thought it would be. And it sure suits you. Are you glad you're back?"

Somewhere a bird sang a lonesome note. "It's home."

"Did you expect to come back so soon?"

"There were a few days in the service I didn't expect to come back at all." The rocks crunched beneath his feet as he walked to the river's edge. He picked up a stone and threw it across the shimmery surface, where it skipped and danced to the other side before sinking to the depths below.

"Are you happy with your life here?" I asked.

"I'm content with seeing Fox Falls doing well."

"That wasn't what I asked." Beau looked like a model for an outdoor catalog—a man almost too handsome to be in the wild—yet one who knew exactly what to do with a fishing pole and hiking boots.

"I'm not that interested in getting all zen and happy," he said. "I have my business, this land, and in a few years I'll build a house out here. I think that should qualify me as happy."

I picked up a rock, the warmth seeping into my skin. "There's one very thin wall that separates your bedroom from mine." With a flick, I released the rock, watching it fly to the water . . . and immediately submerge. "Sometimes I hear you yelling in the middle of the night." His jaw tightened, and I knew I was trespassing on raw, barbed territory. "I can't make out what you're saying, but—"

"We better get back."

I reached for Beau's hand, halting his retreat. "I know you have nightmares. What you experienced in Libya must've been horrific."

"I survived."

There was something about a darkening sky and the sounds of night that loosened a tongue and unlaced inhibitions. I let my fingers slip around Beau's. "Do you see it every night? When you close your eyes, are you right back there?"

His deep breath was audible as he peered up at stars faintly winking in the darkening sky. "It's with me day and night. Whether I'm awake or asleep, that place, that moment, those people are with me."

"Do you want to talk—"

"No." Beau pulled his hand from mine. "No, I don't want to talk about it. I don't want sympathy, I don't want compassion, and I sure don't want to rehash every detail with the idea that it's going to make me feel better. It's not. Good men died that day. They were husbands, fathers, sons, friends. And it lives here." He tapped his temple. "It lives right here. And I'm tired of being asked about it. Tired of it being the unspoken question even when I'm *not* asked about it. I don't owe you or anyone else this story. Do you understand, Paisley?"

"Yes." My heart pounded in my chest, and shame burned my cheeks. "Yes. I'm sorry."

He stood as rigid as the mighty oaks around us. "If I keep you awake at night, then just move to another bedroom. Get some earplugs. Get a radio. Get a different house."

"No, it's fine. It's—"

"It's not fine, but there isn't a thing I can do about it. I'm not taking their meds, and I gave up the whiskey last year. It just is what it is, and that's mine to live with. Not yours, not my family's, and not some therapist's. Mine." He stalked toward the four-wheeler, muttering all the way. "And by the way?" He pivoted and stomped back to where I stood. "You've got a whole grab bag of issues too. You know what I'm hearing through those walls?"

"Me declaring my love to the contents of my refrigerator?"

"You blasting your old albums. Over and over. You think I don't hear *that* late at night? When are you gonna let that go?"

"I have."

"Your days with the band are over."

"I know that. Would I be in Tiny Town, Arkansas, if I didn't?"

"And why *are* you here?"

"Because I need my inheritance."

"But what's it going to do for you? What can that money get you that you couldn't make happen before?"

Beau's words were a rusty arrow piercing my heart. "You don't understand the music business, so I'm not going to bother explaining it to you. But sometimes you have to invest in a new direction."

"A new direction in music?"

"Yes. I'm waiting for a job offer from my agent any day now. What other direction would I be going in?"

"A direction that uses your talent instead of your old fame."

That jerk. If we were in a black-and-white movie, I would slap my palm across his arrogant cheek. "Is this how you deal with a difficult conversation about yourself? You start insulting the other person? I guess it's okay to delve into my life, but heaven forbid we talk about yours." Anger propelled me in his direction, until we stood toe-to-toe. "You got anything else in there for me, Beau?"

"You've lost your twang, you need to stop feeling sorry for yourself, and—" Beau's finger pointed right at my nose. Breath held, I watched as his eyes dropped to my lips.

"And?" I swayed toward him.

"And—" His hand slid up my warm cheek, the touch featherlight. "You can't skip a rock worth a flip."

Beau's mouth dipped toward mine, and I leaned into him, parting my lips for the oncoming kiss. I closed my eyes as his lips hovered, then—

We both jumped as a flock of birds lit from a nearby oak tree, flapping their wings like rude guests leaving a party.

Oh, no.

What had just happened?

"I wasn't going to kiss you." Words fell in a jumbled arrangement. "Right then—when you were all leaning, and I was all leaning, and . . . I'm sure we're both just in the first stages of heatstroke, but I definitely would not have kissed you."

"Of course not." His chest rose in bursts. Sweat beaded at his hairline. "Same here. Sorry if I gave you that impression." He made a lame gesture toward the four-wheeler. "Just part of the tour. We believe in friendliness here."

I swallowed back a laugh. "I'm sorry for the things I said, Beau."

His lopsided grin disappeared. "I'm not. I meant what I said."

How could I want to kiss him senseless one minute and push him in the creek the next? "I am not feeling sorry for myself."

"You are," he said. "And it's going to take you under if you're not careful."

My anger returned with a flash. "You're a fine one to talk."

He nodded toward the ATV. "Get back on the four-wheeler."

"I'd rather not." I lifted my chin. "I'm just going to walk, thank you."

"It's three miles out, you have fifteen minutes of daylight, and last night I saw a bobcat."

The pathway we'd taken had disappeared with the sun, and the terrain seemed indecipherable no matter what direction I looked. "Fine." I climbed back on. "But I'm not touching you. And let the record show after we get back to the lodge, we're no longer speaking."

Beau handed me my helmet, and his voice softened. "Why'd you come out here tonight, Sutton?"

"I—" I started to rehash my earlier excuse—the new tires, the thoughtfulness, the generosity—but instead, I settled on the truth. "I don't know."

"You have a lot going on in there." He ran his finger over my forehead. "But I can't be your diversion. And you can't be mine."

And with that, he revved up the engine and tore off into the field, while I gripped the rack behind my seat.

Dust billowed behind us, covering up the spot where we'd stood. As if we'd never talked.

As if we hadn't *almost* kissed.

CHAPTER TWENTY

MONDAY MORNINGS WERE like too-tight pants. Occasionally you had to wear them, but they sure pinched and pulled.

My hair styled to near-perfection thanks to the long overdue cut and color, I walked out of the house in sequined black leggings, a gunstock gray sleeveless shirt that grazed my knees, and a tailored leather jacket older than most of the brides that came through Enchanted Events. My canary yellow heels landed hard on the concrete as I walked to the car.

I'd managed to get one leg into the driver's side when Beau's truck whipped around the corner and jerked to a stop beside me.

That man had nearly kissed me.

My lips tingled at the memory.

But he'd also said some really hurtful things, and any and all tingling body parts needed to remember we were mad at him.

Shutting myself inside Shirley the Camry, I threw on my sunglasses, started the ignition, and turned up the radio louder than was proper at seven a.m.

I'd just put it in reverse when a shadow fell and a large fist knocked on my window. Beau stood there on the other side, looking annoyingly handsome in dark jeans, Justin work boots, and a faded shirt promoting the high school football team.

"Hey." Beau pounded the glass again. "Stop the car."

I rolled down the window, but I was not turning down Justin Timberlake.

"I'm sorry," Beau said, his voice straining over one fabulous song.

I continued to stare straight ahead, as if the picture window was the most riveting thing.

"Paisley, I said I'm sorry."

The man had told me I was wallowing in self-pity. He'd all but called me lazy, said that I was coasting on who I'd been in the band. I'd lain awake for hours tossing his accusations around in my head.

"Fine." He planted both hands on the window frame and leaned in. "I'll do it."

He smelled like he'd just stepped out of the shower. All Ivory and spice and aftershave and woods.

Beau's hand covered one of mine on the steering wheel. "Will you talk to me?"

With apologies to Mr. Timberlake and his fine groove, I turned the radio off. "This thing you're going to do—what exactly would that be?"

"I'll go to the Mitchell Crawford gala with you."

Oh. Well, wasn't this an interesting and beneficial turn of events? "You sound like you'd rather eat railroad ties and wash them down with battery acid."

His lips quirked. "Maybe just a few swigs of the acid."

I needlessly checked my hair in my visor mirror. "Won't your girlfriend mind?"

"You and I would be going as friends."

"Of course." The visor went up with a snap. "Friends."

"And Haley and I are . . ."

"*Complicated.*"

"Right. And not in a locked-down relationship."

"I'm sure she's completely charmed by your romantic wrestling lingo."

"We're not in a commitment."

"Does she know that?"

"Paisley, do you want me to go to this thing with you or not?"

I pretended to ponder this, as if I now had a handful of other escort options. "I suppose."

He ticked off some ground rules. "We keep our hands off each other, we don't discuss personal crap, and you get three dances."

I angled my head his way. "Four."

"Done." He reached out a hand to shake.

"I would've settled for three."

His fingers gave mine a squeeze. "And I would have gone up to five."

Oh, the charm. It was as if he ate it for breakfast. "Did you leave work just to bring me this apology? You could've texted it." It felt good to repeat his words from last night. "Maybe talked to me tonight when you got home?"

He answered by walking to the other side of the car and getting in. His long frame settled into the passenger seat, and suddenly he was very near, spilling into my space. My rhinestone sunglasses caught his attention. "Did you steal those from a Barbie doll?"

"Did you want something?"

Beau sighed, brushed some dust off the dash, then sighed again. "So last night by the creek . . ." He chewed on his top lip while he decided on some words. "Something weird just came over me, and . . . I wanted to tell you everything. To completely unbuckle all I've held onto and give you every gory detail."

Now I was the one leaning into his space. "What would be so wrong about that?"

"Because I can't let it go. Not yet."

"What do you think is going to happen to you if you talk about it?"

He briefly closed his eyes and shook his head, as if he were seeing snapshots of his past. "I'm sorry I said those things to you. I got defensive, I had a crazy moment, and I was wrong. It was nice of you to come out to Fox Falls."

"That's it? Conversation over?"

Beau's head pressed against the seat, and he studied me while a minivan cruised by. "You're going to pass out from heat exhaustion in that jacket."

Deflection again. "Your counselor must want to shoot himself on a regular basis."

"It's a woman. And I'm pretty sure she started drinking heavily after making my acquaintance."

I knew he was done sharing. "Beau?"

"Yeah?"

"What if you're right?"

"About my shrink being a lush?"

"About my life being nothing more than hits from a decade ago."

"That's not what I said."

"I want to be more than the third girl of Electric Femmes nobody can name. More than a suspected murderess who was embarrassingly wronged by her loser ex-fiancé."

"Then make that happen."

He made it sound so simple. "How'd you pull yourself from the pit after the ambush? How'd you find the will to carry on and start over?"

Beau opened his door, the heat rushing in as he pulled himself out. "One step at a time."

THERE WAS SOMETHING special about Enchanted Events in the mornings when it was just me there. The building was hush quiet except for the settling of old walls, and the light filtered in through all the antique windows like radiant beams from heaven. I could hear my great-aunt Zelda clucking about hemlines and shotgun weddings. Still smell her musty, dusty stack of bridal magazines that were as outdated as her beehive. If I squinted my eyes, I could see my reflection in the lacquer of the hardwood floor and pretend the woman looking back at me was truly the boss, the proprietor, the one who knew what she was doing. The space seemed to welcome me, beckon me. But I wasn't sure what to do with the invitation.

"The minister for the McKenzie wedding unexpectedly moved out of state."

I turned at Henry's voice.

He stood in the doorway, wearing just the hint of a smile

and a charcoal suit that probably cost more than my car. "I'll need you to find a replacement."

I offered a hesitant grin. "I'll get right on that."

"I hear the string quartet we often employ showed up drunk to last Saturday's event. You might call them and give them a warning not to arrive at the Feeney reception in the same manner."

"Nobody wants to hear a tipsy viola."

"Indeed."

"I'm here to work today, Henry." I handed him the bag of muffins I'd picked up at Bugle Boy Bagels. "We have about six weeks left to keep this thing afloat before I can turn it over to you and resume my life. I'll probably screw up a few times before noon. We could have another bride cancel, and I realize right now I'm not exactly good for business. But I'm not leaving."

He held up a blueberry crisp muffin, approval reflecting in those eyes. "I hope you remembered the cream cheese."

"I'm not *that* amateur." I tossed him another bag. "How about I find a preacher for the McKenzie wedding, shadow Layla while she's designing backdrops, and let the Happy Strings Quartet know they need to lay off the hooch?"

"Perfect. And while you're at it, your cousin Emma has just requested a large bachelorette party a week from this Friday."

"That's very short notice."

"Still gives you plenty of time to plan it."

"By myself?"

"Yes. I'll give you all the details I have this morning."

"I'm not sure I'm ready—"

"You are." I wanted to snap a picture and frame the confidence in his face. "And with a schedule that packed, you shouldn't have time to bother me with your little Henry Cole Manners Lessons."

I patted him on the shoulder as I sauntered by. "Never too busy for nagging you, boss."

CHAPTER TWENTY-ONE

I T WAS A long day of bridal shenanigans, and my feet throbbed in my heels. I'd tried to work behind the scenes as much as possible, but occasionally a task did require my appearance in the midst of all the clients. One bride chose not to speak to me, and one made the sign of the cross as I walked by, but most didn't seem to mind my presence.

Exhaustion weighed on my shoulders as I locked up Enchanted Events at seven o'clock and doggedly strolled the two blocks to the Bayonet. Bellying up to the bar, I ordered the evening special of a small sirloin and twice-baked potato. I didn't know what the restaurant put in their potatoes, but I was pretty sure it was a mix of crack and magic.

Five bites into my medium-well steak, my phone trilled. My new agent's name lit up the screen, and I nearly dropped the phone with excitement.

"Hey, Rad." Did he hear me breathing hard? I attempted to modulate my voice so I sounded a little less desperate. "How are you?" The pub noise made it hard to hear, so my phone and I moved to the bathroom hallway.

"Doing good, Pais." Rad Jaxon dragged out the last letter like it was an endless *Zzzzz*. "And yourself?"

"Very busy." Ruining weddings, being accused of murder . . .You know, girl stuff. "Do you have any updates for me?"

"Uh, yeah, not so much. But, I, um, did see something on the internet about you threatening to kill someone? S'at right?"

"No." The talking around me seemed to swell, so I pushed my way through the back exit and stepped into the alley. "Ignore the internet. Just a huge misunderstanding. How are the negotiations with the cruise ship going?"

"Yeah, uh, the Blast From the Past cruise ship has got some really big names signed up."

"Yes, but am I going to be one of them?" It was galling to have an agent who was barely out of high school, and whose name was spelled in such a way he could easily become a rapper if he wanted to switch careers. Plus, I was pretty certain Rad's name was actually Brad.

"Still working on that detail. I'd like to get you in with my image consultant, but she needs a deposit to put you on her schedule. Fatima is super busy. She's booked out for the next twelve months, but she'd do this favor for me and get you in."

I shooed away a fly. "And how much was that again?"

"Five grand."

For a deposit. I didn't even want to know how much the total package would set me back. "It's going to take a few months. Can't she just scribble my name on her calendar in good faith?"

"No can do, Paizzz."

"Okay, how about we talk next week, and you get some info on the cruise for me?"

"Right. Look, um, I gotta go. Lady Gaga's fourth cousin just walked in the office, and I've got a mocha latte getting cold."

"Rad, wait. I think we need to talk about some jobs that—"

Silence. Call over.

Just like my career.

Ten years ago, someone like Rad wouldn't have been good enough to kiss my sparkly shoes, let alone be my agent. And now, here I was, begging for scraps from a man who was too busy shaking Lady Gaga's family tree to even give me five minutes on the phone.

The Arkansas humidity surrounded me like an unwelcome bear hug, and I let my perspiring head lean against the Bayonet's brick wall.

God, if you're listening, I could use some help. I've got to find Sasha's killer and fast. I won't need Rad if I'm rotting in a prison cell. And do they still serve bologna sandwiches daily? You know how I feel about processed meats.

"I said I'd have your money for you."

I ceased my desperate prayer at the intruding loud voice.

"Yeah," yelled a burly voice. "You said you'd have it two weeks ago. Now where is it?"

My ears perked like a dog on point, and I inched closer to the wall to peer around the corner.

And bit back a gasp.

Evan Holbrook stood in the alley, eyes wide and face as pale as meringue. "Just give me a few more weeks, okay? My fiancée just died, for crying out loud. Don't you have any heart?"

"You said you'd have the money for us." This from a man large enough to stuff Evan in his pocket and eat him for dinner. "Boss wants his cash right now."

"I don't have it." Evan held up his hands as if expecting a blow to that pretty face at any moment. "I'm sorry, I just don't have it. But you know I'm good for it. Big Sal knows I'm good for it. I've been faithful to pay."

What in the world was going on? Should I call the police? If this giant killed Evan, with my luck I'd be photographed on the scene and charged with this murder too. I didn't need that kind of stress. Reaching for my phone, I clicked the record button.

"Yeah, you was pretty faithful to pay when your lady was alive to write you the checks, but you're still behind. And while Big Sal sends his condolences, he don't have much confidence in your ability to cough up the funds."

It was a shame Evan would be snuffed out by a man with such deplorable grammar.

The enormous thug gave Evan a hearty shove, slamming him to the brick wall. "You have Big Sal's money by the end of the month."

Evan's head bobbed in a grateful nod. "Yes, I will. I absolutely will."

"And you add five percent."

"That's outrageous!" Evan cried. "I couldn't possibly find an extra—" Giant Thug shoved him again. "Yes, sir. I'll have that for you. And five percent. Five percent will be fine."

"That's what I thought. You let Big Sal down, and we'll have another meeting. That one won't end so well." The man walked away in cinematic villain glory, disappearing into the alley.

I stepped into the light of the street lamp. "What on earth, may I ask, was that?"

Evan pivoted to face me, arms poised like he was ready for another strike. "Paisley! What are you doing here?" His chest beneath that starchy oxford shirt visibly rose and fell.

"I'm listening to you and your best friend. Interesting boys' night you're having."

"It isn't what it seemed."

I walked toward him. "It *seemed* like you owe this guy some money or he's going to toss you like trout food to the bottom of Beaver Lake."

"He was just kidding."

"You always were the worst liar." Like all the times he'd told me he loved me. "What's going on, Evan?"

He hung his head. "I owe some people some money."

"Who?"

"They're in the loan business."

"Pretty sure the Sugar Creek Bank and Trust does not send out henchmen. At worst they dispatch Daisy Patton's grandma from accounting who makes you look at photos of her cross-eyed Siamese cats." While I didn't want Evan to have his limbs rearranged, it was kind of nice to see the preppy, pretty boy sweating profusely. "Tell me what's going on or I share the video footage I just took with our local press."

He ran a hand across his glistening brow. "I said I owe money."

"I got that. What I don't get is why people need to send the brute squad to recoup it."

"It's a long story."

I pushed a few buttons on my phone. "Pardon me while I take a sec and hit send."

"No! No, don't do that." He loosened his tie as if it were a noose. "Political campaigns are very, very expensive. And winning is even more expensive. And when one campaign is over, fund-raising begins immediately for the next term. It's endless! I didn't exactly have a steady stream of contributions coming in for this last election, so I took out a loan or two. And Sasha helped me out. A lot."

"How much do you owe?"

"That's none of your business."

"Should I send the video to the *Sugar Creek Gazette* or just the whole internet universe?"

"Hundreds of thousands of dollars."

I nearly dropped my phone.

"I was already behind on payments to my, um, lender, but now that Sasha's gone"—he mustered the energy to scowl as if it was my fault—"the financial aid obviously stopped. Big Sal assumes I don't have the means to pay now."

"Do you?"

"My bank account could be healthier."

I guessed that crossed Evan off the suspect list. No way would he get rid of the woman floating his campaign. "Where was Sasha getting that kind of cash?"

"I don't know."

I slapped at a mosquito who'd nibbled on my cheek. "You didn't question where she was getting the huge amounts of money to give you?"

"Her dad's rich."

"And bankrupt."

Evan paused, as if surprised I knew that. "His company is. He's probably socked cash away like a squirrel."

"But not to give his stepdaughter to throw into the wind."

"My political career is not wasted money. I work tirelessly for the good people of these United States of—"

"Can it, Evan." Even in this moment, caught with his metaphorical pants down, he was trying to secure a vote. "Did you honestly never think about where those funds came from?"

"I'm telling you, her stepdad."

I doubted it. "He couldn't give her that kind of money without a serious paper trail." Which I would get file-cracking Frannie to dig into. "And does a man who's declaring bankruptcy want to risk moving defunct business funds into family members' accounts?" Totally ignoring Evan, I continued to talk out these plot twists. "Or maybe Mr. Chandler found out how Sasha used the funds, and he was so furious, he killed her. Or his financial officer did. Or your loan shark did, so he could—"

"Do I need to be present for the rest of this conversation?"

Sure, sass from the man *not* facing a murder charge. "What else are you not telling me about Sasha?"

"I wasn't aware I needed to journal our lives for you."

This phone would fit so nicely up that arrogant nose. "You're a politician, so naturally you have enemies. Would anyone go so far as to kill your fiancée to hurt you?"

He spent some time considering this. "I don't think so. I'm still pretty new to the game to have ticked off too many people."

I doubted that.

"What about this Big Sal? Maybe he got tired of your debt."

"Not an option. He knew Sasha was funding most of my payment plan."

"Evan, you know I'm not an option either. I didn't kill Sasha."

He sat down on a bench someone had crafted out of plywood and milk crates. "I mostly believe that."

"Seriously?"

"Fine, I completely believe that," he said. "But you were the last to see her alive. The last to talk to her."

"Except for the killer," I reminded him.

"You were the one who brought in that stupid champagne bottle."

"I certainly never thought it would be used as a weapon." I stepped over a coffee can of cigarette butts and sat down beside him. "Did Sasha act strange in the days leading up the murder?"

"I dunno. Maybe." He swiped at some sweat near his hairline. "She was kind of quiet, now that I think about it. But she was really stressed about wedding planning."

Why? It had all appeared to be done. "What about her enemies?"

"She was a dear, sweet, loving angel—"

"Never mind." Gag. "But if you think of anything, you call me. Got it? No detail too small."

"What about that video? Are you going to erase it?"

"I don't think so." I patted my jacket pocket where I'd slipped my phone. "I kind of like watching you squirm."

CHAPTER TWENTY-TWO

"I CAN DO this." I patted Henry's impressively contoured shoulder. "So you can stop watching me like I'm going to pull a remote out of my pocket and detonate this wedding at any second."

Tuesday evening at six was a weird time to have an outdoor ceremony. I mean, Tuesday? Didn't most brides want a Friday or Saturday? I'd have to research this. And six o'clock in Arkansas . . . well, it was still hot enough to melt your high heels and make demands your deodorant couldn't meet. Yet here we were hours before the event, scurrying around like ants at a church picnic at Shadow Ranch, owned by Mitchell Crawford, for the wedding of one of his employees.

Sweat dotted Henry's forehead. "I don't think you're going to ruin this. I know you'll do fine."

He didn't sound convinced. "Then why don't you give me a job besides unloading the truck?"

"Unloading the truck is very important."

"We could hire teenage kids to do that."

"Paisley, not all parts of this job are glamorous. There's a lot of grunt work. And we used to hire some boys from the high school, but if you want to know the truth, it's not in our budget right now. So if I ask you to unload a box it's because I need you to unload a box."

Heat that had nothing to do with the ninety-degree temps burned my cheeks. "Okay. Sure."

I stormed off toward the Enchanted Events truck, an old moving van that had been repainted white and emblazoned with our logo. It held every possible supply that could be needed for our part of the wedding, from props to lighting to food to stationery. And in this case, custom-printed handheld fans and cases of chilled water bottles. To stave off a heatstroke or cardiac arrest.

"Consider Henry's snippiness a compliment," Alice said as she met me at the truck. "He's rude to all of us from time to time. It's his love language. You learn to ignore it."

"You shouldn't be ignoring it. He should treat his employees as nicely as he treats his clients."

"He gets really wound up right before the wedding. If he gets through tonight without yelling at us, then we'll call the event a success."

I stepped into the back of the truck and grabbed the nearest box. "After last week, it's like he doesn't trust me with anything more than the most basic of tasks. Today he had me stuffing envelopes and refilling the staplers."

"He meant what he said, Paisley." Alice reached for a box marked *votives.* "Right now there are no small jobs here. With all the cancellations we've had, we're lucky he hasn't made any cutbacks. Could he be nicer to me? Yeah. But do I care right now? No. I can't afford to."

A weight heavier than anything in my box settled over my heart. The success of Enchanted Events wasn't just about my life.

Alice and the others were depending on it too. Everyone needed their jobs, their paychecks. They needed Enchanted Events to not only succeed, but flourish. The sooner I cleared my name, the better for my neck *and* the business.

"I'm sorry," I said as we walked together to the rented stage, which a construction team had covered with bleached barn wood. "I know you're probably nervous about the stability of Enchanted Events."

"It's not just where I punch a time clock. I love working here." Alice glanced around, as if seeking out eavesdroppers. "I have ideas, you know? Event planning ideas. But Henry won't hear them, especially now that the company is struggling. So I know this gig is just a hoop you have to jump through to sell and get out, but to me, Enchanted Events is my livelihood, it's what feeds my kids, and it's possibly my ticket to a better life."

I had no idea Alice wanted to be more involved in the business. "When's the last time you talked to Henry about this?"

"Last week." She shrugged. "But it doesn't matter. I don't want to make waves and get tossed overboard."

"He wouldn't fire you."

Alice set her box down on the stage. "He would if he didn't have a choice." She walked back toward the truck, her black flats coughing up tiny plumes of dust.

Many sweltering hours later, I stood beside a headset-wearing Layla and watched the bride and groom say I do. The two were both bodybuilding enthusiasts and had met at the local gym. As the groom dipped his wife and planted a kiss on her lips, the love between them glowed like the sun hovering through the trees. But how did a person know it would last? I'd thought what I had with Evan was the real thing, but what a sham it had been.

I let my eyes wander over the ceremony, surprised to feel a surge of pride over this Enchanted Events accomplishment. Everything had come together so nicely, from the timing of the bride arriving on her favorite horse to the harmonious rendition of "At Last" by a local bluegrass band Layla had found, to the backdrop of flowers where the couple stood and the fairy lights in the trees. The bride wiped away tears throughout the service, and I was happy that her special day, though blazing hot, had gone so beautifully. Henry and his team made dreams happen. And for this small window of time, I got to be a part of it.

As I skimmed the crowd, my eyes widened as I saw a familiar pair in the fifth row, fanning themselves and smiling.

Zoey and her boyfriend, Max.

She wore a strapless dress, while a muscled-up Max donned a skintight blue polo that was surely sticking uncomfortably in this heat. This was my chance to talk to them, as I still had so many questions. I didn't know if they were on Detective Ballantine's suspect list, but they were still on mine.

There was little we could pack up until the photographer finished with the wedding party, so I completed a few odds and ends. Then I made my way to the reception, held beneath an air-conditioned tent and spilling out into the yard, decorated with hay bales for sitting and wildflowers for admiring. Waiters in boots, plaid shirts, and Wranglers wove through the crowd, offering icy drinks and appetizers. At the request of the couple, everything was low-carb. I worried that detail alone would curse their marriage.

"Zoey, Max!" I waved and dodged my way through the crush

of people.

The two stood beneath a shady oak, where Zoey sipped a cucumber-infused water and Max held a beer. Once recognition lit Zoey's features, her smile faded. They did not return my enthusiastic greeting.

"Quite the event, huh?" I grabbed an iced tea from a passing waiter as a country band began to play another love song. "Such a fun wedding."

"Yes, beautiful ceremony." Zoey shifted closer to her boyfriend. "I thought they'd arrested you by now."

I nearly choked on my tea. "Nope. Still here. One of the perks of being innocent, I guess." My goodness, she was frosty tonight. "Are you friends of the bride and groom?"

"They work out at the gym I manage," Max said. "And he's my running buddy."

"What gym is that?"

"Blazing Guns." He fished into his pocket and produced a card. "We're a mile from downtown. Been open six months. We offer personal training if you ever want to try us." He looked at my arms with a disapproving frown. "We could start out light. Like we do for some of our senior citizens."

When a girl passed by with a tray of fruit, I snagged a strawberry and stuck it in my mouth, reminding myself I needed to be nice. A snarky comeback would not get me information.

I swallowed the berry and licked my lips. "So, Zoey, how are you and your family doing?"

She focused on a spot over my head. "We're fine."

"I know these last few weeks have been hard."

"We're getting by, but thank you for asking."

My phone in my pocket buzzed, and I pulled it out to read a text from Henry. Shoot. He needed me at the trailer ASAP.

Well, no time to slowly ease into my questions. "Zoey, can I ask where you were the morning of Sasha's murder?" Her eyes went wide in offense. "I know it's crazy, but I'm just trying to piece together where everyone was."

"I was in a hot yoga class at Surrender, a new studio here in town."

What was it with these people *enjoying* the heat? "Do you have any witnesses to confirm this?"

One eyebrow lifted in disdain. "I don't really know anyone in the class, but I guess I would've signed in when I got there."

How would I check that? The yoga studio wasn't going to hand over their sign-in records.

"And you, Max?" I turned to Mr. Muscles. "Where were you when you got the news?"

"I was at work."

"At Blazing Guns Gym."

"Right."

I swear the man flexed beneath his shirt. "Can anyone vouch for that?"

"Not that it's any of your business, but yeah. The ten people I was teaching in my advanced bodybuilding class. There's one right there."

He pointed to a burly man big enough to lift a refrigerator.

"The guy with the mustache?" I asked. "Wow. He's buff."

"That's Helen," Max said. "My mom."

Oh, my. "And isn't Helen lovely?" Smiling, I retreated a step as my phone continued to buzz. "Sure nice talking to you both.

I've got to get back to work, but thank you for the information and enjoy your evening."

Zoey should definitely give a second thought to ever having children with Max and his Hercules DNA.

My heels spiked into the ground as I walked across the grass toward the Enchanted Events van. Clusters of vertical lights hung from trees like cascading stars, giving the farm setting a magical, romantic glow. My heart pinged for a mere second, the longest I would allow myself to dwell on the fact that I was alone, denied my own wedding. Though Evan ditching me at the altar had really pulled the rug out from beneath me, it had been for the best, and I needed to remember that. Still. It would be nice to have a strong, handsome shoulder to cry on when one faced sad and dramatic days. Like the days that included a murder.

The warm air carried the sounds of the band, their stringed instruments in harmony with their voices. I knew soon a line dance instructor would take the stage, giving everyone in attendance a brief lesson in some easy dances. This wedding was just as fun as Sasha and Evan's formal event would *not* have been. Such a study in contrasts.

I listened to the music a moment and reviewed my suspect list. Evan was no longer a contender, so I could stop fantasizing about him in an orange onesie. I'd make sure Max's alibi checked out, but he, too, seemed to be in the clear. I still needed to verify Phoebe's whereabouts, but could sweet Phoebe really commit murder? She'd gotten so emotional when I'd spoken to her. Almost *too* willing to share information.

Then there was loose-lipped Phoebe's opposite—Raven

Arnett. I got a weird vibe from that girl, but her lack of personality didn't make her guilty. Still, why was she so uncooperative? And if she did kill Sasha, what would be her motive?

Zoey said all the right things, but she had motive. She'd been second fiddle to Sasha for years. That could surely mess with a person's mind. And then there was her father—Mr. Chandler. Maybe he'd gotten tired of his stepdaughter, or maybe he *had* been funneling her money after all. He'd been in an argument with her the night before the murder, a detail I'd yet to explore. It was imperative I find a way to speak to him at the gala.

"Paisley, hello!"

I was saved from my own heavy thoughts as the woman I'd met at the Sugar Creek Library stepped into my path, her smile wide.

"It's so good to see you," Anna Grace said. "This is my husband, Carson Fielding." She nudged the hipster man beside her. "See, honey, I told you I met her!"

"*Professor* Carson Fielding?"

"The one and only," he said with a grin.

The very guy Raven said I should talk to! Finally, something was going my way.

"My wife's a big, big fan." Professor Fielding smelled like expensive cologne and looked like he'd read a fashion blog or two. His dirty-blond hair stopped just short of the collar on a linen jacket that coordinated beautifully with his leather wingtips. "She has all your music. Even has a collector's edition of your debut album on vinyl."

"Wow, not many copies of that around," I said. It was kind of nice for someone to remember the group for what it was and not just the little band that Jaz used to launch her solo career. "Beautiful wedding, wasn't it?"

"It was," Anna Grace said. "Anytime Enchanted Events handles a wedding, you know it's going to be fabulous."

"Thank you." So far, Anna Grace was right. Henry and his crew put on events to rival anything I'd seen back in California.

I turned to her husband. Now that I had this opportunity, I had no idea what to ask. What exactly was his connection to Sasha and why did Raven think he was a person of interest? "You teach at Arkansas A&M, right?"

"Yes. I teach art. Upper-level painting classes mostly. Been there about six years."

"Kind of a random question," I began. "But did you ever have Sasha Chandler in any of your classes?"

The professor's smile flickered. "Ah, I think I might've years ago. I encounter hundreds of students every year, so—"

"But I think you'd remember Sasha, and—"

"Mr. Fielding! Carson Fielding!" A woman in a too-tight pink dress hustled toward us, fan waving and buttons straining.

Anna Grace rolled her eyes at her husband then looked at me. "He has quite the following."

"Hello!" The woman stopped mere inches from Carson, her updo nearly unwound. "Oh, my." One diamond-covered hand fluttered to her bosom. "I just wanted to say how much I adore your current exhibit at the Sugar Creek Gallery."

"Well, thank you." Professor Fielding's easy grin reappeared. "That's a very nice thing to say. And you are?"

"Veda Nelson."

Professor Fielding lifted Veda's right hand and shook it slowly, gently. "Veda. What a lovely name."

The woman had to be old enough to be the man's mother, yet she blushed like a sophomore being asked to prom. "The beach paintings are so real." She flapped her fan, her bangs aflutter. "I can practically smell the ocean."

"Thank you." Fielding's accent was decidedly Midwestern, as no twang dented a single syllable. "May I ask which one is your favorite?"

"*Lonely Woman on the Shore.*" Veda's eyes went distant, as if she were imagining herself there. "She appears to be simply wading, yes? But when you look at the despair on her face, juxtaposed with the ominous cloud above her, you wonder if she'll walk out into those waves and never return."

"I love it when someone gets my work," Fielding said. "You really do understand it."

"Well, what does the woman choose?" Veda rested her hand on his arm. "Does she keep walking into the waves?"

"Whatever you believe. *That* is the answer."

As Veda giggled, I looked at Anna Grace, whose shallow tolerance seemed to have morphed to barely contained annoyance.

I caught Anna Grace's eye and inclined my head toward her husband and his adoring fan. "Does this happen often?"

"He's something of a local celebrity," she said low, not that Veda or Carson were listening. "Especially when he turns on the charm, but I guess it helps him sell his work."

"He's good at it."

"Too good," Anna Grace said before resetting her facial features to their perky default. "Don't mind me." Her laugh was a little too squeaky, a little too loud. "I'm glad he's finally found success in the art world. He's an incredible talent, and we've waited years for everyone to see how brilliant he is. It just comes with some occasional arrogance, and I have to take him down a notch or two by telling the artiste extraordinaire to just unload the darn dishwasher, you know?" She nudged me as if we were best friends and laughed some more.

Bubbly Anna Grace was back, but I still wondered why a senior citizen's attention bothered her to such a degree. Maybe it did happen a lot. Maybe it intruded on their privacy, which I certainly understood. Back in the Electric Femmes' heyday, I couldn't enjoy a quiet dinner in a restaurant without multiple interruptions for photos and autographs. It did get old and annoying, especially to those who were with me and just wanted to eat a burger in peace. Was Professor Fielding really that big of a deal?

"I'm sure you're very proud of your husband," I finally said, still observing his amazing gift of schmooze. He really had some charisma. The romantic kind. Perhaps this was part of his marketing, his brand.

"Yes," Anna Grace said. "We've both taken the slow route to success. I worked and put him through college and grad school. Now that things are going so well with his job at A&M and his showings, it's my turn. Or will be."

"Your turn for what?"

"I took the spring and summer semesters off from school, but I'm going back in the fall. It's my turn to focus on my career."

"That's great," I said, for lack of anything else in my head. I never got the chance to go to college and wondered if it was something I needed to look into when I returned to LA. But I had no idea what I'd major in. I was pretty sure there wasn't a degree plan called Aging Rock Star with Zero Direction.

"Goodbye, dear," Professor Fielding said to Veda Nelson. "Such an absolute joy to talk to you."

"And you as well." Veda looked at the professor like her long, lost love. "I'll be back in the gallery to purchase the next in the series as soon as I can talk my cranky old husband into it."

"I'll rest easier knowing my beloved work will be in your worthy home."

A starry-eyed Veda reluctantly walked away, and I half expected her to turn back and blow a kiss.

"Wow, you have quite the way with the art-loving ladies," I said.

Professor Fielding's mouth paused for a brief second before curving upward. "It's all in good fun."

Anna Grace nodded and threw her arm around her husband's waist. "Whatever sells the goods, right?"

"So, Professor Fielding, you were telling me about Sasha Chandler."

"Ah, yes." He swiped a drink from a passing waiter. "A good student, if I recall correctly. Nothing about her really stands out."

"She was a business major. Why was she in one of your upper-level art classes?"

"Everyone needs electives."

"So no complaints about her?"

"Can't think of any." He took a drink.

"Her death was really tragic," Anna Grace said. "I hope they find her true killer."

"If you think of anything else about Sasha, please let me know."

"I'll do that." Professor Fielding waved to another attendee near us. "I see a friend from work I need to say hello to. Welcome back to Sugar Creek, Miss Sutton. I hope you find all the answers you're looking for."

The couple departed hand in hand, leaving me standing there knowing no more than I had that morning.

The clues were coming slowly, and time was running out.

I needed a break, a piece of information that would open the door to my freedom.

Before it was too late.

CHAPTER TWENTY-THREE

THE REST OF the week passed by in a flutter of activity. Not enough activity to erase the lines of worry that constantly marred Henry's forehead, but enough to keep Enchanted Events in operation. For now.

On Friday night, I left the shop later than I intended, leaving little time to get ready for the Mitchell Crawford gala. Heels in hand, I flew through my front door, took the stairs two at a time, and jumped in the shower. I hated being late and hated being rushed even more. Leaping from the shower, I wrapped my body in a towel, the bathroom turning into a sauna. The mirror fogged over and sweat dampened my underarms. Oh, this would not do.

Desperate for air, I flung open the bathroom door.

And squealed at the man standing there. "Beau!" I clutched my sagging towel with one hand and held the other before my face, ready to defend. "Oh, it's just you." My spine shimmied in relief. "You scared me to death."

Wait a minute.

"What are you doing here?" My heart had yet to resume its normal beating pattern.

Beau's eyes dropped to the top of my towel and back to my face, but not before making a quick detour to my bare legs. "It's, um . . ." Was he struggling for words? "It's time to go."

I glanced down at my chest and realized my yellow towel barely covered up the goods. I yanked it up, anchoring it with both hands. "It can't be. Not yet."

"Yep." His eyes were trained on mine, and his mouth eased into that roguish smile. "Nice legs."

"Thanks. Do you always conduct a little breaking and entering before your dates?"

One dark brow lifted. "Is this a date?"

"An outing. Before an outing."

He stepped closer, and my only thought was that Professor Fielding's deliberate brand of charm couldn't hold a candle to this. Beau didn't have to say pretty words, didn't have to even touch. His magnetism was an invisible force field that held him up like gravity. It was effortless and automatic, something that came to him as naturally as breathing. He wore a dark suit and crisp white shirt, looking like an NFL god whom men wanted to be and women wanted to devour.

"I knocked on your door for a good ten minutes." Beau's voice seemed deeper, softer. "When you didn't answer the door or your phone, I got worried."

"You were worried about me?"

"I hear they're serving prime rib at this gala." He shrugged a shoulder. "I didn't want to miss it."

Was it my imagination, or was Beau standing even closer? "So not worried for my safety?"

He planted a hand on the doorframe over my head, his head angled toward mine. "Just concerned about my ticket. Didn't want it to go to waste."

"Very economical of you." His dimples were disarming. "Did you break my door down, Captain Hudson?"

"Nope." He dangled something silver in his fingers.

"You still have a key?"

"Sylvie thought it would be a good idea."

I cinched my towel in again, and his eyes followed. "Why don't I have your key?"

"Because I don't listen to *all* of Sylvie's ideas."

I'd be talking to my grandmother about this. "Well, as you can see, I'm running behind and am a little underdressed."

"Tardiness looks good on you." His grin was the stuff of Sylvie's romance novels.

"Are you flirting with me, Beau?"

He reached out and traced a curl spiraling near my cheek. "I've been up for thirty-six hours straight dealing with a water leak at Fox Falls. I'm sure it's just the fatigue talking."

He often had shadows beneath his eyes, but now I could see the hint of puffiness and his bloodshot gaze. "Do you want to cancel? I'd understand. Please, go home. Go to bed."

"Not happening," Beau said. "I committed to this, and we're going to your fancy wingding."

"Are you sure?"

"Yes."

"I do so love a good wingding."

And I loved to make him smile.

"Hey," I said, "did I tell you I talked to Zoey and her boy-friend at a wedding earlier this week? Zoey said that—"

"Paisley?"

A drop of water fell from my hair to my bare shoulder.

"Yes?"

"Can we talk about this when you're not naked?"

I blinked. "That seems reasonable."

Beau took one last perusal before retreating. "Meet me downstairs in twenty?"

"I'll bring underwear."

It took me a half hour, but I threw myself together as quickly as I could. With smoky eye makeup and glossy red lips, I slipped into a sparkly full-length gown I'd once worn to Jaz's Grammy party a few years ago. It traveled with me everywhere because one never knew when one needed to celebrate. And because it was the next thing I was going to hock when the money ran out. With no time to straighten my curls, I piled them on top of my head and let the ringlets and waves fall in a messy cascade. A final spritz of perfume, a necklace dripping with stones that wanted to be diamonds, and I slipped into my electric blue heels to glide down the creaking stairs.

Where Beau stood waiting. Like a dark angel come to sweep me away to his mysterious underworld.

"You look . . ." He viewed me the way I imagined Fielding's fans looked at his paintings. "Stunning."

His words were a balm to my thirsty soul. "Thank you. You're quite handsome yourself." And he smelled divine.

"I like the hair." He reached up and plucked a curl again, letting his finger run the length of it before it sprang back to its curvy shape. "You should wear it like this more often."

"And you should wear a suit more often. Might bring more ladies out to Fox Falls."

"Always looking for ways to expand business."

Beau held the door open, and with his hand pressed to my back, we walked to the porch like the couple that we weren't. Like he wasn't sort of dating someone else. Like I wasn't on the verge of being arrested for murder.

As my heels beat a staccato pattern on the wooden planks of the porch, a familiar dark sedan drove by, the windows down.

Beau and I both watched as Detective Ballantine crawled by, his elbow sticking out the window before he threw up a slow wave. I couldn't see his eyes behind his Aviator glasses, but I knew they matched the smirk on his mouth.

"Come on, Sutton." Beau's hand softly rubbed the skin of my bare back as Ballantine cruised past. "Don't think about the investigation tonight."

His fingers sent heated frissons of electricity that almost made me forget about the case.

Almost.

But I had to stay focused and not get distracted.

My life depended on it.

THE SUGAR CREEK Civic Center was a brick and native stone structure designed to blend into the wooded surroundings. It held about three hundred people and had provided a prime celebration location for former presidents, Arkansas celebrities who had made it big, as well as locals who wanted a beautiful location to hold a wedding or reception. Tonight's gala was all about celebrating Mitchell Crawford, a Sugar Creek citizen who'd made his wealth from his cattle ranch and shared his prosperity with numerous recipients such as the library, schools, and local charities. According to Emma, this event commemorated his seventieth birthday, but it also saluted his thirty years of philanthropy.

Beau wheeled his cherry red pickup truck flawlessly into a parking spot, as if it was no bulkier than a Prius. I had no idea how he drove his gigantic beast of a vehicle, let alone parked it between two narrow yellow lines. I could barely park my small car without a few re-dos. What I did know was that I had spent the last five minutes inhaling the scent of him and stealing furtive glances as he drove. The boy sure cleaned up nice.

It was strange to have this impression of high school Beau in my head, a picture I kept comparing to Adult Beau. But Adult Beau was definitely all grown-up, with a strong chin that lifted when he was deep in thought, chiseled cheek bones that beckoned a hand to trace, and those dimples that appeared all too infrequently. His eyes still held mischief, just as they had when we were sparring children, but now they reflected his protective nature, his loyalty, and unspoken stories he unwittingly carried like the shrapnel in his leg. On the drive, I kept finding myself asking Beau questions just to hear his voice. It was a voice that could narrate books—and a girl's fantasies.

Beau shut off the engine, and I realized I was still staring at the man. "Um . . ." I flipped down his visor mirror and pretended to check my makeup. "Thanks again for coming with me tonight."

His eyes found mine in the dimming lights of the cab. "My apology is complete after this."

"Your jerkiness is totally forgiven at the stroke of midnight."

"I'm not staying that long, superstar."

I snapped the mirror shut. "We stay as long as it takes to talk to Mr. Chandler."

"You can, but I'm out of here by ten."

"So you can take your next dose of hemorrhoid meds?"

Beau rolled those beautiful blue eyes. "So I can go to sleep."

He yawned into his hand, and I immediately felt contrite. Poor guy really was exhausted. We needed to go in and conquer while he was still upright and conscious.

Jazz music swelled around us as Beau held open the door and we stepped inside. The place was already packed with the who's who of Sugar Creek and the surrounding cities.

"Paisley! Beau!" Emma, wearing a stunning red gown that showed off her hourglass waist, held out her arms for a hug.

My cousin and I met in a loose embrace, as it went without saying that neither one of us wanted to muss hair or dress. And my dress was a little tight. One wrong move, and my weak seams would call it quits. I'd given up my entertainment biz way of eating since landing in Arkansas, and my clothes were starting to protest.

"Hello, Noah," I said to her handsome fiancé. "Quite the swanky affair for Sugar Creek."

"We know how to throw a party." He looked at his friend Beau. "Didn't expect to see you here."

"TV was all reruns tonight," Beau said dryly.

"Noah, are you counting the days 'til your wedding?" I asked.

"Can't wait to make this woman my wife." He smiled at his fiancée.

Emma grinned. "Since he's my boss, it'll finally put an end to all that workplace harassment."

"But Emma tells me some of your vendors have quit at the last minute, Paisley," Noah said. "Everything's still on track for our big day, right?"

"Of course." I tried to radiate confidence and assurance. "Your wedding's going to be perfect." I hoped.

As the two guys began to talk kayaks and catfish, Emma leaned toward my ear. "Quite hot date you have there."

"We're just friends." And barely that. "He's doing me a favor."

"Uh-huh. Oh, I bet he is."

"Geez, Emma."

"Hey, Sylvie has thrown all her international crime-fighting energy into matchmaking. And if you think it's just coincidence you're living with a mere wall separating you and GI Gorgeous, you are woefully naïve." She inclined her head toward Noah. "How do you think we got together?"

"You shared front row tickets to a Cher concert?"

"Sylvie strategically placed me in a rental house right by Noah."

"She can scheme all she wants. Beau and I are not going to be a couple."

"He hasn't taken his eyes off you."

"He's barely even awake." But when I glanced back Beau's way, those romance hero eyes were watching me. He gave a slow, lazy smile, and set the butterflies in my stomach to flapping. I had to snap out of it. "Have you seen Sasha's father yet?"

"Yes." Emma scanned the crowd. "He got here about a half

hour ago. The bad news is his wife is stuck to his side like Velcro. The good news is the guy is already pretty tipsy."

Maybe that was good. Alcohol could loosen lips.

"Just be careful tonight," Emma said.

"Always."

"So my wedding is still all set, right?"

"It'll be magical," I promised.

She inhaled with relief and nodded. "Okay, Mr. Mayor," she said, rejoining Noah. "Take me to the dance floor."

"Anything for one of my voters." Noah pressed a kiss to her cheek, then led her away.

This left Beau and me standing there under a canopy of balloons and awkwardness. Suddenly I was that twelve-year-old girl at the Sugar Creek Junior High School spring dance, two-stepping with Justin Dashner but wishing that football player Beau Hudson would cut in. But I hadn't been his type. And I still wasn't.

"Well," I said. "What do you want to do?"

"Cruise by the buffet, grab some hot wings, then take a nap in my truck."

"If you're the one in charge of your dating activities with Haley, I can see why you're having problems."

He scrubbed a hand over his face. "Let's get this dancing requirement over with so I can go home and crash."

"If you snore on my shoulder, I get to be mad at you again."

"Deal." His calloused hand reached for mine, a thumb sliding over my palm.

Probably just an accident.

I followed him through the large room of minglers, past

tables of people noshing on appetizers, and finally to the ballroom. With my newly trained event-planning eye, I took in the lighting, the music, the flowers, and the general vibe of the partygoers. I think even Henry would've approved. But he also would've found ten ways to make it better. A few ideas came to my mind, and I smiled at what I'd turned into. This event planning was getting in my blood. Maybe I could somehow use those skills back in Los Angeles.

A fedora-wearing DJ set up in a corner was spinning hits beneath flashing lights. A familiar slow song poured out of the speakers, a tune about a lost love waiting in California. The floor emptied of everyone except couples who immediately entwined and moved to the music.

"Slow dance number one," Beau said, guiding us to an empty spot.

He pulled me in close, with one hand pressed to the low curve of my back and the other bringing my fingers to rest on his heart. He seemed to have this slow dancing thing down, and I wondered where he'd gotten all the practice. My hand on his chest felt the steady rhythm of his heartbeat, but also the firm muscle beneath his shirt.

"So, I guess you go to a gym." My conversation skills were a thing of brilliance tonight.

"Yeah, I suppose," Beau said. "It's called the outdoors."

Well, it was certainly working for him.

"Noah said Detective Ballantine stopped by his office today."

Beau's words were a bucket of ice over my head. "Is it too much to hope for that they talked town infrastructure and zoning ordinances?"

"Said Ballantine really quizzed him about you."

"I barely know Noah." What I knew of him was through Emma.

"Yesterday Ballantine spoke to Patrice Bradshaw at Sugar Creek Winery."

I managed a fake smile for a passing couple. "I don't even know who that is."

"Apparently she's the one who sold you a few cases of champagne."

I'd give anything to get a refund on *that* moment. "The good detective's going to have to expand his suspect list to someone besides me if he's going to solve the murder." This topic was as appetizing as soured milk. "But I don't see signs of that happening. It's like he's already made up his mind. I'm starting to lose hope."

"You have plenty of things to be hopeful about. For one, you have Sylvie and Frannie on your side. On the miniscule chance you go to prison, they'd find a way to overtake the whole place and get you out."

"After you got shot—did you ever want to just give up?"

His arm stiffened around me, but he answered. "Lots of days."

My eyes held Beau's. "How long was your recovery?"

"Physical therapy was six months."

"And you're still working on the emotional aspect?"

His left foot stumbled slightly, and he looked away. "This topic bores me. Did I tell you about the new biking trails at Fox Falls?"

"Do you ever talk to your old Army buddies?"

"No." He sounded completely bored now.

I angled my head to watch him. "Don't they ever call you?"

Those tired eyes hardened. "Sometimes."

"You don't pick up the phone?"

"I'm very busy."

I was close enough to inspect that stubbled, and oh-so-stubborn jaw. "Maybe if you talked to some of your team, you'd feel better. About things."

"I don't need to feel better about anything, Paisley. Next topic."

"Beau, what you went through had to have been devastating on so many levels and—"

"Look, pop princess." Beau brought us to a halt so quickly my heels landed on his shoes. "I promised you my attendance and a few spins around the dance floor. I did not promise conversation that mined the emotional depths. Pick another topic or I'm done."

Pain shimmered like faint snowflakes around him, an almost physical thing I could reach out and touch. "Okay, fine. Cranky." I removed all sympathy from my voice. "What do you want to talk about?"

"Sports."

"How about you talk about it, and I just nod my head like I'm listening?"

His chest beneath my hand rumbled with a laugh as he set us back into motion. "Okay, then you pick the topic. But *not* about me."

"You come with a lot of rules."

"It's part of my allure."

I ignored that sarcasm, my brain still idling on Beau and his battle scars. Swimming for safer shores, I decided to pick a harmless topic, regaling him with details from the very lively steampunk wedding we'd put on that week, a colorful, creative joining of two lit English lit professors. He laughed as I told him about their unusual music choices and the three-year-old golden retriever who wore a monocle and cape as he trotted down the aisle with the rings.

"You sound like you're enjoying the wedding business." Beau's voice tickled my ear.

"It has its moments."

The song ended, and a country ballad took its place. Beau kept us moving, not missing a beat. He might've been all muscle and steel, but even with a slight limp, he moved with a natural grace that defied logic. Held so close, I gave in and rested my head on his chest, feeling both safe and unguarded. I couldn't fall for this man. I needed to keep my eye on my goals. Saving my own neck was priority one. And if I wasn't careful, walking away from Beau could wreck what was left of my heart.

"You're awfully quiet." His voice was rumpled-sheets sexy. "What are you thinking about?"

You. Me. Making a big, hot mistake. "I was wondering why Detective Ballantine cruised by the house earlier."

"Let it go for tonight, Sutton."

Now that I had brought it up, I couldn't. "Was it to intimidate me?"

"Probably."

His agreement came way too easily. "Or because he has new incriminating evidence and wants to arrest me?"

"If he wanted to arrest you, he would."

"But what if he's baiting me? Enjoying this?"

"Maybe he is."

"And what if I go to jail?"

"We won't let that happen."

We. "And what if—"

"Paisley, would you just be quiet?" And with that, Beau lowered his lips to mine, stopping one more word from falling out, and I forgot the rest of my queries.

CHAPTER TWENTY-FOUR

BEAU'S KISS LIT my system with electricity, and every thought leapt from my brain. Every thought but *this man. Oh, this man.* Good heavens, he could kiss. It was fiery, yet tender. Slow, yet pulse frenzying.

His lips slid across mine as though they'd been waiting, wondering, and were going to take their sweet time to explore. My heart dissolved into vapor, and I leaned into the kiss with every bit of neediness, loneliness, and heat I had. It was pleasure to feel his mouth on mine, but even more pleasure to be taken away from dark thoughts that had been swirling in my mind.

My fingertips slipped into the softness of his hair as he changed the angle of the kiss. He held my face in his hands, and his thumbs brushed my cheeks. It was nearly too much, an undertow that wouldn't let me go.

Until Beau's lips stilled.

He lifted his head, his gaze fused to mine.

Breathe, Paisley. I was barely capable of words. "What was that?"

"Distraction technique."

It was hard to play it cool when you were about to have a stroke in his arms. "Something you learned in the military?"

His focus slipped to my lips. "We soldiers do whatever we

need to do."

Slowly, I released my breath. "I thank you for your service."

Beau's hand holding mine, he spun me out, then reeled me back in. "You need to chill out, Sutton."

"And you think that helped?"

"You were two what-ifs from hysterical."

My head filled with glitter and clouds as I mentally replayed that kiss, and I barely heard the DJ announce the next song. I floated on the moment, letting myself enjoy being in a handsome man's arms. A handsome man who had just kissed me.

But then the next song began, and it opened with a too familiar melody.

Because Jaz and I had helped write it.

"Isn't this one of the Electric Femmes' songs?" Beau asked.

I untangled from his arms, but his hand captured mine, holding me to my spot. "Yeah, it went to number one seven years ago." And was now considered retro. Vintage.

"Why don't you sing a little?"

"No, that's okay."

"I never hear you sing."

"It's not like we hang out a lot. Besides, I'd hate to burden you with my brilliance."

"Those walls are paper-thin. I'd hear you if you so much as hummed. Growing up, you'd sing nonstop. In the halls, in class, in church."

I resented the way he could chitchat as though he hadn't just kissed me boneless. "Uh-huh."

His eyes narrowed slightly, as if all the details of my life and career were one big algebraic equation and he was close to filling in all the variables. "You are still going to pursue your music career, right?"

"Yes, of course. Inheriting Enchanted Events hasn't changed that."

The song built to a crescendo, running toward the bridge. And crashing right into my soul. Those days seemed so long ago and far away. It was a distance paved with mistakes, regrets, and a holy and all-too-brief moment in which I held success in my hands for the first time. I knew what I wanted then. Knew who I was. I'd had it all.

And I wanted it back. I wanted the old me back so badly.

Tears pressed at my eyes, and I took a shuddering breath to hold them at bay. I was seconds away from the dam breaking, and I was not going to spastically fall apart in front of Beau.

"I'm going to—" Just as I was about to excuse myself for an escape, a man in a charcoal suit walked past us, making a determined beeline for the bar. "There's Sasha's father." I blinked away a stray tear and forced a smile. "I'll see you in a bit."

"Paisley, wait."

I threw up my hand in a dismissive wave, sidestepping Beau's reach and weaving between groups of happy, dancing people.

Steven Chandler paused only a moment to speak to an elderly couple before continuing on his path. I watched him enter the bar and take a seat on a stool. Not wanting to appear obvious, I waited a good minute before my too-tight dress and I eased onto the seat beside him. I risked a glance at Chandler. His chin in his hand, he looked depressed and slightly foxed.

I blotted the moisture beneath my eyes with a cocktail napkin before turning to him. "How's the wine tonight?"

"Watery." He lifted his head, recognition dawning on his face. "Oh, it's you." He identified me with the same enthusiasm Sylvie had for colonoscopies. Lifting his near-empty glass, he took another drink as if resigned to my intrusive company. "But that's how they get you at these events. Not only do you pay through the nose to get in, but then you fork over wads of cash at the bar to wash away the taste of their complimentary dollar-store wine."

"What a racket."

"You're telling me. If this weren't for the fact that this is a party for my buddy Mitchell and the money's going to his charities, I wouldn't even be here."

"Everyone would understand your not feeling especially social right now. I'm sure this has been a terrible time for you and your family."

"You don't know the half of it."

No, but I wanted to. "I'm a good listener if you'd like to talk."

He swayed my way and wagged a finger. "I know what you're doing. You've been talking to people. You want me to start rambling on in hopes I'll say something revealing, something you can use. That's what you're doing."

"Is it working?"

He laughed and shook his head. "Well, you don't look like a killer to me, if it's any consolation."

"I'll take that." Maybe a jury would think so too.

"I can tell you have questions. I know you've already talked to my Zoey. So just ask your questions so you can get back to the festivities."

I certainly appreciated this man's bluntness. "I know you and Sasha got into a big argument the night before her death."

Surprise struck his features. "Yeah. So? We argued all the time."

"Can I ask what it was about?"

"Why do you want to know?"

"Because I have zero faith in the authorities on this investigation, and I'm trying to piece together the days leading up to Sasha's death. I've talked to enough people to know you were an incredible stepfather to her." I was pouring it on thick as cake batter, but hoping the alcohol would dull Mr. Chandler's common sense enough to talk uninhibited. "I'm sure you want to see justice for your family."

"And what if you're the killer?" he asked.

"Would I be getting in everyone's business and drawing attention to myself if I were?"

"Probably not." He frowned into his drink. "But I've already discussed all I know with the police."

"Then you won't mind rehashing it with me, right? How about I promise to give you a discount on any future weddings."

"I'm never getting married again."

"I meant Zoey."

"Oh. Right." Chandler took a handful of peanuts from a bowl.

"I'll buy you a drink in exchange for a little information."

He paused for consideration. "I'm going to need that drink to be extra-large," Mr. Chandler said. "And none of this wine stuff. Gimme a Jack and Coke, light on the ice, heavy on the

Jack."

"Coming right up." I signaled an oily-skinned bartender who didn't look old enough to drink and ordered a super-grande Jack and Coke, plus a Dr Pepper for me. I didn't want my wits muddled by any more liquor. Just sugary carbs. "So, this argument . . ." I turned my attention back to Mr. Chandler.

He rested an elbow on the bar and popped a peanut in his mouth. "Sasha wanted more money for her wedding. She'd asked for a bump in wedding funds half a dozen times. This was just another attempt, and I told her I was done hearing these requests. I might've said it a little louder than I should have."

"So you told her no more money?"

"I'd cut her off months ago. She knew seventy-five grand was my max. I mean, if you can't get married on that, then there's a problem. And I pride myself on not living large, you know? We Chandlers are not showy, ostentatious people. But Sasha wanted it to be like some sort of Kardashian event."

I did a quick mental review of Sasha's wedding file. Her flowers, music, and catering alone were well over that budget. Who had provided the rest? The event had already been paid in full. Had Evan and his family kicked in some money? I'd have to go back and look at the paper trail, see if Sasha paid with someone's credit card, perhaps. And it still didn't answer the question of where Sasha got the funds for Evan's campaign.

"So that's all the argument was about?"

"Uh-huh."

"You said no to more cash, and she got upset?"

"Right."

I didn't have much of an instinct for crime-solving, but after years in the music biz, my BS-meter was a marvel of accuracy. And it was going off like a tornado siren. "Nothing else was discussed that night?"

"Nope."

Interesting how Mr. Chandler could no longer look me in the eye. "Can I ask where you were at the time of the murder?"

"In a meeting with my management team. Reviewing their severance packages. Some of those people have been with me thirty years when we operated our construction company out of a single-wide trailer on a quarter-acre lot east of town." He downed half his glass.

"I'm sorry about your business." Apparently Mr. Chandler's bankruptcy wasn't the gentler kind.

"It wasn't just a business. It was people's livelihoods. And my dream. The only thing more important to me than Chandler Construction is being a father, and I've even failed in that job too."

"Sir, there's nothing you could have done to save Sasha."

His forehead bunched in a frown as he gestured to the bartender for another drink. "I don't mean Sasha. I'm talking about Zoey." He swirled the remaining liquid in his glass.

I aimed and took a shot in the dark. "Did you and Sasha argue about Zoey the night before she died?"

Mr. Chandler said nothing for a full minute, but continued to sip his Jack and Coke. "I might've brought up Zoey."

He turned unfocused eyes back to mine and dropped his voice to a near-whisper. "She thinks I don't know about the accident, but I do."

"Who?"

"Zoey."

Zoey? "What accident?"

His head bobbed in a woozy nod. "Her car wreck."

"Her DUI from last December?" That was a matter of public record. Of course he would have known about it.

He contemplated his drink an agonizing length of time, then ran his finger over the grain of the walnut bar top. "So many times Zoey took the fall for Sasha," he mumbled. "So many times, and I just turned a blind eye to it. It wasn't worth the wrath of my wife. When the wife's unhappy about her baby Sasha, she makes my life miserable. I just wanted a peaceful home, you know? I wanted everyone to get along, and I guess I thought if I ignored it long enough, the girls would work things out between them." He stopped his inspection of the bar. "But they never did. And that time Sasha went too far. She never thought of anyone but herself."

"Are you saying Zoey wasn't the one behind the wheel that night?"

He shook his dark head. "I should've known sooner, the way Sasha was so sweet to Zoey after that. That wasn't her personality at all. I should've known something was up, and it hadn't just been a change of heart from seeing her life flash before her eyes."

"Did Zoey tell you this?"

"No." He gave a mirthless laugh. "She'd stopped trusting me with her Sasha stories years ago because I'd never do anything about it. She pushed you out of the tree? Aw, just shake it off. She stole your homework? Well, maybe you should keep your backpack in a safer location. She took your date for junior prom? The boys have gotta be lined up for miles to step into his place, babe." Mr. Chandler wrapped his hands around a napkin and crumbled it into a ball. "I did nothing. And look where it got us."

I tried to nudge the super tipsy Mr. Chandler back to my question. "So how did you discover who was really behind the wheel?"

"An anonymous call at the office."

"Male or female?"

"Female. About a week after the accident."

"Young voice? Old? An accent?"

"I don't know. Youngish. Maybe twenties or thirties. No accent that I can remember."

"Why would you believe a person who wouldn't even identify herself?"

"Why wouldn't I? It aligned perfectly with Sasha's character."

"How would this lady know what really happened?"

"I don't know. I didn't really care about that part."

"Did you confront your daughters?"

"Every day I woke up, I'd say, 'This is the day I talk to Sasha.' But I didn't. I couldn't. My business was nose-diving, my wife was remodeling the house for the third time and sneaking out with the pool guy, and . . . I just didn't do it."

"Until the night of your argument with Sasha."

"I finally brought it up. You know what she did? She just blew it off. As if my kid getting arrested for her was no big deal."

"I'm sure that made you furious."

"I told you, Detective Pop Star, I wasn't anywhere near your shop the day of Sasha's murder. I've got about twenty employees to back that up."

Fine. I'd cross Mr. Chandler off my dwindling suspect list. "What incentive would Zoey possibly have for taking Sasha's place behind the wheel?"

He only shrugged. "Zoey's spent a lifetime being the good daughter, trying to win Sasha's affection." He thanked the bartender for his drink. "I guess she doesn't have to worry about that anymore."

"Mr. Chandler, can you think of anyone who'd want to kill Sasha?"

He swiveled his head and trained those heavy-lidded eyes on me. "Not Zoey, if that's what you're thinking."

"I wasn't. I—"

"She didn't do it. She couldn't hurt a fly. My Zoey had been pushed to the limits, but that's my fault. Not hers. She wouldn't kill anyone. She wouldn't. Not even her brat of a sister." He wiped away a tear and sniffed. "Crap." Something behind me snagged his attention. "My wife just spotted me. That harpy can't leave me alone for a second."

"One last thing." I slipped off the barstool. "Evan said Sasha had given him tens of thousands of dollars toward his campaign. Did you provide that money?"

That sobered him. "What are you talking about? Are you sure?"

"Positive."

Mr. Chandler looked genuinely confused. "The only thing I gave Sasha money for was her wedding. Where on earth would she get that much cash?"

"I don't know." I laid down some bills for the man's drinks.

"But I'm trying my best to find out."

I found Beau seated at a table talking to Emma and Noah. Or rather watching them talk as he tried to stay awake. As if he knew I was near, he turned his head, searched the room, and locked his eyes with mine. I wondered what thoughts lit up his eyes, what made his lips curve in a gentle smile. Was he thinking about our kiss? That *distraction*?

By the time I got to the group, Beau stood. "How'd it go?" he asked.

"Not bad. I might possess some of Sylvie's gifts of interrogation."

Emma snuck a shrimp from Noah's plate. "Just make sure you don't also have her gift of hiding lethal weapons in your bra."

Beau pulled out a chair. "Sit. Tell us about Chandler."

"No, I think it's time we called it a night." I patted his chest. "Mr. Outdoorsy is dead on his feet."

"I still owe you a dance, per our agreement."

I knew he'd drag himself back on that dance floor if I asked, but he'd put in his time. "I'll take a rain check."

We bid Emma and Noah goodnight, then stepped outside into the evening air. The Arkansas humidity slipped around us like wool coats, but the moon more than made up for the rudeness. It glowed bright and full, hanging in the star-dotted sky like a disco ball just for the two of us.

The ride home was short, but it provided just enough time to fill Beau in on my conversation with Mr. Chandler. Three country songs on the radio, and we were parked in the driveway.

"So where did Sasha get the money to fund Evan's campaign?" Beau jumped out of the truck and opened my door, reaching out a hand to help me climb down.

"I don't know. It doesn't make sense." I followed him to our front porch. "Maybe she gambled? Maybe she had her own loan shark."

Taking the key from my fingers, Beau opened my front door but didn't walk inside. He stood there beneath the glow of the porch light, blocking my doorway, a heartbeat of space between us. He watched me for a moment, a slight frown marring his features. I wondered if he was contemplating another kiss.

Until he spoke. "You kind of freaked out when your old song came on."

This was a conversational land mine. "It just brings back memories of wild groupies and all the broken hearts I left behind."

He flicked a faux diamond hanging from my neck, his fingers skittering across my skin. "You want to talk about your music career?"

"No."

"What if you didn't go back to it?"

"Music is all I have. It's all I know."

"You know weddings."

"Barely. And I didn't give up ten years of my life to come back home and watch people get married."

Beau's hand slid around mine, then gently opened my fingers. He pressed the house key in my palm. "Whatever your future holds, Paisley, you're going to be okay."

"You're a good man, Beau Hudson." Standing on tiptoe, I kissed his fuzzy cheek. "I do hope you're right."

CHAPTER TWENTY-FIVE

"**D**ON'T YOU AGREE, Paisley?"

"Paisley? Helloooo?" Sylvie waved a hand in front of my face as I drove down Main Street.

"Hey! Trying to drive here." I flicked my turn signal, a driving nuance many people in Sugar Creek didn't seem to observe.

"Emma's been talking to you for a good two miles," Sylvie said.

Now I took my eyes off the road on this sunny Monday morning and glanced at my passengers. Sylvie sat in the passenger seat while Emma perched in the back, her ivory wedding dress hanging up, the bag spilling into her lap like precious cargo.

"Don't mind Paisley." Sylvie tsk-tsked. "She's had her head in the clouds ever since that gala, mooning over that Hudson boy."

"I am not!"

"You are." Emma frowned. "You haven't heard a word I've been saying, have you?"

"Sure. Of course I have." What had they just been saying? "You've been talking about your in-laws, then we moved on to the topic of the best way to tie your ceremony program."

"That was a good ten minutes ago," Emma said.

Sylvie checked her pink lipstick in the visor mirror. "Yeah, we've since moved on to more important stuff, like nightie choices for the honeymoon."

"Paisley, you seem off today," Emma said. "Is something wrong?"

Is something wrong? Was that a rhetorical question?

"I'm fine. I'm sorry. I just have a lot on my mind, that's all." It was certainly true. But with my treasure chest full of problems, Sylvie was right. The thing that occupied most of my brain space was Beau. My lips and I couldn't forget that kiss. He had kissed me like he meant it, yet dismissed it as nothing. Had it truly been nothing? And did I even want it to be something? All I knew was that I'd enjoyed it a little too much and relived it at least a hundred times. "I'm still thinking about my conversation with Steven Chandler, I guess." Which was at least partially true.

"Taking the fall for her sister's DUI is definitely noteworthy, and may I say—good interrogation work on your part, shug. We definitely need to talk to Zoey again," Sylvie said. "If I had access to, say, a truth serum, would you want that? It does involve a needle and has the side effect of the drizzles for days, but what's a little gastrointestinal distress when it gets us our information?"

My fingers tightened on the steering wheel. "I'll deal with Zoey."

"Are you excited for your bachelorette party, Emma?" Sylvie asked.

Enchanted Events was throwing her pre-wedding celebration this Friday, and I was quite nervous about the details. "I think I've got a fun evening lined up," I said. "At least I hope it will be."

"Well, of course it will!" Sylvie slapped her knee. "You are a natural at this event planning stuff. Now, tell me what we're going to do. A hot dude will leap from a cake in his skivvies, of course."

"No!" Emma and I shouted in two-part harmony.

"I trust you completely," Emma said. "I know it's going to be a blast, and I'm so glad you two will be there with me."

While I was grateful to be celebrating with family, I wasn't so certain the party would be up to Enchanted Events standards. Henry was either generous or insane to let me take lead, and except for some pointers, he'd left all the planning completely up to me. It was both thrilling and stomach-churning.

"Turn left here for the church." Emma pointed from the backseat, her garment bag crinkling as she leaned forward and pointed.

We had spent the morning with her at Sugar Creek Formals, helping her with her final fitting. When she'd stepped out of the dressing room in that gown, Sylvie and I had gasped right on cue. Emma was one of the most beautiful brides I'd ever seen, and I experienced a twinge of regret that we hadn't been in each other's lives in the last decade. We'd been such good friends growing up, but the music business had taken me away and life had moved us in different directions. I certainly hadn't done my fair share of maintaining contact, but now that I was in Sugar Creek, I'd been totally blessed to reconnect with my cousin. Not seeing her would definitely be high on the list of things I would miss about this town when I left, a list that was growing by the day.

The Sugar Creek Chapel was a glass structure that sat at the top of the hill overlooking the greenest valley in our corner of Arkansas. With its ability to be both sophisticated and comfortable, it was a popular spot for weddings and attracted brides from all over the state.

"Can we get back to the topic of Beau Hudson?" Emma's voice carried over the radio I had just turned up. "Maybe if you're so distracted with thoughts of him, you should do something about it. Like, I don't know—date him?"

"No!" I said a little too urgently. "No need for that."

"Paisley, there's nothing wrong with a little flingy-ding while you're here in Sugar Creek," said Sylvie. "You two spark like bomb oxidizer to fuel. You would be a fool not to follow up on that."

"There will be no flinging *or* dinging."

"Frannie and I endured bullets, torture, and way too many costume changes to protect this great nation, to protect all your freedoms—life, liberty, and the pursuit of hot dudes."

I parked my Camry in an open spot near the door of the chapel. "Just drop it, you two. Leave it alone."

Sylvie nudged me with her pointy elbow. "I hear Beau planted a big smooch right on your lips at the gala."

"How do you know that?"

"This is Sugar Creek, sugar," Sylvie said. "You can't blow your nose or launch a spy satellite on your cheating ex-boyfriend at the Dixie Dairy without everyone knowing about it."

"It *was* quite the kiss," Emma said. "Noah and I saw it from our spot on the dance floor. We gave it at least a 9.5."

Was everything in my life gossip fodder for this town? "Look, it's nothing. It was just a kiss."

"It looked like more than a kiss to me." Emma stepped onto the sidewalk. "Way more."

Sylvie chortled. "This is better than anything we've ever read in Sexy Book Club. Even that book about the amnesiac viscount who forgot he loved the lowly chambermaid who was on the run from her dastardly stepbrother."

I marched up the sidewalk to the chapel, my pink flats swishing against the concrete. Today was a rare day in which I'd left the high heels at home. I was tired, out of sorts, and just needed the comfort of a good flat.

"There's nothing between Beau and me, so just leave it alone. Please." I flung open the door and stepped inside, the overzealous air conditioner of the chapel immediately soothing my heated skin. This conversation had gone out of control. Just like everything else in my life.

"I think we should talk about this." Sylvie's voice echoed in the hollow of the church.

I turned around and shushed her. "No, we should not. Topic closed. We're here to finalize chapel details, not delve into my love life, analyze the intentions of a kiss, or scrutinize where all hands were located."

"So it was a handsy kiss." Sylvia grinned. "I like it."

The chapel manager, Lynn Rigsby, met us in the foyer, thankfully ending this train wreck of a conversation. "Ladies, welcome. Would anyone care for some tea?"

Would it be rude to ask her to spike it? "None for me, thanks."

"How about we start from the top and discuss the rehearsal?" Lynn led Emma away, leaving Sylvie and me to sit in one of the pews.

Sylvie watched a man near the altar climb on a ladder and replace a lightbulb. "It's okay to let yourself feel something for Beau," she said.

"I don't want to talk about this." I consulted my to-do list on my iPad.

"At some point you gotta get back on the horse again. Take a chance."

"Next week I need to confirm the menu for the rehearsal dinner. And I've been working on ideas for the welcome baskets for Emma's out-of-town guests. I was thinking strawberry jelly from the House of Webster, kettle corn from Bentonville Poppers, maybe some stationery from that place on Second Street."

Sylvie patted my hand. "Not every man is out to break your heart, Paisley."

"Maybe we could get Beau to donate day passes for Fox Falls. It would be a great way to cross promote." I made a note to discuss this with Henry.

"Paisley."

I stopped typing and looked at my grandmother. "Yes, Sylvie?"

"There are worse things than taking a chance on a man and failing."

"And what is that?"

Hands that had probably snuffed out a life gently patted my cheeks. "Missing out on the chance of a lifetime."

"Paisley, where is my dress?" Emma dove into the backseat after our meeting, only to reappear, her face drained of color.

"What do you mean?" I asked. "It's in the car. You left it in the back."

"It's gone." Her voice rose in hysterical alarm. "It's not here!"

"It can't be." Dread poured over me like lava.

"Didn't you lock the car?" Sylvie asked.

"Of course I did." Didn't I? Sweat prickled my brow, and my stomach turned nauseous. This couldn't be happening. "I'm pretty sure I locked the car." I ran around to the trunk and flung it open, knowing full well we hadn't stuck the dress in there. Sure enough, when I looked inside, all I found was an old magazine, two grocery bags, and a faded towel with the words *Redondo Beach*.

"Don't panic, Emma." My words sounded lame even to me. "It has to be around here somewhere."

"I bet the Russians got it." Sylvie nodded her blonde head with certainty. "They're still mad at me over our little tussle in Moscow, and they'll do anything to get to me."

At this point I would accept any theory if it would bring the dress back.

"I don't understand how this could've happened." Emma shook her head, her eyes wide and watery. "That's my dress—the dress I'm getting married in in two weeks."

"I'll fix this. I'll take care of it." I didn't even know what I was saying. I just tossed out promises and assurances like confetti.

"I can't believe you didn't lock your car door. How could you do that? You knew the dress was in there." Emma paced with a fury hotter than the sun above us.

"I'm sorry," I said again. "I don't know what happened, but we need to call the police."

"Hmph." Sylvie snorted. "As if you can trust them. They're probably in bed with my Russian friends. Do you want me to activate my underground network? I can have every home in Sugar Creek turned inside out by this time tomorrow. Linda Dithers borrowed my ice cream scooper last month and never returned it. It would give me a chance to get it back."

"No," Emma cried. "We'll call the police." She sniffed indelicately. "But that doesn't change the fact that the dress is gone. Someone took it. Who would do such a thing?" She turned her accusing eyes to me. She didn't have to say the words, but I heard them all the same. Once again I had screwed up, and this was all my fault.

CHAPTER TWENTY-SIX

E MMA'S DRESS WAS nowhere to be found.

The police filled out a report, but due to an old sow running loose on Halleck Lane, they didn't have time to give it the concern we thought it merited. Chief Mark O'Hara probably chalked it up to my incompetence as a murderous human being. Sylvie and I had marched up and down the streets near the chapel, knocking on doors and asking questions like a vigilante justice league, but nobody had seen a thing. I left a watery-eyed Emma at Sylvie's, then worked until close at Enchanted Events. My guilt over the theft was a shackle I dragged behind me all day until I couldn't take it anymore. At five thirty, I got in my car and drove to Zoey Chandler's, hoping she was home. I didn't know how I'd replace Emma's gown, but working on my own case would at least be a worthwhile distraction.

Zoey answered on the first knock. "What are you doing here?"

"I'd like to talk to you."

"I have nothing more to say, Ms. Sutton. Leave my family alone."

I pushed my hand on the door to stop her from closing it. "Zoey, I don't want to hurt your family. I want to help them, but things do not add up with Sasha."

"When have they ever?" she said.

"I know about the wreck." A raindrop plopped onto my shirt, followed by dozen more. "I know you took the blame for Sasha's DUI."

Irritation sharpened her features. "My dad and his big mouth. He told me he'd spoken to you, but he couldn't recall the conversation. Leave it alone, okay?"

I hated to throw threats around, but right now it was all the ammunition I had. "I think you need to let me in so we can talk. Otherwise . . . I relay your father's revelations to the police."

Zoey heaved a weary sigh and held open the door, revealing stacks of boxes behind her. "Come on in."

"Are you moving?" I stepped around two pink suitcases.

"No, now that the police are done with Sasha's apartment, Max and I cleaned it out and brought some of the stuff back here for my stepmother."

I followed Zoey into the house, taking a seat on a couch covered with clothes that looked like they belonged to Sasha. "So do you want to tell me what happened the night of your car wreck?"

Zoey folded her long legs beneath her in a chair. "We ran into a tree and switched places. What else do you need to know?"

"Why would you take the blame for that? A DUI can ruin your life."

"Because that's the sister I've always been to Sasha—the one who takes care of her, who cleans up her every spill."

"There's a huge difference between helping her with her homework and spending a night in jail on her behalf. Nobody's that magnanimous." She didn't seem to understand my point. "I'm not buying your story, Zoey."

She reached for a stack of fabric samples on the coffee table beside her, her fingers tracing a lace pattern on one she placed in her lap. "I thought my dad's money could get us out of it. I didn't think it would be a big deal, and I thought it would just go away."

"Sasha could've killed somebody. Why get in the car with her after she'd been drinking?"

"We both had. I just hadn't realized she was that far gone. She told me she'd had two drinks."

"What would prompt her to ask you to take the fall?"

"Why wouldn't she? She was newly engaged to Evan, and she began crying hysterically, telling me he would surely break off the engagement if she were charged with a DUI, that a politician's wife couldn't have this hanging over her head."

"You didn't do this solely out of the goodness of your pure heart," I argued. "What could you possibly have gained from taking the blame?"

"It's about a dress, okay? I know it sounds stupid to you— and yes, it's ridiculous."

"A dress?"

Zoey leaned toward me. "I've been working my tail off trying to get my break as a fashion designer, and nobody will take me seriously. I've interned in Paris, Milan, and New York, yet I still can't get my foot in the door at a design house. I'm good, Paisley. And I've been waiting for an opportunity show off my designs. In that time before the police arrived, Sasha told me if I would just trade places with her, she promised to wear one of my wedding dresses when she married Evan."

I had a moment of gratitude for my brother and sister. They might've been obnoxious overachievers who got all the approval of my parents, but at least they'd never sent me to jail.

"I don't expect you to understand," Zoey said. "I mean, you did a choir competition as a teenager and walked right into an international career."

Oh, right. Life had been nothing but rainbows and jackpots for me.

"Sasha and Evan's wedding was going to be the biggest social event to hit Arkansas in years." Zoey's wide eyes implored me to understand. "There would be state dignitaries, people from Washington DC, business associates of my father's from all over the world, probably some press coverage by wedding websites and magazines. And what would they all see? The bride wearing *my dress*. It was a chance of a lifetime. So, yeah, I switched seats with her that night. Even with a broken arm and part of the windshield in my lap, I dusted the glass from my jeans and crawled out of the shattered window to put myself in the driver's seat." Silence pressed down heavy on the room, and for a long moment neither one of us spoke. How had Sasha Chandler managed to manipulate everyone in her life, and get every person close to her to do her bidding, no matter how vile? She was merely a puppeteer holding her friends and family by the strings.

"Zoey, remind me again where you were when Sasha was murdered?"

"I told you. I was at yoga."

I needed to follow up on that, and I had an idea about how to make it happen. "So, I got a copy of Sasha's college transcript.

It reads a little strange."

Zoey puzzled at the swift topic change.

"Did your sister have any artistic abilities?"

"None. She could barely draw a stick figure."

"Then why does she have three advanced art classes on her transcript?" I handed over the record.

"That's impossible." She scanned the document. "She doesn't even have Art 101 here. You can't take higher level classes without taking basic art. And she certainly didn't have the talent to take something like watercolors and Drawing II."

"And if you hadn't taken that prerequisite class, what would you have to do to still get into those advanced courses?"

"Probably get professor approval."

Zoey squinted in concentration as she read each line, her finger following along. "This makes no sense. And look at her grades. A's in the first two art classes, then a W on the third."

"She withdrew from that final class." I knew from Frannie's info mining that Sasha had dropped out with only weeks left in that semester.

"I don't know what this has to do with anything," Zoey said. "But I do know that Sasha wasn't capable of making an A in an advanced art class. It's not something you can skate through. It requires talents and skill, and she didn't have that. Like this one? Advanced water color?" She pointed to an entry on the transcript. "She didn't even own any watercolors that I ever saw. Do you know who any of her professors were?"

"Each class was taught by the same person—Professor Fielding."

"It's almost impossible to get into his classes. He's so in-demand that he selects his students based on their degree of talent. Professor Fielding's an incredibly hard instructor. I took one class with him, and I barely scraped by with a B. . . . And pardon my bragging, but I'm good. There's no way my stepsister could've aced any of these classes."

"What possible motivation would Sasha have for taking art? She was a business major."

"I have no idea. I think I stopped questioning the strange things in Sasha's life a long time ago. To know her was to shrug your shoulders and move on. Why are you even pursuing this?"

"I ran into Professor Fielding last week at the wedding you and I both attended. He said he barely remembered Sasha. Looking at her transcript, I find that very strange."

"He's an odd one." She stood and stretched her back. "Very into himself."

That was one detail we knew for certain.

Following Zoey to the door, I couldn't help but pause at the pile of Sasha's belongings. "She had a lot of books." Four boxes were labeled as such in bold, black marker. Funny, I hadn't pegged Sasha as a big reader.

"Mostly some nonfiction on weddings, politics, and former first ladies," Zoey said. "More pictures than words. Her mom's keeping a few outfits, but all the books, magazines, and excessive amounts of clothing will be donated to Samaritan House."

"Have the police looked through these already?"

"Yep."

"I know this is probably rude, but could I take a peek at the wedding books?"

She hesitated.

I glanced longingly at Sasha's stuff. "If you're just going to give them away . . ."

Zoey's phone rang from the living room. "Yeah, er, I guess. Be right back."

As she rushed to grab her call, I lifted the lid on a box and thumbed through the collection. The political tomes appeared brand-new, with unbroken spines. But the wedding books had dog-eared pages to mark favorite spots. While it was odd to flip through the pages Sasha had highlighted for her wedding to my ex-fiancé, I thrilled at the wealth of information here. I could really put these books to good use for my work at Enchanted Events.

"I'm sorry, I have to go." Zoey reappeared in the foyer, car keys in hand. "Gotta help Max with something at the gym."

"Oh, sure. I'll get out of your way then. Would you mind if I maybe—?"

She snagged her purse off the entry table. "Just take the books, Miss Sutton. I gotta leave."

Zoey waited long enough for me to grab a single box, tossing in a few extra wedding books on top and nearly shoving me out the door.

"Thank you for speaking with me." I fumbled with the heavy load as I stood in the yard and watched her open her car door.

Zoey shut herself inside, then rolled down her window. "Good luck," she said. "I may have disliked my stepsister on a regular basis, but she was my family. I do hope you or the police find her true killer."

"Me too, Zoey." I put the box of books in my backseat, a little pleased with the information I could now share with Sylvie and Frannie. And knowing my next step would be talking to the mysterious Professor Carson Fielding.

CHAPTER TWENTY-SEVEN

"YOUR GRANDMA'S HERE."

I looked up from my desk at Enchanted Events the next day to find a frazzled Alice, holding the doorframe with one hand and a fortifying energy drink with the other.

"Tell her I'll be right out."

"Feel free to hurry." Alice took a pull from her can as if wishing it were something stronger. "She just talked one bride into a prenup and another into what she called a 'level five background check' because her fiancé reminded Mrs. Sutton of a man she knew in Greece who sold olive oil and explosives."

"On my way."

After calling the college and being told Carson Fielding was working from home today, Sylvie and I decided we'd pay him a visit. My grandmother had insisted upon meeting me at Enchanted Events, which clearly was not in the best interests of our altar-bound brides.

I walked into the main area and gently pulled Sylvie away from a thirtysomething woman making her venue selection.

"We'll talk later, dear," Sylvie said to the woman as she waved goodbye.

"Don't harass the clients."

"I'm not. I just noticed she had a few silver fillings and wondered if she knew those could be used as communication devices."

"Okay, let's go." I opened the door and walked outside to my car, grateful she was following.

"Your car's a mess." Sylvie opened the passenger door and found it filled with binders, bags, and fabric samples. "Let me drive. I'll get us there faster."

"Just throw it all in the back."

"Can't," she said. "There's a big box back here. What is all this?" Her face sobered as she watched me over the hood of the car. "Hey, you're not packing up to make a quick getaway, are you?"

"No, I stopped by Zoey's last night. Turns out Sasha was a wedding book collector, so Zoey gave me some of her stash."

"Very generous, given your perilous connection. Anything revealing in there?"

"I don't think so."

But Sylvie didn't take my word for it. She dug through the box as if it held the answer to all my problems. "An etiquette guide—she should've read that one a little closer. A how-to on vow writing, one on reception trends, and . . . what is this?" She held up a smaller red book I hadn't had time to peruse. "Wait a minute."

I dodged a fly and shut my door impatiently. "Let's get going, Sylvie."

"Hold on." She walked to my side with her treasure. "Shug, do you see this?" She flipped open the cover—revealing a mini iPad.

"Well, that's an interesting development." The iPad's protective cover looked just like a novel, and I hadn't even noticed it.

"Want me to take a look at it for you?"

"Should we? I mean, it's private."

"Yes," said Sylvie, "we definitely should."

"Or we could take it back to Zoey. Or to the police."

"You and your conscience. Give Frannie and me a crack at it first."

"No. I need to think about this." It seemed wrong. Yet so did going to prison. Maybe I needed to explore every possibility of information.

"If you're not going to let me snoop on the iPad, then you definitely have to let me drive."

That sounded even riskier.

"Sylvie, can we change the radio station? Maybe some music?"

"My car, my tunes," my grandmother said.

"It's nothing but clicks and static."

"It's coded." She pushed a button on some gizmo she had clipped to her dash, ending the racket. "But excuse me for checking on a hot situation in Istanbul. By all means, let me turn on some George Strait for you and ignore all matters of global security."

"I appreciate your sacrifice." I was having doubts about her so-called retirement.

Before setting out for Fielding's, we'd stopped by the rent house to pick up my mail, including a royalty check from my old label so small it didn't deserve a stamp. While Sylvie was wandering the house in search of bugs, I'd hidden Sasha's iPad beneath my bed. I had no desire for Sylvie to find it if she discreetly let herself into the house later. Which she would.

My grandmother pulled a hard left onto Pope Street, and my head knocked into the passenger window.

"Easy there, Earnhardt." In most people's cars, the overhead handles were for looks. In Sylvie's car, they were sheer necessity. Riding in my grandmother's sports car was like strapping yourself to a rocket. All you could do was hold on—and pray that when you crashed you'd get to keep a limb or two.

Sylvie speared me with a quick glower. "If I'm to be in charge of the getaway car on this mission, then let me do it."

"This isn't a getaway car. We're not robbing a bank. This should be a nice, calm interaction with Fielding, so I don't want to see screeching tires or bullets."

"That's cute how you think fun always equates with *legal*." Her air quotes were an insult to civility.

"Talking to the professor could be a complete fool's errand," I said. "So he lied about knowing Sasha. So she took some art classes that she never qualified for. How is this relevant to the murder?"

"Everything's relevant. Didn't Raven tell you to look into this guy?" Sylvie took her hand off the gearshift and placed it on my leg. "When it comes to protecting my granddaughter from the slammer, I'm gonna leave no stone unturned. Something about this doesn't smell right, and I've smelled a lot of rotten fish in my day. Especially that one time Frannie and I got dumped into a sewage ditch in the Ukraine. I burped green bubbles for a month."

We exited a neighborhood of cheery craftsman homes, newly built to look as if they'd been there since girls wore poodle skirts and boys rolled cigs in their sleeves. The road then emptied out into a less desirable part of town.

"Are you sure you gave me the right address?" Sylvia asked.

I glanced at the address Frannie had texted me. "According to Frannie, this is it."

"Our girl's rarely wrong." Sylvie made another turn, nearly taking the car up on two wheels.

Johnston Street sported so many identical duplexes, it looked as if someone had created one, then done a copy-and-paste all the way down the street. The neighborhood had seen better days and was frequently highlighted in police reports.

Sylvie slowed the car to a respectable speed, but as we neared 310 Johnston, she just kept cruising.

"What are you doing?" I pointed toward her side of the road. "That was the house."

"You never go right to the perp's hideout. You have to do a little surveillance." She slowed the car even more. "Check out the perimeter, scan the area for any danger—like snipers and Chihuahuas."

"Sylvie, a professor and librarian live here. Probably the most hostile thing they might do is throw a textbook at us. Now circle back to the house. I don't have all day."

My grandmother made quick work of her extended tour and finally guided the car into the bumpy driveway. Just as Anna Grace Fielding walked a green bicycle out of her small garage.

"This is going to be awkward." I unbuckled my seatbelt. "Asking her husband about Sasha right in front of her."

"You want me to distract her?" Sylvie asked. "Maybe knock her out with one of my jujitsu moves? She won't remember a thing."

I opened the car door, grateful for terra firma. "No, that won't be necessary. And if you have any explosives on your person, please leave them in the car."

I heard her grumbling as she threw a few items back in the car. "Apparently kissing Beau Hudson makes you extra crabby."

"Paisley Sutton at my house? Pinch me, I'm dreaming!" Anna Grace Fielding popped her kickstand and rushed to us. "Oh my goodness! I cannot believe *the* Paisley Sutton of the Electric Femmes is standing in my driveway. Fifteen-year-old me is just dying right now."

"Hi, Anna Grace." My cheeks had to be as pink as Sylvie's roses. "I called the university, and they said your husband was working from home today. I wondered if I might have a quick word with him?"

Realizing I wasn't there to see her, Anna Grace's bright face fell. "No, I'm sorry. Carson's in Bentonville at Crystal Bridges Museum giving a special lecture on an exhibit. He's supposed to be home in a couple of hours, but he tends to lose all track of time in art museums."

Crystal Bridges was a state-of-the-art museum, strangely located in a small town like a crowning jewel, a gift to the community from the family who had brought us WalMart.

"I see you're on your way out." Sylvie nodded toward the bicycle. "That's quite a bike you have there. A vintage Ladies Royale. I used one of those in Zimbabwe, back in 2010. They're surprisingly agile in quicksand."

Anna Grace laughed. "Carson and I are a one-car family at the moment, but we're hoping to buy a new vehicle soon. We usually carpool to school, so it hasn't been too big of a deal, but I do miss my car. You know, if you're not in a hurry, you ladies should come in and have some tea."

"No, that's okay," I said. "We need to be going and—"

"We'd love to!" Sylvie linked her arm in mine and gave it a tug. "Charming place you have here, dear."

Anna Grace wheeled her bicycle back into the garage as we followed her. "It's not much to look at, but the rent's cheap. We sold our house a year ago. We're trying to save money for another, and we like to travel. But all of that's been curtailed in the last few years. My husband hasn't had a raise at the university in nearly four years. We relied pretty heavily on his art sales, but with the economy as it is, people aren't exactly lining up to pay big bucks for his work like they used to. But it's fine." She opened the door and motioned us in. "It's just a temporary speed bump. When I graduate in a year, we'll be a two-income household and can have all those things that we want."

I'd forgotten to mention to Sylvie that Anna Grace was a fan of some chitchat.

We stepped into the Fieldings' kitchen, an outdated eat-in with sagging cabinets and countertops the color of depressed pine trees.

"So you said you wanted to talk to my husband?" Anna Grace reached into the refrigerator and procured a water bottle, offering it to me.

I declined with a shake of my head. "Yeah, a bride wants a themed backdrop for a wedding, and it's just completely out of my range of ability. I was hoping to get some art direction, maybe even see if your husband would be interested in doing some freelance work for Enchanted Events."

Sylvie gave a barely perceptible nod of approval to my story. "We also had a few questions about Sasha Chandler," she said.

My eyes went wide, and I smashed her toe with my foot. What was she doing?

"Sasha Chandler?" Anna Grace cracked open her own water. "What more can Carson tell you about her?"

"When I last spoke to Professor Fielding, he acted like he hardly remembered Sasha," I said. "But she attended three of his classes, including some upper-level courses she would've needed his permission to get into."

Anna Grace took throat-pulsing gulps of water, then daintily wiped her mouth. "Let's go sit in the living room, shall we?"

I sat on the couch next to Sylvie, who was pulled taut as a violin string, ready to jump on any suspicious information.

Anna Grace rested her sweating bottle on a coaster bearing Jane Austen's face. "I think you'll find, Paisley, that people around here don't relish talking about Sasha Chandler, especially now that there's a murderer at large. But I can tell you my husband did, in fact, know Sasha." Shadows fell across eyes devoid of any makeup. "It was quite a dark time in our lives."

Sylvia scooted closer, the thrill of the hunt evident on her face. "What happened?"

Mrs. Fielding pressed her lips together, her eyes drifting to the floor as if gathering difficult memories. "My husband and Sasha met at one of those faculty-student government events at the beginning of the school year some time ago. I believe Sasha was probably a sophomore. Carson, as you may have noticed, can be incredibly charming. And not that he acts on it, but he has quite the way with the ladies. Really with anyone. He's just an effusively friendly guy. Sasha walked away from an innocent conversation with Carson and assumed he was interested in her. He hadn't been at Arkansas A&M long, so he wasn't going to be dumb enough to date a student. But Sasha seemed smitten, so she took some of his classes."

"But she couldn't have gotten in those classes if he hadn't approved her," I said.

Anna Grace released a ragged breath and contemplated her wedding ring, twirling it around her finger. "This is where it gets a little tricky," she said. "And I don't expect you to understand or agree with this. Money has always been tight for us. We've been on our own since we were nineteen. Neither one of us has much family to speak of, and all we've known is struggle. Carson's student loan debts were astronomical. Five years of undergrad, two years of the Masters program and then his PhD? We were drowning in debt. So when Sasha Chandler came along and asked my husband to let her into his class, he said no way. He knew that art had nothing to do with her major, and he didn't have enough space as it was for all the students he wanted to reach. But then she offered to buy a handful of his paintings—for a large sum of money." Anna Grace laughed. "Can you believe that? This rich, spoiled college girl offered my broke husband the chance to sell his work in exchange for a seat in his class. And he took her up on it."

"Why would she do that?" Sylvie asked.

"I have no idea," Anna Grace said. "I guess just to be close to my husband? He's known for being a dynamic professor, so even if she couldn't keep up with the art projects, she would've enjoyed learning from him. Right now at the museum, there are probably two hundred people listening to his lecture. So, maybe it was unethical to make the exchange, knowing she had a crush on him. But he also knew he was never going to act on it."

Sylvia and I both looked at each other with matching frowns. "Didn't someone at the university question that?" I asked.

"No," she said. "Nobody said a word."

"Anna Grace, are you sure nothing ever developed between your husband and Sasha?" Sylvie asked.

"I assure you, crazy as it sounds, that my husband did not ever so much as touch Sasha Chandler. Here was a girl throwing money at him, so confident in her own female wiles, that she thought she could wear him down. But she couldn't. The only thing unethical about Carson is that he would sell paintings and take money from a rich girl who thought she might have a chance. It was pocket change to her, but it ended up being close to a thousand dollars for us. We were able to pay off a long overdue medical bill that had been hanging over our heads. He assured me, no matter how many tricks Sasha tried, he was never alone in a room with her, and I believed him. I'd even routinely drop by campus just to check."

"You mentioned Sasha pulling stunts," Sylvie said. "Like skydiving into his classroom from a fighter jet? What are we talking about here?"

"She'd send him flowers."

My grandmother's cheeks blew out in a plume of disapproval. "Amateur stuff."

Anna Grace turned to me and continued. "She'd have expensive art supplies delivered to him in perfume-scented boxes. Bring him lunch. Tape little notes to his door. She was relentless in her pursuit of him for a good year and a half, and we used that to our advantage. It was a rare, weird opportunity, and, I'm ashamed to say, we ran with it."

"The transcript says that Sasha dropped out of her third art class with your husband a few weeks before semester's end. What happened?" I asked.

Anna Grace peeled the label off her water bottle and curled it in her fingers. "One afternoon Carson came back to his office, only to find Sasha dressed in a trench coat and little else, reclined on his desk. She had paid some janitor to let her in. I was with him. He told her in no uncertain terms to get out and that there would never be a future for them. She ran off and never returned to his class." Her volume dropped, as if someone might overhear. "If the college found out that my husband sold seats to his class, he'd be fired. It's a blatant ethical violation, and he'd lose his job." Her hand gripped mine with a strength reserved for lady wrestlers. "I'm asking you, as the idol of my teen years, as the good woman I know you are, and as someone who understands a desperate situation, to please not tell anyone. Nobody can know about this. Even though it was a long time ago, Carson could still get fired. What he did was stupid. We've regretted it and have just been waiting for it to come back around and bite us, but it never did. Please understand we were flat broke, and it just seemed to be an answered prayer at the time. One we couldn't turn down."

"Where was your husband the morning of the murder?" I

asked.

Anna Grace sat back, as if the weight of the question offended with a shove. "He was at his monthly department meeting on campus. First Tuesday of the month at ten o'clock. Without fail."

All of this was so very strange and nonsensical. How had Sasha Chandler managed to exploit everyone in town? One thing I did understand was the desperation to get back on track and pay your bills. If someone threw cash at me to bask in my presence, I'd probably sign up for the arrangement as well.

"Promise me our secret is safe with you." Anna Grace's voice was fraught with alarm. "Carson would kill me if he knew I was telling you this, but it's important you understand why he did it. And why he didn't want to admit his connection to Sasha."

"I don't see any need to share this information yet," I said.

"Oh, thank you. Thank you so much." Anna Grace turned expectant eyes to Sylvie.

Sylvie rolled her eyes. "All right," she said. "I'll keep my yapper shut too."

"You're just as wonderful in person as I knew you would be." Anna Grace threw her arms around me and squeezed. "You're the best, and I can't wait until your next album. Tell me you're going solo. You are going solo, right?"

I was about as solo as it got. "Goodbye, Mrs. Fielding." I rose and walked to the door. "Thank you for the information."

She stood in her driveway and waved with impressive enthusiasm until our car was out of sight.

"Well, what did you think?" Sylvie asked as she dodged a pothole a little too aggressively.

"She's a strange bird," I said. "I'm not sure how I feel about her story."

"Agreed." She braked to allow a child on a bike to cross, nearly sending me into the windshield. "Let's do some research to see how much of her story holds up. We'll let Frannie do some fact-checking."

"Frannie does her research legally, doesn't she?"

"We're not afraid of little roadblocks called laws." Sylvie stomped on the gas. "Now let's get you back to Enchanted Events so you can work on throwing Emma the best bachelorette party this town's ever seen."

CHAPTER TWENTY-EIGHT

"SOME OF THE ladies are trickling in."

I looked up from my computer Friday to find Henry standing in the doorway of our office. "Wow, the day flew. How is it five o'clock already?" I stood up, stretched, and pressed a hand to my aching back. We had been hustling day and night this week, and between the stress of work and the case, sleep had been a fickle friend.

"Your first solo event." Henry settled himself into the tufted chair in front of my desk. "How does it feel?"

"Like I'm about to throw up." Tonight was Emma's bachelorette party, and my gift to her was to give her the best pre-wedding bash this town had ever seen. One that was fun yet functional. One that entertained and fit my cousin's eclectic interests. "I've reviewed my list a million times today, and I *think* I've got it all together, but I've probably forgotten something." Because it would be so like me to screw it up. "Emma's only now speaking to me since the dress disappeared."

"Any word on that?"

"None. Nobody saw a thing, which is strange in a town that prides itself on minding everyone else's business. Sugar Creek Formals said they couldn't get that exact dress, but they think they can get one very similar. I insisted on handling it for

Emma." My cousin pretty much bursts into tears every time she had to talk about her missing wedding gown.

"You've got this, Paisley." Henry gave me a bolstering smile.

"Do I?" I had discarded exactly fifty-seven ideas before coming up with something that got me energized, and now that it was show time, I doubted every single detail I'd devised.

"Well, for one, I am quite proud of your end product. It's creative, it's different. Maybe a little violent for my taste, but you are Sylvie Sutton's granddaughter. After tonight, our phones will be ringing off the hook for bachelorette party requests."

"Thanks, Henry." I walked around the desk and wrapped my arms around him. "Don't pull away there, big guy. We're hugging this out." I smiled as he predictably squirmed. "Just gonna stay like this until I squeeze every ounce of my gratefulness right into that snobby suit and chilly heart of yours."

"Uh-huh. Okay, that's enough." One arm came around and stiffly patted me on the back. "Enough huggy stuff. We're cool. We're good. Paisley, let go, now. All right, I'm about three seconds away from having an allergic reaction. *Paisley!*"

Laughing, I released my stoic partner. I would surely miss him when I was gone. Henry was a whiz at the event planning business, and he got stuff done. He could be as prickly as a corsage pin, but he was also as reliable as a wedding march.

Layla popped her head around the door. "Some ladies just walked in wearing some seriously frightening bridesmaid dresses." She visibly shivered.

I straightened the butt bow on my moss green tea-length gown, and gave my rhinestone-covered bodice a tug. "Perfect!"

Within the next ten minutes, every able-bodied person

who'd been invited for the party had arrived looking adorably awful in their ugliest bridesmaid dress. Henry and Layla helped me serve drinks in to-go cups with glittery straws. With Enchanted Events closed, the noise level swelled with the buzz of excitement and the shared laughter over their punishing attire.

"Good evening, friends and family of our beloved Emma Sutton." I stepped into the center of the room, my volume finally getting everyone's attention. "We are all gathered here tonight to celebrate our dear friend and my cousin—a woman who's incredibly smart, sassy, *and* snagged herself one fine fellow."

"Aw, thanks, Paisley." Emma blew a kiss my way.

"And a lady who has a mere nine days left as a single lady."

"Enjoy it while you can!" Frannie yelled.

"I'd like to welcome you all to Sequins and Starlight," I said. "You're in for a ton of surprises and even more fun. Tonight we'll share some good food, some sweet memories, and a lot of adventure. Are you ready?"

A mob of about twenty-five women cheered, and some of my anxiety flittered away on dragonfly wings.

I could do this. I'd poured all my spare time and energy into a solid plan, and it was going to be a success, by gosh. Now I had to just repeat that in my head one hundred more times, and I'd be good to go.

We herded the women to the parking lot, where a zebra-striped party bus waited to take us to our first destination.

The old zebra tossed and jostled like it was mid-seizure, but none of the ladies seemed to mind. We looked like a bunch of misfit beauty queens as the bus rambled down a series of dirt roads.

Frannie sat across the aisle and tugged at her sleeve. She wore a peach chiffon confection that could've been the height of fashion when Madonna still crooned about virgins. Her shoes were dyed to match, and if I looked closely, I was pretty sure the heel had a tiny compartment—probably customized for some mode of malice.

The large bow decorating my derrière ground into my back as we were jimmied about. "This dress is uncomfortable," I said to Sylvie, my seat mate.

"What do you have to complain about?" She wore an intricately detailed red kimono with a samurai sword looped to her waist.

"Is that thing real?" I asked with a pointed look at her weapon.

"Of course it's real. And it's digging into my hip." Sylvie adjusted the holster. "I was the bridesmaid for a PSIA." She frowned at the blank look on my face. "Public Security Intelligence Agency? Japan's version of the FBI? Anyway, like all good nuptials, it was a secret wedding, and Akeno and her sweetie were only hitched ten minutes before her father found out, dissolved the marriage, and married her off to a short, fat prince from Kyoto. Prince Chubby mysteriously died in his sleep six months later, but I know nothing about that."

When we finally arrived at Shadow Ranch, the bus doors wheezed open. I followed a whistling Frannie down the steps to get a closer look at her wig and the peach chiffon monstrosity she wore. Bridesmaids' dresses were often such cruel and unusual punishment.

A muscular man in full camo rose from his seated position on a hay bale. "Hello, there, Ms. Sutton. I'm John Simpson." He shook my hand, his fingers curving around mine with an impressively, firm grip. "So glad to see you haven't backed out yet. You ladies are going to have so much fun."

Sylvie elbowed me. "As long as Sargent Sexy Stuff is with us, I know it'll be a good time."

Frannie's eyes twinkled. "He can check my pistols anytime."

"Are y'all ready to get a little rowdy?" John called out.

The bevy of ladies clapped and hooted, Emma leading the pack.

"Paisley here has quite an evening planned for you." John took off his sunglasses. "First we're going to start with a little target practice."

"Otherwise known as my daily workout," Sylvie said.

"I'm from Splat Paintball Academy. And with thanks to Shadow Ranch for allowing us to set up here today, we have fully customized a great time for the bride and her friends. To begin, you'll be split into groups. While I'm training one group, the other half of you will go into the barn, where we have a photographer waiting. Then you'll get some . . ." He lifted his camo hat and scratched his head. "What did you call those things, Miss Paisley?"

"Glamour shots," I said. "And if you walk inside this barn, not only will you find all the props and backdrops you need to take the most beautiful bridesmaid photos, but you'll also see a selection of hors d'oeuvres and drinks."

"So this is a scavenger hunt," John said. "And the first to get the most items without being taken out by paint is the grand prize winner." John explained the rules, passing out a list of things we were to find around the ranch.

Emma perused her list. "A bottle of champagne, a beach towel, a travel journal . . . Aw, they're all things we can use on the honeymoon, aren't they?"

I nodded.

Her eyes misted. "This is awesome already, Paisley."

Later I would analyze that warm, cozy feeling in my chest, but right now, I was still on the job. "The winner tonight gets a two-night stay at the Sugar Creek Bed and Breakfast, as well dinner at the Bayonet," I announced.

After half of the ladies departed into John's care, I went inside the barn. Stopping in the doorway, I looked around, a smile lifting my lips. A powerful feeling welled up within me, one I hadn't experienced in so long I barely recognized it.

It was pride.

I was proud of what I'd created here.

The barn had been completely transformed. To one side was a series of rustic farmhouse tables filled with chilled drinks and hors d'oeuvres. In the center I'd set up elegant Lucite chairs and tables, Tiffany-blue floral centerpieces blooming on each one. In another corner, where the ceiling dipped, floated hundreds of blue-and-white balloons—with trailing strings to which I'd attached black-and-white snapshots of Noah and Emma.

Laughter bubbled from another corner, where ladies posed and the photographer styled them in various tableaus of mock-sexiness. Sylvie was already arguing at the photographer's request for her to drop the samurai sword.

"This looks real good, hon." Frannie sipped on a piña colada as she stood beside me. "You did a real nice job."

"Thank you." I smiled. "I think the best is yet to come."

She hugged me to her and kissed my cheek. "Oh, sugar. It certainly is."

The phone in my hand vibrated, and I didn't even bother checking the display. "It's going fine, Henry."

Crackling on the other end. "Um, is this Paisley Sutton?"

That wasn't Henry. "Yes."

"This is Raven Arnett. I was wondering if you had some time to talk."

Four women in flouncy taffeta ran by giggling, drinks in hand. "I'm working an event right now. Can I call you back later?"

"I'd rather discuss this in person."

"Okay." My barely existent sleuthing senses tingled.

"I'll be home all day Saturday." Raven rattled off an address. "Can you stop by?"

"Can I ask what this is concerning?"

I heard her exhale. "Sasha Chandler."

CHAPTER TWENTY-NINE

AN HOUR LATER, the bridesmaid brigade reassembled in the barn, dripping with sweat and clutching battered helmets. Our dresses were torn and covered in splatters of paint. We looked like we'd been assaulted by rainbows and dropkicked by Crayola.

"I see Emma got the grand prize." Sylvie sat at one of the Lucite tables, her arms crossed over her bosom. Beside her Frannie munched on a plate of stuffed mushrooms.

"What place did you get?" Emma asked as we sat down and joined them.

"It doesn't matter," Sylvie said. "I am your grandmother—and Frannie's your dear aunt. What kind of matriarchs would we be if we had showed you girls up with our unfair advantage?"

Frannie popped another mushroom. "Yeah, not to mention that little first-grade teacher over there is a crazy sharpshooter. Took us both out like it was our first day on the job. If she's not careful she's gonna blow her cover."

"First grade teacher, my tush." Sylvie threw the woman a dirty look. "She's got NSA written all over her."

Emma reached for a cupcake on Sylvie's plate and took a bite. "What is this heaven I'm tasting?"

"Frannie made them," I said. "We still haven't found a bakery up to our standards who'll do business with us, so Frannie volunteered."

"It was nothing." Frannie blushed.

"You should open a shop," Emma said.

"I'm pretty busy with my neighborhood watch and Sexy Book Club." Frannie blotted her lips with a napkin. "But I might give that some thought."

When dinner was over we loaded our tired bodies back onto the bus. As we cruised over the dirt roads, I stood and announced our next stop.

"Tonight is about celebrating Emma, and I wanted to give her one adventure that was unexpected." I brushed at my arm, which was decorated with paint. "In the last six months, Emma has taken up yoga, so we're all going to join in her new hobby. But this isn't regular yoga Emma will be practicing this evening. No, tonight we'll be trying . . . *aerial* yoga."

With twitters of trepidation, the ladies and I unloaded from the bus and marched single file into Surrender Yoga. The very studio where Zoey Chandler had a membership.

An employee handed us shorts and cotton T-shirts bearing Emma's and Noah's faces.

"I'm so glad you could join us tonight," the instructor said as we walked past the office and into the class. "Aerial yoga is brand-new to our studio, and you're gonna be one of the first classes to try it out. We hope you like it so much that you want to return."

"I just hope I don't wind up in the hospital," Emma said.

Though yoga was the chic thing to do in LA and among the music crowd, I had very little experience with it. I wasn't exactly super-bendy.

Inside the classroom, fabric harnesses hung from the ceiling like narrow hammocks. Gentle music wafted above us as the instructor began.

"Let's start with some basic stretches."

A half hour later, I wanted to cry. The twiggy instructor had us suspended in the air, knees pointed east and west like a frog. I expected to split in half at any second, which was really going to stink as I had terrible health insurance that did not cover midair yoga catastrophes.

"You ladies are doing lovely." The instructor's voice was as Zen as an NPR radio host's. "I can tell you're ready to move on. Now I'd like for you to drop down and dive to the floor, letting your legs in the fabric catch you. And there you'll just hang."

And hang I did. My fabric wrapped around my ankles, and I began to swing by one leg. I knocked into Sylvie next to me, who hung like a bat—perfectly graceful, as if she were meant to contemplate the earth from upside down.

The material around my ankle decided to release me, and I hit the mat below us with a loud thud.

"You okay down there?" Sylvie asked.

"Couldn't be better." I rubbed my sore tush. "I'm going to get a drink."

Limping out the door and into the hallway, I found a fountain and let the cool water glide over my lips as exhaustion washed over me. I was tired, I was dirty, and I clearly wasn't cut out for hanging upside down spread-eagled. Plus, it was time to get down to business of why I was really here.

Glancing about to confirm no one was around, I then padded on bare feet toward the office at the front of the building. My aching hands twisted the doorknob, and disappointment speared through me to see it was locked. I rattled the knob again.

"What do you think you're doing?"

I spun around and swallowed my heart.

Only to find Sylvie. "I asked you what you think you're doing . . . without asking for my assistance, that is."

"It's locked."

"Only to you mere mortals." She reached into her shirt and extracted a silver object. "Stand back and observe some greatness."

"Did you just pull that thing from your bra?"

She patted her bosom. "It's like a treasure chest down there."

"Wait." I grabbed her hand on the door. "There could be cameras on us right now." I furiously looked about.

"There's not. I assessed the place within sixty seconds of walking in the door."

"Are you sure?"

"As sure as I was about there being an underground city beneath the Chicago subway system."

"I've never once heard this claim."

"Oh, it's there." She patted my back like a coddling parent. "Scoot out of the way so I can get us inside." She paused. "By the way, what are you breaking in for?"

Now that was family. My grandmother would commit a crime for me without even knowing the cause. "This is where Zoey takes yoga. I want to get a look at their studio sign-in sheets on the day Sasha was murdered."

"Have you asked the studio for this information?"

"No."

"My girl going the route of espionage." Sylvie looked toward the ceiling, blinking back tears. "I'm so proud."

Only my grandmother. "Let's move this along before we get arrested."

"Stop blowing out my happy candles." But she turned to the task, and before I could say *maybe we can be cell mates*, Sylvie had unlocked the office.

We slipped inside, shutting the door behind us. We walked past a barren reception area to the main office. We found two desks, a printer, a vintage poster of Olivia Newton John in a wedgie-revealing leotard, and four full-sized file cabinets.

"I was hoping there would just be a file labeled 'Sign-in sheets' sitting on a desk," I whispered.

Sylvie dug into the pockets of her silk kimono, producing two pairs of latex gloves. "Get to looking, Sherlock."

My grandmother's outfit was like the Mary Poppins bag of bridesmaids' dresses. We had to make this quick before she produced homing pigeons, dynamite, or a stink bomb.

"I've got nothing," Sylvie said five long minutes later, extracting her arm from a desk drawer. "Except for some peanut butter crackers I'm confiscating for my trouble."

I stood next to file cabinet number three, a gray metal thing with little personality. "Mostly bills, invoices, and—wait a minute." My fingers riffled through one file, then another. "Jackpot." It was a collection of sign-ins for the entire year. "This could take awhile."

A voice broke through the hush of the office. Someone was talking on the other side of the door.

"Shoot." Sylvie tiptoed toward me, cracker crumbs dotting her upper lip. "Someone's coming."

"Let's go." I furiously looked for another exit.

"No!" She aimed her finger toward the files. "Not 'til you find that sign-in sheet."

"Sylvie!"

"Just do it! Leave the rest to me."

Oh, my gosh! This was insanity. Cardiac arrest was as imminent as my criminal arrest.

But I obeyed, flipping through page after page, my ear pealed for the voice getting nearer. Was it wrong to pray for God to help you pull off a theft?

Probably, but I did it anyway.

"Here!" I cried. "Here's the date!"

The sound of a squeaking door in the outer room had me clutching Sylvie's arm in a death grip. *What do we do?*

Taking a page from Sylvie's playbook, I crumpled up a handful of the sign-ins and shoved them into my bra.

"No! We can't do that." Sylvie reached into my top and plucked them out. "The police will eventually confiscate them for evidence." She whipped out her cell phone and snapped what I thought was way too many photos.

"We don't have time for this," I hissed. "We need to go!"

"Come on." My grandmother grabbed my hand and pulled me toward the back of the room. "You know what's behind Olivia Newton John?"

"An eight-by-ten glossy of Richard Simmons?"

"A window."

Her eye for detail was not to be underestimated. "That's well over my head."

She rubbed a hand over the bookcase beside it. "Seems sturdy enough. Start climbing."

"No!" I'd never make it.

"Fine." She hoisted one foot onto the first shelf and proceeded to scale the furniture like a geriatric Spiderman. "See you on the other side."

"Wait!"

A woman's voice grew louder as she spoke in the outer room. "Yes, Janet, I definitely want to talk to the city about our next yoga in the park . . ."

I leapt onto the bookcase, the white shelving wobbling as if trying to buck me off.

"Just a minute," the woman said. "Let me go into the office and check my calendar."

I climbed the remaining shelves like a deranged spider monkey, finally reaching the top and catapulting myself to the window.

"You can do it!" Sylvie yelled from the ground below.

With little space to hang on the window, I threw a leg over, my toes touching air. *Lord, I'd like to get through tonight without an arrest or broken neck.*

My hands clutched the base of the window like a life raft, and I eased the rest of my body over, just as the yoga employee entered the office.

I let my feet dangle for four heartbeats.

Before gravity pulled my fingers loose, and I dropped to the ground.

And took off running.

CHAPTER THIRTY

M Y CAR WHEEZED as it inched into the driveway, as if she, too, were only capable of crawling at this late hour. After hurling ourselves out the yoga studio window, Sylvie and I had sprinted to the party bus, still idling from its recent arrival. We seated ourselves in the back, me—completely freaked and out of breath, and Sylvie—eating the last of her stale crackers. When the ladies were finally released from their yoga class, they stepped onto the bus in a painfully slow fashion.

"Zoey's alibi seems to check out." Sylvie discreetly slid me her phone.

I enlarged a picture to see clearer. The lighting was terrible, but Zoey's name was unmistakable. "She signed into a yoga class—just like she said."

"We'll find the killer, shug." Sylvie slipped the phone back into her purse. "Don't you worry."

I was starting to have some serious doubts. Everywhere we turned—a dead end.

As the zebra bus drove us back to Enchanted Events, I kept looking over my shoulder, fully expecting to see blue lights. Surely the studio employee would know someone had broken into the office. Was it simply a matter of time before the police came knocking on my door?

By the time I drove home and pulled into my own driveway, the dashboard clock said it was ten minutes after midnight, yet the air still sweltered with the heat of the afternoon. Unbuckling my seatbelt, I lifted bleary eyes to the porch—

And froze.

My front door swung wide open, flapping in the night breeze like an ominous invitation.

What do I do?

Reason screamed loud and shrill in my ear, telling me to put the car back in drive and go directly to Sylvie's.

But this was my house.

And it could be nothing.

Though it sure didn't feel like nothing.

I slowly stepped from the car, my high heels long discarded in the backseat. My feet slip-slapped on the driveway as I shined my phone's flashlight along the path, entering the carport. In the dark of night, every shadow loomed, menacing and predatory. Chill bumps scattered along my arms. I grabbed Beau's shovel and propped it on my aching shoulder like a baseball bat.

Creeping toward the front door, I whispered a quick plea for protection to a God who hopefully hadn't tired of my Hail Mary prayers. Then I took one step inside, my shovel locked and loaded.

A wasteland of debris surrounded me.

My TV broken and tossed on the floor. The couch cushions in tatters, as if someone had slit them with a blade. The drawers of my coffee table emptied, papers and Post-its scattered everywhere. My ears on alert like a coon dog's, I heard nothing but my own ragged breathing as I took a few more steps into the space so I could see the kitchen. Anger overtook fear as I beheld the sight of my beloved great-grandmother's dishes resting in a pile of shards on the wood floor. Every cabinet hung open as if screaming for help. The drawers had been yanked out and cast out to join the dishes, making a mess of silverware, tongs, and no end of knives.

I knew I had to get out. I had to call the police.

I swiveled on my bare heel as I turned, giving a small arc of the shovel for good measure, and bolted for the door.

Three steps from my escape and I heard it.

A crash from outside, like someone playing cymbals with trash can lids.

"Who's out there?" I ran outside, shining my weak beam of a light. "I'm calling the police!" I saw a faint shadow round the corner of the house and took off in pursuit. Rocks and grass bit into my feet as I ran, but it didn't slow me down.

The tree root did.

In cheap horror-film fashion, my body went airborne and my arms reached out for the ground, the shovel landing somewhere nearby. "Ow!" My knees struck with a hard crack, and my hands slid into landscaping rocks that bit into my skin. With no time to lose, I pulled myself back to my feet, shook off the pain, grabbed my garden tool, and gingerly walked the length of the side of the house, where I stopped and peered into the night, watching and listening like an avenging superhero.

When I felt the very human tap on my shoulder, I'm pretty sure super girl tinkled in her pants.

My scream rent the air, and I lashed out with the rusty shovel. "Get back!"

"Paisley!" Beau stood wide-eyed with his hands up. "What in the world is going on here?" He jerked his shovel from my grip. "What do you think you're doing? You could've brained me."

I bent over, hands on my knees, my breath heaving in rapid gusts. "What . . . what are *you* doing?"

He settled a hand on my back. "Checking on you. I saw your door open and went in. I got worried when I couldn't find you." He stepped closer, and the faint scent of his cologne was an instant comfort. "What happened in there?"

"Someone broke into the house. I think the intruder just left." I flailed a finger toward the backyard. "Went that direction. I saw a shadow. Heard somebody moving."

"Are you okay?" Beau glanced beyond me, into the darkness.

"I think so." I straightened my spine. "We need to call 911."

He swiftly guided me back to the porch and pressed a key into my palm. "Lock yourself in my house."

"But—"

"Get inside, Paisley."

Adrenaline slam-danced in my head. "Stop telling me what to do. I've had an *insane* night and—"

He leaned down. His mouth was so close to my ear, I felt his lips graze my skin. "Either you get inside and lock yourself in, or I tell your grandmother you'd like her to be your full-time bodyguard."

"Going inside." The jerk. I twisted his key in the lock. "No need to mention this to Sylvie. Feel free to scurry along now."

"I'll go when I hear the click of the lock."

"Beau?"

His sigh could've shaved the bark from the trees. "Yes?"

"Be careful, okay?"

He gave me that flash of a smile, then, with a pronounced limp, tore off the porch like a man on fire, his dark form swallowed up by the night.

With trembling hands, I called 911, reported the break-in, then collapsed on his couch. I pulled a thick-yarned afghan around me and proceeded to shake and startle at every noise and shift of light.

I could've died tonight. A few times.

What if I'd been home? Would the intruder have come in anyway? Were they armed?

And what if they were still out there, and Beau was running right toward them?

Ten different variations of Beau's demise played out in my head like cinematic tragedies, until my nerves nearly overheated. Pacing seemed like a better idea, so I wore out the floor, walking back and forth across his living room, sending up even more prayers. *Please let him be okay. Please let him not get shot. Please let him not get maimed because that boy has one pretty face.*

Minutes and eons later, footsteps thudded on the porch, and I stilled mid pace.

Then came the knock. "Paisley? It's me." Beau's beautiful voice. "Let me in."

He was alive!

I flung open the door, grabbed Beau's left hand, and pulled him inside. "Thank God, you're alive." He barely had the door closed before I launched myself into his arms, my hands snaking around his back and hugging him to me like my missing piece, the source of my next breath, the hero who'd rescued me.

"Can't breathe here, Sutton."

I pressed my cheek to his chest and closed my eyes, drawing my first easy breath since I'd pulled into the driveway. Tears pressed at my lids, and I was helpless to stop their escape. I was so tired. So scared. And so tired of *being* scared.

"Paisley?" Beau pulled back, running a hand over the back of my head, his touch featherlight. "Hey." His gaze studied my face, his eyes narrowing in scrutiny. "What's this?" He brushed a finger across my cheek. "Why are your arms covered in blue paint?"

"Bridesmaids' paintball war."

"Perfectly logical explanation."

"And to think it was the easy part of my evening."

"You're okay," he said. "You're safe now."

I released my hold and stepped away, sniffing as I averted my gaze. "Yeah, I'm fine. Sorry, just nerves. And worried about you." I blindly reached out, my hands fluttering over his face, his shoulders, his chest. "You seem to be in one piece. Well done, Beau. Well done, indeed."

He captured my shaking hands in his own. His hands were so warm, strong, and steady. "There wasn't anyone out there."

"Right. Of course. I'm sure I scared them off. Shovels show you mean business, right? Who needs a gun? I mean, Sylvie does, I guess, but she knows how to work those things. Keeps at least two or three on her person at all times in really uncomfortable places." A traitorous tear slipped past my nose. "My house is trashed."

"Look at me." Beau gently lifted my chin, his eyes searching mine. "Are you crying?"

"Allergies." I shook my head. "Pollen. Mold spores. Arkansas."

A strand of hair had escaped the constraints of my updo, and Beau slowly tucked it behind my ear. "I'm not going to let anything happen to you."

Good heavens, were there any sweeter words? "It's just . . . everything. Moving back, my career in the toilet, the murder, an intruder. Then you."

That sultry frown could've melted a snow cone. "What about me?"

"You just ran out there without any concern for your own safety. What if they'd had a gun and—"

He shrugged as if it were a totally normal thing to do. "I've dodged a few bullets in my day."

And still carried those scars. "Thank you, Beau. I'm glad you were here."

"Me too." His gaze lingered. "You'll sleep here tonight."

"Wait, what? No, I'm fine."

"It's too late to call your grandma and worry her at this hour. Take the guest bedroom."

I couldn't imagine sleeping a wink. "I'm going to go assess the damage."

"Just wait 'til the cops arrive," Beau said. "You don't want to mess up the crime scene." He smiled. "I learned that on TV last week."

I went to the living room window to watch for the police. "If there's one bright spot about tonight, I did manage to see the yoga studio's sign-in sheet for the day of Sasha's murder."

"To confirm Zoey's alibi?"

"Exactly."

"How'd you get that?"

"It's best you don't know. I will say this: Sylvie and her Bra of Wonderment were involved." I updated Beau on what we knew so far.

"Zoey could've left the class," Beau said.

"But it's looking unlikely." On one hand I was glad she didn't do it. On the other, her innocence did nothing for my possible conviction.

And then another dreadful thought hit me like a meteorite. "I'll be back."

Sirens wailed in the distance, as I bypassed Beau and ran out his door.

"Paisley, wait!" he called.

Ignoring the blue lights in the distance, I barreled into my own living room, making a beeline for my bedroom.

And I knew.

I just knew.

Diving to the floor, ignoring the sound of ripping satin, I held the shattered pieces of Sasha's iPad in my hands.

It had been smashed to dust particles.

CHAPTER THIRTY-ONE

"NO, AARON, STOP!"

My eyes shot open, and my brain fought wildly to orient myself. My heart galloped like a derby horse as I sat up, the puzzle pieces shifting into place.

The break-in. My ransacked house. I was at Beau's.

And he was . . . yelling?

I heard it again—Beau's voice. Anguished. Tormented.

And distant—slurred. Not the voice of someone addressing an intruder. But the sound of someone in the tight grip of a nightmare.

I rubbed a hand over my face, my fingers trailing over the swell of my sleep-deprived eyelids. Then I swung my feet over the side of the four-poster bed. Padding out of the room and down the hall, I stood in front of Beau's room. The door was ajar, so I eased it open and stepped inside.

Beau was sitting up in bed, his lamp glowing. His gaze glowering.

"Hey," I said softly, uncertain where to go from here.

"Paisley?" His hair tousled from sleep, he blinked a few times, trying to focus. "Everything okay?" He reached for the phone beside his bed. "Almost four o'clock."

I stood there in my *Golden Girls* T-shirt and running shorts, looking like a gym flunkey. "I was just checking to see if you were all right."

He said nothing, but his face pinched in a severe frown.

"I think you were having a nightmare." I took three more steps into the room.

"So you came to check on me?" He was clearly less than thrilled for me to see this side of him. "Tuck me back in?"

"And to make sure it wasn't actually an intruder in the house."

"What would you have done? Brained them with a heel?"

"I'm glad you're finally acknowledging the efficiency of my shoe choices."

He dropped his head back to his pillow, his back hitting the mattress with a thud. "You can go away now."

"It happens a lot?"

"What? Finding annoying women in my bedroom?"

"These nightmares."

"Go back to bed, Paisley."

"Maybe I can help."

He propped his elbow behind his head and cracked open an eye. "Your hair looks Medusa met a hurricane."

"Your swoony compliments aren't going to distract me from the topic at hand, Beauregard."

"You're not going to take my advice to go back to sleep, are you?"

"I can't. I've been awake for most of the night anyway."

"Me too."

I figured that was probably nothing unusual for him. "So you were going to tell me about this dream. It seemed like a bad one."

"It was horrible. It was about a nosy pop star who wouldn't leave me alone."

"I bet she has a good heart."

At that he smiled, his eyes holding mine. "Turns out she does."

Oh, gosh. He was devilishly handsome in the dark of morning. "Okay, well." I took two steps in retreat. "I'll mosey back down the hall. My bedroom is very comfy, by the way. For a lumberjacky, outdoorsy dude, you sure do have luxurious sheets."

"Sutton?"

I had just made it to the door and turned around. "Yes?"

Beau sat up, the sheet pooling at his waist, and the lamp throwing beams on his sculpted abs like a shrine. "Would you like to forget all about your troubles and do something . . . crazy?"

"What . . ." I licked my suddenly parched lips. "What did you have in mind?"

He crooked a finger and beckoned me to come near.

I obeyed, as if in a trance of trampiness.

"Yes?" I sat on the edge of the bed, his sheets cool against my bare legs.

Beau balanced on an arm, leaning close. "Want to do something fun?" He stroked a finger from my wrist to the hem of my sleeve. "Something to take our minds off all our troubles?" That early morning rasp unfurled a curious heat in my stomach. "Something kind of . . ." His finger slipped back down my arm. "Hot?"

I could barely form sentences right now. "What did you have mind?"

Beau let his gaze slide over me nice and slow. His hand covered mine before his full lips drew toward my cheek, pausing at my ear. "Let's go fishing."

FISHING.

Not my first choice. Ever. But if you've been raised in the Ozarks, you most likely spent some time fishing as a child. Even though I didn't especially want to be out with pole in hand at this unholy hour today, I had fond memories of my grandfather, Sylvie's husband, giving me my own army green pole and a tackle box filled with some of his favorite lures.

"See?" Beau bumped me with his shoulder. "You're smiling already."

"When you said hot, this wasn't what I had in mind." The heat and humidity rarely slept in an Arkansas summer.

"Fishing's the answer to most of a man's problems."

I stood beside him, ankle deep in Sugar Creek, a five-minute ride from Fox Falls. "I believe we both got baptized in this creek during our church youth group days."

"Yeah, God's out here." He nodded toward the landscape. "In the trees. In the sound of the babbling creek. Some days I think it's the only place I can sense Him."

"I'm sure you've questioned a lot of things since you got back from Libya."

Beau pointed toward the water. "Cast your line. Aim for the

center of the creek."

I reared back my pole, let my thumb off the button, and did my Southern girl best. The lure plopped three feet in front of me, making a small tremor in the shallow water.

"Have you forgotten how to fish, city girl?"

"No. It's just hard to see. Maybe if we didn't do this during vampire hours—" I closed my lips on a yelp as Beau stepped directly behind, his arms slipping around me.

"The things LA did to you." His words were a breeze against my cheek. "Your form is a disgrace."

"Just what every girl wants to hear."

His laugh was low and quiet. "Swing it back and forth a few times." One of his hands rested on my hip while the other covered mine on the grip of the pole. "Press that thumb bar down onto the spool. Easy, easy. Control your line."

Who knew fishing terminology could be so hot?

"Bring it forward, and now." His voice reminded me of a dark whiskey, the kind you steal a sip of when no one's looking. "Lift your thumb. Gently. Don't force it."

My lure hit the water at the end of a beautiful arc, bobbing there proudly in the deepest part of the creek. The blush sky dimmed in surrender, and the crickets and frogs chirped their approval.

And Beau still had his arms around me.

My heart beat a wild staccato, and I knew it was more than the sticky humidity making it difficult to draw a full breath.

I slowly turned to face him, letting him take hold of the fishing pole. "Beau?"

He looked down, his warrior's gaze searing into mine. "This

is probably not a good idea."

I placed one hand on his chest. "You and I never were."

"I can't give you what you want, Paisley."

"And what is that?"

"Permanence."

It was a lemon-doused slice to the heart, but it shouldn't have been. I tried to shove that feeling aside. Did I not inspire a yearning for commitment with any man on this planet? What was it about me that said "just keep on walking"?

"I guess you're right." I took back my fishing pole, the hook and bobber dangling. "I obviously couldn't give you permanence either." I said this as if he'd requested it. "My time in Sugar Creek has been nothing but drama and chaos, and it's probably dulled my common sense." With some satisfaction, I watched his brows slam together. "Probably turned me into someone who's a little bit too needy."

"You haven't been needy. Far from it." He secured my hook to my pole. "Except maybe for your fishing prowess. You could use some lessons."

"I'm sure it will come back to me." For some reason, even *that* wounded. "Not that I need it to."

"Right. Because you're leaving soon."

"Exactly."

"Well, while you're still here, you need to hook Sylvie's security system back up. Get the police to patrol Enchanted Events, as well as the house more often."

"I'm fine. I don't need any home alarm designed by my Inspector Gadget of a grandmother."

"What if you'd been home when the burglar had broken in?"

You're totally unarmed."

"I have you next door."

"I wasn't home. I'm rarely home. Get serious." He walked to the shore and laid his fishing pole on the rocks. "You need to learn some self-defense."

"Oh, and who's going to teach me?"

He planted his fists at his hips. "I think I'm more than qualified. The question is, can you handle it?"

I quickly calculated the total mass of his muscles, multiplied by how often this would involve him touching me, then divided by the square root of my weakening resistance. "Maybe we should head back home."

"Either you learn a few moves, or I'm telling Sylvie you're ready to move in with her."

She'd love that. "Let's make it quick."

In the high beams of Beau's four-wheeler, we spent the next twenty minutes doing a very aggressive watoosie, with moves I'd probably never remember in a real assault.

"Try it again," Beau said. "You forgot to knee me in the face."

"Oh, for heaven's sake, we've done this move three times."

But Beau started the process all over again. "If I grab your shoulder, what do you do?"

I slapped my hand over his, grabbing his thumb. "I bend your wrist back toward you, then twist your arm toward the ground."

"And if you see I'm bent down in pain, utilize that knee. Right in the nose. Hard."

I simulated the movement, then let him go. "Got it."

"And use those elbows when you strike. It's all about throwing your body weight into it. Where do you hit?"

Running on fumes and exhaustion, my brain grasped for answers. "Um, the throat, the temple, and . . ."

"The chin. Let's go over it all again."

"Enough. I'm tired. You're tired. You need to get to Fox Falls." And I needed to visit Raven Arnett.

"I just think you should try—"

"Beau, look." I pointed toward the east. "Look at that beautiful sky." The sun peeked out from a hill, a radiant beam of yellow just warming up for the day, the clouds gathering around it in little worshipping puffs. "My word, isn't that view incredible?"

He closed the distance between us, his side pressed to mine. We stood there for a long moment, taking it in.

When Beau finally spoke, his voice was hushed as the river. "I promised myself if I made it out alive, I wouldn't take anything for granted. Things like this—a sunrise, a sunset, the serenade of crickets, the feel of the creek on my skin. Things the guys we lost would never get the chance to experience again. But I let go of that. Got busy with life and the business . . . and just forgot."

I gave the words a moment to linger between us before responding. "But I know you didn't forget those men for a second. They're with you all the time. Even when you're asleep." I rubbed my hand across his strong back. "You're a good man, Beau Hudson."

"I wasn't good enough."

"How can you say that? You saved lives and—"

"Drop it." The gravel crunched beneath his feet as he swiftly walked back to the ATV.

"Beau."

But he climbed onto the four-wheeler and revved up the engine 'til it roared, drowning out anything else I had to say.

CHAPTER THIRTY-TWO

T HE GOLDEN SUNSET that followed us home Saturday morning was no match for the dark cloud hovering in the cab of Beau's truck. Conversation was cold as a forgotten coffee, the radio played terrible songs, and we nearly ran over Mrs. Ruckle's aging poodle, Mr. Curly Pants.

When I saw two familiar senior citizens sitting on our front porch, I knew my morning sprinkle of awkward was about to turn into a full-on shower.

"Don't make any sudden movements," I said as we got out of his Ford. "They're likely packing heat."

Beau opened his car door as if grateful for the escape.

Sylvie stood up from the mint green glider. "Your house gets burgled, and I gotta hear about it from Maria Jiménez's daughter's loser husband Barney, who always shorts me on the bacon on my breakfast burrito at the diner?"

Frannie fanned herself. "If a man shorted me bacon, I'd introduce him to my four friends: righty, lefty, Smith, and Wesson."

"It was late." I stepped onto the porch. "I didn't want to worry you."

"You didn't have to," Sylvie said. "Bacon Stealing Barney did it for you." She slid those sly eyes between Beau and me.

"Where've you two been?"

"The creek." Beau settled himself into a metal chair, a grin back on his face as he enjoyed the show. "A little early morning fishing."

Sylvie's eyes narrowed like a viper primed to strike. "Where'd you sleep last night, Paisley?"

"With me." Beau slipped on his Ray-Bans.

"That's not true." I gave his shoulder a smack. "But I did sleep at his house."

"You rake!" Sylvie leapt to her feet. "You've compromised my granddaughter."

"You've sullied her reputation!" Frannie threw her hands wide. "She'll be cut off from all society and forever left on the shelf."

I bit back a giggle.

"She was a diamond of the first water!" Sylvie cried. "I insist you marry her!"

"Or pistols at dawn!" Frannie said. "Name your seconds!"

From behind those sunglasses, Beau's eyes met mine. And we both laughed.

The earlier tension evaporated like the light morning fog. "Don't mind these two," I said. "They've read way too much historical romance lately." I wrapped my arms around my grandmother and leaned my tired head on her shoulder. "And Sylvie, unless you're willing to pony up for a really big dowry to give us, we're not getting married."

She sighed dramatically. "It was worth a shot. Was there at least some hanky-panky?"

"None," I said.

Frannie shook her head in disgust. "Sometimes it's like we're not even related."

"Did *The Sheik's Pregnant Secretary* teach you nothing?" Sylvie asked.

"Beau never once asked me to join his harem."

"Young people today." Sylvie shot Beau a withering look. "You bore me."

"So, a break-in, huh?" Thankfully, Frannie was ready to get back to business.

"The place is pretty trashed." I pulled my house key out of my purse and opened the door, the others following.

"Holy detonator buttons." Sylvie turned a full circle in my living room. "This is almost as bad as that time Frannie and I accidentally detonated that tiny explsoive in a Topeka KMart."

"Right in the ladies' undergarment section." Frannie stepped over a ripped couch cushion. "There were bras and frillies all the way to the garden center."

"Bloomers as far as the eye could see." My grandmother made her way to the kitchen and stopped when she saw the dishes in the floor. "My mother's china."

"I'm sorry," I said.

Sylvie sighed. "They're just things. What matters is that you and Mr. Morality are okay." She then regarded Beau. "Thank you for looking out for my granddaughter."

Beau smiled. "Anytime."

"I still think you should marry her within the hour."

"I'm giving a fish-gutting workshop at Fox Falls."

"Maybe another time." She inspected the drawers on the floor, careful not to touch anything with her hands. "I'll have some friends stop by to see if they get any prints."

"I think the police have already done that," Beau said.

Sylvie's look clearly said *bless your simple little heart.* "What was taken?"

"As far as I can tell, nothing," I said. "It's going to take some time to know for sure, but my diamond earrings are still sitting on the bathroom counter, the TV's still here, though in pieces, and even the ring Mom and Dad gave me for my first Grammy is right where I left it. I did a quick inventory of my shoe collection, and not so much as one heel is missing."

Beau rubbed his chin. "So the robber has taste . . ."

Funny. "The bad news is Sasha's iPad is now a useless heap of trash—and I never got to fully check it out."

"That could've been your perp's target," Frannie said. "We'll still have to inspect everything to see if this was a ploy to install bugs or cameras, but what if your intruder wanted to toss the place to make it look like simple vandalism?"

Beau let his weary eyes rest on me. "Or what if they just wanted to scare Paisley off the case?"

"A very viable option." Sylvie pulled a pair of latex gloves from her pocket as if carrying them was as normal as having a tissue or Chapstick. "Where's the iPad?"

"My bedroom floor."

We followed my grandmother down the hall. "This poor bedroom surely got the worst of it."

"Actually this is pretty much what it always looks like." I popped a sagging drawer back into place with my hip. "Just the iPad and a mirror got smashed."

Frannie gloved up and retrieved the white tablet from a pile of laundry. "Not much left of it. That hard drive looks like it went through the woodchipper."

"So it's hopeless?" I asked. "I'd barely looked at it."

Frannie picked up a few more pieces. "I'd categorize it as impossible."

"Which happens to be her specialty." Sylvie winked. "Now don't you worry about a thing, shug. By the time you get home tonight, my friends will have analyzed this crime scene, put a new security system in place, and set everything back to rights. If there's any evidence here, they'll find it."

"Who are these people?" I asked.

Sylvie and Frannie ignored my question and escorted us out of the bedroom.

"Thank you again for taking care of my granddaughter last night, Beau," Sylvie said as we returned to the front porch.

"He was great." I smiled at Beau, who leaned against the porch rail, his hands shoved in the pockets of his jeans. "He even taught me some self-defense moves."

"How to use a water bottle as a silencer?" Frannie asked.

Beau arched a brow. "No."

Sylvie's eyes lit. "How to make a lead pipe out of wrenches and an umbrella?"

"The old jab-a-pen-in-the-throat trick?" Frannie suggested.

Sylvie shooed a fly. "Did he at least teach you to build a Molotov cocktail with fuel and a tampon?"

"Fresh out of feminine products," Beau said.

"And you call yourself a soldier." Sylvie stepped off the porch. "Come on, Frannie, we have work to do."

Her friend followed behind her. "Crime is so invigorating."

We watched them drive away in Frannie's minivan, windows rolled down, vintage Jay Z bumping from the speakers.

"They're kind of frightening," Beau said.

"They are." I thought of the jigsaw puzzle that was the iPad. "Let's just hope they're effective."

CHAPTER THIRTY-THREE

A T TEN A.M. I mashed my finger on Raven Arnett's doorbell, uncertain as to what was waiting for me on the other side.

Raven opened the door, her face pale and devoid of expression. "Hey, Paisley. Thanks for stopping by, but I'm afraid I've come down with something and don't feel so well. Is it okay if we talk another time?"

"Oh." *Seriously?* "Um, okay. Sure."

"Thanks. I'll call you later and—"

"Let her in, Raven." Phoebe Chen butted her way into the entrance, looking nothing like the apprehensive young woman I'd met before. "If you don't tell her, I will."

Tell me what?

Raven's posture deflated. "Come on in." Her tone carried a root-canal level of enthusiasm. "Can I get you something to drink? Some snacks? Chips? A peek at my new *People* magazine, which mentions you finding a dead body on page 97?"

"Quit stalling." Phoebe speared her friend with a harsh look. "Why don't we all just take a seat?"

I followed the two through the small entryway to the living room. The decorating style came as a shock, as it was as vivid and colorful as Raven's personality was not. I knew she'd just graduated with a law degree, but if her legal endeavors didn't work out, she definitely had career potential in interior design.

"I love what you've done with the place." She had taken a cookie-cutter apartment and made it her own.

"Thank you," Raven said. "Decorating is a hobby of mine."

The couch was accented with navy and coral pillows, made of material and patterns that shouldn't have matched but somehow did. Over a chipped white mantel hung a wooden sign emblazoned with a Jane Austen quote in an elegant and whimsical font. Bookshelves to the right and left of the couch were painted a pale cream and trimmed in eclectic hardware. Raven was one of those who, unlike me, didn't use her book-shelves to store books and stack junk she didn't want to deal with, but instead staged them with quirky items such as a jar of seashells, a glitter dipped globe, and an old red typewriter. She clearly had a brilliant grasp of balance and symmetry, and I stepped closer to get a better view of some of her framed photos on the shelves.

"I need you to decorate my house," I said. "I'm kinda going with a moving boxes and lawn chair motif right now." I inspected an eye-catching photo on the top shelf in front of me. "Venice, Italy. That was one of my favorite places when I used to tour."

She spoke quietly behind me. "My father took me there for my high school graduation."

"Why don't you sit down, Paisley?" Phoebe asked.

"Oh, and this photo here." I tapped on the glass of a frame. "I love the angle in which you've captured the skirts of the Eiffel Tower. The lighting is incredible. Did you use a filter? Because—" My lips shut on the next words as I got a look at the picture beside it.

Raven cleared her throat. "Why don't we just sit down and talk for a minute?"

"What is this?" I grabbed a photo of a couple embracing, the sun shining a halo of light around them. A man held Raven close, his lips parted in laughter, an unmistakable glow of love in Raven's eyes. "This is you and Evan. When was this taken?"

"A little over a year ago." Raven wilted onto the love seat like a flower.

"Raven, did *you* kill Sasha?" I really needed to work on my delivery, but the question tumbled out and demanded to be heard.

Raven's long, black hair swished as she shook her head. "No, I didn't. And I've been afraid that someone would think I did." She glanced at Phoebe, whose wide eyes were telling her to get on with it. "I've been withholding information that may be helpful to your case."

Phoebe gestured for me to join her on the couch. "Raven saw something the morning of Sasha's murder." She nudged her friend. "Tell her. Tell her what you told me."

Raven reached for the photo in my hand and studied it wistfully, as if wishing she could jump back into that moment. "You have to understand that Evan was mine. I dated him first. We met at a party a year and half ago to celebrate the hundredth birthday of the law school. We struck up a conversation at the punch bowl and somehow ended up talking all night. You can't understand how captivating he was."

I'd hocked a two-carat engagement ring last year that said

differently. "What is it with Evan seducing every female from Sugar Creek?"

"What we had was real. It transcended anything Sasha thought she felt for him. He and I only dated for two months, and it may have been a very short time, but it was long enough to fall madly in love with one another. And then she came along."

"Sasha stole him from you?" I asked.

"More like a ripped him from my arms." The stoic Raven wiped away tears. "A group of us went out to eat one night— Evan and me, a few other couples, Sasha and whatever boy she was dating that week. Sasha flirted with all of the men there. She thrived on turning any guy's head, on being the center of attention. I was pretty used to it. I even made the mistake of thinking Evan loved me too much for the extra attention he was giving her to mean anything. Two weeks later Evan broke up with me, telling me that he had deep feelings for Sasha and had to follow his heart."

I rolled my eyes. "Evan and his wandering heart line. When will women stop falling for his crap?" For a moment, I thought he deserved whatever fate his loan sharks would deal him. "You're better off without him. Trust me."

"You don't understand. We had a soul connection. We could talk for hours. Anything from classical music to the Constitution. He had nothing in common with Sasha, the girl who was supposed to be my friend. All she wanted was to be the arm candy of someone important. And he wanted a trophy wife. But I would've been more than that. We could have been a political power couple."

"But he chose her," I said. "So you got angry, and you got revenge."

"No!" Phoebe said. "She did go off the deep end just a little bit—I'll give her that. But Raven is not a killer. Tell her, Raven."

"I kind of stalked Sasha the last few weeks of her life," Raven said. "I'm not proud of it, and I know it makes me look mentally unbalanced and a prime candidate for offing my ex-friend, but I didn't do it. But I did see something that day you should probably know about."

"And what is that?"

"I saw someone run into Enchanted Events that morning during the time Sasha had an appointment, then exit your business not five minutes later. Someone who would've had no reason being there unless it was to speak to Sasha."

"And who was that? Evan?"

"No." Raven set her photo on the coffee table. "Professor Fielding."

I straightened my spine, my every limb and cell alert with attention. "Was that why you mentioned him in the salon? Were they having an affair?"

"They definitely had a relationship before," Raven said, "and I don't know what happened inside the building—but I do know he came out very upset."

"How do you know they had an affair?"

"We both knew," Phoebe said. "It was years ago, but she did very little to hide it. Forcing her way into his classes, spending time in his office, showing up at school events where he'd be. It was a strange game of cat and mouse to her. And I'm not sure she ever let go of that."

"Do you think they were still seeing each other?" I asked. "Maybe Professor Fielding went to end it or demand Sasha break up with Evan."

"I don't know." Disgust laced Raven's voice. "She never would've broken her engagement to Evan. She thought she finally had it all, and that together they'd take on Washington and be the most glamorous couple to hit Pennsylvania Avenue. But whether she still felt anything for Fielding, I'm not sure. I got the impression he was more of a game she once played."

"Yeah," Phoebe said. "I think she genuinely liked the professor and pursued him years ago, and even though she told the story differently, our theory is the professor broke up with her and she never got over it. I'm not sure she'd ever been rejected by a man in her life."

Raven sighed, as if unfolding the details exhausted her. "Sasha would say weird things like, 'I'm going to make him sorry.' Or, 'He'll regret that he doesn't have me in his life anymore.' And then she would just laugh."

"I need to go to the police with this information," I said. "Do you have any photos of the professor entering or leaving the building?"

"I don't," Raven said.

"You're kind of a crappy stalker."

"I'll go to the police myself," Raven said. "I just thought you should hear this from me." Phoebe cleared her throat again. "Okay, *Phoebe* thought you should hear this from me."

"I know you've put your detective hat on," Phoebe said, "so I was hoping this would be useful for you."

"The Professor Fielding angle is something I definitely need to pursue further. I think it's time he and I had another chat." As I stood, Raven continued to clutch her beloved photo. "I know you don't believe me now, Raven, but you're better off without Evan. He's only interested in his own gain, and he'll do anything and hurt anyone to get to the top. Somewhere out there is a good man, a man of integrity, and he's gonna love you more than you ever loved Evan. And he'll be worth the wait."

With trembling lips, a teary-eyed Raven nodded. "Thank you."

"By the way," I said, "would either of you happen to know anything about an anonymous phone call to Mr. Chandler with a tip about Zoey and Sasha's car accident?"

The two looked at one another.

"Mr. Chandler needed to know Zoey was innocent," Raven said.

Phoebe walked me to the door. "Thank you for coming. And thank you for not tearing into Raven for withholding that information."

"I gotta know what secret Sasha held over Raven's head all these years."

"I barely recall." Phoebe's face was angelic innocence. "Might've been something about a paper-writing business at the university. Such a long time ago . . . Who can remember now?"

I was pretty sure one Phoebe Chen did. "Well, I won't keep the information about Professor Fielding to myself, but I don't see any reason to pass anything else on."

"Be careful, Paisley. I don't have a good feeling about Fielding, and I never have."

I waited until I was out of the neighborhood before I rang up

Sylvie. "I have some news to share with you."

"Bring it to my house," she said. "Frannie and I have some vital intel for you as well."

CHAPTER THIRTY-FOUR

I STOOD ON Sylvie's front porch and had barely lifted a fist to knock when the door flew open.

Frannie scanned the outside perimeter, then whisked me inside. "What took you so long?"

"I got stuck behind traffic." Which in this town meant either a school bus or J.C. Beazer's cows crossing Lee Town Road for their twice-daily milking.

Sylvie stepped into the foyer. "Pat her down."

Frannie immediately complied, her hands roaming like an overzealous TSA agent.

I slapped her away. "Hey! Watch it!"

"She's clear." Frannie stepped back. "Commence with the full body scan."

"Nobody is scanning this body. I'm leaving if—" But my grandmother whipped out a flashing gadget that whined with the exuberance of a dying bagpipe, tracing the air around my clothes.

Sylvie stuffed the device in the pocket of her skinny capris. "Clear."

"Enough." I threw up my hands. "All I wanted to do was talk to you. Can I just quickly share some information before I have to give you my bra size and a urine sample?"

"Urine sample." Sylvie looked at Frannie and laughed. "That's so 2005."

"We're checking you for any bugs or traces you might unknowingly be carrying," Frannie said. "It's befallen many an unsuspecting heroine."

"In Sugar Creek?"

Sylvie lifted her spa-sculpted chin. "I think the events of the last month prove you cannot trust this seemingly quaint hamlet."

"The living room has been cleared for further discourse," Frannie said. "Let us adjourn there." She pressed her fingers to her lips in a silent *shhh* and motioned for us to follow.

"Okay, now we can talk." Sylvie closed the double doors behind us as we entered the sanctuary. "You may scoff at our security measures, but clearing your name and keeping you safe are priority one."

"I'm sorry." I righted my rumpled shirt. "What is it you need to tell me?"

"You first, shug." Sylvie gracefully descended into a chair and picked up a tea glass sweating on a coaster. "Wha'cha got?"

"I just came from Raven Arnett's house and had quite the interesting conversation with her and Phoebe." As Sylvie and Frannie listened with rapt attention, I filled them in on all I'd learned. "Why would the professor go talk to Sasha at Enchanted Events?"

"We might be able to shed some light on that," Sylvie said. "But first, Frannie called in a favor and got us a peek at Carson Fielding's bank accounts."

I took a step back. "Is this one of those things where I wake up in the morning with no memory of having this information?"

"Mr. Fielding has a few accounts, but he has one in his name only at the Ozark National Bank." Sylvie arched a brow. "Mr. Down on His Luck gets a bimonthly deposit from the Sugar Creek Gallery in very large amounts."

"Like five-figure deposits," Frannie said. "I called a friend at the gallery who confirmed the man's paintings still sell like he's Picasso."

"So he's not flat broke," I said. "I wonder if his wife knows that."

"Let's move on to our biggest news. Frannie was able to salvage Sasha's iPad carcass." Sylvie cleared a spot on the coffee table. "You're not going to believe our good fortune. Frannie, show her the goods."

"The iPad itself is a loss, but I was able to resurrect her hard drive." Frannie lifted the hem of her floral shirt, exposing a pink tank and a laptop secured to her tummy with giant straps of Velcro. "I transferred the data to my own computer, but I had to make a quick run to the Dixie Dairy for half-price shakes. I wanted to keep this thing safe." She undid the first strap. "Though it might be a tad sweaty."

"Ew."

"Be grateful," Frannie said. "Sylvie wanted to stuff it down my britches, but I told her no. Obviously that's where I keep my burner cell phone and switchblade." She rested the laptop on top of a magazine with Oprah's smiling face. "Sasha's hard drive wasn't in the worst shape, but the girl did have a brain and managed to hide some pretty important files she'd deleted."

"But Frannie here found them," Sylvie said. "Get a load of these pictures."

High-def images popped onto the screen. "Whoa!" I shielded my eyes. "Too much skin! Make it go away!"

"Sorry." Frannie's fingers flew over the keys. "Those are my dating profile pics for Sexy Single Seniors. Moving on!"

"Good heavens," Sylvie said. "Will you stay focused? And I told you that was too much cleavage. Now, Paisley, allow us to present your next plot twist."

The file opened, and Frannie supersized one photo, then another.

Photos of Sasha lip-locked with a man.

"Professor Fielding." I moved in closer for a better look as she scrolled through snapshots of the duo embracing and kissing at various locations, a handful in Sugar Creek, a few even on campus. "They were clearly in a relationship."

"And not a professional one," Sylvie said.

I pointed to a photo of some serious canoodling. "One that could totally tank a career."

"Or provide fuel for a good blackmail scheme," Frannie said. "These were taken over two years ago."

"Someone was blackmailing Sasha?" I asked.

Frannie opened her mouth to respond, only to be interrupted. "No," Sylvie said. "Let Paisley think about this."

The two women watched me expectantly, as if it was the final round of *Jeopardy!* and I'd just been handed the easy topic of Things That Meow. "So if you don't think someone was blackmailing Sasha, then . . . *oh*." The light bulb finally sparked. "You think Sasha was blackmailing the professor."

Sylvie sniffed indelicately. "Frannie, I do believe she's one of us."

Her best friend blinked her misty eyes. "So proud."

"It certainly makes a twisted sort of sense." I clicked through more photos. "The professor should've been making a killing selling his art, but instead he lives like he's fallen on hard times. It would explain where Sasha got the large sums of money she'd been giving Evan. And also how she funded a wedding big enough to rival any British monarch's. I know the professor abused his authority, and his behavior is deplorable, but the photos don't paint her in a flattering light either. Why would she risk her own reputation?"

"Classic narcissistic personality," Sylvie said. "From what we've learned of her, she was manipulative enough to have played the victim if the photos were released. But in Sasha's brain, I'm sure she thrived on the control and never thought her plan wouldn't work. Failure wasn't a consideration."

"Everything else had certainly worked for her in life," I said. "Every single scheme Sasha concocted. She'd had a lifetime of people bowing to her pressure and bidding."

Frannie tapped a photo on the screen. "Until the good professor snapped."

"Tell Paisley the rest of it, Frannie."

"Photos weren't the only things I discovered." Frannie's hot pink nails clacked on the keyboard. "I might've hacked into Sasha's web-based email account."

"How?" This sounded shady.

"I found a document she'd saved with all her passwords on it," Frannie said.

Sylvie's eyes rolled skyward. "Oh, the young, foolish, and digitally naïve."

"I did a history search using the name of the photo files, and voilà!" Frannie opened a series of documents. "Sasha didn't even bother using a dummy account to send her blackmail messages. Just her own email. She'd trashed them, but they were no match for my recovery skills." She pushed up her bifocals. "Also in her email I found a Groupon for half-off pole dancing classes—so, Sylvie, get your spandex ready."

"Send all those files to me," I said.

"You want in on the discount?" Frannie asked. "I can get you a referral code. Gets me another five percent off."

I hugged my aunt. "You two are the best. It's quite possible you've just saved my life."

Sylvie stepped in and joined the huddle. "So that's a yes on the classes?"

"No."

"Might help things along with your Beau," Frannie said.

"He's not my Beau." I swatted each of them on the tush. "I need to get going."

Sylvie rushed to stand in the doorway. "Do *not* go see the professor by yourself."

"Wouldn't dream of it." Freedom was so close, I wanted to sing. "I plan on inviting the police."

CHAPTER THIRTY-FIVE

I T WAS A great day to catch a killer.

Shirley the Camry shimmied as I pulled into the parking lot of the Arkansas A&M art gallery. It had been easy to get Carson Fielding's location, after sixty seconds of talking with the grad student who manned the phones in the departmental office.

My cell trilled with an unidentified number as I reached for the door handle. "Hello?"

"Paisley? This is Carol at Sugar Creek Formals."

"Hey, Carol." This was a horrible time to talk. "Can I call you back later?"

"I have a dress coming in that I'd like you to look at. I think it's a pretty good match to Emma's first pick."

"Yeah, sure. When should I stop by?"

"It should be here by Friday morning."

"I'll be there."

"I think you're going to love it!"

My goodness. Everything was looking up. "Great. See you then."

I grabbed my purse, which contained some pepper spray and a random screwdriver, then waited for the familiar beep as I locked my car. After living in LA, locking my car was just a mindless habit—so I was almost certain Shirley had been broken into the day Emma's dress had been stolen. It had to be related to the investigation, but why would the professor steal a wedding dress?

Following the cracked sidewalk, I walked up the geranium-lined path to the gallery. I pulled on the double doors and paused as I stepped inside. The grad student had said I'd find the professor inside setting up new displays, so I continued past the small lobby. The gallery provided a chilly contrast to the sweltering heat outside. It was eerily quiet, save for the *click-clomp* of my heels on the floor, and the air carried the scent of paint and glue. I breezed past a white canvas with a red dot in the center. The placard stated that it was a famous piece on loan from the Met. It looked more like an accidental drip from a paintbrush. Some of the work I passed put my stick-figure drawing to shame, but other items looked like the results of a drunken trip to the craft store.

Rounding a corner, the hall led me to a well-lit wing of paintings and enlarged photos. I stopped and took a quick peek.

"That's a Japanese internment camp in southeastern Arkansas."

Startled, I trained my features before turning. And found Professor Fielding before me.

"What you're looking at here is a senior project by Tyler, one of my students. I'm really proud of it." He nodded to one of the paintings, done mostly in black, white, and gray. "The photos are of the location now, juxtaposed with paintings that capture recollections of Tyler's great-grandfather, who was imprisoned there."

It was hard to focus on the art when I was most likely standing next to a cold-blooded killer. "I vaguely remember learning about this place in school."

"It's not talked about much, and isn't a part of history the state's proud of, but the camp was open for a solid three years. I think he's captured so much here—the pain of losing your home and all your belongings, of being herded up like criminals, and even some of the beauty as they worked to stay together as a family."

"I definitely understand people labeling you, thinking you're someone you're not." I ventured to another set, stalling for time. The police had to be en route soon. "Tyler's work is brilliant." I took a detailed inspection of the paintings and photography. Chief O'Hara had warned me to stay away from Fielding when Sylvie and I had tracked the sleeping policeman down at midnight last night. He'd been none too happy to see us on his doorstep, but thanks to whatever strings Sylvie pulled with the judge and the information she forked over, an arrest warrant had been issued within the last hour. According to my grandmother's last text, the arresting cavalry were on their way.

"This is the kind of art I enjoy. The red dot back there?" I jerked my head toward the entrance. "Totally beyond me."

"The beautiful thing about art is there's something for everyone." Fielding dropped his voice to a stage whisper. "And that painting from the Met baffles most of us." He straightened a painting of a Japanese woman standing in front of a barrack, her red ribbon the only color in the piece. "But I don't think you're here to get a tour of the summer school projects, are you?"

My pulse stuttered, and I glanced at the phone in my palm. With one push of a button, I'd have 911. "No, I didn't drop by to peruse some art, beautiful though it may be. I'm sure your wife mentioned I stopped by your house to talk to you."

He looked genuinely puzzled. Fielding was very good at this. "No, she didn't."

"I had some questions about Sasha Chandler suspiciously taking some of your art classes, and Anna Grace was able to shed a little light."

"Was she? And what exactly did she tell you?"

"That you allowed Sasha into your classes because you were a broke teacher, and she paid you—or purchased your artwork as a gift of her . . . appreciation."

"I'm not really comfortable commenting on that."

"Your wife assured me it was strictly platonic between you and Sasha." I watched the professor's mouth tighten. "But it wasn't, was it?"

"I don't know what you mean."

"You don't want to talk about that? Okay, how about we discuss something else? Like how you were in Sugar Creek at the time of Sasha's death." It was satisfying to watch his arrogant face pale.

"Again, I'm not sure what you mean."

"Did you forget you were at Enchanted Events?"

His Adam's apple bobbed as he swallowed.

"I have a witness who can place you at my shop minutes before Sasha keeled over."

"I didn't kill her," he said. "Why would I kill her?"

"Because she was blackmailing you. I know you broke into my house and destroyed Sasha's iPad."

"What?" His voice rose above the hush of the gallery. "How

would I know you had her iPad, or know where you live, or . . . Why on earth would I even want her iPad?"

"It's where she stored the photos of the two of you together. The very photos she used to extort a lot of money."

He combed his fingers through his shoulder-length hair and huffed a breath. "Okay, I went to see her. I followed her that morning and knew when she went into Enchanted Events. I finally had my opportunity to get her attention, to get her to listen to me. Over the last few weeks she'd refused my calls, avoided all of my attempts to see her in person. I went there knowing I'd stand in the middle of your store and shout out my message if I had to. But when I found her in that little room, it was perfect. Just the two of us."

"Yeah, perfect for distracting her with an argument, then bashing her over the head with a champagne bottle."

"I don't recall a bottle in there. I don't recall anything on the table."

"And what did you tell Sasha?"

"I told her I was done giving her money, that she could go to the public with the photos for all I cared. I'd been so stupid. I kept meeting her outrageous demands, and I realized way too late that she'd never go public with those photos after she got engaged to Evan Holbrook. She wouldn't want to sully her image as a politician's wife. So I confronted her and called her bluff. I'd spent two years paying that witch off, and I was through. It felt good to say the words. And yes, it felt good to see her squirm. But I didn't kill her. I'm not a murderer. I'm an artist and a simple professor."

"A professor who has affairs with students."

His eyes flashed. "I'm not proud of that."

"If this got out, you'd most likely lose your job here."

"I make a killing with my paintings. And if I wasn't handing Sasha over a monthly wad of cash, I wouldn't even have to work here."

"How much did you pay her?"

"Thirty grand a month."

Geez. I'm not sure I made that much after my first gold record. "That's a significant amount of money over a couple of years. Lots of debt you had to take on. It probably took a toll on your marriage, your personal life. Naturally that would make you angry and bitter. Wanting a little revenge."

"Yes, Sasha drained me of a lot of cash. But I decided I didn't care anymore."

"How convenient." My ears perked at the sound of wailing sirens. "Then you made everyone think I killed her. Let's stick it to the new girl in town, right? The one who already had a reputation of being unbalanced."

"What? No."

"You came into Enchanted Events that morning and killed Sasha, knowing whoever had served her would take the fall."

The professor's face flushed red, and he'd lost all of that schmoozing charm. "I went to talk to her. That's all. She was certainly alive when I left."

"Then when you realized I was digging around to clear my name, you tried to scare me off."

"I'm telling you, I had no motive to kill Sasha."

The sirens grew closer, louder. "I guess you can tell that to the police."

As Professor Fielding's visible panic grew, my own anxiety ebbed. There was something morbidly satisfying about watching the man who would've let me go to jail for life get his just desserts. He'd stalked me, invaded my home, and given me nightmares about orange jumpsuits and iron bars.

When the police escorted him out, I knew I'd sleep well for the first night since Sasha's death.

CHAPTER THIRTY-SIX

I AWOKE MONDAY morning with a song in my spirit and a skip in my step. It was one of those times you wanted a movie soundtrack to highlight your life because it would be glorious, it would be snappy, and it would involve doing spritely leaps across the entire yard until you spun, arms outstretched, like Julie Andrews in *The Sound of Music*.

I was free!

Thanks to the good Lord, gun-toting grannies, and one spurned ex-girlfriend of Evan's, I was free.

Up earlier than usual, I couldn't wait to get to Enchanted Events and start finalizing Emma's wedding. After showering in speedy fashion, I made quick work of getting ready. Letting my curls go as free as I felt, I piled them on top of my head and slipped into a hot pink pencil skirt, a tank, and a fuchsia blazer with giant onyx buttons. I'd worn the piece when the Electric Femmes had played Madison Square Garden ten years ago. It was a little tight, but who cared? I wasn't going to jail!

Stepping onto the porch at six a.m., purse hanging from my shoulder and coffee in hand, I stopped and inhaled the fresh-cut grass and the roses that skirted the porch. Was it just me, or was the sun brighter than usual? Were the birds singing more melodiously than ever? Were those clouds extra puffy and white?

The door beside mine opened, and out spilled Beau wearing boots, faded jeans, a Razorback ball cap, and a sleepy grin. "Mornin'."

My heart floated toward the sky. "Good morning. This is kind of late for you."

"And early for you." Like old times, he reached for my coffee, sealed his lips to the lid, and took a long sip. "I hear they arrested Professor Fielding this weekend."

"You won't have visit me in prison with a pocketful of nail files."

He eyed me over the cup. "Saves me from getting a new neighbor."

"Your enthusiastic compassion will be the air I breathe all day."

His grin deepened, dimpling his left cheek. "Congratulations, Paisley. I know you're relieved." He slipped his arms around me and pulled me to his chest. "We all are."

My hands automatically went around his waist, as if that's where they naturally belonged. I lifted my face, only to find Beau's lips hovering—

Ring! Ring!

He took a step back and another drink of my coffee. "You should probably get that."

As my phone continued its untimely, rude intrusion, I watched the fire in Beau's eyes cooling. "Right. Good idea." I cleared my throat as I read the display. My agent. "Hello?"

"Great news, Paizzzz!"

"Hey, Rad."

"Guess who had a terrific phone call with Riviera Cruises las night? Me! And you know what? They've finally offered you a gig with the Blast From the Past tour and agreed to bring you on with no expectations of you singing any solos. You can sing harmony all day long. Isn't that fab? Didn't I tell ya I'd take care of you? Didn't I swear I'd get you back on track?"

I wasn't sure singing in a venue that was basically a floating buffet was "back on track." "Thanks, Rad."

"What? That's all I get? No tears of joy? No squeals of delight?"

"I'm . . . I'm really pleased. When would I start?"

"You sail out of New Orleans in six weeks."

"Nice." I waited for the elation and relief to hit. I had a job in the entertainment field, and I should be happy.

"Now about that image consultant I've talked to you about. You really need to let her and her people get a hold of you before you embark on this next phase of your career. It's not just a hair trim and some makeup we're talking about here. She does brand management, a Hollywood level makeover, and for an additional $199.99, she'll throw in her patented colon cleanse."

I didn't even want to know.

"You just need to get me a check for five big ones pronto."

I had that much saved up finally.

"I'm telling you, Paizzz, Fatima is a miracle worker. Do you remember that child actress Darita Boles? She had that triumphant burst back into movies, right? Guess who gave her a total image face-lift?"

"Fatima?"

"Totes. And Billy McGee, the kid who had two number-one hits ten years ago when he was sixteen? The guy who's now sitting at the top of the Billboard chart and just signed a modeling deal with Ralph Lauren? He was a nobody 'til Fatima got a hold of him. Five grand may seem like a large deposit, but it'll be a drop in the bucket to the eventual windfall." His guffaws bellowed in my ear. "After I take my twenty percent, that is."

"I think you mean fifteen."

He continued his off-key chortles. "Right, Paiz. Right."

"Okay, Rad." I locked eyes with Beau, who stood there with one eyebrow lifted and apparently no intention of giving me some privacy. "Thanks for the update. I'll get back with you."

"Wait, I need a verbal commitment from you. What do I tell Riviera Cruises?"

Tell them they're the direction I never want to sail to. "Tell them I'm checking my schedule."

I ended the call and leaned against a porch post, grateful for the light breeze that slid over my skin.

"Is that the call you've been waiting for?" Beau asked. "The agent?"

"Yeah." I stuffed the phone in my jacket pocket. "The cruise line finally met my terms and offered me a job."

"Good." He watched me a little too closely. "I'm sure that makes you really happy."

A duo of robins sang from a nearby oak tree. "Yes."

"So I guess you'll be selling Enchanted Events."

"I have to meet with the attorney next week, but if it's back in the black, then . . . that's what I'll do."

"Is that what you want?"

"Of course it is. The cruise is a humble restart, but it's a step in the right direction."

"Is it?"

"What's that supposed to mean?"

"It means you're leaving this town, your family, your friends, and a career you've grown to love to go sing on a cruise ship."

"There's nothing wrong with my new job."

"No, not if that's what you really want to do."

"It is."

"I watched your face the entire phone call. Between your expression and your dismal tone, I assumed he'd given you bad news."

"So because I didn't break out into cartwheels, you think I don't want to leave Sugar Creek? Excuse me for being sleep-deprived from working in a business I have no experience with and trying to keep myself out of jail in my precious off-hours."

"Your lack of enthusiasm for the cruise job has nothing to do with any of that."

"Oh, and what does it have to do with?"

"You—you're scared to take a chance on a new life."

"What did you just say?" I advanced on the man like I was going to take him to the floor. "I am *not* scared. I may be scared of sleeping in a house that's been broken into, but I think I'm owed that one. Scared of the security system my grandmother installed malfunctioning and deploying missile launchers in the middle of the night? Absolutely. But scared of the opportunity my agent brought me? That would be a big fat *no*."

"Did you catch the part where I said you were unwilling to take a chance?"

"Too ridiculous to even acknowledge."

"I think the words you're looking for are 'spot on.' You have a good thing going here in Sugar Creek, and you're too chicken to stay and see it through. This bridal planning thing may not have been your first pick of careers, but you're doing it, Paisley, and you're doing it well."

"I've nearly taken the business under. I don't call that doing it well."

"That has everything to do with Sasha's murder and nothing to do with your ability. You have great ideas, your staff loves you, and you work your butt off. Why would you want to leave that?"

"Because weddings are not what I want to do with my life." Didn't anyone understand? "All I know is the music business. I didn't go to college, I didn't learn some trade. I didn't even marry well. Ten years invested in the music business is all I have. And I want to go back and start again. I can rebuild and rebrand."

"Not if you won't even sing solo on that cruise." He gestured to my phone. "I could hear everything your agent said."

I snatched what was left of my coffee from his hand. "That's my preference. I've always sung backup."

"Is that all there is to it?"

"So maybe I have a little performance anxiety after being gone from the stage so long. Is it wrong to want to ease my way back in?"

Beau glanced over at the neighbor, Babs Honeydew, watering her hostas and watching the drama unfold on our porch. "Something doesn't add up, and I don't know what it is—"

"I don't remember it ever being any of your business anyway."

"But what I do know is that you have a life here in Sugar Creek—one you're too afraid to live. If you stayed here, you could have your business. There's no limit to what you and Henry could accomplish with Enchanted Events."

"Did it ever occur to you that maybe I don't want to stay in Arkansas? That I don't want *People* magazine to do a 'Where Are They Now' series and see some tiny footnote about how I screwed up the music business so badly that I settled down in a tiny town in *Arkansas*!"

"You like this place."

"And I like Los Angeles. The nightlife. The restaurants. The culture. The close proximity to everything I need for my music career. It's where my life is. I have friends there. And as long as we're playing front porch therapy here, what about you?" I pointed my cup at him. "You're standing here telling me that I'm running away from the commitment of a business, when you can't even kiss me without following it up with a disclaimer."

Babs Honeydew dropped her garden hose with a clatter.

"I've never been anything but honest with you," Beau said.

"Maybe, but have you ever been honest with yourself? Huh? If I'm running, let me assure you, I'm in good company. You, sir, are sprinting from a whole pack of issues. You won't talk about your experience in Libya, and you're still not over it."

"I don't have to be over it."

"You do nothing to deal with it."

"You think I don't know that? I've seen a real counselor, Dr. None of Your Business, and I'm fully aware of my problem."

"When's the last time you saw this counselor? When's the

last time you had a decent night's sleep?"

"Sure as heck not since you moved to town."

"You work morning and night—"

"Because I have a business to run."

"But you do it so you won't have to stop and think—and feel. I don't know what you saw that day, and I'll never know that kind of emotional torture, but you are a hero, Beau Hudson. Those men didn't die so that you could come back and live out the rest of your days in self-punishing misery."

"You have no idea what you're talking about."

"Maybe I don't, but neither do you. My future isn't here, Beau. I love Sylvie and my family, and I've even learned to love that mess of a wedding business. But Enchanted Events could go under any day, and then what would I have? I've got too much time and talent invested in music to not go back and see that through. I can't throw that away. Music is my life. Not Enchanted Events. Not Sugar Creek." *And not you.*

I stomped off the porch, my heels teetering with every angry step. "The show's over, Mrs. Honeydew!"

Shirley the Camry roared to life, as if she, too, were furious. I peeled out of the driveway, not even bothering to look back toward the porch.

Pulling over a half-mile later, I dialed a familiar number. "Rad?" I wiped away the falling tears. "Tell Riviera Cruises . . . I'm in."

CHAPTER THIRTY-SEVEN

"PAISLEY, I THOUGHT you'd be happier about not being shipped to the Big House for murder." Sylvie sipped her vanilla Dr Pepper, then popped a fry between her red lips.

"Me too." Frannie accepted another glass of sweet tea from the waitress. "Yeah, Paisley, has something dimmed your happiness? Did Fielding's arrest interfere with some plans to bedazzle a prison uniform?"

"No, of course I'm thrilled to be cleared." Still, something nagged at me. Doubts of my own fate moving forward, I was sure. And a little sadness over departing soon. Not to mention, I definitely didn't like how I'd left things with Beau. I'd spent the last few days alternating between ignoring him and listening for the slightest sounds of his existence next door. We'd yet to run into one another, yet to speak again.

"Want to tell us about your fight with Captain Cutie?" Sylvie asked.

I stabbed a piece of romaine from my Cobb salad. "I won't bother asking how you know about that." While I was still wrestling with the idea of going back to Los Angeles in a few weeks, I'd be grateful to leave small-town gossip far behind. "We got in a fight. End of story."

Sylvie turned to me in the booth, her face way too close.

"Babs Honeydew said you kids made out before you started all the yelling."

Frannie nodded. "Said it got very PG-13."

"We just want you to know we approve," Sylvie remarked.

"Two thumbs up." Frannie demonstrated.

"No," I snapped. "Thumbs down. There was no making out. A little yelling, yes. But that's it."

"No kissy face?" Sylvie asked.

I glared at my grandmother until she returned her attention back to her cheeseburger.

"Okay, okay." Sylvie exchanged a disappointed look with Frannie. "Did Beau say hurtful things to you? Do you need us to take care of him?"

Frannie grabbed a napkin. "I know a guy in Des Moines who, for a nominal charge, can make his drinking water taste like dog pee."

The idea had some merit. "Beau heard me talking to my agent about the cruise gig. He said I didn't really want to take the job, that I was just doing it out of fear."

Sylvie bit into another fry. "Interesting."

"Who is he to tell me I'm living my life wrong? That *I'm* the one scared of a new direction? He knows nothing about my past or what's ahead for me." I'd peaked young, but my star had dimmed quickly. Jaz got to be the celebrity, the giant musical success, while I got hit with a hurricane and was expected to form a life with the debris. I was rather proud of myself for joining the cruise tour. "The cruise isn't my dream job, but it's a full-time income and nothing to be ashamed of."

"Nothing at all," Sylvie said. "Especially if it's what you

want. Instinct rarely steers you wrong. Just promise me you'll listen to your gut."

"Mine's a little hard to hear when I take so many antacids," Frannie said. "But she's right. Women like us have some serious intuition."

"I'm doing the right thing. Tomorrow I meet with my attorney and accountant, so it's not as if I'm not taking advisement from professionals." I was certain the peace and happiness of my decision would hit me at any moment. I probably had some lingering anxiety symptoms from the whole murder thing.

Not that leaving was going to be easy. I'd miss Sylvie and my family. I'd miss this town, which resembled nothing of the Sugar Creek I'd left years ago. I'd even grown to—dare I say it?—*love* it a tiny bit. While I was sailing the choppy seas and popping Dramamine like Tic Tacs, I'd think of the day I walked into Enchanted Events, expecting to find a mothball-scented, run-down office, but instead discovered an alternate universe where a model-gorgeous black man stood in the place of my great-aunt Zelda and created confectionary dream weddings. I'd think of the ladies who worked for us, who kept me on my toes and pushed me to dive in with all I had, whether I'd wanted to or not. I'd think of their own aspirations and ideas, just waiting for someone to give them wings.

I'd miss the blue skies, the clean air, the deer tiptoeing through my backyard, the rustic landscape of hills and trees, the chirps of birds, the bluegrass I could sometimes hear from the square.

A place that asked me to call it home. Made me consider, if only for a moment, settling in and rerouting my life's GPS for a brand-new path.

But I couldn't.

Music had been my life since I was sixteen, and despite the odds, it somehow wasn't through with me yet.

"We'll miss you, shug, but you need to do what's best for you." Sylvie reached for my hand on the table. "I love you, and I'm so grateful for the time we've had together, even if it did involve murder and some drama."

"Same here, babe," Frannie said. "I love you like my own. Probably more than my own, but that's the fault of my ex-husband's DNA. Anyway, you brought me and Sylvie the greatest gift."

I sniffed and dabbed at my eyes with a napkin. "What's that?"

"Shenanigans." Frannie joined her hand with ours. "We love our shenanigans."

"We've been so bored, and then you showed up." Sylvie rested her cheek against mine. "Thank you for finding a dead body."

"Amen." Frannie lifted a praise hand. "Thank you, Lord."

Good heavens, I would miss these two. "I love you guys too. So much." I hugged Sylvie and held onto Frannie.

Sylvie kissed my temple, and I breathed in the scent that was my beloved grandma. "As for Beau, sometimes it's easier to stay in your own pit and tell others how to get out of their foxholes," she said.

"What?"

Sylvie patted my leg. "I mean, sometimes we can't see how to get out of our own trouble, but we can clearly see how others can avoid it. It's quite possible he wants the best for you, that he cares about you enough to want you to have it all. Who knows?" She went back to her burger. "Maybe he's even right."

An alarm dinged on my phone, saving Sylvie from my blistering retort. "He's not right." I slipped my phone back into my purse. "I need to head over to Sugar Creek Formals. Carol's got that dress she wants to show me."

"I hope it's a match for Emma's," Frannie said.

"Me too." Sylvie stood to let me out of the booth. "Let me know if I can chip in."

"That's sweet of you to offer, but I can handle it by myself."

"I know you can." Sylvie clasped my shoulders. "But that's the beauty of home and family—you don't have to handle anything alone."

My throat thickened and I didn't trust myself to speak. So I hugged my grandmother again and slipped outside, scattering pieces of my heart behind me as I left.

"NOW THIS DRESS is a size ten, but you get the idea. I tracked this one down in Conway, but it's the only one they had. Looking at the picture of Emma's dress, I think it's darn near close."

I stood in the pink chiffon pouf ball that was Sugar Creek Formals while "Chapel of Love" serenaded us from speakers in the ceiling. "It's beautiful, Carol." The gown was nearly a duplicate, save for a subtle pattern difference in the beading.

Carol held a strapless A-line gown with lace appliqués, covered in thousands of beads and sequins in a floral design. She whished her hand over the skirt. "It has that blush color she wanted."

"And with the rose gold that's been so hard to find. How much is it?"

Carol sucked in her bottom lip, a sure sign of imminent bad news. "We could do a payment plan."

"How much?"

"It's a Gustav Renaldi, I'm afraid. I tried to find something cheaper, but nothing came as close to Emma's dress."

"How much?"

"Six thousand." She caught my grimace. "Her original cost at least that."

Emma had purchased another dress only last weekend, but when she'd shown it to me, she hadn't been able to cover her lack of enthusiasm for her last-minute selection.

"You say the word go, and I can have this altered to her measurements within a day," Carol said. "But you're running out of time."

"I'll think about it."

"Maybe we should tell Emma. Give her the option of buying it."

"No." I gave the gown one last look. "I'll let you know by this afternoon."

"And the wedding's in two days? That's really pushing it," Carol said. "Don't sit on this too long, Paisley, or your opportunity will be gone."

I let that thought roll around in my brain. "Thanks for finding it."

"Sure thing, hon." Carol smacked a wad of gum. "Oh, wait." She motioned me back, her eyes darting about for eavesdroppers. "We still have Sasha Chandler's wedding dress here. I've called her mother a few times, but she's yet to pick it up. What do you think I should do?"

"You mean it's here for alterations?"

"No, we hadn't gotten to that point yet."

Now I was confused. "The dress her sister Zoey made for her?"

She shook her head. "The custom Zalinza gown she ordered from London." Her voice dropped to a faint whisper. "The price tag makes our dress for Emma look like a garage sale find."

"You're saying Sasha intended to wear this Zalinza dress?"

"Come take a look."

I followed Carol past rows of gowns, back into a hallway where the air-conditioning rattled with chilly exuberance. We came to a storage area that surrounded us with racks and racks of dresses and suits. It seemed like a giant mess to me, but Carol walked right to a section and pulled out a bagged dress as if she had the key to this organization system.

"Over here." She gently rested the bag on a table, unzipped it, and held up its contents.

It was a gown fit for a queen. It shimmered. It sparkled. It was an ivory mix of bling and antique lace, with dainty cap sleeves and a train that would make a chapel aisle sigh with its caress.

"That's not the dress Zoey designed." I touched the crystals on the waistline.

"Far from it." Carol eased the gown back inside its protective cocoon. "And when Zoey found out her sister wasn't wearing her creation, she was as mad as a cat in a bubble bath."

"I'm not following. I saw Sasha's bridal book, the binder where she kept all her plans and ideas. She clearly had a photo of Zoey's dress. And Zoey told me herself her sister was wearing it." At the cost of Zoey's DUI. "She went to great lengths to get her sister to agree."

"Sasha had me handle the ordering of her Zalinza gown," Carol said. "We were to receive it and do the alterations. She came in almost daily, and we all dreaded the diva's frequent appearances. About a week before her death, Sasha did one of her drop-ins to see if the dress had arrived. It just so happened that UPS had delivered it that morning. I had no more taken it out of the bag than Zoey walked into my shop, searching for her sister. Zoey put two and two together, and the sisters had a giant row right next to the push-up bras and girdles. I had to grab that Zalinza dress and take it to safety because I wasn't paying for that thing if it got mangled."

"Are you certain you have this right? Some brides wear two dresses—one for the ceremony and one for the reception. Maybe that was Sasha's plan?"

"Nope. She looked her sister in the eye and bold as brass told her she had zero intention of wearing Zoey's dress. Sasha said the dress hadn't met her expectations, and it was her sister's own fault. The look on Zoey's face about broke my heart, the poor girl."

So Zoey knew her sister hadn't intended to wear her design.

Unease walked spiky fingers up my spine.

Sylvie had said to go with my instinct.

And right now that instinct said something was quite amiss.

CHAPTER THIRTY-EIGHT

"MR. JEFFCOAT AND Mr. Higgins are here for your nine o'clock," Layla said from the doorway of my office the next morning.

I held up a finger and finished my voicemail message. "So if you could call me back, Detective Ballantine, that would be great. It's imperative I talk to you." Ending the call, I sighed. I'd only called the man half a dozen times since yesterday. "Send them in, please."

She hesitated as she neared my desk. "These men are here to talk about selling Enchanted Events, aren't they?"

I felt like I was breaking up with everyone. "Yes. My two months is nearly up, and they're here to give me a status update and point me to the next step."

"I want you to know that yesterday Henry bought my kid a birthday present."

I blinked in confusion. "Okay."

"And last week when you were at an event, he had lunch delivered for everyone. And he promised Alice an hour of his undivided attention Monday to hear her ideas."

"I'm glad to hear that." I stood and smoothed my black faux-snakeskin pants. "Henry's a brilliant businessman, and I'm convinced there's a softy in there."

"You don't understand," Layla said. "He never acted like this 'til you came along. Paisley, you've changed him. I mean, sure he snapped at me this morning for parking in his spot and ordering invitations in the color of lemon cream when he requested lemon tart, and most people would still think he's this gorgeous, grouchy blowhard, but to us—he's changed. All thanks to you."

I would not cry in the office today. "Thank you, Layla. You guys have been so wonderful to me, and I know Enchanted Events has bigger and better things ahead. I'm incredibly grateful for all you've done for me." My eyes stung as I hugged my employee and friend. "Don't take any crap from Henry after I'm gone, okay?"

She gave a watery nod. "Sure thing, boss. And I'm sorry I thought you were a murderer."

"It's okay. I'm glad I could prove you wrong."

"That makes two of us. Though I did lose the betting pool we had going at the VFW."

A moment later, Layla escorted my attorney and accountant in.

"Good morning, gentlemen." I shook both their hands. "Please, take a seat."

"We have good news for you today," Brian Higgins said. I'd gone to school with Higgins, and it was hard to believe this boy who'd offered the home base for wild parties in high school was now deacon of his church, father of two, and my accountant. "Enchanted Events took quite a tumble in profit after the little murder mishap."

Mishap? Someone had lost her life, and I'd nearly been sen

up the river for the rest of my days. "It affected a lot of things, for sure."

"Right," said Brian. "And it's unfortunate that we have such a small snapshot of time for us to declare your time at Enchanted Events profitable or not. But in the last few weeks you've booked out future events having nothing to do with weddings, which was incredibly wise strategy on your part."

He said that as if we'd only done it to stay afloat for my sake. "Henry and the staff really want to explore event planning—and not just weddings."

"Sure you do," Brian said. "When you combine that with the profits Enchanted Events was already maintaining before you arrived, it averages out to a bottom line that's in the black. And get this"—he slapped his knee—"it's by one dollar!"

"So you're free to sell the company and the property," my attorney said.

"Oh." They were the words I'd hoped and prayed for since I'd stepped foot back in Sugar Creek. "That is good news." Though the peace and relief I'd expected seemed tardy in its appearance. "Mr. Jeffcoat, I assume you brought the paperwork so I can sell—" My cell phone chimed on my desk, flashing Sylvie's name. "So I can sell Enchanted Events to Henry Cole."

"I've reviewed his offer," Mr. Jeffcoat said. "And it's a fair one."

I silenced my ringer. I'd call Sylvie later. "Good. Let's get the ball rolling and—"

"But, Ms. Sutton, in the last week you've received two higher offers." He slid a piece of paper to me with a lot of zeroes. "And I received this offer from an investor just last night."

Holy Mercedes-Benz. The dollar amount I was looking at would set me up for years in Los Angeles. All my sleepless nights, tossing and turning over how I'd pay the bills would be over. I hadn't had that kind of security since I was a child under my parents' roof.

I startled as Henry's office phone rang shrilly, but I ignored it, knowing one of the girls would get it.

"You don't have to give me an answer now," the attorney said. "But the offer does expire in three days." He tapped the paper. "I'll leave that with you."

"Sounds like a no-brainer to me," Brian Higgins said as he rose. "You're one lucky lady."

I walked them to the door, only to have Alice follow me back to the office. "Your grandmother's called five times."

"I'll call her later." I had way too much on my mind right now and needed some quiet.

"She said she won't give up 'til you answer."

"Okay." I sighed and reached for my cell. "Thank you." As Alice departed, I dialed Sylvie's number. "There better be a good reason you're blowing up my phone."

"Hugs and kisses to you, too, pumpkin," Sylvie said. "Shug, we've overlooked something so simple."

"The fact that you're not really retired from the CIA?" A few seconds of dead air followed.

"I don't know what you're talking about," Sylvie finally said "But I looked at our photos of the yoga class sign-in sheet."

"Yes?"

"We failed to compare Zoey's signature on the day in question to her signature on any of the other days."

"I compared them. Looked the same to me."

"Not if you look closely. They're different—just slightly. But I'm telling you the signature on the day of the murder is not the same as Zoey's signature on the other days I photographed."

"So someone signed in for her?"

"Looks like it."

"I can't sit here any longer." I gathered my purse. "If the police won't call me back, then I'm going to talk to them in person."

I barreled through the lobby of Enchanted Events, gunning for the door.

"Paisley, what's wrong?" Henry blocked my path, his eyebrows rising in concern.

"I can't talk right now. I'll be back."

He opened the door for me, and warm air blew in. "Can't you at least tell me how the meeting with Higgins and Jeffcoat went?"

"I will. Later, I promise." Then I burst into tears, sidestepped Henry, and made an escape for my Camry. I took a drive with the windows down, aiming my car towards the Sugar Creek Police Station, my head aching from an overcrowding of worries. I couldn't even think about the offers on Enchanted Events right now. Not when we might've locked up the wrong person for Sasha Chandler's murder.

My heeled sandals beat a hasty rhythm as I sprinted up the sidewalk and through the doors. The department didn't see a lot of action beyond speeding tickets and the occasional disorderly conduct, so every uniformed person in the building turned my way as I flew in like a 747 ready to crash land.

"I want to see Chief Mark O'Hara," I loudly proclaimed "And I want to see him now."

"Are you wearing explosives?" A receptionist stood. "I wen to a training on crisis demands, and I can help you."

"No." I walked toward her and watched her retreat. "I'n Paisley Sutton, and I have information Chief O'Hara needs."

"Is this about the Girl Scout cookies?"

"Can I just talk to the man?"

"He's busy right now. If you leave your name and number—"

"I've already done that."

"He's working on some time-sensitive stuff right now," the wirehaired woman said. "A skunk broke into his ex-wife's house last night, and he's reviewing the procedure for bestowing a town medal of honor."

"To his ex-wife?"

"No, the skunk."

I so did not have time for this. "My grandmother is Sylvi Sutton. If you don't get me into Chief's office in two minutes I'll have her take down the city's power grid and go to Faceboo! with the neighborhood watch file she calls 'Naughty Secrets tha Would Ruin Many Lives.'"

The receptionist blanched. "Let's get to stepping."

I followed her down the linoleum-tiled hallway to the offic of the man in charge.

"Ms. Sutton." Chief Mark O'Hara lowered his phone and glared at his employee. "What an unscheduled pleasure."

"I've called you repeatedly."

"I've been busy."

"I have information that's relevant to the Sasha Chandle

murder."

"We have our man, Ms. Sutton." O'Hara twirled a pencil between his stubby fingers as he sat at his file-stacked desk. "We even have you to thank for that."

"Please, just let me talk to Detective Ballantine."

"Detective Ballantine doesn't work out of this office on the daily. He's only here when there's a murder. Or when you come to town. Are you planning on leaving soon, by the way? You don't do good things for our crime rates."

"I've left five messages for him, and he's yet to call me."

"Because he's done with this case. Probably on his way to Gulf Shores for his yearly beach vacation."

"Chief O'Hara, I was convinced Carson Fielding murdered Sasha, and evidence definitely looks condemning, but it's certainly not conclusive."

"His own wife says he went to Enchanted Events and got in a fight with Sasha Chandler. Between that, the pictures, the copied hard drive Frannie gave us, and the blackmail letters, I'd say this case is wrapped up."

"I think we have the wrong person behind bars."

He leaned back in his chair, hands bracketed behind his head. "And who would you like to swap out for Fielding?"

"Zoey Chandler—Sasha's stepsister."

"Impossible."

"It's not."

I sat down in a cracked-vinyl chair and shared all I'd discovered—except the detail about Sylvie and me breaking into the yoga studio office. Why incriminate ourselves with that?

"So you think because Carol overheard a tussle over a wedding dress, Sasha's sister killed her?"

It sounded so stupid. "Yes."

O'Hara scratched the skin behind his ear. "Would a dress really drive a woman to kill?"

Had he not heard a word I'd said? "It's not just the dress. The dress was just the tipping point. I'm not sitting here saying I know without a doubt Zoey killed Sasha. What I am saying is that there are things at play you and Detective Ballantine need to consider. Zoey has motive and—"

"She also has an alibi. She said she was at yoga, and as far as the instructor recalled, she was."

"Someone could have easily signed in for her. I think you should check the sign-in on the date of the murder and compare it with previous days." My eyes bore into his with a fierce intensity. "Please."

"Okay . . ."

I knew he was only agreeing to get me out of the office. "I think you need to look at the evidence again, Chief O'Hara."

"And we will. In a court of law."

"I'm talking about the evidence against Zoey. Maybe she was an accomplice."

"And maybe she's just a young lady who got treated like Cinderella when daddy remarried."

"Which provides motive."

"I'll take this all into consideration." He smiled and gestured to the door. "Get on outta here. It's a beautiful day, and I hear you have our mayor's wedding to prepare for. My son's doing the photos for the event, so it better be good."

Something niggled at the outer edges of my thoughts. An

idea that was so close, but it had yet to fully materialize. "Please have Detective Ballantine call me. Tell him it's urgent."

"Yeah, yeah. I'll pass that along."

All eyes were on me as I walked through the lobby of the police department. I knew they thought I was taking this sleuthing thing a little too far.

And maybe I was.

But if I was right, there was still a killer running free in our town.

CHAPTER THIRTY-NINE

T HE SUGAR CREEK Chapel sat like a beacon on a hill, the light from within radiating through the glass walls like a prism in the night. A place where decades of love had seeped into the steel, board, and mortar, where hope hung from every shingle. It was a beautiful setting to begin a marriage and a new life.

The acoustics were also fabulous for singing.

Or so Alice told me.

"Come on!" Her phone played a catchy Timberlake song, and she shook her groove thang as she fused tulle to burlap with a hot glue gun on the last pew decoration. "Sing with me, Paisley!"

"Too busy!" I climbed down from the ladder, satisfied with the fabric we'd draped from the ceiling. Alice and I had been at the chapel since three, and with the assistance of some hired help, we'd transformed an already gorgeous setting into a pastel fantasy.

"Come on," Alice said. "Let's hear that golden voice."

It was more of a rusty, tarnished voice these days. "Can you help me with these candelabra?"

"Sure thing. I—" She stilled as her phone pinged, then grabbed it from the floor. "Crap. Sick kid. I gotta go."

It was nearly nine. "No, not yet. Give me thirty more minutes, and we'll finish together." I didn't want to admit to her that I was afraid to be in the chapel alone.

"Paisley, Levi just barfed all over my living room. I can't stay." She gathered her event notes and shoved them in her purse. "If I can get him settled, I'll have the neighbor sit with him. Otherwise, I'll call Layla to take my place."

"Okay." So far Detective Ballantine had yet to call me back. I'd phoned him another four times and popped into the station again on my way to the chapel. They were satisfied with their arrest of Professor Fielding. But I still wasn't.

"It looks like we're almost done. Relax, okay? I'll leave you with my cherished glue gun and bag of tools. This wedding's going to be phenomenal. Girl, look at this place." With her hands on my arms, Alice forced me to do a slow turn. "Huh? Is this stunning or what?"

I'd been working nonstop, one hyperfocused task at a time. Now that I surveyed the chapel as a whole, it really was something. "We did pretty good."

"Pretty good?" Alice laughed. "We did amazing. *You* did amazing. You're a natural at this, Paisley. You took Emma's plans and supersized them. How can you look at this and not be proud of yourself?" She pulled me in for a warm side hug. "Let me hear you say you're proud of yourself."

I shooed her toward the door. "Go home to your sick boy."

But Alice wasn't relenting. "Say it."

Such a simple thing, but why was it so hard? "I am . . ." The girl who never felt good enough. The one who couldn't compete. The one who wanted to make her parents proud, but rarely did. The one who thought she'd finally, *finally* arrived when the record deals came. Only to lose that too.

Then along came a little wedding planning business. Falling into my lap like manna from the sky.

Here I was, a former pop star, running a business so well I'd received multiple offers on the sale. "I am . . . proud. I'm proud!" Now I was laughing, delirious giggles of wonderment. "I had no idea how this wedding stuff worked, and I'd wanted no part in running Enchanted Events. But it came together. I'd stuck with it, and everything was working out—including Emma's wedding."

"Feels good, doesn't it?" Alice moved toward the large double doors. "How about you give staying in Sugar Creek some thought?"

"Let's not go too far with this. I'm glad it was a job well done, but my life is in California."

"Is it?" She gave a pointed look, opened a door, and stepped out. "Don't work too late, boss."

I spent the next ten minutes straightening pew decorations, climbing up the ladder once more for a final adjustment, and setting up the candelabra. Wanting to dust the backdrop free of sawdust before I called it a night, I pulled a microfiber cloth from Alice's Enchanted Events bag of tricks and gently cleaned humming the song stuck in my head.

"Hello, Paisley."

My heart leapt at that familiar voice, and I turned, nearly falling from my place on the altar platform. "Zoey. Hi." Why hadn't I locked the doors? "What are you doing here?"

With her hair in a pink ball cap, Zoey wore black yoga pants and an oversized sweatshirt, despite the heat. "I just came from the police station."

It took a Herculean effort to keep my face neutral. "You did?"

"I went to pick up a few of my sister's effects, now that the investigation is over. They said you'd solved the case." She smiled and walked the aisle to me. "When I drove through town and saw your car here, I thought I'd stop in and thank you myself."

No matter where Zoey had been headed, this chapel would not have been on her path. "No thanks needed." I dusted my hands against my pants. "I obviously had selfish motives for finding the real killer."

"The police said they were now in possession of Sasha's old iPad."

"Yeah, funny thing. I found it in that collection of books you gave me." I watched her face for a reaction, but found none. "It got pretty bashed up when my house got broken into." Did she know about that? Was Zoey the culprit?

She roamed her fingers over the material at the end of a pew. "Amazing that you were able to recover any data on the thing."

"I have two family members who are former CIA. They're pretty handy. Annoying, but mostly handy." I was rambling. Confronting a possible murderess did that to a girl.

"I should get home," Zoey said. "But on behalf of the Chandler family, thank you. We owe you a debt of gratitude."

She turned to go, the echo of her shoes like a ticking clock. It would be so easy to let this go—to close the chapter and get on with my life.

"We were able to do a thorough inspection of the hard drive." The words flew out of my mouth, and I desperately wanted to grab them back.

Zoey's steps faltered and she stopped. "Oh?"

"Yes," I said. "It's interesting what you can find on someone's device, isn't it? So personal." I was pretty sure I had not worn enough deodorant for this task, but when one dove into the deep end, one had to keep swimming. "Did you know Sasha had blackmailed Professor Fielding?"

Zoey didn't so much as blink. "No, but I guess I'm not surprised."

"It all fit so perfectly. Sasha blackmails her former fling, and he kills her to shut her up."

She gave a tight-lipped smile. "The answer was right under our noses the whole time."

"Yes," I said. "Almost so close we couldn't see it."

"Well, nice to see you again." Zoey glanced toward the door. "Max and I have a party to go to."

Let her go, Paisley. Do not handle this alone! "Remember when I delivered Sasha's bridal book to you?" My brain and my mouth were in a battle for control, and my mouth was definitely overruling.

Zoey's lip curled. "You mean the one she stole from me?"

"Yes," I said. "It was so impressive. So detailed. I'd never seen anything quite like it."

Zoey's face looked mildly impatient.

"I especially enjoyed the photos you had in there. The one of the dress Sasha would wear, the venues you'd liked, you creative décor choices. Your photography skills are really something. I can barely work my iPhone camera, so I admire that."

"Thank you."

"But I noticed something on the photos." Zoey stilled, and I knew I was on to something. That little detail that had finally clicked into place. "A small watermark in the bottom right corner. So faint, it would be easy to miss."

"It's from my editing program. Something I put on there so people don't rip them off from social media without giving me credit."

"Very smart. You can't trust anyone these days. But you know where else I saw that watermark?"

"No."

"On Sasha's blackmail photos."

Her gaze never wavered. "I'm sure you're mistaken."

"Bottom right-hand corner—your little symbol. A heart with your initials in it, I think? Almost invisible. I'm guessing the program you run your photos through is set to watermark by default, am I right?"

Zoey reached a hand to her ponytail and combed her nails through. "Yeah, I knew about the blackmail. So what? It was just another day in the life of being Sasha's stepsister."

"And you knew she had no intention of wearing the dress you designed for her." I reached into my back pocket and gently retrieved my phone, holding it behind my back.

All warmth left her countenance. "Where did you get an idea like that?"

"I was at the dress shop yesterday. They're still holding the Zalinza gown your sister intended to wear. The lady who runs the place heard your argument in the store. I know Sasha told you she wouldn't wear the dress you'd created." I pressed a button on my phone, activating the voice recorder. "That must've been quite the blow. You'd allowed yourself to trust her one more time, and she stabbed you in the back—again."

"I got over it."

"Did you? Here was the big opportunity she'd promised you. Your chance for the who's who of Sasha and Evan's political circles to see your work. And when you found out she'd ordered a gown from London, you knew she'd never intended to follow through on her vow to help you."

Zoey's lashes fluttered as she rapidly blinked tears.

"You took a DUI for Sasha. Ruined your record for her. Took the fall for her again and fell for her lies."

"Yes! I did! I did all of that. And got burned every time. But I didn't kill her."

Why couldn't she confess already? This never went so slowly on television! Was I wrong? "Did you know I got access to the sign-in sheets for your yoga studio?"

Zoey's left eye twitched. "Pretty sure those are confidential."

"They probably are. But a few sort of fell into my possession—including the sign-in from the day of Sasha's murder."

"I signed in to my yoga class. Because that's where I was when Sasha died."

"You mean *someone* signed in for you. The signature for that day is different from the other days you'd signed in. You didn't go to yoga, did you, Zoey?"

She dropped her fancy purse on the ground with a clank. " guess you think you've got this all figured out." She suddenly seemed much taller than I, as she confidently straightened her shoulders and met my stare, unfiltered hatred flaming in her brown eyes. "I wasn't feeling especially Zen that day."

"What were you feeling? Murderous?"

"A little."

I quickly peeked at my cell phone, my thumb accessing the keypad to dial 911. "Are you going to kill me too?"

"No." Zoey's attention shifted past my shoulder. "She is."

A hand wrenched my phone from my grip, and I spun around.

Anna Grace Fielding stood behind me like a demented fangirl.

"Hello, Paisley." She waggled her fingers in a wave with one hand and held a gun in the other. "You really shouldn't have gone to the police about Zoey. It's a shame things now have to end like this." Her fist shot out, connected with my jaw, and spun my body toward the rock floor.

Blood seeped into my mouth as I struggled to push myself up. The church tilted and spun while black dots swam in my vision.

Anna Grace leaned over me. "I truly love your music, and I hope you don't take any of this personally."

They were the last words I heard before her fist again smashed into my face.

And someone turned out the lights.

CHAPTER FORTY

MY EYELIDS LIFTED slowly, as my sluggish brain chugged to life. My face felt like I'd been hit by an anvil, and blood pooled near my mouth on the floor. Where was I?

Awareness wavered like a bad Wi-Fi connection, until I looked through the curtain of my hair and saw the chapel.

And it all came back to me. Zoey. Anna Grace. A very pointy gun.

I struggled to rise, and pain shot through my wrists as I realized they were bound—and with the cord of my own glue gun, no less. I blinked against the pungent aroma that hit my nostrils. Smoke!

I had to get out of here now—and fast.

"Look who's awake." Anna Grace climbed down from my ladder, a cigarette lighter in one hand, her gun in the other. "Just stay right where you are, okay?"

My head pounding, I looked up to see the canopy of fabric above us, almost completely engulfed. "Are you insane?"

"My husband thinks so." Debris fell from the ceiling. "My counselor thinks with the meds that I'm just fine though."

I assumed she was definitely off the meds. "Where's Zoey?"

"She had a date." Anna Grace did a swooping circle toward me with her weapon. "This sort of thing isn't her speed."

"But it's yours?" I pushed myself to a seated position, spitting blood to the floor. Running my tongue across my teeth, I was grateful to not find any gaps.

"Don't move another inch. I like you and all, but I won't hesitate to use my gun." She sighed heavily. "You were supposed to stay unconscious. Now I'm going to feel bad."

I regarded her through one very swollen eye. "And why is that?"

"Being trapped in a burning building is not something you want to be awake for."

It hurt to talk. "You don't think people are going to be suspicious when they find my body in a burned wedding chapel?"

"Not really." Anna Grace sidestepped a fireball of tulle that fell, barely missing her. "You were lighting the candelabra, and one fell and lit the building on fire. In your haste to get out, you slipped and hit your head." She tsk-tsked. "Darn that stone floor. Pretty, but not sensible. It could trip anyone up. Especially someone who wears such impractical shoes."

Right now I wanted to stab the heel of my impractical shoe right through Anna Grace's forehead. "I still don't understand your connection here. Did your husband have anything to do with Sasha's murder?"

"Not a thing. He loves the ladies. You think he'd purposely kill one off?" Her hyena-cackle didn't slow her down from lighting the first candle. "Lots of fabric you have there." She pointed her gun to the dropped ceiling above us. "Highly flammable—and highly convenient. Thank you."

I was desperate to stall Anna Grace or at least distract her. My phone rested a few feet away, and if I could grab it, I could call for help. I prayed feverishly for divine intervention—or at least some participating sprinklers. "Humor me as I fill in the blanks before I die." My fingers tugged on the knotted cord at my wrists. "Zoey was the master planner, and you're just the hired help?" One thing I had in my favor was that Anna Grace loved to talk.

She admired her fiery handiwork. "Zoey and I met at a university art event a few months ago. We had a few too many cocktails and traded Sasha Chandler sob stories. Zoey was torqued over her sister's lies and abuse, and I was sick of my husband handing that witch every dime we made. That gal lived like a queen, while I had to sell my house and car? I was done." She lit two more candles with one hand, the gun still trained on me. "Then Zoey offered me a sum of money I couldn't refuse."

"To do her dirty work?"

"It wasn't that hard. I started following Sasha around, carrying a few options for her death—poison, a bullet, a setup for a fake a suicide. But when I saw Carson go into your shop after her, I lost it. How dare he still talk to her? It was as though he couldn't stay away."

"He said he told Sasha he was done paying her," I said.

"Do you think I'd believe a word he says after all this time?" Anna Grace yelled. "After all his infidelities?" She shook her head and mumbled to herself. "You and your employees were so busy that no one noticed me coming in with the florist's crew. I found them in that little room. He left, and she got up to go fix her makeup. As if her tears were even real! When she came back in, she was delightfully tipsy. We swapped a few insults, and when swung that champagne bottle, she didn't even have the reflexes to move."

"And Zoey's role?"

"I called her after the fact, and she was my getaway car."

Something loosened in the cording, and I continued to pull and jerk every time Anna Grace took her eyes off me. "Is this really worth your going to prison?"

Anna grace grabbed a fat ivory candle and dropped it in the fabric seat of a pew, then walked toward me, hatred punching her every word. "I put my dreams on hold for eight years while he went to school, and *I* paid the bills. And what do I get in return? Just when we finally start making some bank on his art, this bimbo comes along and tears him away from me. Then has the nerve to *charge* us for it?"

"You couldn't just divorce the man?"

"I didn't intend to set him up for Sasha's murder. I'm not *that* good at this." Her words were so dry, so droll. "It just happened. And it worked perfectly in my favor. My husband rots in a cold cell while I cash in on all his stupid artwork. He's got a whole basement of those paintings, and I'm unloading every one of them and taking a long European vacation."

"It's not too late. You can still make things right and let me go."

"Nah." She coughed and covered her mouth with the collar of her shirt. "This is probably my cue to leave."

"Do you really want to be the one person responsible for making a future Electric Femmes reunion tour impossible?"

A beam above our heads buckled. "Don't think I don't feel contrite," she said as she moved out of range. "I do. Just as I felt bad about slashing your tires and trashing your house. But the good news is, rock stars and authors are often more famous after their death. Maybe they'll name a flavor of Ben and Jerry's ice cream after you."

Wasn't that just a comforting thought?

"You can quit waiting for the fire alarms to turn on, by the way. I've disabled them. Heaven knows we don't want the police to join our party too soon."

Smoke filled the space as surely as it filled my lungs. "Can I make"—a violent cough seized my lungs—"one dying request?"

She lit two more pews. "I guess."

"I'm going to need you to coldcock me again so I'm not conscious when the fire gets me."

Her eyes narrowed, but she relented. "That seems fair."

Anna Grace strolled toward me with all the confidence of one getting away with murder. Her gun barrel close to my head, she leaned down and drew back her fist. A loud groan sounded above us, and as the fire-drenched ceiling beam wrenched free of its steel shackles and catapulted toward us, I knew this was my moment.

I launched my body into Anna Grace, my head plowing into her gut. We both went tumbling to the floor, and her gun skidded beneath a pew as the beam crashed to the ground—an explosion of wood and flame, shaking us like an earthquake. I cried out as a piece splintered and struck my leg.

"Get off me!" she yelled. "It's over!"

"Not for me!" I shouted aloud for the sake of my own ears. I couldn't be over for me. I kicked and thrashed with my leg while jerking on my restraints. A relentless scream sounded over the roar of the fire, and I realized it was coming from my lips.

Anna Grace had a good twenty-five pounds on me and used that advantage to heave me up by the arms. "I never liked the song 'Band Boys Make Better Boyfriends'!" Her right hook connected with my cheek.

Pain seared my bones, and I fought for consciousness. "That song bought me my first BMW." Fabric from the ceiling fell in hot licks of fire at our feet, and I kicked out to drive my heel into Anna Grace's thigh.

"Ow!" Coughing and sputtering, she pulled my left arm, angling my body for her next blow.

And loosening the cord that held me captive.

Freedom!

As smoke threatened to swallow us, Beau's self-defense lesson became a spasm of images in my brain. Elbow down? Twist an arm? Grab her head? What was I supposed to do?

The pew beside us exploded into a fireball, as Anna Grace clutched my shoulder. Muscle memory and panic fused, energizing my hand to slap over hers. With a mighty yell, I bent her wrist toward her body, thrilling at the sound of her scream. Taking advantage of her pause, I yanked her toward the ground. As her crazy head passed my waist, I lifted my knee and plowed it right into her nose.

Use your elbows! Use your elbows! Beau's instructions became a litany in my frenzied thoughts, and I swung madly, making wild arcs with my pointy elbows, pummeling Anna Grace's face, her ear, her throat—until she collapsed into a heap to the floor.

I leapt away from her, grabbed my cell phone, shoved it down my shirt, and began to run, dodging debris and particles dripping from the portal of hell above me that was the ceiling.

Anna Grace called out, but I kept moving, my eyes nearly swollen shut from abuse and smoke. As I made my way toward the front doors, the air became too thick, too heavy to breathe. Dropping to all fours, I crawled, coughed, and prayed.

Please, God, let me get out of here alive. I have so much to live for.

Images of my time here floated before me. My grandmother, Frannie, even Beau.

I thought of all I'd miss, all I had yet to do. Emma's wedding. Enchanted Events. The beauty that was Sugar Creek, Arkansas.

Coughs racked my body, and tears burned dirty trails down my cheeks.

Almost there.

Not much further.

Visibility down to nothing, I used my hands to feel for the path. I had to be near the door.

Behind me the fire roared like a demented monster, and he was consuming everything in his path as he came to get me.

My hands slapped at the floor, and my head bumped into a pew.

Keep going, Paisley. You can do this. You have to.

Breaking every rule of fire survival, I opened my mouth and began to sing, something I hadn't done in nearly a year. It was a silly little tune from my total flop of a solo album. A song that had helped tank my career, but I warbled out its words of love and hope, of power and freedom.

My fingers finally hit smooth wood, and I knew I'd reached the doors.

Still singing, I stood on wobbly legs and swayed.

Then peeled one of the giant doors open.

The fresh air rushed to greet me, but it couldn't hold me, and my body lurched.

As darkness swam around me, I stumbled onto the pavement, music still on my lips.

I had made it.

I had escaped.

Death had not won.

CHAPTER FORTY-ONE

I AWOKE TO sirens. And pain.

"Just breathe, ma'am." From the one bleary eye that seemed to be working, I saw an attractive man in a navy uniform holding an oxygen mask over my face. "Don't try to move."

Move? I wanted to sleep for a hundred years.

"Stay with us." He shined a light in my face. "Can you tell us your name?"

I mumbled something I hoped was coherent, then let my eyelids drift closed. "Too bright."

"We're taking you to Mercy Hospital. We'll be there soon You're going to be okay."

You're going to be okay.

Tears slipped down my cheeks.

I was safe. I was alive. With my whole life ahead of me.

"Phone. In my bra."

"Ma'am?"

"Please. Get phone. Play voice memo."

"That was some fire," his female partner said as she took hesitant peek down my shirt. "You're lucky to have made it out."

I nodded as best as I could with the brace around my neck "Someone else in the church," I managed.

The cute EMT shook his head. "As far as I know, you're the

only one who made it out."

TIME SLIPPED AWAY from me like fog in my hand.

When I roused again, I found myself in a pale green hospital room with an oxygen tube rudely stuck up my nostrils and three anxious faces nearby.

"Hey, shug." Sylvie lightly patted my bruised hand. "How you feeling? You've got quite the shiner."

"I took a picture of it," Frannie told her. "That's one for the wall of fame."

Emma rose from her chair beside the bed. "You gave us quite a scare."

"I heard it all on my scanner," Sylvie said. "It's the reason we got here with the ambulance."

"That and Sylvie driving fast enough to break the sound barrier." Frannie brushed a strand of hair from my forehead. "Saw you hoisted out of that ambulance like a champ."

I licked my busted lip and tasted copper. "How long have I been out?"

"About four hours." Sylvie held my hand. "Your face looks like pulverized meat, sweet thing, and once the swelling goes down, they want to check for a break in your nose and jaw. But you're alive." She lightly kissed the top of my head. "Thank the good Lord you're alive."

"Not much left of the chapel," Frannie said.

"Emma." I rested a moment and breathed. "Your wedding."

She gave a lopsided grin. "It's fine. We'll postpone it and

find a new location. The important thing is you're safe."

"Zoey Chandler." I started to rise, but Sylvie held me down.

"You stay put. The police took Zoey into custody." Gratitude shone in her blue eyes. "I'm so proud of you."

Frannie grinned. "You cracked the case."

"Barely." The sludge in my brain started to clear. "Just throwing darts at a hunch."

"Well, it worked," Sylvie said. "Because you're one of us. You've got a nose for trouble."

Frannie tilted her head. "I hope the fact that it's now a little crooked doesn't affect that."

Sylvie walked to the door and stuck her head out. "She's awake now," I heard her say.

Moments later Beau walked in, wearing faded jeans and a face of concern.

"Why don't we go get some coffee and talk about alternate wedding locations?" Sylvie reached for her purse.

"Great idea," Emma said, following Sylvie and Frannie outside.

The man sure knew how to fill a room. I was sure I looked like a train had mowed me down—yet he was a sight for my very sore eyes.

"Hey, there." Beau's soft voice was a caress to my frayed nerves. "You gave us quite a scare, Paisley." He leaned over the bed, his hand bracing near my pillow. "I know I'm supposed to say sympathetic things here, but . . . all I can think is if you ever go rogue like that again, I'll put you on a plane and send you back to Los Angeles myself. You could've been killed."

I looked into those sea glass blue eyes so steady on mine

"You care."

His frown deepened. "Of course I care."

I nodded, the motion rattling everything in my head. "I feel more than a little vulnerable here in a hospital bed, braless and in a gown big enough to house the both of us, but . . . you're right."

His dark brow arched and he lowered himself to a seated position on the bed. "I'm too focused on the fact that someone busted up your face to check out the boobs right now, but do go on about how I'm right."

My fingers traced the edge of the sheet pulled to my waist, as I edited my story before finally setting it free. "I can't sing anymore."

"Sure you can," he said. "So you fell off the horse. You pick yourself back up and—"

"No, I mean I'm not physically able. Not the way I used to, anyway." I paused to let the familiar, bitter pain put its stranglehold on my heart. "About a year ago I started having issues and went to the doctor. He found a cyst near the ligament of my vocal cord, which doesn't have to be a big deal. It's not that unusual for singers. He set me up for surgery." The sheet was a wad in my fists. "There's always a small chance of complications, and . . . it didn't go well."

"Aw, Paisley—"

"No, it's okay." Or maybe one day it would be. "I did a bunch of therapy, but I never recovered my singing voice. There's nothing they can do. And I miss it, you know?" I lifted a hand to swipe a tear, only to find some weird contraption holding my finger hostage. "It sounds silly, but I miss the sound of my own voice when I sing in the car."

"It doesn't sound silly at all."

I sniffed, then winced at the shock of pain.

"Take it easy." His fingers covered mine. "We can talk about this later."

"But you were right—I was scared. As if my music career wasn't doomed enough, then to lose my voice? I had no idea how I'd work, how I'd support myself. I found this jerk of an agent, and I told him my conditions. I could basically only get jobs on my old image—people more interested in nostalgia than hearing my voice. But I knew that would only last so long. I thought taking this cruise ship gig would give me time to clear my head and come up with a new plan. A new life."

"I'm sorry," Beau said. "I had no idea."

"I wanted that music career more than anything."

His thumb slid across my hand. "I know you did."

"I had no clue who I was without the music. But then the rug got pulled out from under me, and I was in the middle of a really good depression when I got word I'd just inherited my great-aunt's business. Life's just thrown me a lot of curveballs lately." I took a tissue from the box he offered. "Tonight when was trapped in the church with that crazy woman, my life flashed before my eyes like some big ol' cliché. And very little of it was my music career. It was here. Sugar Creek." *And even you, Beau.* "When the flames were getting closer, I started thinking about all I had left to do in this life, and all the things I still wanted to accomplish. And every bit of that can happen right here."

Beau's lips slipped into a smile. "You're staying?"

"I'm still scared." I attempted a laugh, but it hurt my chest. "But I'm through running. I have an opportunity to make something of myself here—something new, something better. And I'm taking it."

He watched me for a moment, and I wondered what was going through that complicated brain of his. "I'm glad you're staying."

I yawned and blinked the eye that wasn't swollen shut. "I guess you won't have to find a new neighbor."

Standing, Beau pulled the sheet to my neck and pressed a light kiss to my cheek. "Good. You're the neighbor I want."

Later, I would unpack that line and look at it over and over.

"Goodnight, Paisley." He brushed his hand over my hair. "Get some sleep."

"Goodnight." I snuggled into my pillow and watched him walk to the door.

Beau paused, his hand on the knob. He inspected the floor for five ticks of the clock above me before lifting his gaze to mine. "Over two years ago I lost my best friend in Libya." He stepped back into the room, but didn't come near the bed. "My Special Forces team had been away from the US compound all day. We'd been outside the grid and were finally on our way back from a pretty stressful job. There were about three trucks carrying me and my guys as we made it to the checkpoint. It had been an adrenaline high all day, and now that we were almost home, we were all powering down—joking on the radio, laughing, ready to get something to eat. The sniper fire caught us totally off guard."

Fatigue fuzzed the edges of my consciousness, but I had to

hear this story. "I'm listening," I said.

"Injuries happen when you get too comfortable, you know?" Beau stared at a spot on the shiny floor. "The checkpoint was compromised, and shots hit the first truck. Took out two of my guys." He stopped and breathed.

"But you got out of your vehicle and fired back," I said. "How many guys did you save?"

"I'm not sure it matters." Beau's voice softened. "One of the people I couldn't save was one I would've died for. He had a wife and a brand-new baby."

Words seemed trite and inadequate, so I said nothing.

"His name was Wyatt Fox."

"Did you name your property after him?" Oh, my heart. "Wyatt would be so proud of you—and of Fox Falls." I wanted to throw off all these tubes and hobble to Beau and hug him tight. "Thank you—for telling me."

Nodding, he rubbed the back of his neck and reached again for the door. "I just thought one hard story deserved another." He opened the door, and the hall light poured in. "Get some rest, city girl. You've got a lot to do when you get out of here."

"Beau?" The painkillers had created such a delicious buzz.

"Yes?"

"You know one day you're going to kiss me again, don' you?"

"We'll see about that, Paisley." He laughed as he stepped outside. "We'll just see."

CHAPTER FORTY-TWO

"**G**OOD MORNING, HENRY."

I slipped into our shared space of an office one week after the fire. The morning light streamed in through the old windows with golden encouragement, as I handed Henry a bag from Bugle Boy Bagels. It was my first day back, and my purple, bruised face and I moved at a sloth's pace.

"Paisley." He jumped from his leather seat. "I was just re-working plans for Emma and Noah's rescheduled wedding. Sit. Sit. Are you sure you should be back already?"

"I'm fine."

He gave a pointed look at my nose. "So, surgery, huh?"

"Broken nose." I tapped the splint covering the center of my face. "Funny it took me leaving LA to get a nose job." I collapsed into his chair, noticing his seat was superior to mine. That would have to be remedied. "Can I talk to you?"

His smile faded. "This is it, isn't it? You're about to break up with us, aren't you?"

"I'm sorry," I said. "But I can't sell you Enchanted Events."

His lips pressed thin. "But you gave me your word."

"I know." Seeing his reaction pierced like the stitches in my forehead. "But I have to do what's best. For all of us."

"I got outbid." He dropped his head and paced a few steps

before circling back. "I know the property alone is worth twice what I offered, but I thought this place had come to mean something to you. I hoped *we'd* come to mean something to you. That you cared what happened to Enchanted Events and everyone working here. But yeah, I guess I get it. Money talks. And if you're going back to Los Angeles, you're certainly going to need some." Henry leaned both hands on my desk, quiet with his brooding thoughts. "Let me be the one to break it to the staff."

"I agree," I said. "They should hear it from you."

"Right. Good. Great." He went back to pacing, fists clenched as if wishing for a good punch. "And what do I tell them about the new owner? Did you at least sell to someone who knows what they're doing?"

"I'm afraid the owner will probably need a lot of help."

"Paisley, for the love of—"

"That's why she's bringing in a partner. She understands her limitations. Knows she has a lot to learn."

Henry stopped pacing, his fiery eyes intense on mine. "What are you saying?"

I handed Henry a stack of papers I'd barely read. "This is the sales agreement. I'm offering you the chance to buy forty-nine percent of the company."

"Forty-nine?"

"We'll be equal partners as far as anyone else knows. I just wanted to take the lead, have the edge." For the first time in my life. "But I know I can't run Enchanted Events without you. I wouldn't want to."

"You're staying?"

"I'm staying. For now."

He turned away then, sniffed once, and I saw his strong hand rub over his clean-shaven face.

I reached out, my fingers giving his shoulder a light squeeze. "It's not what you wanted, but I thought we'd worked so well together. I know I'm a disaster magnet, and I jacked a lot of things up. But we have so much potential here. Like you said, weddings are just the beginning, right?" A faint laugh escaped my busted lips. "In the end, I couldn't walk away. This town, this business got to me. I realized I feel alive when we're working on an event. It's hard work with insane hours, but I like it. I might even kind of love it. And who'd have thought, huh? Me, jilted Paisley, planning weddings?" With Henry's back turned, I spoke to his broad shoulders. "Can you just take some time to think about it? Don't say no right now. Please?"

Henry slowly pivoted, his gaze glazed. "Think about it?"

I nodded meekly, about ready to cry myself.

"Paisley." He took a contemplative breath. "Do you know what my grandma Dottie did for a living?"

"I don't believe I do."

"She was a maid," he said, his voice a raw whisper. "She worked as a maid who didn't make enough to keep her five kids out of poverty, putting in ten-hour days for rich folks. She had a ninth grade education and cleaned until her hands were nothing but callouses. And when my momma had me at seventeen, Grandma Dottie took care of me, even after my mother ran off and never looked back. Grandma Dottie would come in late from work, cook my dinner, then sit at the old Formica table in the kitchen, making sure I finished every bit of my homework. If she thought my penmanship was sloppy, she'd make me copy it all again. 'You're going to be something important,' she'd tell me. 'You'll go to college if I have to carry you there myself.'"

"And look how that paid off," I said.

"I wanted to go right to work after high school and help my grandma out. I had no plans for college, but she wouldn't hear of it. Even got on a bus and came on campus a few times to box my ears."

I smiled, uncertain where this was heading. "Is your grandma still alive?"

"She has a small house in Little Rock. I'm going to call her tonight."

"And what are you going to tell her, Henry Cole?"

"That I'm now co-owner of Enchanted Events."

Relief filled my bruised chest. "You are?"

"I am."

"Oh, thank goodness."

"And I'll tell Grandma Dottie that I made it. That everything she ever did for me paid off." He glanced at the papers in his hands. "My plans were to run this myself, but you came along and messed everything up."

"I'm kind of good at that."

"But you messed it up in a good way. You've taught me to think outside the box. And you're right—you've got a lot to learn still. But so do I, I guess. Though it makes no sense—we are a good team."

"It makes a little sense."

"This region's on fire, and together, I know we can become the premiere event planning business in the four-state area."

"Maybe the whole South."

"Okay, the whole South."

"Maybe the whole nation."

"Don't ruin my moment with your hyperbole."

I laughed, joy floating around me like confetti. "You won't regret this, Henry."

"By this time next year, I want to be able to buy Grandma Dottie a new car."

"Then let's see that she gets it." I stuck out my hand. "Partners?"

His fingers clasped mine. "Partners."

"I think we should start dressing alike. Really get simpatico."

"Don't make me rip this contract up."

I couldn't help it. I threw my arms around Henry and hugged him as tight as my injuries would allow.

He patted my back, stiff, robotic whacks punctuated with a few sighs. "Okay, gushy time over. That's it." *Pat. Pat.* "Seriously, Paisley, let go." He squirmed out of my embrace, brushing any evidence of contact off his tailored jacket. "And if you ever tell anyone I got a little choked up, Sasha Chandler won't be the last murder victim here."

"Now there's the surly Henry we know and tolerate."

"It means a lot that you'd make me partner."

"Enchanted Events is going to be great."

He smiled and surveyed our office, his eyes alive with the hopes of our future. "We'll make sure of it."

CHAPTER FORTY-THREE

Two Weeks Later

"EMMA'S WEDDING TURNED out beautiful." Sylvie clinked her champagne glass to mine. "You and the team have really outdone yourselves, Paisley."

On Friday evening, we stood in the prettiest dale in Suga Creek, located right on Fox Falls. As if the weather wanted to bless the union, the temperature was unseasonably mild, and the stars twinkled and danced above us. I'd gotten hundreds of pew from local churches and antique shops, and we'd set them in the newly shorn field. Emma and Noah had been able to expand their guest list, and most of the town had shown up to see their mayor and his sweetheart say their I Dos. Stringed light crisscrossed overhead, strung from oak tree to oak tree, swinging in the breeze. I'd called in a few favors, and a band I'd worked with years ago had flown in from Nashville to sing their bluegrass-infused indie rock while Emma and Noah swayed to their first dance.

"I think we just pulled off the event of the season," Henr said as he joined us. "Beau's barn cleaned up good." We' moved out all of the four-wheelers and other equipment to us the rustic building for the cakes and catering.

"Frannie, your cakes tasted like heaven," Sylvie said. Eve

though Measuring Cup Bakery had agreed to lift their ban on working with Enchanted Events, we weren't sure we were ready to reconcile.

"The groom's cake is especially tasty," Sylvie said. "I love the hint of pineapple. And something else I can't put my finger on, but such a familiar flavor."

Frannie grinned. "Remember that secret aphrodisiac ingredient we learned in Nepal, Sylvie?" She waited for my grandmother's nod. "I might've thrown a little of that in the batter."

"Lord help us all," Henry muttered.

Frannie laughed. "So if you see all the menfolk throwing themselves at me tonight, just stand back and let nature take its course."

Henry took two steps away from my aunt. "Did you hear the crazy story about Emma finding a duplicate of her original wedding dress hanging in her closet last week?"

"How wonderful." Sylvie caught my eye and smiled. "I wonder where it came from. Any ideas, Paisley?"

I swayed to the band's love song. "Just one of life's little mysteries."

"You seem to be good at solving those." She hugged me to her.

"Woo, look at that handsome fellow." Frannie pointed across the way.

Standing beneath a tree dotted with lanterns, Beau chatted with Chief O'Hara and Emma's father. A breeze lifted the mighty oak's limbs, and Beau turned, his eyes scanning the crowd before lighting on me. His gaze held mine for a moment before he gave a slow, heart-melting wink.

Missing nothing, Sylvie waved at Beau before linking her arm through mine. "Don't give up on that one," she whispered.

I inhaled the fresh air, contentment infusing my spirit. I'd like to think I was through giving up on anything. No more running, no more quitting. I had staked my claim in this town and I was here to stay. And if the love of a man had eluded me, the love of a town certainly hadn't.

Sugar Creek had captured my heart.

It was the home I'd run from, yet it had welcomed me back and offered me sanctuary and solace, a chance to rethink how I'd catalog the rest of my days. It gave me a place to unpack my bags, and people to call my own. People who didn't care if I could fit into a size two or hit that high E.

It was true—sometimes you had to leave to come home again. Lose it all to appreciate the bounty being offered.

To witness kindness, I only had to stop in at the auto parts store where Randall Crawford would give me a cup of coffee, sell me a battery, then install it for the price of a thank-you and a conversation. To hear beauty, one only had to listen to the midnight train, calling into the star-dotted sky all the way over from the next town. I loved the unexpected joy of picking up dinner from the high school FFA, who sold BBQ chicken from a grill in the ditch in front of the grocery store, using a seventy-year-old recipe that was still top-secret to this day. I could buy farm fresh eggs from the feed store downtown, who did business beneath a faded checkerboard sign, then walk through the library with the tin ceiling. My mother had taken me to read there from the time I could toddle around the books.

Home was a gas station that offered fried chicken and live bait. It was a Sunday handshake in church from someone who knew you before and after you'd risen from the baptismal waters as a Barbie-toting seven-year-old. It was a walk to the Civil War battlefield, where oak and maple trees joined hands and lucky day-trippers still happened upon arrowheads and musket balls—reminders that life does go on, yet a part of us will always remain. It was sitting on the front porch on a fall Friday night, where you could hear the high school football game, the announcer's rich voice carried on the backs of fireflies and evening breezes. It was driving by a white house that used to be pink, and every time you passed you thought of a beloved great-aunt and her deft way with a piecrust.

This was home.

For most of my life I'd wanted nothing to do with it.

But it welcomed me back all the same, gathered me to its freshly laundered bosom, and said, "Child, I'm gonna love you anyway."

Home.

Dear Reader,

The *Enchanted Events* series is my love letter to my home and small towns everywhere. I grew up in a small town and still love the life. Though Sugar Creek is a fictional town, Sugar Creek itself is a very real geographic area and water system in the northwest corner of Arkansas. My imaginary Sugar Creek is located by a real city called Bentonville, which, as the series states, is a unique mix of Mayberry meets Los Angeles. Due to Bentonville being the home base of WalMart, it's not uncommon to go to the picturesque town square and see a celebrity or two, especially during certain times of the year. This corner of Arkansas is an odd (but fun) mix of rural and city, and I hope you enjoyed reading about it as much as I loved writing about it.

The sweet town of Sugar Creek can also be found in *A Sugar Creek Christmas*, Emma and Noah's romance, as well as *Wild Heart Summer*, a romance novella set on Mitchell Crawford's ranch. And don't forget Sylvie has a crazy sister Maxine, who stars in her own series, *A Katie Parker Production*.

Stay tuned for more mystery and mayhem with the next *Enchanted Events* mystery, hitting shelves late this summer. Sign up for my newsletter to get a free ebook and be the first to know when new books are on the horizon.

Happy reading to you all!

Jenny

ACKNOWLEDGEMENTS

I had a lot of help writing this book. Enormous thanks to:

Beverly Jones, for making sure your kids knew who Miss Marple and Jessica Fletcher are.

Kristin Kathryn Rusch, for totally kicking my tail in a mystery writing intensive and being the first to say, "Hey, have you thought about writing cozies?"

Sibella Giorello, for holding my hand during that destined writing intensive we both barely survived. (Have we picked our tattoos out for that yet?) Thank you for all your advice and encouragement.

Officer Will Gardner, for letting me throw a hundred legal questions at you and for answering every one.

Army Lieutenant Colonel Brian Easley, who was a HUGE help in creating the character Beau Hudson's backstory. Thanks for "getting it" and for the info. It was a missing piece (or two) I needed. Hey, have you ever been to San Antonio. . .?

Michael Simonson, for your help with medical procedure, as my own knowledge base didn't go beyond Ninja Turtle Band-Aids.

Jocelyn Bailey, for your friendship, your support, and for making this book so much better, thanks to your editing eagle eye.

Rel Mollet, for catching manuscript errors, for your Richard Armitage appreciation, and for the way you encourage and promote authors.

Carina Paredes, for giving me the name Bayonet for a Sugar Creek restaurant. I appreciate your creativity!

Reba Buhr, a fabulous actress and a genius at audio book narration. Thank you for bringing the series alive.

My beloved readers, who are simply the best. That you'd give up moments of your life to read words I wrote never ceases to humble me (and baffle me). Thank you for every book, every page turn, every review, every email, and every kind word.

And finally, thanks be to God for giving me the opportunity to write about kissing and killing.

ABOUT THE AUTHOR

Award-winning, best-selling author Jenny B. Jones writes romance with sass and Southern charm. Since she has very little free time, Jenny believes in spending her spare hours in meaningful, intellectual pursuits, such as eating ice cream, watching puppy videos, and reading celebrity gossip. She lives in the beautiful state of Arkansas and has worked in public education for half of forever. She loves bluegrass, a good laugh, and strong tea. She adores hearing from readers.

www.jennybjones.com

22322191R00218

Printed in Poland
by Amazon Fulfillment
Poland Sp. z o.o., Wrocław